I0607653

BORDER SLOT

Also by Jack Lyndon Thomas

The Monsoon Killed the Tiger (Novel/A Thriller)

Whirling Fire (Poetry on the Vietnam War)

Coyote Jack/Drawing Meaning from Life and Vietnam: A Memoir

Training Runs: The Regenerative Power of Motorcycling Back Roads (eBook)

Lights on the Water/Impressions in the Sand: A Motorcycling Odyssey (eBook)

BORDER SLOT

By

JACK LYNDON THOMAS

lyndonjacks publications
www.JackLyndonThomas.com
lyndonjacks@att.net

Copyright © 2020 by Jack Lyndon Thomas

All rights reserved. No part of this book may be reproduced or transmitted in any form or by any means, electronic or mechanical, including photocopying or recording by any information storage or retrieval system, without written permission from the publisher.

ISBN 978-1-7340993-2-4 (paperback)
ISBN 978-1-7340993-3-1 (eBook)
Library of Congress Control Number:2019915500

Thomas, Jack Lyndon, 1944-
Border Slot by Jack Lyndon Thomas

lyndonjacks publications
1681 River Rd #3110
Boerne, Texas 78006

This is a work of fiction. Names, characters, businesses, places, events, and incidents are either the products of the author's imagination or used fictitiously. Any resemblance to actual persons, living or dead, or actual events is purely coincidental.

Message to Readers

The use of coarse language and negative references to minorities reflects how I believe certain characters would act, think, and speak in respect to the milieu in which this novel takes place. The negative references do not reflect the personal beliefs of the author.

Acknowledgments

I appreciate the dedication to excellence from members of the writing critique groups I have participated in over the years. Their sharp, unbiased readings, suggestions, and comments have improved this work: JP Goggin, Stephen Eagles, James Lopez, Linda Robinson, Tina Mollie Fisher, Mike Ley, Jerry McFarland, Carolyn Owens, Constance Lopez, Rick Nelson, Charlotte Jones, John Oehler, and Marcia Gerhardt. Any screwups or omissions are mine.

Special thanks go to Chris Rogers: editor and reader, an excellent teacher, a talented writer, and an eclectic artist; and to JP Goggin for the book cover design. Also, I am grateful for the efforts of the following volunteer readers, who have given candid, useful feedback: James C. Smith and Katharina Guttenberg.

Dedicated To

Steve, Harry, Richard, & Jim
Summer & Allison
Mason & Ava

Combat senses—the smells of gunpowder, charred earth, and shit; the visuals of gunships and helpless villagers; the sounds of explosions and screams; the tastes of bitter nước mắm *sauce and warm beer; the touches of hot metal and the cold bodies of the dead— conspired to rewire my brain circuitry to overreact to those same stimuli in current, far less dangerous circumstances. Not to worry, Lan, I won't surrender to inappropriate triggers.*

Kannon Ballard

One

Saturday, 17 October 2009, Texas Hill Country

On his way to meet Streak, the man to whom he owed his life, Kannon Ballard countered-steered his motorcycle off Texas FM 187 and entered the Lost Maples State Natural Area. After checking in at the ranger station, he traversed a low water crossing and rode into the east parking lot. He switched off the ignition, heeled the side stand into position, and dismounted.

Kannon removed his helmet, placed it on the ground, then took off his black leather jacket and laid it on the saddle. He filled his lungs with a mass of clean Hill Country air and smiled at its rejuvenating effect.

A noonday sun bathed the grasslands and wooded hills beneath a deep blue sky. Sycamores and rusty-hued oaks stippled the rolling terrain, while broad-leafed cottonwoods and Bigtooth maples lined the Sabinal riverbank.

Great weather for renewing a friendship. But there's more. I owe Streak, big time.

Nicknamed for his speed, Streak had been one of Kannon's classmates in Infantry Officer Candidate School at Fort Benning, Georgia. That was the era when most graduates were commissioned in the infantry and sent to Việt Nam. Like lots of veterans, they had lost touch with each other.

In early 2004, unexpectedly, Streak called. He had stumbled across an online publication that highlighted Kannon's return to Việt

1

Nam two years before. The caption read: "A Veteran Clears his Name," followed by a subtitle: "Ugly Skirmishes in Two Countries."

Unfortunately, the article stirred controversy over circumstances Kannon had hoped would never resurface. If not for the write-up, though, he and Streak wouldn't have reconnected.

Intending to get together, they had exchanged several phone calls, but that connection ended abruptly three years ago. Kannon's last call to Streak prompted the not-a-working-number message. An online search also proved fruitless.

It'll be good to see you again, my friend.

Kannon scanned the picnic area. Other than two couples and their kids occupying one table at the far end, no one else was in sight. He whipped out his cellphone and placed a call to Lan, his Vietnamese wife going on six years. She was less than pleased with the timing of this rendezvous because it interfered with family time.

"Hey, it's me. I'm here. Safe and sound."

"I am glad," Lan said. "I understand meeting this man is important to you, but I worry you will be drawn into another escapade, which will escalate."

"I won't get sucked into anything," he said a bit too quickly. "I've got a handle on the PTSD thing. I'm not susceptible to the triggers anymore."

Lan sighed. "Please be careful."

"Will do. And I'll take you and Derrick to Austin—"

The unmistakable rumble of a Harley running through its gears caught his attention, the sound of harnessed thunder. Kannon turned in time to see a helmetless rider downshift and churn fantails across the low-water river crossing.

As the rider accelerated along the winding road, Kannon glanced at a photograph sandwiched inside his wallet. Yep, the approaching motorcyclist was the man he hadn't seen for nearly forty years.

"Gotta go," Kannon said to Lan. "Will call you later."

Streak, astride his growling Harley, entered the parking area and stopped beside Kannon's BMW K1200 RS. Gleaming from its silver-toned finish, Streak's motorcycle exuded power and class.

"Great to see you," a clean-shaven Streak said, swinging his leg over the seat.

"Likewise," Kannon said, aware now that he'd looked forward to this casual reunion more than he realized. They shook hands. "Good looking steed you got there. New V-Rod?"

"Nah! It's a two-thousand-six model."

"You obviously take good care of it. Liquid-cooled, right?" Kannon asked.

"Roger! Your mount's not bad either."

"Thanks. Except for the wire-rimmed glasses and salt and pepper hair, you haven't changed."

"Tip the scales at one hundred sixty pounds." Wearing ragged blue jeans, a crisp khaki shirt with epaulets, and spit-shined Corcoran Jump Boots, Streak stood a good four inches shorter than Kannon's six-foot two-inch frame, yet his fellow veteran appeared tall because of his slender physique.

"You haven't lost your Kentucky draw," Kannon said, pleased by the intense, warm feelings flooding his body at seeing his old comrade.

"It's not as drawn out like yours." Streak whipped out a tin of chewing tobacco, grabbed a pinch, and plugged it into his mouth. "And your mustache has turned silver."

"Changes color in late fall," Kannon said. He grabbed his jacket off the seat and reached for his Meerschaum pipe tucked inside an inner pocket. He tamped in pinches of Mark Twain-branded tobacco and lit up, releasing an aromatic puff of smoke.

"Can't believe it's been forty years since Officer Candidate School," Streak said.

"Yeah," Kannon said. "Remember the time we nailed our tactical officer's extra pair of boots to the floor."

"The whole platoon paid for it," Streak said, laughing.

"And then our coup d'état." One night, at 0300 hours, the two of them had infiltrated another training company's barracks, mixed cement in the commanding officer's commode, and then planted a third company's guidon in the center of it.

"I'll never forget it," Streak said. "I wonder if that company ever got its banner back."

Streak dipped into a leather-fringed saddlebag and withdrew

a soft-shelled cooler containing a six-pack of Shiner Bock. With his back turned, Kannon noticed a slingshot protruding from his friend's back pocket. A tad strange, he thought. They moseyed away from their motorcycles toward a vacant concrete picnic table and took seats opposite each other. Streak slapped two bottles on the table.

"Normally, I don't drink when I ride." Kannon grabbed a chilled beer. "But it's a hot day."

Streak nodded.

"I was concerned when we lost contact," Kannon said.

Streak looked down at his beer. "Had some difficulties."

An involuntary tic tweaked Kannon's right hand. His friend's statement, tone, and expression suggested more substantial needs than Kannon wanted to address, at least this soon. He moved the conversation in a different direction.

"During our first talk, I thought it cool to learn you'd gone to flight school."

"Well . . ." Streak hesitated as if deciding whether to follow Kannon's lead. "I went through general flight training on rotary aircraft before being assigned to fly Huey Cobra gunships. In Việt Nam, they assigned me to the 25th Aviation Battalion."

"It's ironic you flew out of Cu Chi."

As revealed during their first phone conversation, Streak had been on station the night Kannon's outpost was nearly overrun. Fortunately, one of the aviation battalion's missions was to support advisors serving with South Vietnamese Regional Forces in Hau Nghia Province.

Streak and his wing-mate had deftly outmaneuvered the tracers and B-40 rockets the Việt Cộng unleashed that night. The pilots accurately engaged their targets, which saved Kannon's and his South Vietnamese irregulars' asses. At the time, he had no idea who had been piloting one of the choppers. Voice recognition was impossible, due to static between air and ground radio transmissions, and radio call signs further obstructed identification.

"We couldn't rely on South Vietnam's artillery or gunship support," Kannon added. "Their logistics weren't reliable."

"The sky was lit up like a fourth of July celebration," Streak said, also appearing *lit up* by the recollections.

"Artillery shells, whirling blades, flares, strobe lights, tracers, rockets . . . I can see it all." Kannon's nerve endings buzzed with adrenaline as he recalled the deafening sounds from the Huey Cobras' rockets and wingstub-mounted machine guns, the choppers' slender fuselages stenciled with shark's teeth, all of it instilling fear in the retreating Việt Cộng.

"One hell of a year," Streak said.

"And a hellish postwar aftermath." Kannon raised his beer to Streak. "Thanks for saving my ass."

They clanked bottlenecks in a toast.

"About the online article," Streak said, "a lot of it was redacted. What led you to return to 'Nam? Give me a sitrep."

Kannon flashed a nostalgic grin. He hadn't heard the abbreviated term for *Situation Report* in a long time. "In two thousand-two, I got a cryptic, one-liner note from my former interpreter."

"Really?"

"Yep. The message read, 'We have unfinished business.' Long story short, late in my tour, we were under attack when the Việt Cộng suddenly withdrew. My CO ordered me to pursue them. I and the other American on station led a reaction team of regional force soldiers. We were ambushed. Everyone was killed except . . ."

"You."

"Yeah." Kannon clamped down on the pipe stem so hard it cracked. "The CO threatened to court-martial me."

"Wow."

"I returned to 'Nam, only to find the interpreter near death. He gave a couple of scant clues, then died."

"Jesus!" Streak said. "Then what happened?"

"My old interpreter had a sister, Lan, who was caring for him. We clicked, and she helped me trace the faint leads in 'Nam." Kannon always considered it odd that his interpreter, the man to whom he dedicated his Silver Star for an earlier engagement, had been ill the night of the subsequent ambush. While unraveling the past, he, along with Lan, had recovered the Star, which now hung on his study wall.

"Heavy stuff." Streak removed a blue- and green-checkered bandanna from around his neck and wrapped it around his Shiner

5

Bock. Kannon noticed the missing index finger on Streak's left hand.

"Back in the States," Kannon continued, "I tracked down the CO and his . . . let's just say I uncovered what happened and cleared my name."

Streak nodded. "The woman? Is she—"

"Yes. Lan is my wife." Kannon smiled at recalling the imagery attached to her flower name, Orchid. Her color was pink, standing for femininity and grace, among other meanings. "I'd fallen in love but didn't know if I'd ever see her again. So, there I was, months after returning to the States, recovering from a gunshot wound, and she appears on my doorstep, pregnant. We married a month later. Twice. The first, a Christian ceremony. The second, Buddhist."

"Again, wow," Streak said.

"Lan speaks perfect English. No accent." Kannon let seep a wry smile, thinking about his meager vocabulary regarding the Vietnamese language. It wasn't one of his skill sets. "We have a six-year-old boy, Derrick. And I have a grown son from my first marriage. He's a lawyer working in Dallas. But enough about me. What's up with you?"

Streak frowned, shook his head.

Kannon tried again. "I noticed you've lost a finger. Did it happen in the war?"

"Nope. Besides, it's not relative."

Okay, we're not clicking on all cylinders.

"Surely, you've been doing something, even if you've retired."

"Wish I *could* retire. I'd spend my time fishing." Streak wiped his broad forehead. His expression was dour. The corners of his lips pointed south.

Perhaps the former chopper pilot's life hadn't turned out as well as his. "Something is bothering you. Right?"

Streak didn't answer.

Must be touching raw nerves. I'm not reaching him.

Sipping from his beer, Kannon wondered whether his efforts to connect with Streak were too intrusive. Yet, for Kannon, silence bred anxiety. He wanted to unclog the conversation. If he kept throwing out salvos, maybe one would dislodge whatever was going on in Streak's head.

"Did you continue flying after the war? You know, civilian medevac?"

The ex-Cobra jockey fixed him with sad eyes.

"I'm a contract pilot. I fly an old helicopter."

"Sounds cool."

"It's nothing but an old clunker." Streak placed his elbows on the rough concrete table surface. "Remember the Jolly Green Giant."

"Yeah. I flew in one on occasion. It's a twin-turbine, right?"

Streak nodded. His cheeks twitched like disturbed spider webs, and tobacco juice dribbled onto his chin. He wiped it clean with his bare right hand.

Glad we shook hands earlier.

"How in the world did you acquire it?" Kannon asked.

"They did, not me. Black market. Alberta Province."

Kannon's antennae spiked. *Who's they?* "Where are you going with this?"

"I'm in a bind," Streak said.

"Your turn for a sitrep." Kannon pressed the cool bottle of beer against his forehead.

"You know the job I mentioned, contract pilot?"

"Right."

"I signed on with an outfit to fly hunters and adventurers to remote destinations in Montana and Wyoming, even western Canadian Provinces." Streak drained his Bock and opened another. "'Rugged Men Lead Rugged Adventure and Hunting Expeditions into the Remote Wilderness' is the company's mission statement. That's not exactly what the group does."

"What does the group do, exactly?"

"Border location, unspecified group activities. You figure it out."

Kannon raked his hands through his hair. Streak's tone had grown more acerbic, changed from reconnection-fueled excitement to cool detachment. The vibrancy of their past was wearing thin, scattered. *It's like trying to regroup cattail pods gone to seed.*

Lan had warned Kannon about high expectations running

afoul, but had he listened? Of course not.

"We're wasting time, Streak. What do you want?"

Immersed in his own closed world, Streak didn't respond. His gaze was distant, lost. It reminded Kannon of the thousand-yard-stare. Was he trying to remember or forget?

"I can't help," Kannon said, "if I don't know what's going on."

Streak drummed his boots on the ground as if stamping out a fire. "You've always accomplished everything you set out to do."

"What's your point?"

"I need money."

"For what?"

"Resettlement."

"You mean like a plane ticket? Moving costs?" If that was all Streak needed . . . "I could lend you money for the airfare." It was the least he could do. "As for contacts, I really don't—"

"It's bigger than that," Streak said, wringing his hands. "I need to leave the country."

Kannon arched his eyebrows. "What the hell are you talking about? Don't tell me you've gotten involved in drug trafficking."

"The less you know, the better." Streak drained his second beer and reached for a third.

"All right." Kannon tried puffing on his pipe, then remembered the cracked stem. He set it down. "I assume you're involved in something illegal. Why not just go to the police? You've got a clean record, right?"

"Nope."

"Christ! You did time?"

"Yeah. I did time."

For what? Kannon wanted more explanation, but none came. And he wouldn't probe. "You don't have any family or friends to help out?"

"No."

"How much do you need?"

The sound of children's bantering sailed past. A mockingbird mimicked another bird's song. Frowning, Streak turned toward the sound and muttered, "Stupid bird."

Why the distraction? Kannon wondered. Was he too embarrassed to answer?

"It's okay. How—"

"Twenty-five thousand."

Much?

"Jeez, Streak! Are you crazy?"

"Do I look crazy?"

"No. You look desperate. But you're asking for too much cash. I won't do it." Kannon tugged on the end of his mustache. It was apparent Streak was running. "I could put you in contact with a good lawyer."

"Fucking lawyer wouldn't do any good."

"I don't know what else to say, Streak. I'm not going to get involved."

The chopper jockey glowered. "You committed a crime in getting your precious wife out of Việt Nam. And in New Mexico you killed—"

"You're out of bounds!" Kannon said, rising. "Whatever happened in Việt Nam and New Mexico is irrelevant to your situation."

Streak, too, rose and faced Kannon. "We leave no one behind. Remember?"

Kannon recoiled from Streak's breath. It carried an *old man's death scent*.

Streak grasped Kannon's lapels. "I need help." His voice was coarse and brittle.

"As I said, no way. I won't risk it."

"Bastard. I saved your life!" The words spewed from Streak's mouth like a snake's venom.

"This meeting is over," Kannon said.

"There will be . . . shall we say . . . consequences."

Kannon refused to bite. He wouldn't add more fuel to Streak's virulent, raging cocktail.

"Looking out for number one, right? Fuck your fellow man." Streak tightened his grip.

Kannon wrested free, flung Streak to the ground. "You're a walking timebomb."

Streak scrambled up, returned to the picnic table, picked up his beer, and slammed it on the concrete table. The bottle shattered, sending glass shards flying. A large sliver gashed Streak's hand and blood spurted from the wound.

"Good grief." Kannon reached forward to help.

Streak brushed Kannon off, then removed the embedded glass shard and wrapped the injury with a kerchief. Using his free hand and teeth, he tied it in place.

Kannon wondered if a broken beer bottle had been the cause of Streak's lost finger.

All the while the mockingbird kept trilling.

"Shut up! Shut up!"

"You guys get a grip," one of the nearby picnickers said.

"Fuck you!" Streak charged toward the group but stopped as a predator would in a bluff. Instead, he did an about face and plucked the slingshot from his back pocket.

"Sorry, folks," Kannon said, attempting to mollify the offended party. "We're out of line."

Thwack!

Turning, Kannon saw the mockingbird plummet to the ground. He spun toward Streak, only to see him pocketing the powerful slingshot, bloodied hand and all. "Why in hell did you do that?"

"Noisy bastard annoyed me."

"You need the kind of help I can't give," Kannon said.

Kannon strode to the occupied picnic table and again offered his apologies. By the time he returned to his own table, Streak was straddling his V-Rod. He fired it to life and, before riding off, hollered, "You'll be seeing me again."

"What?"

"Keep a close eye on your wife and kid."

It was like he'd stumbled into an irate, vengeful dimension. Jaw muscles clenched, Kannon watched Streak depart Lost Maples, half tempted to chase after the asshole.

Instead, he drew a deep breath and exhaled. Most folks responded to adversity with growth, but not Streak. Apparently, he was one of those combat veterans who'd never faced his demons. Or, if Streak had confronted them, he'd lost the battle and was languishing in bitterness. Worst of all, he had apparently turned criminal. What in hell had happened to him?

In OCS, Streak had earned respect from his fellow candidates for demonstrating command presence, composure, and attention to detail. And now he'd morphed into desperation. It was a familiar state to Kannon. He'd suffered despair himself but, fortunately, hadn't succumbed to it.

Shaking his head, he gathered the beer bottles and dumped them in a trash can. He shifted his gaze toward a cluster of broad-leafed maples. The wind kicked up and sent sycamore leaves fluttering to the ground while the sweet smell of cottonwood trees wafted past. Nearby, a squirrel scampered across a stout limb toward its hoard.

After the reunion, he'd intended to hike along the dry, dusty Maple Trail and photograph the trees lining the Sabinal River that wound among the variegated limestone cliffs. He'd brought along his Mamiya 645 Medium Format camera for that purpose, even though the fall colors hadn't arrived.

Instead, feeling like he'd bitten into a spoiled grapefruit, Kannon returned to his K1200 RS. Leaning on the handlebar for support, he stooped and whacked his damaged Meerschaum pipe against the heel of his boot, then ground the tobacco ash into the pebbled concrete. Reaching into the rear pannier to put away his pipe, he heard an ominous hiss. Air was spewing from the rear tire. He knelt to discover a missing valve cap and a loosened valve stem.

"You sorry SOB!"

Two

Sweat dripped down Kannon's cheeks. Pissed, he removed the tire-plugging kit stored beneath the seat. In addition to usual repair items, the kit contained extra caps, valve stems, and a valve attachment tool for the CO_2 cartridges. He tightened the valve stem. As he reached for a sixteen-gram cartridge, an aging blue Camaro rattled into the parking lot. Rolling down a tinted window, a round-faced woman with thick black hair swept back in a ponytail peered at him.

"Trouble?" she asked.

"Flat."

Leaving the engine running, she opened the door and got out. Dressed in a bulging sweatsuit, she appeared to be Asian, probably Filipino.

"Got a bicycle pump if you need it," she said.

Her thick accent suggested English as her second language.

"You bet." Kannon set the cylinders aside and accepted the air pump. "These gas cylinders can be tricky to handle."

He pumped in the correct pressure and then capped the valve stem. Kannon returned the pump, which she tossed onto the rear seat. The woman slipped behind the steering wheel and shut the car door.

"Much obliged," Kannon said. "Few good Samaritans these days."

Diverting her attention from an open notebook lying on the passenger seat, she tilted her head back and stared straight ahead. "If I were you, I'd be more careful with whom I associate." The woman shifted into gear and sped off.

Kannon stroked his mustache. What was that about? The woman's timing seemed strange. It was as if she had appeared from nowhere. Had she been watching them? Possibly she had seen Streak vandalize Kannon's tire.

Regardless, the woman's grammar was fairly good for an ESL speaker. His cellphone chimed. It was his brother Roger.

"How did your reunion go?" his brother asked.

"Horrible!" Kannon recapped the encounter.

"You were able to fix your tire, right?"

"Yeah."

"At least you can get home. Thinking about that guy's threat, have you considered canceling tomorrow's trip to SyncTrak?"

"I've thought about it," Kannon said. "I need to talk to Lan."

"If I were you, I'd cancel it."

Kannon sighed. "It's an important meeting. We're to review marketing plans. Conduct an R and D session on implantable child-tracking devices."

"Use video conferencing."

"Good suggestion, but the Board won't like it if I'm not there."

Roger, Professor Emeritus of Accounting at the University of Texas—he held a doctorate—had run across SyncTrak while researching emerging high-tech firms and suggested Kannon take a look. Kannon did and liked what he saw. And now he was a paid consultant for a firm that manufactured electronics—from GPSs, tracking and monitoring devices, and cellphones to niche products such as prepaid cellphones—burners they called them.

"Tomorrow's agenda includes a breakout session with venture capitalists for additional financing. I need to see these guys face to face." The company was private, but there was a strong possibility of its going public. Kannon also wanted to negotiate equity positions for Roger and himself.

"Maybe Karen and I could chaperone Lan and the kid while you're gone," Roger said.

"Appreciate the offer. I'll run it by Lan and get back to you."

"Okie dokie," his brother said.

"Roger, Roger." Though his brother had never served in the military, Kannon enjoyed niggling him by using the military term for affirmation along with his name.

"Cute. Out," Roger said.

Kannon keyed Lan's speed dial. What was he going to tell her? *Stand guard! Look out for a nutcase riding a silver Harley V-Rod.*

"Yes, Kannon?"

"I'm running late."

13

"Is anything wrong?"

"Flat tire." Warn, not alarm, he thought. "Oh, be sure the security monitors are on."

"Why?"

"I worry about you and Derrick."

"Kannon—"

"Okay, Streak turned out to be a frigging nightmare. I shouldn't have come. I doubt he'll try anything but stay alert."

An exasperated sigh ensued, the type of sigh signaling, "This isn't over." He'd screwed up. Nevertheless, he'd placed his wife on edge and couldn't leave her hanging. Reiterating the encounter, he described Streak's appearance and riding mount.

"Keep your revolver handy," Kannon said. "I'll be home as soon as possible."

"When you get here, we will talk further."

"Okay."

"Do not worry about me," Lan said. "You know I can handle M-16s and AK47s, and I am a better shot than you with a revolver."

Touché.

After signing off, Kannon slipped the cellphone inside his jacket, then donned his riding gear. He mounted the K-bike, started it, and shifted into first gear. He crossed the shallow river and headed north. Five miles further, Kannon stopped to inspect his tire. After spreading saliva across the valve, he looked for bubbles and didn't find any.

Kannon resumed the three-hour ride home, leaving behind Lost Maples, now tainted with a bad memory. He flicked east on State Highway 39, proceeded alongside the South Fork of the Guadalupe River, and cruised past rolling hills stippled with cedar, mesquite, and red oak. On a long straightaway, his K-bike's shadow paralleled the fence line like an amorphous specter.

When he entered Fredericksburg, a mesquite-scented breeze enveloped him. The town was composed of historic buildings, boutiques, and antiques, as well as tasty German food. Along Main Street, decorative lights sparkled like sequined dancers. Buyers toting shopping bags and licking ice cream cones crowded the sidewalks.

Up ahead, a patrol car's lights flashed. Kannon downshifted

to cut speed. A state highway patrol officer was talking to a bunch of bikers whose motorcycles were angled three abreast and sardined into parking slots for customers of the Black Forest Restaurant. There didn't appear to be any serious confrontation.

Off to one side, Kannon noticed a lone Harley parked butt to curb. It was a silver V-Rod, and it was Streak's.

Kannon's heart rate accelerated. This could be an opportunity to resolve the not-so-subtle threat to his family. He wheeled beside the V-Rod and shut off the engine. After securing his helmet to the luggage rack, he strode toward the restaurant. A sauerkraut-laced odor, his one objection to German food, permeated the air like a pesticide and aggravated his lousy mood.

A waist-high rock fence skirted the limestone- and rough-pine structure. Kannon passed through a metal gate and entered the dimly lit restaurant, which consisted of two dining rooms linked by a stone fireplace.

Streak wasn't among the diners sitting at oval-shaped tables covered in checkered cloths. An overhead sign pointed to an outdoor rear patio. Kannon shuffled across the hardwood floor and outside encountered a hard-packed dirt surface, reminiscent of the earthen-floored homes in rural South Việt Nam.

One of the kitchen staff was leaning against a post, smoking a cigarette. A young couple seated at a spool table was holding hands.

No Streak.

A country and western song piped through outside speakers. The singer's words about forgiveness and letting go resonated, reminding Kannon of the first time he'd taken Lan country and western dancing. He was the klutz. They laughed about it, which wound up in his taking lessons—he, the man from Texas, she, the woman from Việt Nam. This made him smile.

So, what good would it do to confront Streak? It might only further sour the whole situation.

Lead me not into temptation!

Kannon walked to an empty table and grabbed a handful of shelled peanuts from a bowl. He cracked open a couple and popped them into his mouth—salty good. From his vantage point, he could see the street. The patrol car drove off. One of the bikers shot the finger at the departing officers.

Cowardly, he thought, like Streak, who had threatened his family and deflated his tire. Kannon dropped the remaining peanuts onto the dirt and ground them in with his boot heel. The PTSD trigger-activation that typically required four pounds of pressure pull now only required four ounces.

Lips compressed, he reentered the main restaurant. He wanted more data to assess Streak's threat. How serious had it been?

A narrow door, one he'd not noticed before, caught his attention. Above it, an unlit sign read, *Bar*.

Kannon opened the door and peered inside. In contrast to the darkened dining rooms, the homespun bar was well lit. Odd, he thought. Two women occupied one of five tables several feet away. The rest were vacant.

Perched on a barstool, tending a draft beer, sausage and sauerkraut, and a steaming peach cobbler, was the man Kannon sought. He sidled up to the empty stool on Streak's right and sat, shaking his head to ward off the bartender.

"I'll be in the supply room," the bartender said. "Ring the bell if you want anything." He slapped an old-time tap bell on the mahogany bar.

Kannon turned to Streak. "Who the hell do you think you are, threatening my wife and boy?"

The chopper pilot turned, arched his eyebrows. "Get the fuck out of here."

"Not until we settle up. Ever touch a piece of my property again, I'll beat the crap out of you. If you come close to or harm any member of my family, I'll kill you."

Streak sawed off a piece of sausage and popped it in his mouth. "Ask me if I give a shit."

Kannon wanted to shove the sausage up Streak's ass. "I don't know what happened that's turned you inside out and made you ugly, but it doesn't matter. Stay away!"

"I'll do what needs to be done," Streak said, glaring at Kannon.

This was not the assurance Kannon wanted. He should leave before doing something he'd later regret.

Streak reached toward an ominous bulge in his jacket pocket. Senses heightened, Kannon braced for action.

"Cigarettes, dumb ass," Streak said, with a mocking smile.

His knuckles turning white, Kannon slid off the stool and stood behind Streak. "Acknowledge what I've said, or—"

Streak spun the barstool around at Mach speed and brandished a six-inch-long K-bar. "Or what? You don't know what you're up against."

The women gasped. The bartender was nowhere in sight. Kannon motioned palm down, trying to convey for the women not to make any sudden movement.

He stared at the blade, then at Streak. "Let's see how good you are."

For a moment, it looked as though Streak might lunge, but Kannon, feeling quick and alert, held steady. As the faceoff continued, Kannon saw in Streak's eyes more misery than hate.

"Ah, screw this," Kannon said. Turning on his heels, he headed for the exit. A knife whizzed by his ear and embedded in the doorframe.

"Oh, my God!" one of the women hollered. "Call nine eleven."

Kannon pivoted in time to see Streak swiveling on his stool to face the bar. *Not falling for it, old boy.* Just as well the bartender was in the back, he thought. He didn't need more aggravation. To the ladies, "Don't bother. Just a disgruntled vet down on his luck."

Kannon grabbed the knife handle and yanked the blade out of the frame. He slid the weapon up his jacket sleeve as he exited the restaurant. What a waste of time, time which would have been much better spent with his wife and son.

He hurdled the rock fence and walked to his motorcycle. After stashing the knife in a side pannier, Kannon straddled the bike and hit the starter. He engaged the clutch and shifted into first, then twisted the throttle and shot down the main thoroughfare. Once on the highway, he quickly ratcheted into sixth gear, leaving Fredericksburg in the rearview.

Chilly air buffeted Kannon's body and dark clouds scudded across the sky, obliterating the late groping shadows. Oncoming

17

headlight beams refracted off his windshield like starbursts. Insects smacked against the windshield, and the odorous trail from a passing skunk polluted his nostrils. A fitting stench, Kannon thought. He'd come close to losing control inside the Black Forest, resurrecting and releasing his own destructive venom. If he'd reacted violently to Streak's provocation, well, it would've resulted in a backslide to recovery.

Feeling like he could bite a nail in two, Kannon clutched the handlebars in a vice-like grip and swung wide on a curve. He had to execute an abrupt counter-steer to return to his lane. *Calm down, idiot, unless you want to give a frozen-in-the-headlight deer a ride.*

Kannon reduced his cruising speed and raised his faceshield to sweep in the fresh air. Was he excessively worried? Perhaps. Looking at it more rationally, and based on Streak's skill with the slingshot, Kannon didn't doubt his classmate could have nailed him with the knife if he'd wanted to. The toss could've been a final act of frustration and resignation.

After passing through Llano, Kannon continued east on State Highway 29. Two hours later, he reached the turnoff to his home. It was a one-story ranch-style house constructed of cedar, pine, and limestone, which sat on a fifteen-acre granite plot carved from former ranch land. His lot fronted the highway and featured a half-mile-long private drive. A dry streambed ran through the property, filling and running only after a hard rain.

He loved the isolation, Lan, not so much. It was one of many unresolved issues piling up. "Derrick needs to be closer to children his own age," she'd said, more than once. Yes, they needed to have a long talk.

As Kannon rode up the long drive, the K-bike's engine hummed its steady rhythm. He stopped short of the garage door beneath the overhanging floodlight, slipped off his modular helmet, and hit the kill switch.

He dismounted. It was quiet, a state he usually favored. Tonight, though, the silence stoked melancholy.

Gone was the song of the cicadas, whose chirping rise-and-fall cadence reminded him of lazy, late summer evenings and portended the metamorphosis into autumn. Also gone was the simplicity of those times. Gone, as was his youth. Gone, as was his anticipated pleasant reunion with Streak.

He looked to the sky, now free of clouds. Unsettledness plagued him as he gazed at the stars. It was like a night patrol when all movement and noise ceased. You sensed a foreign, shadowy presence, but couldn't see beyond your man in front or behind.

Pursing his lips, Kannon returned to his motorcycle, keyed the remote to open the garage door, and manhandled the bike inside. He emptied both panniers and stashed the contents inside a collapsible carry bag.

"Knock, knock," he said, entering the kitchen through the connecting door. The light was off, but one glowed from the den. He walked in and found Lan asleep in her leather recliner. In her lap lay *Spring Essence,* a book of poetry she loved written by a Vietnamese woman two hundred years ago.

Kannon decided not to disturb her. They could talk later.

He carried the bag into his study and emptied the contents. A polished, gleaming steel blade tumbled out. Streak's knife. Kannon examined the weapon. Six inches long, the blade was razor sharp. The handle was made of bone-white ivory and contained an inscription: *Long Live the Posse Comitatus.*

What the hell? He was familiar with the term, Posse Comitatus, but lacked detailed knowledge.

Kannon flipped open his laptop. He signed on to the Internet and Googled *Posse Comitatus*. There were hits, lots, and he didn't like what he saw. A quick read led him to conclude that several current groups operating under the concept were extremists. They'd marginalized the original intent of the 1878 Act narrowly passed by the Forty-Fifth Congress, which was to preclude armed forces of the federal government being used for police actions. Law enforcement belonged under the purview of states and counties.

Far rightwing groups wanted complete power—to the exclusion of any federal government interference.

Streak, college graduate and veteran helicopter pilot, had fallen from grace and, whether by intent or by bad judgement, joined a militia group.

Damn! I've figured this wrong.

Three

Saturday, 17 October 2009, Bitterroot Mountains, Montana

Duncan Crandle, Commander of Border Slot Militia, pivoted in the pilot's seat and stared into the Jolly Green Giant's huge cargo hold. Nine armed militiamen occupied the starboard bench, while six unarmed candidates sat opposite. The gear needed to set up the training field was stashed in the center of the helicopter.

The candidates had mastered tactics and marksmanship but failed the standard obstacle course, a three-acre range that looped back on itself like a motocross dirt track. The course was sandwiched between mountain cliffs, granite boulders, and copses of trees at their forty-acre compound. The trials consisted of sprints, hurdles, rope climbs, water obstacles, tree climbing, low-crawling, and weight training—five successive runs. Thirty-nine minutes allotted time.

The candidates were being afforded one more chance to prove themselves worthy, worthy of joining the *White Might* movement. In Crandle's program, you either made the cut or disappeared.

Crandle turned away from the candidates and glanced at Spencer Whitehead, his second-in-command and acting copilot. A stout six-footer with curly brown hair, blackish handlebar mustache, high cheekbones, and square chin, Whitehead could be obstinate but was a capable leader with proven loyalty.

Shifting his gaze to the terrain below, Crandle's muscles tightened as a wave of anger swept over him. He spoke through his headset. "Flying over *our* land reminds me how the federal government confiscated my family's property in the early seventies. The Bastards!"

"Yeah, for not paying taxes and grazing fees. As if the Feds are entitled to the money," Whitehead said.

"The Feds aren't entitled to shit."

A strong cash base and subsequent ongoing cash flows were critical to financing his operation. Baseline funding had originated from the eighty-million-dollar lawsuit settlement against the driver and trucking company responsible for killing his wife and son. The at-fault truck driver was a nigger talking on his cellphone during an ice storm.

Crandle stared at the photograph taped below the instrument panel, a snapshot of his five-year-old son, Patterson. He had planned on grooming Patterson to take over Border Slot. Feeling his blood starting to boil, Crandle turned it down a notch by reminding himself what had evolved from the accident. *Without the settlement, I might never have gotten Border Slot off the ground.*

Bitter over the government land grab in the seventies, his dad had become a follower of the Posse Comitatus—restoring power to the county. William Potter Gale, an angry half-Jew disillusioned with his military career, was a principal proponent of the movement and an inspiration. His dad, who just stewed in misery, kept an autographed photo of Gale on his roll-top desk. But neither man ever acquired sufficient funds to take action.

I am different. This country was founded upon county sovereignty—ruled by White Might. Supplying trained militiamen, initiating racial violence, and employing electromagnetic weapons to destroy America's infrastructure is my way of supporting the Lord's will.

The helicopter entered a cloud bank. Crandle turned back to the candidates. "Think any of these guys will finish the course?"

"One, maybe two," Whitehead said.

"Our graduates are among the most competent and fearless white fighters in the world."

"I'm aware, Commander."

"We need more of 'em."

"I'm aware of that too. You don't have to pound it in."

"You need to recruit better. Too many rejects."

"I do my best," Whitehead said, frowning. "Besides, this upcoming exercise always eliminates some otherwise qualified applicants."

Crandle lashed out with a backhand to Whitehead's shoulder. "Don't be a prick. It's necessary."

The helicopter dropped beneath the cloud cover, revealing Montana's rugged Bitterroot Mountains. The rattling inside the HH-3E's cockpit battered his hearing like the din from machinegun bursts.

Crandle slipped off the headphones and massaged his earlobes. He repositioned his headset, then zipped his jacket to the collar to keep out the chill.

"When was the last time you saw Streak?" Crandle manipulated the cyclic stick and collective pitch control to level the chopper.

"Last Sunday, when you were in Spokane," Whitehead said, keeping his head buried in the sectional map. "Besides, we don't know for sure Streak's AWOL."

"Bullshit!" Crandle switched from instruments to visual navigation. "He is. And it pisses me off. His absence distracts from our mission planning."

Whitehead didn't respond.

"And you were off fishing," Crandle said, glaring at Whitehead.

"You sanctioned my leave. Remember? Besides, I left Hatfield in charge."

A mistake, Crandle thought.

"None of the others saw Streak afterward?"

"He flew the bird solo on Monday and returned late."

"Solo?"

"Yep."

Crandle grumbled. One person could handle the Jolly Green Giant on short jaunts, but technical specs called for a four-man crew—three, sans gunner.

"On Wednesday," Whitehead added, "Streak left a note on the barracks door saying his mother was ill and took off in that dilapidated Jeep of his."

"No one's heard from him since?"

"Nope! When I got back Thursday night, Hatfield brought me up to date."

"Why the hell didn't Hatfield call you beforehand?" Working the collective with his left hand, Crandle decreased the pitch angle to maneuver the helicopter into a slight descent. "Why the hell didn't you call me?"

"Damnit, Commander. You were due back last night, and Streak's note indicated he'd return in time to fly this mission."

Crandle stroked his chin. "I don't buy the sick mother bullshit."

"It's possible Streak's mother really is ill," Whitehead said. "You lost yours to cancer."

"Yeah, yeah." Crandle was glad none of his regular militiamen, who chatted among themselves, wore headsets. They didn't need to monitor this conversation.

"For all we know, he might be with his mom in a hospital," Whitehead said.

"With no commo? Get real. Streak's been gone three days."

Whitehead shrugged.

"He's your responsibility," Crandle added. "You mishandled the situation."

"What do you want me to do . . . shackle him at night? He's one of the guys. I can't maintain watch twenty-four-seven." Whitehead twisted one end of his handlebar mustache, his standard operating procedure when thinking or on the defensive. "After returning to the compound, I spent my time coordinating this training exercise. I can't do everything, be everywhere, at once."

Point taken, Crandle thought. "I'm sure you've called his satphone."

"Of course." Whitehead let out a deep, noisy breath. "No answer."

"What if the bastard has contacted the Feds?"

"Streak's not stupid."

"Neither am I. If word leaks, we could be in deep shit," Crandle said.

"Money, pride, and fear of death will keep him in line."

"Are you nuts?"

"Border Slot will remain intact."

"We can't take that gamble." Crandle's grip tightened on the cyclic control between his legs. The chopper lurched to the right and responded sluggishly as he fought to steady it. "The fuel mix may be off," he interjected. "Another reason I'm pissed. Streak's the only one who knows how to adjust it."

"I know, Commander." Whitehead squared his shoulders. "Maybe you shouldn't have exempted Streak from the normal training routine, including this final exercise."

"We needed a pilot! It's a mistake I won't make again."

Streak's AWOL status put Border Slot in a pinch. Crandle needed a full-time pilot so he and Whitehead could devote more time to militia tactics and strategy. And while Streak had taught them both how to fly, neither knew how to pull maintenance. If his pilot didn't return, Crandle would have to recruit another one, along with a mechanic.

"Find the son of a bitch," Crandle said.

Whitehead spat a glob of tobacco juice into a can wedged in his crotch and then glared at Crandle. His amber-colored goggles didn't mask his anger.

Let him steam.

"Fifteen miles from the landing zone," Whitehead said, folding his sectional map. "Turn to a two-two-five heading."

"Roger." Crandle repositioned his voice-activated intercom, setting aside their argument for later.

Through the front Plexiglas, Crandle noticed thickening nimbostratus clouds encroaching from the North. Clear visibility would be short-lived. The talus slopes and rugged mountain crests towering above the 8500-foot timberline would soon be shrouded in clouds.

He lowered the collective control lever to lose more altitude. The aerial panorama provided a much broader perspective of the scoured surface than when he and Whitehead had hunted bear and wolves at ground level.

Ironically, their relationship had begun years earlier on a hunt, when Crandle happened upon him in prayer position, paying homage to a wolf he'd killed. The muscular Whitehead, already sporting a handlebar mustache, was wearing jump boots, the kind paratroopers wore, and was shirtless. A tattoo on his back depicting an eagle holding a swastika in its talons caught Crandle's attention. Military, retired military, or paramilitary? In their talk, he learned Whitehead had been raised by the Nez Percé, a Native American tribe, which in the old days subsisted on hunting and fishing.

What Crandle hadn't understood at the time was the contrast between the Nez Percé's nonaggressive nature versus Whitehead's

24

right-leaning tendencies and loathing of minorities, Native Americans excluded. Over time Crandle learned that Whitehead was a former special forces candidate who had drummed out of the program due to insubordination and fighting against blacks and Hispanics. That explained some of it.

The young man had earned his stripes as a mercenary fighting alongside rightwing Contras against the Nicaraguan Sandinistas during the mid-eighties. Since then, he had performed *contractor* work, most recently in Afghanistan and Iraq. That explained a little more.

It wasn't until Whitehead revealed the details about his parents' murders at the hands of two Mexicans that Crandle realized the source and depth of Whitehead's animosity toward minorities.

Once that pattern was in place, he treated Whitehead like the son he'd lost, although at times, Crandle worried this rebellious trait might flare up. Whitehead also displayed an in-depth knowledge of military protocol, which helped instill discipline in both candidates and graduates. Border Slot wouldn't be Border Slot without his second-in-command.

Crandle returned his attention to the mission at hand. Ahead, a glacier-scooped, U-shaped basin popped into view.

"There's Trapper Peak." Whitehead spat another glob into the can.

"Got it," Crandle said, slipping into place purple-tinted goggles. With his left hand working the collective and his right manipulating the cyclic, Crandle altered the chopper's heading toward the box canyon-like cirque selected and prepped during an earlier recon.

The 10,200-foot-high mountain, which capped western Montana's Bitterroot Range, loomed closer. In the foreground, Engelmann spruce and subalpine fir bordered a secluded clearing dominated by a level granite shelf. The scarcity of roads in this pristine wilderness impeded detection, providing additional security.

Manipulating the cyclic and left pedal to keep the nose pointed into the prevailing wind, Crandle descended toward the LZ. He flattened the pitch angle and landed the six-ton chopper. As tree limbs recoiled from the backwash, Crandle activated the hydraulically operated rear ramp and shut down the bird. The five-bladed rotor wound down.

Crandle removed his headset and goggles. Whitehead did the same.

They disembarked through the starboard side door. Crandle's nine militiamen, wearing green and brown camouflage fatigues, black berets, and olive-green scarves, piled out the rear and formed a cordon behind the Jolly Green Giant. Badger, the dog handler, exited and ushered his German shepherd into position. The dog, Brick, also wore an olive-green scarf.

The sky darkened. Large, fluffy snowflakes began to fall. Crandle brushed the flakes off his jacket.

"Candidates, remove your blindfolds," Crandle commanded.

"Attention!" Whitehead barked.

The candidates snapped to, rising from their bench seats inside the cargo space, which was longer than some tractor-trailers.

"Right face! Forward march!"

Thirty-year-old Candidate Mandell called cadence, no surprise to Crandle, who had reluctantly accepted the recruit as a favor to OT, Mandell's older brother and a Border Slot graduate. During OT's post overseas, he had developed international connections with anti-government players promoting electronic warfare. Crandle found the idea intriguing, thus the favor.

Mandell wanted to lead, and Crandle hoped he would measure up. The other five candidates ranged in age from nineteen to twenty-eight. In addition to Mandell, Crandle eyed two others he hoped would survive the final exercise. Both had been successful in the mainstream world before finding their true paths. The athletic Drake possessed a bright, quick mind. The owner and manager of a seafood restaurant, he had gone home early one night and found his wife giving head to a neighbor. He dismembered them both.

The other favored candidate, Jason, was tough, determined, and as agile as a panther. After earning a college degree in marketing, he decided to test his shooting prowess in a road rage incident.

"Border Slot's a haven for those with righteous views and no place else to go," Crandle said.

"Don't I know it," Whitehead said, watching the candidates

disembark.

Recruiting by reputation, word of mouth, and exploiting existing contacts, Whitehead sought capable candidates whose lives were shattered in the conventional sense. All viewed violence as the necessary means to an end. The majority were violent offenders, either on the run or in violation of parole. That didn't mean they lacked talent.

While this group of recycled candidates looked promising, Crandle worried about Drake's and Jason's stamina, thus their failing grades on the obstacle course. As for Mandell, Crandle hoped he would succeed simply because of his regard for OT, who, like all graduates, was sworn to secrecy regarding this exercise.

By principle, Crandle couldn't reveal the context of his training range in advance. A candidate either completed the course alive or not. Graduates were sworn to secrecy, or else.

"Candidates," Crandle bit off the end of a Honduran Corona cigar, "I want street-smart guys with physical agility, ingenuity, and mental toughness. This is your last opportunity to prove you're worthy."

The candidates nodded in unison.

"Take charge," Crandle said to Whitehead.

"Under my supervision, assisted by Border Slot militiamen, you will set up a training field," Whitehead said, facing the applicants.

"Whatever the drill," Candidate Drake said, a smirk on his face. "I'm ready."

Confronting Drake, Whitehead jabbed his finger into the man's chest. "You think this is funny! We'll see how ready you are."

"Yes, sir," Drake said. "Meant no disrespect."

Crandle gave a head shake, indicating for Whitehead to let it ride.

"The gear's in the cargo compartment," his second-in-command said. "You've got fifteen minutes. Move it."

Double-timing to the chopper, the candidates hustled to the loading ramp and removed the equipment. They unrolled and erected a three-sided, twelve-foot-high reinforced steel-mesh barrier, which they anchored into position using steel rods inserted into pre-drilled postholes placed ten feet apart. Ropes knotted to ground-embedded stakes, using round turns and two half hitches, secured the assemblage.

Measuring fifty-feet wide by ninety-feet long, the field approximated the size of a basketball court—a sport Crandle loved as a kid. His father, though, had other ideas. He considered basketball a sissy sport and used a twelve-gauge to shatter the backboards in the high school gym to illustrate his point. To toughen up Crandle, his father subjected him to bull riding and calf roping at rodeos in Montana and Wyoming, as well as to rightwing agenda.

And here I am.

While the militiamen supervised and performed quality checks, Crandle and Whitehead retrieved from the chopper a large but lightweight camouflage netting, which was packed tight like a parachute. They grabbed their bows and one arrow each. Positioning themselves on either side of the Jolly Green Giant, in a synchronized release, they shot the netting over the bird. After securing the cover, they returned to the field.

The wind blew colder as the sky grew darker. The density of snowfall thickened, capping the needled conifers in a white glaze and blanketing the uncovered ground.

Crandle breathed in the sharp scent of fir and spruce as his men readied the field. A swell of pride filled his chest. Energized by the cold air, he grabbed his lariat, twirled it, and let fly. The lasso snared one of Brick's legs. The dog yelped.

The dog handler swore.

Crandle laughed.

"Launchers there," he heard Whitehead command.

Crandle returned his attention to the setup. After toying with manually cocked skeet launchers, he had developed more sophisticated models and fabricated modified, sequentially wired, generator-powered portable mobile launchers mounted on separate platforms with lockable wheels.

The electronically activated throwing arms were programmed to sling six-inch-diameter glass discs at a velocity of ninety-five miles an hour. The discs, an inch thick in the middle, were tapered to a razor-sharp edge at the disc's circumference. While the skeet launchers were relatively stable, sometimes discs were thrown erratically.

Now, under Whitehead's supervision, the candidates stabilized five launchers at the open end of the training field. Next, militiamen placed a two-foot-high, two-foot-wide trampoline at the fenced-in rear of the field before rejoining the group. Crandle grew amused when he noticed candidate Mandell staring at the trampoline with an inquisitive expression.

"Commander, what's going on?" the candidate asked.

"You'll see."

Putting away his lariat, Crandle walked toward an open, seven-foot-tall shelter erected behind the launchers. When he entered, the top of his head brushed against the canvas sagging from collected snowfall. He reached overhead and pushed against the top to clear it.

Whitehead switched on the portable boom box sitting on an improvised table. Wagner's *Die Meistersinger* trumpeted loud and sharp. After letting it play a minute, he decreased the volume.

Crandle lit the cigar.

"Candidates, October seventeenth is a day you'll remember the rest of your lives. This is your final test. If you fail, you will be drummed out. There is no second chance."

He motioned for Whitehead to retake charge.

"If you succeed," Whitehead said, "you will become a highly regarded graduate of Border Slot Militia, with lucrative compensation packages."

"Sir, what's the purpose of those launchers and the trampoline?" Withers asked.

"To test your stamina, determination, and agility," Crandle said, scowling.

His second-in-command handed each candidate a round, fourteen-inch diameter carbon-fiber shield with a handgrip on the concave side. Caruthers tossed his in the air and caught it like he would a Frisbee.

Crandle signaled to Whitehead, who blew a sharp whistle blast. Nolan and McAfee, militia sharpshooters, worked their way up stout spruce trees. Five others shielded themselves among conifer-sheltered rocky placements on the surrounding slopes. To complete security, Badger and his dog, Brick, took position behind the steel

29

mesh rear barrier.

Up front, Garrett would operate the launch controller. He started the generator. Its sound was unobtrusive.

His men carried the ubiquitous AK47 assault rifles equipped with standard thirty-round banana-shaped mags filled with 7.62 mm rounds. Despite the cumbersome three-position fire selector on the right side of the weapon—up safe, middle full auto, down semiautomatic—the AK was rugged and reliable, if not the most accurate rifle. Fitted with threaded suppressors, the rifles' retorts were muted somewhat but still allowed distinctive *pops*. The sharpshooters' rifles were scoped.

"Remember," Crandle said, "stay alert to low-flying aircraft and hunters."

He paused to let this sink in. They had been surprised once before. A twin-engine Piper Cheyenne invaded their space just as they were dismantling the setup at another site. After circling, the pilot moved on and nothing had come of it.

"Show the candidates their places." Crandle increased the volume on the boom box. Once again, Wagner's opera blasted into the wilderness, despite Whitehead's objection to the noise pollution, as he called it, that might draw unwanted attention.

Herding the candidates to the middle of the field, Whitehead placed them in a staggered semi-circle, eight feet apart from each other, and then joined his Commander underneath the canvas shelter.

"There is one rule," Crandle said. "You may not assume the prone position."

"Why?" one of them asked.

"Cause you'll be shot." Crandle's pulse quickened as fear crept into the candidates' eyes. "As I said . . . no more fucking questions."

A current of mumbling broke out.

"Ah, he's just kidding," Mandell said to his co-candidates. "Good joke, Commander."

"Think so?" Crandle cocked his left arm, then straightened his elbow. One sharpshooter fired a shot that ricocheted off a rock at Mandell's feet.

"Jesus Christ!" Caruthers jumped aside. Mandell didn't move.

Crandle motioned to the disc-launch controller. "Fire one!"

"What the hell?" Drake yelled.

Molded from glass, the saucer-shaped projectiles ripped through the chilling mist. Programmed to throw two discs at twenty-second intervals, a total of ten per round, the five catapults flung razor-edged discs from one- to eight-feet above ground level. The candidates would face seven rounds in total.

The first fusillade sliced forward. It was almost comical to watch the candidates brandish their shields.

One candidate suffered a nicked ear. No others were wounded.

"This is bullshit!" Candidate Jason yelled. "We didn't sign up for slaughter." He bolted toward the non-barricaded end of the field. Two other candidates followed.

A burst of automatic weapons fire raked the ground. The three froze in place, but their mouths didn't. It was as if they were prattling in tongues.

"I suggest you fuckers stop yapping and concentrate on avoiding discs," Whitehead said.

"You sons-a-bitches think you're tough? I'll show you tough." At Crandle's command, the controller activated the second round.

"Bring it on!" Mandell sidestepped a head-high projectile and hop-skipped a second disc. Positioning himself on the balls of his feet, he poised, fierce and determined, to face the next challenge.

Jason dodged one but got whacked in the arm by another. Blood spurted from below his elbow as his severed forearm flopped to the ground.

"My God . . . my arm," Jason screamed, his face contorted in pain.

"I'm disappointed, Candidate." Crandle tossed his lariat at him, but the noose fell short.

"He blocked his line of sight with his shield," Whitehead said, commenting like an analyst covering a boxing match.

Next came the part of survival training Crandle found fascinating, seeing how a wannabe combatant reacted to a near-crippling injury. Signaling to halt the launchers, he noticed the other candidates standing by, seemingly shell-shocked.

Indicted for second-degree murder, Jason whipped a

bandanna from his pocket, wrapped a tourniquet around his arm, and sprinted for the trampoline, which in theory enabled a candidate to vault the twelve-foot-high steel-mesh screen.

Jason reached the vaulting platform and bounded aloft, but a militiaman with his suppressed AK47 shot him in mid-air. The body impaled on a tree stump. Crandle needn't worry about him vanishing into the wilderness.

Though one candidate had successfully vaulted the wall in the past, the watchdog Brick had run him down. The wannabe was brought back to finish the course, which he did in fine fashion, enriching the forest floor with his blood.

Four

Crandle drew on his cigar, blew smoke rings, and glowered at the five remaining candidates. Their stunned expressions stoked his adrenaline. He liked the powerful feeling surging through him.

Whitehead, his cheek bulging from a chew, joined him alongside the disc-launch line. "Fall in," his second-in-command ordered.

The five remaining candidates formed a line. They were shivering from both fear and the cold. Crandle could have supplied jackets, but hell, Navy Seal wannabes weren't issued wetsuits when spending hours in the frigid ocean.

Snowfall continued, coagulating on the ground. Wagner's opera still streamed from the boom box. Crandle elevated his gaze and scanned the evergreens and rises to check how well his seven marksmen blended with the snow-covered trees and rocky outcrops. He could barely see his guys.

"Get the idea, gentlemen?" Crandle said to the aspiring militiamen. "Jason was too slow. Stay alert. Concentrate. Only five rounds to go. Negotiate these, and you're in."

"You bastards aren't combat leaders," candidate Stitch shouted. "You're nothing but a bunch of sociopaths."

Crandle shook his head. "You guys know as well as I do, we're talking about survival of the fittest."

"It's not a matter of if you die, it's when," Whitehead added.

"Death is about timing." Crandle thought about his Father in heaven. God would welcome these boys. He'd let 'em in because they were white and right. "If you don't pass the cut today, a better life awaits you."

Angry, determined looks spread across the candidates' faces.

"Next, you're gonna give us your *White Might is Right* version of the Islamic virgin shit. How many are waiting for us?" It was Caruthers.

"All your needs will be taken care of." Crandle kicked a mound of stones. "Enough talk. Let's get on with it."

"Launch round three," Whitehead shouted.

Except for Stitch, the other candidates sprinted to the rear of the field. Razor-edged saucers slashed through the snow-laden air as icy instruments of death. Stitch deftly sidestepped one missile, and, using his shield, blocked another.

Drake rolled to the ground but leaped up before being penalized for violation. Mandell darted and jigged, eluding all discs.

Caruthers got clipped in the foot. Another disc sliced his jugular. As Caruthers' blood flowed onto the white-crusted granite, Crandle halted the round. Withers and the other three remained unscathed.

"Mandell and Drake . . . clear the field," Crandle commanded.

His rifle leveled, Whitehead herded the two candidates to Caruthers' corpse, where they picked it up and carried the failed candidate to an array of body bags stashed near the chopper. After securing the body and zipping up the bag, his second-in-command led Mandell and Drake back to the field.

"Ready, Commander," Whitehead said, returning to his side.

"Count off," Crandle ordered his militiamen.

Garrett, Porter, Badger, Wolfhound, Hatfield, McAfee, Smitty, Timmons, and Nolan counted off in pre-established sequence, confirming their positions. Brick barked, confirming his.

"You're fucking crazy," Candidate Withers yelled. "You might as well burn us at the stake."

"He's doing right for *White Might*," Mandell said.

"God's work," Crandle said.

"Hooah," the militiamen shouted.

"Launch round four!" Crandle hollered to the controller.

Drake, the five-foot ten-inch ex-handball champ, recruited through a coded ad in *Soldier of Fortune*, deflected a disc with his shield. It caromed into Withers' side.

"Redheaded devil!" With blood gushing from the wound, the injured candidate withdrew the six-inch disc, and, brandishing it like a meat cleaver, charged Crandle.

Crandle drew his Colt .45-caliber semiautomatic and shot Withers in the middle of his forehead. Mouth yawing, the candidate dropped, his reddish-black blood seeping into the snow.

The Commander holstered his pistol. His second-in-command

winced as Crandle crossed Withers' name off the list.

Even though it was hard to see through the white-blanketed air, Crandle wasn't canceling the exercise. Two killers and one rapist vied for survival and the ultimate prize—graduation. Crandle paced behind the disc launchers as the fifth of seven volleys erupted.

A candidate dove to the ground and remained there. Whitehead blew his whistle. "Violation!"

It was Stitch, the midget-sized rapist. Recruited after defecting from a skinhead youth gang, Stitch had earned his nickname due to the number of stitches prison doctors used to patch up his knife wounds.

As he lay prone beneath the bottom tier of flying glass discs, rifle shots thudded into the ground around him. Stitch leaped to his feet just as the sixth round released. A disc whacked him in the forehead and embedded there. The rest of the glass projectiles slammed against the barriers and shattered.

"Another one down," Crandle said, frowning.

"Hell, Commander, what do you expect?"

Crandle's face turned livid red. He drew on his cigar, exhaled, and watched the cigar smoke swirl into the mountain air.

"Are you challenging my operation?"

"It just seems there's a more humane way to dispose of these guys."

"You're insubordinate. Who are you to challenge God's way? Is that why you washed out of Special Forces? Couldn't follow orders? Or just couldn't cut it?"

"That's a low blow. We said the past was past."

Crandle cocked his head toward his second-in-command. He didn't want this to go any further. "All right. Forget it. Let's finish our business here."

Whitehead hooked his thumbs on his pistol belt and scuffed the ground. "These guys are desperate, anyway. Most of them should be on death row."

"We're giving them a chance they would've never had otherwise," Crandle said.

Whitehead shrugged.

"Launch round seven," Crandle commanded.

"For God's sake . . ." Panting heavily, Drake leaned over and upchucked, then straightened and faced Crandle. "Time out!"

Hoots and shouts came from the tree-mounted militiamen. They sounded like a squad of raucous owls. "Come on, Drake, you can do it," one of them shouted.

A razor-edged glass disc caught Drake in the heart. Without a whimper, the candidate went limp like a sleeping child and collapsed to the ground.

It was over. One man stood—Mandell. Squat as a fireplug at five feet eight, crested with obsidian-black hair, the square-jawed man oozed violence. Twenty-five years old, a former high school football star, the man had cut the throats of three pro-abortionists at minority clinics, snuffed out one pedophile priest, and taken out two Muslims fingered as terrorists. It turned out they were only students, but no matter.

OT had expressed concern about his brother's recklessness. Even though Crandle had undermined Whitehead by accepting Mandell as a candidate, it appeared things might work out.

Satisfied, Crandle looked up in time to see Hatfield and Badger escort Mandell to a tree stump and motioned for him to sit.

"Have a beer," Whitehead said.

Mandell, eyes glazed and body heaving, accepted the beer, ripped off the top, and chugged the brew. When finished, he crushed the can and tossed it in the snow. Badger's dog, Brick, broke ranks, padded to the can, picked it up, and returned it to Mandell. This time the newbie put the flattened empty in his back pocket.

"You motherfuckers are crazy," Mandell said.

"No. We're God's supremacists, the chosen ones. Now, you're one too." Crandle enjoyed rewarding a new graduate. "We have something for you. Whitehead . . ."

His second-in-command jogged to the chopper and disappeared inside. He double-timed back, holding at port arms a brand-new AK. He handled it to Crandle, who motioned for Mandell to come forward.

Whitehead called the veteran militiamen to formation. Brick fronted Mandell.

"Don't sweat the dog," Crandle said. "He won't bite unless

ordered to. Right, Badger?"

"Right."

Crandle stubbed out his spent cigar and fieldstripped it. He placed a fresh one in his mouth and lit up. Next, he saluted Mandell and presented the new rifle, sans loaded magazine. "Congratulations."

Eyes fixed upon the dazzling rifle, Mandell took the weapon, worked the bolt mechanism, and stroked the barrel. Next, he loosened the strap, tightened it, and slung the weapon over his shoulder.

Crandle handed over a thick, sealed envelope. Mandell took the envelope and held it up to the gunmetal sky before ripping it open. "Hooah!"

"Twenty-five grand," Crandle said, "in cash."

"With no fucking taxes," Whitehead added.

A saucer-wide smile spread across the fucking new guy's face.

Crandle remembered seeing bull caricatures tattooed on Mandell's forearms. While he allowed his men to be tattooed—his own was the simple 88 on the back of his neck, which stood for Heil Hitler—he wanted his men's tats to be discreet. Mandell's, though, gave him an idea.

"Based upon your performance on the range and your tattoos, from now on, you will be called Bull," Crandle said.

"Hooah!"

Crandle took Bull aside and spoke in a low voice. "Let me remind you. No one knows you're OT's brother. And they won't. Don't let me down."

"I won't, sir."

We'll see.

* * *

The snowfall abated. Granite rocks, fir, larch, and pine were covered entirely and beginning to ice over. Worried about the white background increasing their vulnerability to detection, Crandle raised his binoculars and scanned the sky for aircraft, then the terrain for intruders. Visibility was limited, but he didn't notice any planes or any intruders.

I need to get these guys snowsuits.

Leaning on a russet-colored tree trunk beneath a needled canopy, Crandle reflected on Whitehead's ongoing complaint:

Putting candidates through this exercise makes no sense financially.

To waste resources was sinful, a lesson lashed into Crandle from his father's belt. Yet, he couldn't allow failed candidates to whistle-blow about Border Slot's mission, which could destroy everything. The solution was to kill those who flunked, and the training range was an excellent way to do it. Besides, setting up and maintaining operational control was good organizational practice for his home-based graduates, who were now laboring to clear the area.

This involved retrieving the cartridge shells for all seventeen rounds expended. Crandle didn't want a wandering forest ranger to stumble upon a shell casing. After completing this exercise, his militiamen began disassembling the field. They flattened the camouflaged steel-mesh walls and rolled them tightly. Next, they removed the corner and interim supports, all the while exchanging corny jokes.

"Did you hear the one about the candidate who was so dumb he thought ping pong balls was a Japanese venereal disease?" Hatfield asked.

Crandle closed his eyes and tuned it out. He heard only the crisp crunch of combat boots over crusted terrain. He smelled only the sharp scent of his cigar, salivating from its aroma, and considered the future.

Border Slot's militia output was growing. Along with the collapse of the Cold War, the traditional black market for major arms deals had morphed into a free market. Got money? You got weaponry, which fueled the demand for skilled fighters.

All told, his Border Slot home core numbered twelve, including Bull. Before this final training exercise, twenty-seven men had successfully completed the tactical coursework, firing exercises, field patrols, and obstacle courses and had been farmed out.

Within the U.S., drug gangs and complex-structured corporations paid as high as three hundred thousand dollars a pop to purchase one of his grads. Outside the U.S., he'd placed men in Germany, France, the Balkans, and in former states of the Soviet Union, usually bartering through Canadian contacts.

Crandle retained seventy percent of the contract price. The balance went to the militiaman. Casualties inevitably occurred. If his guy died or became incapacitated, that was it. No refunds.

Could he hold on to his niche? Crandle worried whether his operation could keep up with demand. If he failed to fill enough orders, clients might feed elsewhere. Yet, if he cranked out inferior graduates, trash talk could decimate his organization. And he still needed to maintain and expand his militia's core on the home front.

"We've completed the takedown, Commander," Whitehead said as he approached. "Equipment's loaded. The area's been policed."

Crandle nodded. Checked his watch. "The takedown process took twenty minutes. What's our goal?"

"Fifteen minutes," Whitehead said.

"Don't give me the cold temperature routine. No excuses."

"Commander . . ." Whitehead balled his fists.

Crandle shot him a glare and turned away.

* * *

Militiamen Wolfhound and Timmons carried the final corpse stuffed in a sagging body bag and dumped it into the cargo hold. The dog handler blew his silent whistle. Brick ceased prancing in the snow and trotted to one side of the rear ramp, where he assumed a wolf-like stance. Nine tired militiamen, one of them carrying the boom box, and an exhausted new graduate trudged into the cargo hold, followed by Brick.

Crandle hung back, staring at the sky, then at Whitehead. "Hold on a minute. Need to talk to you about Spokane."

"You mean the meeting with OT . . . how did it go?"

"Productive. OT has come up with a new wrinkle. It's a real opportunity, beyond what I expected."

Whitehead lifted his cap and scratched his scalp as if to say what now?

"Electromagnetic pulse weapons," Crandle added.

"Really! Are you reading science fiction again?"

"Don't go jerking my chain, Whitehead. EMP weapons are real. If employed properly, they'll fry electrical circuits, computer chips, and modern vehicle electronics."

"Okay, okay, I understand. Actually, I heard one intel source say EMPs were employed during the Bosnian conflict."

"According to OT, the U.S. Military, Israeli special ops, and Pakistan have all used them. You just don't hear about it." Crandle locked eyes with Whitehead. "I want you to learn all you can about the concept."

"Will do." Whitehead again stroked his handlebar mustache. Crandle knew the wheels in his head were turning. "Electromagnetic pulse weapons must be expensive."

"Don't worry about it. You just continue to bring in quality recruits. You know as well as I do cash is king. And I have the cash."

Crandle had liquidated his bearer bonds and stashed one million in his study wall safe, and another fifteen million in the vault inside the armory at the base of the cliff. Only Whitehead knew about it. The rest of his funds, some sixty-four million, were deposited in offshore accounts and in Swiss banks. What with expenses, his cash balance remained close to what he'd received in the lawsuit, but the growth opportunity loomed large.

"And you expect to get these EMP weapons . . . when?" Whitehead asked.

"This month."

"Are you serious!"

"Deadly serious."

"You're talking about a crash course in electronic warfare," Whitehead said.

"Cram for the exam." Crandle flicked cigar ash to the ground. "It won't be that hard. We're going to deploy the devices, not develop."

Whitehead eyeballed him with skepticism.

"Later, we'll work on developing our own in the workshop," which was where they modified the disc launchers and made silencers, among other aids. That reminded Crandle. It was time to reorder additional discs from their Canadian supplier.

"After you nab Streak," Crandle added, "we're going to disable a city."

"Which one?"

"Kalispell, Montana."

"That's right in our backyard."

"Roger that. A practice run will help us iron out the kinks, test

40

our logistics."

"So you say."

"If successful, we'll target larger cities. It's the fastest way to create chaos. Destroy infrastructure. Races will congregate. Let the riots begin. Whites against niggers, slant-eyes, spics, wetbacks, ragheads, and misguided Shields of David."

"I get it," Whitehead said, boarding the helicopter.

The ceiling was low due to the crappy weather. With high humidity and low temperature, icing was a possibility.

"Whitehead, I hate flying in this crappy weather. We need to closely monitor our velocity, air pressure, and temperature. We don't want to have to set the chopper down."

"Roger."

After taking a final puff on his cigar, Crandle snuffed and fieldstripped it. Then he scattered the ashes in the wind, just as he had done with Patterson's cremated remains. If alive, his son would be thirty-one, a pilot, and a leader in the Border Slot Militia. For Crandle, it was ordained for them to reunite in heaven because *White Might is Right*. Streak, though, was destined for hell.

I'll dump his ashes at the bottom of a shithouse.

Five

Saturday Night, 17 October 2009, Fredericksburg, Texas

Elbows planted on the Black Forest Restaurant's bar, Streak propped his chin on one hand and reached for his beer with the other. Willie Nelson's melodic "Red Headed Stranger" played in the background.

The music saddened him.

After taking a swig of beer, he slumped. He wasn't a has-been but a never-was. His Việt Nam exploits meant nada. The grim future awaiting him consisted of jail, life on the streets, or death by the Border Slot Militia, perhaps a combination of all three and in short order. No one was going to help. He was destined to finish life as a maggot in a shithole.

Might as well kill myself. Kannon could've at least left my knife.

Frowning, he swiveled on the barstool and hopped off. Ambling toward the jukebox, Streak noticed the two women, one of whom had screeched, "Call nine-eleven," exchange warning glances. In unison, with the screech of wood grating on wood, they scooted back their chairs.

As they hurried toward the exit, the bartender returned from the supply room. "Whoa, ladies. Where're you going? It's early."

"Not with that nut case here, it isn't," one of them said.

Bitches all! If you want to see real nut cases, you should meet Crandle and the rest of the psychos.

"What's that all about?" the bartender asked him.

"Haven't the foggiest," Streak said over his shoulder. He slipped several quarters into the coin slot and selected an array of Willie Nelson's and Merle Haggard's more upbeat classics. There weren't that many uplifting tunes.

"You hit on those gals?"

"Nope." Streak resumed his post at the bar. Abstaining from his now lukewarm sausage, he fiddled with his dessert. The sweet-smelling peach cobbler had melted the vanilla ice cream and turned the concoction into a syrupy slush. He scooped a mouthful.

He'd screwed up big time at Lost Maples by trying to force Kannon to fork over twenty-five K. Yet, what could he have done differently? He could've revealed more about his militia connection, or just asked for ten grand, or come up with a better lie, like needing money to cover tuition for his kid's final year of college.

Or just tell the truth—how he didn't want to pilot for a hate group whose goals included killing all minorities and destroying the electronic world—how badly he wanted to leave behind three years of misery and escape Border Slot—and how the fear reprisal of by death kept him from doing so.

"You can leave anytime," Crandle had said while tapping on a model coffin sitting at the edge of his desk.

Streak shook his head. What about the CIA's Sindy Zeller? He wasn't sure she was who she claimed to be, even with her allotting him a crappy thousand-dollar advance. Should he continue playing her game? Would she, could she, really put him in jail? After all, he had a rap sheet.

"Another draft?" asked the bartender.

"Yeah."

His hand hurt. Throwing the knife had aggravated the wound, causing it to bleed again. Streak slipped off the barstool and entered the restroom. His mirrored reflection showed a gaunt man. After washing his bloodied handkerchief and hand, he dressed the injury. Probably should visit an emergency room, he thought. Yeah, right. Without insurance, it would be cash only. And the advance Zeller had given him was dwindling. Forget it. Drugstore meds would have to suffice.

Back to the future. What should he do? Call Whitehead? Buy more time? "Hey, this is Streak. My mother died. Just need a couple more days to wrap things up."

Yeah, call Whitehead. That's it. He tapped the keypad on his cellphone, then shut it off. Whitehead would ask questions, questions he didn't want to answer. Why didn't you call sooner? Where are you? Ad infinitum. And then Crandle would put him on the range.

Streak exited the restroom. A fresh draft beer, condensation beading on the glass, awaited him. He wrapped his injured hand around the cold glass. Not much relief.

He sipped his beer. The antique wall clock ticked. All he wanted to do was escape the militia, escape Sindy Zeller. If only he hadn't picked her up—or rather—it was the other way around.

* * *

It began on Saturday, 3 October. Streak, down in Missoula on a weekend pass from Border Slot, sat on a barstool at a crowded sports club near the Clark Fork River. Half watching a pro football game through a haze of cigar and cigarette smoke, he was surprised when a woman approached.

"You look like an interesting guy," she said.

He scoped her out. A tall, slender gal with blue-gray eyes and close-cropped, russet-colored hair, she smiled at him in a sensuous, mischievous way. His gaze trailed past parted lips, beyond hard nipples pushing against her sweater, and stopped at the slit in her tight-fitting, long black skirt.

"Hey! I'm up here," she said.

The woman appeared to be in her late twenties or early thirties.

Streak extended his hand. She responded with a double-hand clasp. His antennae telescoped. So did his dick.

"What brings you to Missoula?" Streak asked.

"Lame," she said. The woman placed her left foot on the rung of his stool, which exposed her creamy thigh adorned with an iron cross tattoo. "I expected better."

Streak shrugged. "Your hair says dyke. Are you?"

"Would you like to find out?"

"How much?"

Oh, man, I shouldn't have said that. Think entrapment.

"I should slap you."

A chorus of shouts erupted. The favored team must've scored because the neon Budweiser sign flashed on and off like an electronic scoreboard.

"Actually," she went on, "I'm here to organize a motorcycle rally for next spring."

"Oh?" Streak raised his eyebrows.

"Do you mind?"

Before he could respond, the gal grabbed the empty stool next

44

to his. Her perfume, which smelled like wild lime, cut through the acrid smoke. The blend reminded him of poignant scents in Southeast Asia.

"Name's Sindy Zeller . . . That's Sindy with an *S*. She drew out the letter in a long hiss, like a viper.

Ms. Zeller ordered a Glenlivet neat. "Another beer for him," she said.

Streak lifted his draft in acknowledgment before gulping the rest of it down.

"What happened to your finger?"

"Industrial accident." He'd lost it handling one of Crandle's death discs. "Are you really in Missoula to organize a motorcycle rally? You don't look like a biker."

"Honey, I can dress up. I can dress down." She touched his arm. "I bet that's your V-Rod out there."

Streak nodded. He imagined Ms. Zeller, legs spread wide, riding pillion.

"Hot," Zeller said.

"So are you." Not particularly pretty, her appeal was raw, sexual, the type who *did things* to guys. It'd been months since he had sex.

The bartender delivered the scotch neat and another draft beer. Zeller swept her tongue across her lower lip. "You're probably wondering why I approached you."

"The question crossed my mind."

"I've made inquiries and understand you're a helicopter pilot."

"Yep." Inquiries from whom? Streak wondered. In addition to rally organizer and-or hooker, he added the possibility of *Federales*. Maybe he wasn't going to get laid. "I'm a contract pilot, props and choppers."

"You work for a wilderness outfit, right?"

"Roger. Groups hire us to transport hunters, wilderness skiers, that sort of thing," which is what he thought the Border Slot group to be when signing on, a nondescript company that ran wilderness adventure trips. "What do you want with me?"

"I need to transport a couple of bikes to the rally site."

"Why not hire a trucker? It'd be cheaper."

"These are special motorcycles."

Streak narrowed his eyes. "How special?"

"Two custom-made bikes await pickup at a warehouse in Calgary."

"Again, why not hire a trucker?" The only reason to jump the border was to avoid detection or customs. Yet he'd never heard of motorcycles being used as euphemisms for contraband.

Walk away.

"Well, if you're not interested . . ." Zeller swiveled on her bar stool and pressed her knees against his leg.

"I didn't say I wasn't interested."

He'd have to evaluate logistics—distance, chopper speed, headwinds, tailwinds, fuel capacity, and cost. It wouldn't be wise, but thought he could do it, make a pickup and delivery in four to six hours. He'd flown the chopper solo before, for refueling mostly, and once into Canada. He would have to arrange the flight when both Crandle and Whitehead were away from Border Slot, which was rare.

"What's in it for me?" he asked. A crescendo of boos arose from other patrons, perhaps disputing an official's call.

She leaned close and brushed her mouth across his ear. "I'll make it worthwhile."

The scent of wild lime lingered. He wanted more of it, in fact, hoped her pussy carried the same fragrance.

While consuming a couple more drinks, they negotiated a time frame and fixed price—an initial fifteen grand via certified check, to be released upon taking possession of the product in Calgary, plus the cost of transport fuel, then an additional sixty grand upon delivery. The more they talked, the more he doubted any Fed connection. It seemed like a drug deal. Yet, with seventy-five thousand bucks, he could escape the militia and recover his life.

"I'll pay the tab," Zeller said, patting his thigh.

This is too good to be true.

Six

It was too good to be true.

Following the lure of sex and money, he had mounted his V-Rod and trailed Zeller's black Toyota Tundra to her Missoula hotel room. Once inside, she opened a suitcase and tossed two pairs of handcuffs on the four-poster bed.

"Clothes off," she said.

Streak couldn't disrobe fast enough. He flopped on the bed and spread his limbs. Zeller cuffed his wrists to the posts, then staked each leg to the nearest post. His dick was as hard as a steel pipe. She stroked his penis at a teasingly slow pace, almost making him come.

"Would you like me to finish with my mouth?" Her voice was husky, her eyes smoky.

"Oh, God, yes."

Zeller unbuttoned her shirt and hiked up her skirt, revealing caramel-colored skin. She knelt between his legs and lowered her head as if to go down on him but stopped. "We have a little business to conduct first," she said.

"What? Are you crazy?"

"Like a fox."

She rose, withdrew documents from a briefcase, and placed a ballpoint in his cuffed hand. "You're the designated carrier. I am the consignee. After landing in Calgary, you'll present a transfer bill of lading to the consignor, where you will receive a certified check for fifteen grand drawn on the Calgary Royal International Bank."

"Oh, come on . . ." Streak fixed his sight on the *V* between her thighs. "Please . . . finish me."

"I'll finish you all right," Zeller said.

She freed his right hand, then guided his signature three times. Of course, he couldn't read the papers, much less have a clue what they contained. It never crossed his mind to question Zeller about her sources.

After that, the touch of her sucking, probing lips commanded his attention, as did the taste and smell of her lime-scented pussy. And all he saw was dollar green and a way to desert the militia.

Seven days later, on Saturday the 10th, he'd dropped off his V-Rod at a motorcycle shop in Kalispell for new tires, then rented a truck and parked it at a private airstrip north of town. He drove his Willys Jeep back to Border Slot. On the 12th, with Crandle in Washington State and Whitehead on an extended hunting trip, Streak bit deeper.

Early Monday morning, after telling the militiamen of the need to keep sharp his flying skills, Streak grabbed his passport and took off in the Jolly Green Giant. Upon reaching Calgary, he navigated southeast of the city to a helipad and landed. A fuel tanker and a two-and-a-half-ton truck were parked at a nearby warehouse.

Streak lowered the rear ramp to the cargo hold and, planning on completing a quick turnaround, kept the blades turning. Striding toward the warehouse, he encountered a rough-cut, burly man wearing a plaid mackinaw who initialed Streak's bill of lading. "Take these papers to the bank there, while I load the cargo and refuel your bird," Rough Cut said.

"That's a branch bank? It looks more like a massage parlor."

Streak shifted his gaze to the truck, which had a hydraulic lift. A hand-operated pallet jack sat nearby. Two large wooden crates sealed with padlocked chains occupied the lift.

Custom motorcycles my ass, he thought.

Inside the "bank," a dipshit wearing a pinstriped suit, granny glasses, and a bowtie stood beside a barren desk. Streak forked over the documents.

"The bills of lading, release forms, and ID appear to be in order, sir." The clerk handed him a certified check.

"An account was to have been set up in my name," Streak said.

"Yes, sir. Just need you to sign this new account form."

Streak did. "I'd like to withdraw the funds now."

"I can't do that without Ms. Zeller's signature, sir."

Streak examined the check, held it up to the light. It was payable to him but required two signatures, the first by a representative of Calgary Royal International Bank and the second by Sindy Zeller. The latter's signature was missing.

Streak swore, slammed his fist on the desk.

"This check lacks Zeller's signature. That's not the

arrangement."

"Yes, it is."

"The hell it is, you pompous asshole!" Streak reached for the clerk's lapel, but a viselike grip clamped his wrist.

"You should have asked Ms. Zeller for a cashier's check," the clerk said, releasing his hold.

"Go fuck yourself."

"A pleasure doing business with you, sir," the clerk said.

Streak glared at the bank clerk, wanting to soak the man's balls in acid. Instead, he stuffed the check inside his jacket and retraced his steps to the chopper.

His satellite phone buzzed. "Caller ID blocked," the display read, but Streak answered.

"All locked and loaded, I understand." It was Zeller.

"You're screwing with me," Streak said.

"I'm just ensuring delivery, dear. You'll get your money."

"You f—." The Viper bitch clicked off.

Shit! What could he do? The truck was gone. No one was in sight, and he couldn't offload the cargo by himself. How could he have been so stupid! Zeller now held him in virtual handcuffs.

Settling into the cockpit, Streak lifted off. He took advantage of a tailwind and pushed the chopper's speed to its max of one hundred sixty-four miles per hour. Two hundred miles approximated a ninety-minute flight.

At 1800 hours, he landed the helicopter at the private airstrip north of Kalispell and, using a pallet jack stashed inside the rental truck, unloaded the two crates from the chopper.

An hour later he began the three-hour drive to Missoula. It took him four. He reached Zeller's rendezvous point on Mullan Road west of Missoula around 2300.

Sindy Zeller emerged from one of the "abandoned" offices. Gone were the tight-fitting blouse, black skirt, and spiked hair. Instead, she wore camouflaged fatigues, her hair blond and long. Ten yards behind Zeller stood three stout-looking men wearing crew cuts, full battle gear, weapons, but no insignia.

Zeller greeted him with a drawn weapon and flex-cuffs. "No blow job this time," she said, out of earshot of the three men. "Arms behind you."

He complied, and she slipped on the cuffs. Even without makeup and dressed like a guerrilla, she looked sexy as hell.

"Why are you arresting me?"

"Transporting illegal weapons."

Streak stiffened. "Illegal weapons?" So, it wasn't a drug deal after all. "The unsigned certified check, the additional sixty thousand bucks upon delivery . . . total bullshit, right?"

She sniggered.

"Are you really CIA?"

Zeller flashed an ID. It appeared to be CIA, but who in hell knew what was official.

Her three *whatevers* encircled him. One of them emptied Streak's pockets, including his passport, and handed it to Zeller. "For safekeeping," she said.

"Well done, bitch."

"Thank you." To her men, "Unload the truck."

"What the hell's in those crates?" Streak asked.

"Stinger missiles." Zeller's parted lips morphed into a thin line. "Here's the deal. Reveal the militiamen's names and the militia's location. You will testify against them or spend the rest of your life in prison."

"I'm not involved with a militia." Even if Zeller was CIA, how did she know this crap?

"Not buying it, Streak." She paused, her eyes steely like ball bearings. "I'll cut you a better deal if you go undercover."

"You mean, wear a wire?"

"Oh, you're quick."

Streak's throat constricted. If he ratted on Crandle and the others, could the Feds round up—indict, convict, and sentence—the Border Slot Militia? He doubted it. Besides, the militia's tentacles reached into and out of prisons. He'd never be free.

"I want a lawyer," he said.

"Better you cut the deal."

"They'll kill me." Streak winced as the flex-cuffs bit into his wrists.

Zeller shrugged.

"Why can't you use one of your own professionals?"

"We prefer you."

Streak shuffled his feet. He stared at the men unloading the crates and wished he were fishing for trout on the Cumberland River in Kentucky. "I want witness protection."

"My, we're plucky aren't we?" Zeller turned and hollered at her comrades. "Hurry up." Then she faced Streak and removed the cuffs. "Witness protection? No. You don't rank that high."

"A one-way ticket to Brazil?"

"Nice try."

"I can't believe this," Streak said.

"It's your decision."

"What choice do I have? Okay, I'll wire up."

She brought out the wire and showed him its mechanics and how to mount it beneath his clothes. Zeller also advanced him one grand in cash.

"Spend it wisely," she said.

"That's it?"

"Complete the mission, and we get a conviction, there's more in store."

Yeah, like I believe you.

Exhausted, instead of driving back, he turned in the rental truck at a Missoula U-Haul and, saddled with an invalidated passport and a probable worthless promise of money, hopped a flight to Kalispell. It was there he decided to bolt. Before flying the Jolly Green Giant back to Border Slot, he debated whether to discard the wire apparatus Zeller intended for him to use to entrap Crandle—or keep it. He chunked it.

Early Tuesday morning he called every number in his address book—people he hadn't talked to in years—which he kept in a hollowed-out book in his footlocker. No family members could help, and only Kannon Ballard had agreed to meet.

Before leaving, he'd cleaned and straightened his place, but left a half-eaten sandwich and an opened beer on his table. He wrote a "sick mother" note and taped it to the barracks door, locked his cabin, and took off at 1200 hours on Wednesday the 14th. He drove his World War II-era Willys Jeep into Kalispell, picked up his V-Rod with the new tires, and then trailered the bike to Whitefish, where he garaged the Willys. He offloaded his motorcycle, ditched the trailer, and took off for Texas on two wheels.

* * *

17 October was drawing to a close. Half his advance was gone. He needed a revised plan.

The Black Forest Restaurant and Bar was filling up, the noise escalating. Streak's blood-soaked-kerchief-wrapped hand throbbed.

He took another drink of beer and contemplated the messages left on his satphone by both the CIA and Border Slot. Sindy Zeller's last voice message troubled him most. "We know you're in the Texas Hill Country, that you've contacted one Kannon Ballard. We've checked him out. He has a checkered past. It seems his Vietnamese wife may have entered the U.S. under suspicious circumstances."

Zeller or one of her group was tracking him. How? Had someone else been at Lost Maples? The picnickers were there before he arrived. Couldn't be one of them. He remembered seeing a rattletrap blue Camaro, but never saw the driver. Streak shook his head. No way a battered vehicle would be involved in government surveillance. Yet, some government freak might be observing him in the restaurant now. Scanning the patrons, he saw no one who appeared out of character.

Streak rehashed all the events, all the key players. The more he considered Zeller's comments about Kannon, the odder they seemed. Yet Kannon remained his best hope to flee the country. Leverage, he needed leverage.

Maybe Sindy Zeller considered Kannon a militia contact if not a member. Whether she did or not was irrelevant. Streak could twist the information to his advantage.

Kannon is a loner, a maverick. Streak doubted Kannon wanted any of his dirty laundry scrutinized by the Feds. So, give me bucks, or I'll inform Sindy Zeller you're a front man for the militia. Also, exploit Kannon's New Mexico gunfight incident. Even better, threaten to expose his Vietnamese wife for illegal entry. Explain that!

Streak paid the tab and exited the restaurant. Other motorcycles rumbled past as he walked to his V-Rod, straddled it, and fired her up. He'd pay another visit to Kannon Ballard.

Seven

Sunday, 18 October 2009, Kannon Ballard's Residence, Texas Hill Country

Oak leaves fluttered in the pre-dawn breeze as Kannon completed his five-mile run. Slowing his pace to a brisk walk, he collected his breath, then removed a water bottle from his waist pack and took two sips. The water went down cool and refreshing, a cleansing wash from Streak's unexpected bile.

He capped the bottle and stuffed it in his pack. His perspiration evaporated in the crisp, dry air, which was a brief respite because the days still grew warm. He rounded a bend and paused at a rise overlooking his property. Kneeling, he picked up a handful of pebbles and sifted them between his fingers.

Gritty. Like the infantry.

The jog cleared his mind. Despite the declining physical intimacy and other issues in his marriage, Kannon thought himself a lucky man. Second marriage. Second child. It was like being reborn.

It was clear Lan was pissed that he'd put his trek to Los Maples ahead of her desire to take a family trip to Austin. "I want to take Derrick to see a movie and then go to BookLitls," she had said.

Streak's not-so-veiled threats added to her discomfort. And he was scheduled to leave town later today for the SyncTrak meeting in San Jose. He hoped Roger's offer to stay with Lan and Derrick was still on the table. If not, Kannon would stay home.

He stood, brushed the grit from his hands, and resumed walking. Family! What could he do to enhance it in the near term?

Lan missed her brother terribly, as well as her deceased parents, sister, and cousins, and considered her new family priority number one. As his shirt flapped in the breeze, an idea took shape, one he figured would please Lan, because there was one other family member to consider—her nephew.

Chấn, Kannon's interpreter during the war and Lan's brother, had borne a son. His name was Đăng Đạo, and he had been two years old when kidnapped by the Việt Cộng. Kannon was made aware of him during his 2002 return to that country.

In a bizarre twist of events, Đăng Đạo had wound up in America running a New Mexico-based criminal organization dealing in narcotics and weapons, using an import/export business as a cover. Despite being reared by the Việt Cộng—America's enemy during the Việt Nam War—Đăng Đạo had earned an MBA on top of an undergraduate degree in linguistics and computer science. He was also a ninja.

When Kannon tracked down his American nemesis from the War, he discovered Đăng Đạo was carrying out a proxy vendetta against the same guy. It was a long, complicated story, but at the time he and Đăng Đạo fought on opposite sides—even though they had a common enemy. The "kid" gang leader had left him with a lingering threat: "We must never meet again. I will not spare you next time."

Lan knew this.

Kannon was aware they were having ongoing phone conversations. He didn't mind as long as he was kept out of it, even though, allegedly, Đăng Đạo's businesses had transitioned into legitimacy. Thus, although Đăng Đạo's kill threat had supposedly expired, Kannon remained wary.

Up to now, out of respect for Kannon's feelings, Lan had never met her nephew face-to-face. Time heals. *If I suggest she meet her nephew in person, it might mollify her frustration at my absences.*

Kannon reached the attached garage and squeezed between his Jeep Cherokee and Lan's yellow Volkswagen. He recalled his wife's excitement after completing her first significant purchase. Fascinated with her brother-in-law's VW, Lan wanted one as well, only in a different color.

Slipping into the utility bathroom, Kannon showered, then pulled on a pair of blue jeans and a damp T-shirt from a disrupted dryer load. He grabbed his cellphone and placed a call.

"Hey, Roger, it's me. Your offer to stay with Lan still good?"

"You bet. Karen too."

"Great. I'll discuss it with her and get back to you."

Kannon rang off and strolled into the roomy kitchen, Lan's household focal point, along with their son's room.

"Did you have a good run?" Standing at the kitchen sink, Lan was hand washing Derrick's breakfast dishes. She insisted on this practice because she didn't trust the dishwasher to do it as well, and Kannon had given up trying to convince her otherwise.

"Yes, thank you."

She offered him a glass of orange juice, which he gulped down. Kannon gave her a quick hug, his moist T clinging to her ankle-length silk robe like melted chocolate.

A sweet aroma from Derrick's leftover oatmeal permeated the kitchen. Lan always added imported Vietnamese honey. At least it smelled good. To Kannon, the oatmeal tasted like sweetened cardboard, but Derrick lapped it up as his father did ice cream.

"I am sorry your reunion with Streak did not go well."

"Me too."

"You and I have come a long way in six years," she said, her eyes fixed on his. "We have cleaned up our lives and distanced ourselves from the pain and suffering we underwent in Việt Nam. My biggest blessing is Derrick."

"I know." Her implication being, Kannon interpreted, their sex life was still relegated to the back burner.

As she turned toward the refrigerator, her billowing robe parted at the waist, exposing buttery-smooth thighs. At age forty-seven, his exotic-looking wife still turned heads—and with little makeup. Her skin shone of henna and copper, while auburn-colored eyebrows shaded dark brown irises, and her long hair accented full lips and well-defined cheekbones. Her partial French ancestry added a luster that would make Van Gogh proud.

Kannon missed the days when she'd greet him wearing a sheer negligee and panties. Of course, there was now an inquisitive son to consider. Parading around half-nude was off the table. But routine had invaded their marriage until it was like being roommates, dressing and undressing in separate closets, reading while eating, watching TV.

"Most important," Lan continued, "is to provide a safe, learning-friendly environment for our son. Why complicate matters?"

"I'm sorry. I screwed up. How was I to know what Streak had become! It's hard to lose a friend." Kannon swallowed the lump in his throat. If anyone knew about losses—

"I do understand," Lan said.

Of course you do.

"About my business trip . . ." Kannon said.

Lan turned, folded her arms, and narrowed her eyes like she was zeroing in on a dartboard.

"Roger and Karen have agreed to come and stay with you while I'm gone. Is that okay? If not, I'll cancel the trip to San Jose if it'll make you feel more comfortable."

"Well, that is all right. Derrick loves them both, and I enjoy their company. Are you sure it is okay with them?"

"Yes. And I'll be back Tuesday afternoon." Kannon made another quick call to confirm the arrangement. After he rang off, "I have another suggestion."

Lan arched her eyebrows, gave him a what-next stare.

"Why don't you track down Đăng Đạo and arrange for a visit while I'm in Silicon Valley?"

"My nephew?" Her eyes widened. "I thought you did not want me to see him."

"Well, you said he's legit now. Besides, he threatened me, not you. No reason you couldn't meet him alone."

She gave him an inscrutable look, but he understood from experience that behind her expression lay truckloads of emotion.

"Kannon . . ." Lan clucked her tongue, perhaps considering what to say next. Instead, turning back to the sink, she picked up a soapy glass, which slipped through her fingers and shattered on the tile floor. Staring at the mess, Lan compressed her lips as if to stifle any expletive that might erupt. She took a deep breath and strode to the pantry to retrieve the dustpan and whiskbroom.

"Let me do it," Kannon said, taking the items from her.

"All right."

Kannon wielded the whisk broom and swept glass shards into the pan, then raked the floor with a moist dishcloth. "Done," he said, wiping his hands on his jeans.

"Thank you," Lan said. "Derrick has been asking for you."

So much for the nephew suggestion.

"Where is he?"

"In the den watching cartoons."

Kannon plodded into the den and dropped beside the shirtless Derrick. His son sat cross-legged in the middle of a thick Asian throw rug that covered part of the polished pinewood floor.

"Hey, dude," Kannon said.

Derrick cut his eyes away from the television. "Hi, Daddy K. Let's wrestle."

Grasping his son's ribs, Kannon kneaded them like a baker kneading dough. Derrick giggled. Then, letting his boy pin him like a triumphant wrestler, Kannon noticed Derrick's developing muscles. He was all boy. His hair color, fullness, and length mirrored Lan's, while his skin tone, facial features, and eyes resembled Kannon's. Absorbed with board games and computers, Derrick demonstrated an agile mind, but he also displayed an interest in the physicality of sports. There was still father-son cuddling, but Kannon understood that would soon pass.

"Let's throw the football," Derrick said.

"Can't today, son. I'm flying to California on a business trip."

"I want to go."

"Sorry, not this time."

The gleam vanished from Derrick's eyes.

Kannon's hand itched, an aftereffect of Derrick's bite three years ago after being refused another scoop of ice cream. The bite had penetrated his skin and left three nice teeth imprints. It drew blood. Not having dressed the wound properly, Kannon ended up with an infection and an ugly scar.

He massaged it.

"Daddy K, are you still mad at me for biting you?"

"No, Chomp . . ." He'd started to say Chomper, the moniker he had assigned to Derrick's biting prowess. Lan didn't like the word, saying it was derogatory and that humor shouldn't be used to downplay a punishable incident.

"Chomper is not a word anyway," she had said. "If I hear you call him Chomper again, I will chomp on you."

The Vietnamese word for bite is *Cắn*! Since Derrick was too young to write, Lan made Derrick say, *"Đừng cắn!"* (Do not bite!) twenty times.

"That's not it, Derrick. I've long since forgiven you." Kannon

57

stood, picked up the boy, and nuzzled his cheek. "You know what, sport? We'll toss the football after I return from California. And guess what, Roger and Karen are going to stay with you while I'm gone."

That brought a token grin. Kannon set Derrick down, and the boy ran to the patio. A blown opportunity, Kannon realized. He followed his son outside and watched him plunder a castle in his sandbox.

Lan walked onto the patio and came to Kannon's side.

"I believe you think you are being kind by suggesting I contact Đăng Đạo, but I feel manipulated."

Her strident tone increased his discomfort. Guilt, self-indulgence came to mind, oft-repeated criticisms made by his first wife.

"I'm not trying to manipulate you," Kannon said.

Lan stiffened. Doubt clouded her eyes.

"I don't understand your reaction," Kannon said, puzzled by Lan's exasperation.

"I know." Lan sighed. "I appreciate your idea, but I feel like you are trying to distract me from what is going on between us, or rather, what is not going on between us."

Kannon's involuntary hand tic returned.

"You mean family time?"

"I am not talking about family time."

"What then?" Kannon wished he was playing with Derrick in the sandbox.

"Our relationship. You and me. I have been talking to this friend of mine—"

"Who?"

"A lady. She teaches a class in Austin on Native American culture and artifacts. Her name is Belynda Blu. I have told you about her. She is coming for a visit Tuesday."

"What for?"

"To talk."

Something else he didn't get.

"About?"

"Woman talk. About things . . . you know, life, kids, family, you."

"Our relationship?" Kannon began feeling queasy. Better stop pressing, he thought. He remembered a stunt he'd pulled with his first wife. He kept questioning why she wouldn't open her mouth, until finally, she did, only to blurt our tears of frustration over feeling *forced* to talk. Why? She had just applied a transparent face mask, which was destroyed when she spoke. Good job, there, by Kannon. He decided to shut up.

His cell rang. Thank God. It was the airline confirming his flight. "I need to get ready. Can we continue after my return?"

Lan sighed, a deep, deep sigh, followed by a frown. "The issues will remain," she said.

No doubt.

He left the patio and worked his way into the master bathroom. As he reached for his Dobb kit, unwelcome thoughts rattled his consciousness. She and this Belynda were going to discuss *him* and the relationship. What if Lan didn't find him attractive anymore? Maybe he was no longer the partner she wanted. Staring into the mirror, he furrowed his brow. Despite good genes, more lines appeared, defiling creases etched by time. Slapping on lotion or "Old West" aftershave didn't fill the cracks. Mostly gone was the sun-like color of his hair, replaced by wispy gray strands. His silver-toned mustache, thick and well-groomed, in certain lighting, appeared platinum. Big deal. Maybe he should color his hair.

He finished packing, then walked back outside. The sun was high, the air cool. Oak leaves fluttered in the wind. The bougainvillea and rose vines clung to their trellises.

Lan and Derrick were seated at the patio table, engaged in a game of chess. Already competent in both Vietnamese and English, his son also loved math and had learned the basics of the four-player Chinese game—mahjong—something he would probably play later with Lan, Roger, and Karen. Yeah, he was bright.

"See you later, son," he said, scratching the scruff of Derrick's neck. "We'll play ball when I get back."

"Later, gator." Derrick maintained his focus on the tiles and chessboard.

Kannon approached his wife's side and leaned in. "Goodbye."

"Have a good flight." A light kiss, but with cool lips, not the inviting warmth he desired.

As he started toward the garage, Kannon overheard Derrick's soft voice, "Mama Lan, Daddy K sure is gone a lot."

"He is not here when he is here."

"What do you mean?" Derrick asked.

Kannon looked back. "Next weekend, football and Austin."

* * *

Lan stared across the chessboard, past Derrick's shoulder, and watched Kannon walk away. She thought about her little guy's comment, "Later, gator." It was her son's effort to present a devil-may-care attitude, a phrase Kannon often used to describe Derrick's demeanor. But did her husband never notice their boy's downcast eyes and quivering lips when trying to mask his disappointment?

She was not sure.

"Mama Lan, it's your move."

"Oh, sorry." Lan picked up a captured pawn and squeezed it between her thumb and forefinger.

Next weekend, next this and next that, Kannon was avoiding their communication issue by suggesting she contact her nephew. He avoids intimacy by trying to placate me.

"Ha." Derrick slid his rook forward and captured her bishop.

"I will surprise you with my next play." She moved her remaining bishop and seized another of Derrick's pawns. Once she removed her finger from the piece, she realized her mistake.

"Oh, ho. I've got you." Then, "Uh-oh." Derrick scooted back his chair and ran toward the patio door. "I have to go to the bathroom."

"Do not slam the—"

Blam!

Door.

Reminding herself Derrick was only six, Lan could not help but smile. She loved his confidence, his logical thought processes, and his mannerisms—the strutting walk, his squared-up shoulders, the forceful way he pumped his little arms when running—my husband's clone, she thought.

Lan lit a stalk of sage incense and placed the stick in a Buddha holder. She wafted the aroma to her nostrils and sat back.

She and Kannon had come so far. Then Derrick had been born,

and they were family, what she always wanted. Feelings of love and gratitude welled up inside, but there was a chasm that needed fixing.

She sighed. Derrick had been borne out of her love for Kannon. When he appeared in Việt Nam at the request of her dying brother, Lan felt the affection between the two men. They had been through and were still going through hell. It was her brother's death wish to reveal information that might enable Kannon to send his war demons back to where they belonged.

Remembering when they first had locked eyes, Lan was touched by Kannon's tenderness toward her brother and herself. When she decided to help Kannon, they had traipsed to the rice fields of her distant cousin's rural home to gather more information, which led to what she described as the cooking-over-a-wood-fire closeness.

And then she got kidnapped and was held in an awful underground crypt, complete with a slithering cobra. At extreme risk, Kannon had crawled through a booby-trapped minefield, worked his way underground, and rescued her.

Days later, they celebrated with dinner and dancing on the rooftop bar of the best hotel in Sài Gòn. It was a glorious evening. Her body was suffused with the glow. Yes, she was pregnant but refused to tell Kannon because he had one last demon to face in America. Had she told him, he might have stayed with her and never found his peace.

Months passed. After everything was done, Lan had *worked* her way out of Việt Nam and, belly showing, showed up at his doorstep. And oh, the beatific look on his face. Kannon was not a shining knight, but he was her knight, and she loved him. They had grown close in many important ways. Perhaps one person can never know another completely, but her love would heal this chasm.

For now, Lan looked forward to discussing her relationship and self with Belynda, a wonderful sounding board.

Derrick banged open the patio door and came prancing back. "Did you wash your hands?"

He backtracked. Upon returning, he said, "I'm going to win." Derrick did. Then Roger and Karen arrived.

Eight

Sunday, 18 October 2009, Middle Fork of the Flathead River, Montana

At a secluded drop-off point in the Flathead National Forest, Spencer Whitehead backed his pickup against a berm, which allowed him to offload his ATV. The Battle Tank, as he called it, was his means of tackling rough terrain.

Exhausted from lack of sleep, he exited the pickup, stretched and yawned, then lowered the tailgate. Whitehead straddled the Battle Tank, started it, and backed out. Slipping it into gear, he headed for the Middle Fork of the Flathead River, which drilled into the wilderness east of Flathead Lake.

He had a lot on his mind. It was the day after the end of the training session, and he thought about their one graduate, Bull, a misanthrope among misanthropes.

Whitehead twisted the throttle and crashed through the underbrush. He'd rather be here camping and fishing, but that wasn't the plan. Crandle wanted to nail down a strategy for hunting Streak as well as to discuss further the use of electromagnetic pulse weapons. At least it was a break from flying discs and fallen candidates.

As the sun crested the tree line, the lingering smell of damp earth released by the pre-dawn mist drew Whitehead deeper into the wilderness. Ten minutes later, he reached the rendezvous point on the bank of the Flathead, where Crandle was to join him. He killed the engine and unzipped his fatigue jacket, then grabbed a pinch of Redman and placed it in his mouth. The tingling made his mouth salivate.

A gentle slope led toward the river. Across the Flathead, the bank was steeper. Black cottonwood trees, having lost their flaming yellow and orange tinge, were dropping leaves amid the green groves of Engelmann spruce.

Whitehead slid from behind the steering column. He retrieved his AK assault rifle from the mounted scabbard and trailed into the brush alongside the river. Wild grasses, crowned with frost, crackled underfoot.

Facing a stretch of whitewater, he listened to its melody. Due to unseasonably heavy rains and premature melt from an early snowfall, the river ran high for this time of year. Rafting season was over, but it was still possible for mavericks to run the rapids. A hunting party could also bungle his solitude.

Whitehead checked his watch. Crandle, who maintained a bequeathed family cabin outside Whitefish, was past due. It wouldn't surprise him if Crandle arrived late because he'd been banging Anh, a Vietnamese woman from a Thailand refugee camp. When it came to sex, Crandle's *White Might* mantra dissolved.

This is bullshit!

Crossing his arms, Whitehead considered restarting the engine and hauling ass. But then the hunt would be on for him. Besides, the Commander's voice had carried an edgier than usual tone.

Finally, the familiar sound of Crandle's Polaris Sportsman engine reached his ear. A 500cc four-stroke like his, the bog hog thrashed like an angry bear through thatches of shrub alder and red osier dogwood. Whitehead reached the Battle Tank just as Crandle pulled alongside.

Wearing camouflage fatigues, an Army-green cap, field jacket, and combat boots, Crandle mirrored Whitehead's uniform, standard dress when in the wilderness. The clean-shaven Commander chucked his field jacket, snatched up his twenty-foot lariat, and climbed off his ATV. His jaw jutted out far enough to unhinge.

"Streak's in the wind," Crandle said.

"He knows what will happen to anyone who betrays us," Whitehead said, raising his voice. "If he's not with his mom, maybe he's holed up with a friend."

"Goddamnit, Whitehead. Sometimes you need a case of lockjaw." Crandle's breath vaporized in the forty-degree air. "You're thinking like a damn idiot. Streak's got no friends. You know as well as I do, people who join us, they ain't got no fucking friends." The Commander's venomous breath smelled sour.

"Did you put out a BOLO?"

"Of course I did. From my Ham shack."

They walked southeast along the riverbank. Even though

Crandle had never served in the military, he insisted on following the junior rank to-the-left tradition. Begrudgingly, Whitehead assumed the subordinate position, his feet at water's edge.

"If Streak's absence turns out to be legit, would you reestablish him as our pilot?"

Crandle spun around, blocking his path. "Whitehead," his Commander tensed as if wanting to choke him, "just reel him in. You've had time to develop a plan for capturing Streak. What is it?"

Whitehead's stomach knotted up. "Nothing specific. I can't lead our militiamen, train our FNG, and bone up on EMPs all at the same time."

"Streak takes precedence. The sooner you nail him, the sooner the electronic mission gets underway. I'll handle the guys."

"And the newbie?"

"Bull will assist in your search," Crandle said.

"You're kidding."

Crandle shook his head. "On-the-job training. Kill two birds with one stone."

Whitehead balled his fists. He didn't like being held responsible for Streak's disappearance, a man over whom he had no real authority, because he reported directly to Crandle. Besides, going after him might be akin to chasing a wild turkey. And to be saddled with an unproven Bull added insult to injury.

They resumed trekking.

"Yo, Whitehead, I can tell your mind's drifting. Tune in. Need to talk about electromagnetic pulse weapons," Crandle said while fashioning a running noose on his lariat.

"All right." Whitehead was surprised. Why the sudden switch of topics? He recalled Crandle's intent to employ chemical and biological agents, ideas they'd discarded once they factored in logistical barriers and containment risks. In the end, he'd convinced Crandle they would more likely kill themselves than the enemy unless they could bring in expertise regarding the use and handling of lethal agents. EMP weapons, to the contrary, might be safer to employ and activate.

Crandle lassoed a tree stump.

"There's a huge markup for large, fully assembled weapons.

The cost of production isn't high. EMP units aren't that difficult to construct." He snapped the noose loose and coiled his lariat. "Therefore—"

"You want me to learn how to construct them."

"Exactly. E-bombs are clean weapons. We'll force people back to basics. It'll be the new form of guerrilla tactics to fulfill our strategy."

"Global warfare," Whitehead said through compressed lips. Crandle's egomania and grandiose schemes heightened their risk of exposure. As far as he knew, they weren't on any FBI watch list. Disregarding the use of newsletters published by many rightwing groups, Border Slot worked to remain reclusive and anonymous, except to their clients. Not only did their unit leave few paperwork trails, they shunned direct connection to media-hungry Christian-based white supremacy groups that preached militancy but didn't practice it.

A red-tail hawk soared overhead. Whitehead watched it dive after its prey. He preferred the natural order of life in the wilderness as opposed to urban chaos.

"It's an interesting idea, but—"

"But what?"

"The risk. It means operating in more populated areas."

"So?" Crandle said, a sardonic smile revealing his even, white teeth. "You can't run around in the woods all your life if you want to accomplish your goals."

A pink sheen rose above the treetops. The haze dissipated, replaced by a pastel blue sky. Across the river came the cry of an owl. As he and Crandle stood side-by-side facing the Middle Fork of the Flatfoot, Whitehead reflected. He was already concerned about their recent shift to funnel militia graduates to in-country drug dealers and renegade corporations as well as to foreign cells.

"I'm worried we're spreading ourselves too thin. Make a mistake, and the Feds come running."

"You're not getting it. The Feds! We destroy their electronic tools. They can't find us." He tapped Whitehead with the coiled rope. "Streak's a major risk. If he's contacted the Feds, they could destroy us before we destroy them."

Ah, now back on point. Whitehead spat a glob of tobacco juice on the ground. "Commander, I understand your concern about Streak. I just don't see how I can—"

"You scared?"

The blood in Whitehead's veins boiled. Never had Crandle taunted him like this. The Commander's derisive comments grated as if he were screeching chalk on a blackboard.

Whitehead gripped his rifle, wanting to wield it like a club.

Crandle's satphone beeped. He removed it from his belt holster.

"Yeah?" His eyes lit up, then he turned his back and walked several yards away, stopping at the edge of a copse of trees. When he returned, his chest puffed out like a bullmastiff, he said, "Chaos!"

Whitehead issued a mock salute.

Crandle's eyes turned as cold as ball bearings. "I need to take a shit. We'll settle this when I get back."

Nine

Whitehead propped his rifle against a tree, sat on a rock, and absently tossed stones into the river, thinking the Border Slot Militia couldn't exist without him. He was the one who executed complicated operations.

The militia trained for field combat, not urban warfare, much less for the employment of EMP weapons. Exasperated, he released a long sigh. Crandle's dumps could take up to ten minutes. What if the Commander had to drop *trou* in the middle of an operation? He chuckled at the thought but steered himself back to the issues. Crandle was goading him, sure, but this was outright serious. Border Slot was at a crisis point.

Hell, I'm at a crisis point.

He studied a thicket of red osier dogwood. Crimson berries dangled like tinged dewdrops from branches shaking in the wind. The crimson color reminded him of the blood that once had flowed through the veins of his "adoptive" parents. They treasured the land's resources and valued all creatures living on it. Illiterate, they insisted he attend school, where at age thirteen he became interested in literature. The public library became his second home. On occasion, Whitehead speculated about his life before the "adoption," but clear-cut visions never came, only fleeting memories of ragged men and gruff women moving in shadows.

The wind whipped cottonwood leaves around his feet. Whitehead cupped a handful and brought them to his nose, recalling how his mother would gather batches of leaves and herbs, crush and compress them, and make her own incense. She would let him light the irregularly shaped blocks, filling their home for hours with a tangy aroma.

And then she and his father were gone. What vicious unnatural deaths they had suffered.

Whitehead stood and flung his knife into a dead tree. The handle quivered like a plucked bowstring. He'd never intended to violate Nez Percé beliefs or betray their teachings, but in 1978, on his eighteenth birthday, his life changed forever. It happened on a day when white-plumed clouds filled the sky and crisp air portended the arrival of fall.

After dispatching a good-sized wolf with his new Winchester 70, a .30-06 bolt-action rifle, he'd returned from the hunt bringing home the skin to his mother and father, wanting to celebrate his life by honoring theirs. As he approached the sodded-roof cabin, he heard tortured screams, then dead silence. Dropping the skin, he raced to the cabin and arrived in time to see blood spurting from his father's lacerated throat.

There were two killers. Both were Mexicans.

One of them stood laughing, while the other, naked from the waist down, lifted himself off Whitehead's dead mother. Seeing the bloody knife and his mother's eyes locked open in fear, Whitehead lost it. He drilled a .30-06 caliber hole into the standing man's forehead. The second man rushed him. Whitehead fumbled the bolt-action, and, instead, clubbed the killer with the rifle butt. Then he grabbed his father's tomahawk from a wall and planted the blade deep in the dying man's chest. The shock frozen on the killers' faces instilled in him an intense gratification he still carried.

He had placed his parents in a deep grave, piled forest detritus on top, doused everything with kerosene, and struck a match. When the putrid odor from the burning corpses made him vomit, he disgorged his grief as well. There'd been no relatives, no celebratory feast, and no shaman.

Next, he dismembered the killer's bodies and scattered their remains throughout the forest for predator consumption. He torched the cabin and never returned. Killing his parents' murderers had been satiating. It was also the origin of his hatred of minorities.

The next year Whitehead enlisted in the Army. Because of his weapons proficiency, he was quickly promoted to Specialist 4. He applied for Special Forces training and was accepted, but soon washed out for insubordination and fighting. He received an Other Than Honorable Discharge, which ended any chance of a typical career.

Two years later, in the Bitterroots, Crandle stumbled upon him kneeling before the wolf he had killed. Crandle didn't understand why anyone would pray over a slain animal. Whitehead never explained but continued the practice to honor his mom and dad.

Over time, he and Crandle solidified their relationship while sharing pitchers of beer in Missoula bars. Early on, Crandle revealed the loss of his wife and son when a truck carrying toxic waste plowed into their pickup. Agreeing that it was futile to live by rules implemented and enforced by a manipulative, lying government, they concocted their plan to purge their country of scum and reclaim it in the name of the Border Slot Militia—their version of the *Posse Comitatus.*

Arms hanging at his sides, Whitehead walked to the dead tree and extracted his knife. He spat on the blade and wiped it clean on his fatigues. Admittedly, Border Slot had been good to him. He'd met every challenge and earned a chunk of money.

Now, here he was, with new weapons, clean weapons, at his disposal. Would this work be as satisfying, chipping away at traditional man-to-man fighting in which he loved to participate? There was nothing like it. Feeling the awesome power released from an automatic weapon by a simple trigger pull was better than sex.

The sound of an airliner cruising overhead distracted him. It was probably filled with corporate fat cats and middle-income Americans who'd never sacrificed for their country. What if the airlines couldn't get their planes in the air? It would be interesting to see how companies performed without computer flight schedules and air traffic control. "Chaos," as Crandle said, would follow. Opportunities for guerrilla tactics and man-to-man combat stood a good chance of increasing.

From what, then, stemmed his hesitancy? He spat out another sluice of tobacco juice, its bitter taste reflecting his indecision. Part of him wasn't ready to give up all electronics, credit cards, and library visits.

The pungent smell of Cradle's cigar announced his return. "Coming in, you brown-headed banger."

The Commander must've come up with the new tag while taking his dump. Often, Whitehead viewed Crandle like a recalcitrant uncle who sometimes praised him while at other times chastised and provoked him. It was then Whitehead wanted to plunge a knife into Crandle's gut.

69

"I'm not apologizing for standing my ground," Whitehead said.

"Point taken." Crandle squared his shoulders. "But listen. We've got crackheads, niggers, spics, slant eyes, and homos holding office. Next thing you know, ragheads will be on the ballot."

"Don't want those bastards in our country," Whitehead said.

"The fucking government wants to tag and track everybody," Crandle added. "You won't be able to take a shit without them knowing it."

Whitehead nodded.

"EMP bombs," Crandle said, "are the way to go."

"I remember those floppy discs, how they'd be erased if you positioned them too close to a strong magnetic force. I guess EMP weapons would have a much broader effect."

"Like comparing an ant to a dinosaur," Crandle said, puffing on a cigar. "The greater the electromagnetic pulse, the more destruction."

While the Commander prattled on about flux compression generators, dirty bombs, and agents, Whitehead questioned whether all devices containing electronic chips would become disabled. The idea seemed radical, but yeah, he'd study on it.

A rough, fibrous coil encircled his neck. It was Crandle's stupid rope.

"You're not listening," Crandle said.

Whitehead calmly removed the noose, walked to the nearby tree where he'd propped his rifle, and retrieved it.

"I was thinking about electronic weapons and that one day you might push me too far."

Ten

Seething from Crandle's degrading action, Whitehead clutched the hilt of his hunting knife and scowled, wanting to slash the Commander's rope into pieces. How much more could he take?

Screw this!

Slinging his AK47 over his shoulder, he brushed past Crandle into the red osier dogwoods and scrubby chokecherry, where brush-laden moisture licked at his Army jump boots. A bruising autumn wind lashed out and rattled clumps of alder and dogwood branches. Fallen leaves scuttled across the ground. Nearby, a bold deer nosed around a huckleberry bush. Whitehead savored a deep breath and zipped up his jacket. The natural environment calmed him.

Upon reaching the bank, he gazed upriver. A kayaker was paddling an inflatable down the rippling Middle Fork. The kayak reminded Whitehead of when, as a child, he had helped his Nez Percé parents carve a canoe from a felled black cottonwood tree.

"You're pissed," Crandle said.

Startled by Crandle's approach, Whitehead jerked around. He was embarrassed at being caught off guard. Despite his bulky size, the Commander could move like a cat when he wanted.

"You think?" Shuffling pebbles with his boot, Whitehead watched the kayaker paddle closer.

Crandle, obviously not having fully emptied his bladder when taking a crap moments ago, whipped out his pecker and took a piss at the river's edge. The man would pee in front of anyone, almost anywhere.

The kayaker, navigating rapids, dressed in a black and yellow wetsuit, dipped one end of the paddle into the water, then the other, and came abreast. "Stop polluting the river, asshole." The paddler shot the finger and resumed his course downriver.

Red-faced, Crandle high-stepped into the Flathead in pursuit. "Let's get the fucker! I don't want anybody yapping about seeing us out here."

Whitehead clenched his jaw. Probably some egghead environmentalist, he thought, but Crandle was right. The kayaker

71

must have sensed trouble because he ramped up his counter-dipping paddling.

Standing in ankle-deep water, Crandle slipped the rope off his shoulder, twirled the lariat and unleashed it, lassoing the unsuspecting river pilot. He pulled tight, pinning the man's upper arms against his chest.

Flailing, the kayaker's hands flopped around like grounded fish. He lost his paddle.

Working in concert with the swift current, Crandle maintained pressure and kept the lariat taut. The kayaker tried to plunge his hands in the water and back-paddle, gave up, then attempted to wrest the rope from around his shoulders. The Commander pulled tighter as the current worked to his benefit.

Whitehead scanned both sides of the river, hoping not to see anyone else. He didn't.

"Get my other rope," Crandle said. His upper lip curled into a sneer, a look that could curdle milk.

Whitehead set his rifle down and ran to Crandle's ATV. He unhooked a second lariat secured to the rear luggage rack and raced back. He tossed the rope to his Commander.

"Hold this," Crandle said.

Whitehead waded into the river and took hold of the first rope, held it fast. The kayaker bucked and twisted his upper body trying to shake loose of the mummy-shaped craft. Crandle threw the second lasso, looping it around the kayak's bow, and yanked.

The force spun the kayak one hundred eighty degrees, which positioned the victim into a linear view. Eyes wide in fear, the man bared his palms as if pleading to be set free.

Crandle smiled and waved. Then the current swung the kayak back again so that the operator faced downstream. Crandle tied his end of the lariat to a nearby tree stump on the riverbank. He motioned Whitehead to secure the other rope.

Frantic, the kayaker again tried to free his legs and vacate the cockpit. No luck.

"It's an inflatable, puncture it," Crandle said, glaring like a cougar stalking prey.

Once more, Whitehead studied the terrain for possible

witnesses.

Can't stop now. It's gone too far.

He retrieved his silenced AK, pulled back and released the charging handle to chamber a round, then placed the fire selector on full auto. He brought the rifle to his shoulder. Whitehead couldn't help smiling as he pulled the trigger, firing a five-round burst that ripped into the man's legs and shredded the bow of the boat. With the kayak collapsing, along with the strong current, the lasso slipped from the kayaker's chest and settled around his neck.

"Reel him in," Crandle said.

The two of them tugged on their respective ropes hand over hand. The kayaker—tongue protruding, dark fluid seeping from his mouth—sank below the surface. They lugged him and his kayak onto the bank.

"No pulse," Whitehead said.

"Any ID?"

Whitehead dragged the body free of the inflatable. He examined the wetsuit-clad corpse. "Nope"

"Dump him," Crandle said.

Gripping the rope to keep from being swept downstream, Whitehead fed himself into the river as if tethered by a stout fishing line on an oversized reel. The water level peaked at his waist when he released the dead kayaker to the Middle Fork of the Flathead.

"Somebody might find the guy," Whitehead said, pulling himself free of the river. He began rolling the deflated kayak into a manageable bundle.

Crandle clapped him on the shoulder.

"What if they do? He won't be telling anybody anything."

Unless a medical examiner determines the bullets came from an AK. Oh well. Collateral damage. A casualty of war.

Despite his earlier anger, Whitehead felt gratified. Working out differences. Positive energy flooded his mind and body. The more he considered Streak's excuse, the lamer it sounded. And Bull possessed skills but needed discipline. It was up to Whitehead to train him. As for EMP devices, Hooah!

Eleven

Whitehead retrieved the spent shell casings from the rounds fired at the kayaker and his inflatable, then wiped out their boot tracks along the riverbank. They trekked to their ATVs, keeping to the rocks until reaching the brush, Crandle in the lead, smacking the lariats against his thigh.

"Set up a militia assembly for thirteen hundred hours Wednesday afternoon," Crandle said, upon reaching the vehicles. "Give you time to talk to OT and study up on EMP stuff."

"Roger," Whitehead said. "Planning session for the EMP attack on Kalispell, I presume."

"Correct." Mounting his four-wheeler, Crandle keyed the ignition, his clipped red hair standing as stiff as cribbage pegs. "I want Streak captured."

"Will do," Whitehead said.

Crandle's green eyes, usually bright and piercing, appeared sunken and as dull as bleached acorns. Perhaps he was suffering a letdown after the adrenaline-induced killing. Nevertheless, Crandle extended a hand. Whitehead shook it, which was as rough as number twelve-grit sandpaper. He executed a half-ass salute as Crandle drove off.

Whitehead pinched a fresh plug of Redman and placed it between his cheek and gum. Nailing Streak presented a difficult challenge, but he'd tear Streak's cabin apart, do a little Q and A with the militiamen. Search the chopper. Maybe find a clue or two.

Streak will pay for causing trouble. So will anybody else who gets in the way. And it'll be interesting to see how well the FNG performs.

After loading the Battle Tank onto his pickup, Whitehead left the Flathead River behind and hightailed it to Border Slot, stopping only for snacks and gas along the way. It was dark by the time he reached the box-shaped compound. After activating the gate entrance—for the outside world, to appear as the adventure guides they professed to be, Border Slot seldom posted guards or practiced blackout conditions—he parked his truck beside his cabin and went inside to kindle a fire before inspecting the facilities.

Outside, barren tree branches rattled from a steady breeze. Filtered moonlight heightened the shadows. Whitehead trekked to the main cabin. Crandle wasn't due back for a couple more hours, but Anh should be inside. He knocked. A few seconds later, he heard footsteps shuffling toward the door.

"Boss Man not here."

An aria from one of Wagner's operas filtered through the door. Why was she playing Wagner? Even at low volume, the sound annoyed him, but Crandle worshipped Hitler as Hitler idolized Wagner. He guessed Anh, a purchased slave straight from a Thai refugee camp, had been indoctrinated to the music, not knowing what it represented.

"I know, Anh. It's Whitehead."

She opened the door. Indoctrinated or not, she'd been wearing the same look of sadness for six months. Whitehead again questioned how Crandle could put aside his hatred for other races when it came to a piece of ass. "Is everything all right?"

"Yes. All right."

"Crandle will be back soon. He'll want dinner."

"Okay, I get ready."

He left her alone. Everyone did except the *Boss Man*.

Walking toward the barracks, Whitehead noted that the solar panels, installed on a raised platform free of the tall trees, were done collecting energy for the day. There was no connection here to the Internet, which Crandle intended to destroy anyway. All their information was provided by satellite phones, satellite TV, client contacts, and off-site supporters of Border Slot.

The smell of cigar smoke reached his nostrils. Several yards away, two small, orange-red orbs glowed in the growing darkness. It was Hatfield and Porter, smoking stogies. Their faces were bronzed by the outside yellow bulb dangling from a tree limb.

"Saw you drive up. What's happening, bro'?"

"Same-o, same-o," Whitehead said. "Any trouble?"

"Been quiet," Porter said.

"How'd things go with the Commander?" It was Hatfield.

"Smooth as silk." Whitehead wanted to get into the Streak

issue. "Rest of the guys inside?"

"Yeah," Porter said. "When are we going on an operation? Getting bored sitting on our asses."

"Sooner than you think, so stop bitching," Whitehead said. "Follow me."

Whitehead entered the barracks, Hatfield and Porter in tow. A crackling fire inside the stone fireplace made it toasty.

Wolfhound, Nolan, Timmons, McAfee, and Smitty were playing five-card stud while Garrett and Badger looked on. The number of empty beer bottles indicated they'd been at it a while. Crumpled bills lay in the pot like discarded trash. Otherwise, the place was clean but smelled of Clorox, gun oil, and cigar smoke. "He's in the Jailhouse Now" by Webb Pierce blasted from a boom box.

"Listen up," Whitehead said. "We've got an assembly at thirteen hundred hours Wednesday." The muster came at a good time. It didn't sit well for the men to remain idle long.

"Roger that" and "affirmative" were the militiamen's responses.

"Where's Bull?" Whitehead asked.

Nine thumbs pointed toward the rear. Whitehead found Bull sitting in his cubicle. "We've got a mission," he said, tugging on his handlebar mustache.

"What's up?" Unshaven, the squat, broad Bull was wearing skivvies—not a pleasant sight—and cleaning a Colt .45. Skulls and crossbones, along with bull-shaped tattoos covered his forearms and biceps. His black hair was shorn short, like a sheep without its wool. Polished boots lay beside his bunk on the rough hardwood floor. Crandle let the guys maintain handguns and hunting rifles but kept the automatic weapons and other military hardware in the armory.

"Get your ass up front."

"Do I need my weapon?"

"No." Jesus, sometimes these guys acted like refugees in a chow line, only the militiamen were hungry for action, not food.

"Okay," Whitehead said, "now that our newbie's here, I need to pick your brains before Wednesday's assembly."

"It's about Streak, right?" Hatfield asked, his mouth twisted into a sneer.

"Yep."

"I knew Crandle was pissed cause he had to fly the chopper," Wolfhound said.

"Yeah," mumbled several men.

Whitehead sounded the call. Did Streak have a sick mother? Did anyone know where she lived? Any unusual actions, associations lately on his part? Phone contacts? Other addresses?

"He kept to himself," Badger said, shuffling the deck of cards. "Never confided in anyone."

"I'll take that as a no," Whitehead said. "Crandle's afraid he may be talking to the Feds. Any thoughts?"

"He knows we'd kill him," Wolfhound said.

The others concurred.

"Bull and I are going to track him down," Whitehead said.

Smitty plopped his five cards face down in the center of the table. "I'm out."

Timmons remained stone-faced while examining his dealt hand.

"Crandle wants him brought back to the range," Whitehead said.

"Torture the fucker," McAfee said, thumbing his cards.

Whitehead ignored the remark. He motioned for Hatfield to follow him outside as he exited the barracks.

"Hey, man. I'm sorry. I didn't think Streak would run," Hatfield said.

"None of us did," Whitehead said. "Don't worry. I'll take care of it."

Hatfield nodded, puffed on his cigar.

"Get the gear cleaned up tomorrow and ready the guys for the muster," Whitehead said, "and don't leave any cigar butts on the ground. Fieldstrip those babies."

"Roger."

"Send Bull out."

Hatfield entered the barracks and out came the rookie, fully dressed.

"Where are we going?" Bull asked.

"I'll explain on the way to the chopper pad." Leading Bull

77

along the hundred-yard path toward the hanger, Whitehead pointed out another trail. "That leads to the armory. It's in an old reinforced mine shaft dug out of the mountain."

"Is it secure?"

"Like a fortress. The trail flares out before the entrance, which is camouflaged."

"I'd like to see it," Bull said.

"Another time. Let's move on."

Despite Bull's bulk, he moved with stealth. They reached the hanger, a prefab metal shelter on rollers that had to be wheeled manually, both to cover and to uncover the Jolly Green Giant. At either position, the shelter was anchored to iron rings embedded in concrete.

Whitehead directed Bull toward a twenty-foot by forty-foot log structure located ten yards from the hanger. Beyond that lay the *practice* killing field and obstacle course.

Streak's cabin had two bullet-proof windows and a heavy wooden door. An unlit bare light bulb hung above it. "Let's take a look inside Streak's cabin."

"Clues," Bull said.

"Roger."

A padlock secured an old-fashioned hasp and stable combo attached to the frame and door. Whitehead didn't have a key. Had Streak set a booby trap? *Fuck it.*

"Kick the damn thing open," he said to Bull, stepping back.

Bull came to a partial crouch, balanced on one foot, and leg-whipped the lock. The latch assembly exploded, and the door swung open.

"Impressive," Whitehead said.

"Just one of my skills," Bull snapped back.

Whitehead edged his way inside. Bull, his shoulders touching both sides of the doorframe, followed.

The one-room cabin smelled of fresh earth and canvas. Partial window light illuminated a hard-packed dirt floor, uneven but swept clean. An oversized cot sat along one wall, and a wall-mounted oil lamp hung between the cot and an easy chair. Scattered books occupied a makeshift bookshelf resting on cinder blocks. In the corner opposite the easy chair sat an LCD television supported by two-by-fours and cinder blocks. An electrical cord led to an outside generator, which was silent. A vintage school desk occupied another corner. A small sink and wood-burning stove completed the interior. Except for Crandle and Whitehead, everybody else used outdoor shitters.

Whitehead liked Streak's place, because, except for the TV, it reminded him of his adoptive parents' home in Idaho. He walked to the bookshelf and knelt. Riffling through paperback westerns, books on military history and helicopter flight, Whitehead realized he really didn't know much about Streak, who lived like a hermit among hermits.

"Here's a footlocker," Bull said. It lay underneath the cot.

"Open 'er up," Whitehead said.

Bull slid it out and rammed his fist through the wooden lid.

Whitehead clicked on his flash and splayed the light. "Let's see what we got."

He pored through Streak's meager belongings—mostly Army paraphernalia, framed photos of what appeared to be long-ago family life, a couple of slingshots, and an object suspended in a liquid-filled jar. Picking up the jar for a closer look, he laughed aloud. "Look at this," he said, "Streak saved his fucking finger."

"A nutcase," Bull said, cracking his knuckles.

Whitehead replaced the jar and examined the last item. It was a hardback entitled *Street without Joy*, only the guts were hollowed out. He removed a weathered address book from the cavity and handed it over to Bull. "See what you make of it."

Bull took the address book and Whitehead's flash. He squeezed into the school desk and proceeded to skim through the pages. A few moments later . . . "All but two names are crossed out. This one, here, Kannon Ballard, has an address and phone number. The other, Sindy Zeller, doesn't. I think maybe Streak called his old friends. Maybe the Kannon dude was the only one who talked to him." Bull scratched his chin. "You guys check phone bills?"

They hadn't.

Militiamen maintained separate satphone accounts. Whitehead needed to follow up on that.

"Any mention of relatives?"

79

Bull scratched his chin. "Don't see any."

"Interesting," Whitehead said, taking the book back from Bull. "Ballard's in Texas. As for Zeller, there're only initials, a *C*, a dot, and an *A*." He looked closer. What did the initials stand for—a nickname, location, or just scribbles?

"What if that dot caps an *I*?" Bull asked. "Could stand for CIA."

Whitehead bristled. Bull was smarter than he looked. Maybe Crandle had been right all along about the Feds and wrong about militiamen having no friends. Not all guys were without contacts in the outside world. Besides hanging out at barrooms, a militiaman might seek a distant family member or another militia hotspot for refuge. Groups existed in the Northwest, the mid-West, Arizona, and New Mexico, as well as in the Southeast. In Texas, elements of the *Republic* might hole up in the Guadalupe or Davis Mountains, even in the Ft. Hood area near Killeen.

"If Streak ran," Bull said, "why leave this behind? It's a trail."

"Fear, carelessness, desperation, stupidity, or maybe these are false trails." In the three years he'd known Streak, his aloof behavior wasn't out of the ordinary for guys choosing this life. He was an excellent pilot, but, other than ferrying Border Slot militiamen, had never participated in missions. Yet, Streak really didn't choose this life. Thinking the group was an adventure guide outfit, he fell into it. And Crandle hadn't put him through the drills, just posed death threats.

Regardless, I've been wrong.

"Streak's AWOL."

"What next?" Bull was breathing heavy.

"Wait one." Whitehead stepped outside, placed a call to Crandle, and told him what they had found.

"Got a mission," Whitehead said as Bull joined him.

"Before the EMP attack?" Bull said.

"Yep. We'll depart Thursday at o-six hundred."

"Where to?"

"Texas."

Whitehead pocketed the address book.

Twelve

Tuesday, 20 October 2009, Kannon Ballard's Residence, Texas Hill Country

Roger's and Karen's presence had been comforting. The time passed without incident. They had played mahjong, and Derrick did well. Lan bade them goodbye around noon.

Now, standing in front of her bedroom mirror, Lan smoothed her pale pink slacks and straightened her purple áo dài. She fastened it at the collar—like a tunic—and ran a brush through her hair a final time, then dabbed on a touch of Cinnabar. Even though she carried five extra pounds, Lan thought she looked good for a forty-seven-year-old mother of a six-year-old.

Nervous but excited about the upcoming visit from Belynda Blu, she left the bedroom, walked down the hall, through the den, and into the kitchen to check on the herbal tea. She had chosen jasmine for its sweet flavor and aroma. While it steeped, Lan contemplated on her marriage.

She wanted Kannon to grow in his capacity to be involved with family. His running off last Saturday to renew an acquaintance interfered with closeness, as did his Sunday business trip to San Jose. Lan needed more than his physical presence, she longed for emotional intimacy.

I need to concentrate on my guest. What else do I need to do? Finger sandwiches.

Opening the refrigerator, she retrieved cucumber and basil, then opened the bread box and pulled out her favorite white grain bread. Trimming off the crust, Lan considered Kannon's suggestion about contacting Đăng Đạo. They were enticing words but lacked feeling and were nothing more than an attempt, whether conscious or not, to distract her from the real issue at hand.

I would like to see Đăng Đạo, though.

Lan looked at her watch. She needed to hustle, as Kannon would say. Completing preparations, she placed the teapot and two cups on a sterling platter, added the covered finger sandwiches, and carried all to the patio.

Upon reentering the house, she stopped to look in on her son, home from school. Propped against his pillow, Derrick was reading aloud from a second level book given him by his uncle Roger. Her son's facial expression reminded Lan of her husband's, a look conveying his readiness to engage the world.

An irony struck her like a hot wind. She felt lifted by the joy of motherhood but deflated by the ache of alienation from Kannon.

Lan padded to Derrick's bed and sat beside him. Stroking hair away from his forehead, she whispered, "I never thought I would have you, little one. I love you."

"Momma Lan, give me some space."

Oh, my. He is growing too fast.

Shaking her head, Lan left Derrick's room, entered the living area, and walked past her gleaming black Steinway. A wedding gift from Kannon, it was a special treasure because she had mentioned during their first meeting in Việt Nam that one of her dreams was to own a piano. That he remembered her wish meant a lot, and her lips trembled at the sweet memory.

She moved past the remembrance and went to the front window to peer through the gossamer curtains. Belynda Blu's purple van was coming up the drive. She went outside to greet her guest. The dissonant sound of the van's motor reminded Lan of three-wheeled Lambrettas in her native country.

Like Lan, Belynda Blu was a minority, a Navajo, one of the Dine'é People. Belynda taught a course on Native American culture and artifacts at St. Edward's University in northwest Austin. They had become acquainted after Lan signed up for her class.

She liked the way Belynda carried herself in the classroom and her manner of instruction. It gave Lan the feeling that nothing daunted her, that she accepted life as it came—like a maturing Buddhist.

Lan's interest in Indian lore grew during visits with Kannon to Native American historic sites in the Southwest. The fascinating observation she embraced was the similarity between Native Americans and Vietnamese—the height, the absence of facial hair, the suppleness.

"Yá'át'ééh," Belynda said, exiting the van, showing gleaming white teeth and syrupy brown eyes. Belynda Blu's jet-black hair purled past her shoulders and fell upon a simple white cotton blouse offset by a long, billowing floral-print skirt. She carried a tan canvas satchel in her left hand.

"Chào bạn của tôi," Lan responded.

They hugged, exchanging a laugh at greeting each other in their respective languages. Lan saw in her a kindred soul who seemed to be a wise and spiritual woman in whom she could confide.

Lan stepped aside, motioning Belynda to enter. Her friend glided through the door with a swanlike grace.

"What a wonderful piano," Belynda Blu exclaimed as Lan led her through the living room. "Do you play?"

"Yes. Mostly classical and show tunes. I played a lot before Derrick was born, but not so much after his birth."

"I get that," Belynda said, "but I bet you would enjoy playing again."

It would soothe my soul, Lan thought.

She guided Belynda to their backyard covered patio and motioned for her to sit in one of the cedar rockers, while she leaned over the patio table and removed three cylindrical pillars of incense. Clicking the barbeque lighter, she lit the slow-burning sticks and placed them in a miniature adobe cabin. Lan waved the spiraling column of incense vapor to her nostrils and inhaled the calming aroma of sage, hoping this would help overcome the reticence emboldened by her culture.

When Lan sat in the other cedar rocker, she noticed Belynda's beaded moccasins. "How lovely."

"They're handmade by my father. Dine'é beadwork is rare. A Shoshone my father met in military service taught him."

A work of love, Lan thought.

"Would you like some tea? Sandwiches?"

"Please."

Lan poured two cups of the freshly brewed Vietnamese tea and served it mild and tepid, as was her native country's custom.

As the two of them sipped from their cups, their conversation turned more personal. Belynda revealed she was divorced from an archaeologist and had twin sons. "One is a dentist who works on the Navajo Reservation, while the other, a computer scientist, works and lives in Austin."

"I am glad for you."

"My ex," Belynda continued, "was a jerk I met on a whitewater rafting trip through the Grand Canyon. Once, he fell into the river, and I pulled him back into the raft. I should have left him in the river."

Lan was startled. "Was he a bad man?"

Belynda laughed. "No. But all he wanted to do was talk about excavations of historical sites and calibrated radiocarbon dates versus uncalibrated ones. We grew apart after he worked a dig in the Middle East, Jordan, I think it was. The romance between us died."

How familiar this sounds.

Encouraged by Belynda's candidness, Lan felt open to share a little of her own story.

"My mother was born in Corse, a French-owned island south of Italy. I never knew my paternal grandparents. My maternal grandmother was Vietnamese, and my maternal grandfather was French. I would love to visit Corse and trace my grandfather's ancestry."

"A great idea."

As they rocked beneath the covered patio's whirling ceiling fan, Lan provided a brief explanation of the flavor of her life in Việt Nam. "My father was a teacher, as was I."

"I thought as much. What did you teach?"

"English, until the Communists overran Sài Gòn." Lan stirred her tea into a swirl, wanting to change the subject. "Please tell me more about your family."

"I'd be delighted." Belynda paused a moment, perhaps to gather memories, and then began. "Navajo children are considered born into their mother's clan and take the maternal name."

"I like the concept," Lan said. If she had kept her "clan" name, perhaps she would not feel such loss of identity. However, even the meaning behind her first name, Orchid, meant little in her new country.

"I'm part of the Táchii'nii clan," Belynda went on, "which

translates to Red-Running-Into-The-Water."

"The name sounds mystical." Red was also the passion color in Buddhism.

"It is mystical. I'm from the Bííh Dine'é, which means Deer People of Táchii'nii."

Belynda explained in more detail how Native Americans were driven from their lands, of a father who abstained from alcohol and eked out a living dry farming and raising goats on the barren Navajo Indian Reservation in the Four Corners area. She spoke about her mother, teacher of goodness and love, and who valued education. Growing up, deprived of amenities such as indoor plumbing and running water, Belynda spent her time reading library books, sand painting, and riding horses. "As a child, I rode a pony to school."

"I can only imagine."

"If we'd been born white-skinned, it would have become red from the dirt and clay embedded in our pores."

"You could have used our monsoon rains."

"Yes," Belynda said. "Later, we learned our nation dwelled on top of oil, gas, and uranium fields, but that didn't help our family."

"I do not understand."

"We resented the desecration of sacred land, and there were royalty disputes." Belynda continued, telling Lan she'd been fortunate enough to earn a scholarship to the University of New Mexico, where she received an undergraduate degree in political science. "I couldn't get a decent job," Belynda said, "so, I went back to school and got my master's in social work. At first, I thought I knew everything. Then I started counseling young Navajos about drugs and alcohol. I was the one who learned."

Lan knew little about the Dine'é, but how familiar the story sounded. Japan, China, France, and America all caused ruin in Việt Nam, but that paled in comparison to the horrific slaughtering of her people by the Vietnamese Communists. Was it really that different from what White America did to Native Americans?

"Too much tragedy," Lan said.

Belynda nodded. "Now, it's your turn."

A breeze whisked through the patio, tousling her friend's hair and scattering fallen leaves across the mahogany-stained concrete floor. Belynda smiled as if welcoming both the wind and Lan's tale to come.

"The heart of the story . . . I had a brother, Chấn, who served as Kannon's interpreter, but was imprisoned after the war ended. Years later, when released from the reeducation camp, Chấn found me, and I welcomed him." She searched Belynda's eyes, wondering if she was revealing too much.

"You must go on." Belynda grabbed a sandwich and began nibbling on it.

Grateful, Lan continued. "Chấn was dying a terrible death from hepatitis, but he held a secret. His Buddhist background motivated him to send a letter to Kannon. He wanted to make things right."

"And Kannon returned to Việt Nam?"

Lan nodded. "When he arrived in Sài Gòn to reunite with Chấn, I sensed deep affection between the two men. But my brother died, unable to reveal anything specific. Kannon was crestfallen."

"I am so sorry." Belynda looked downcast. "I, too, lost a brother."

"How?" Lan worried she had brought too heavy a cloud to their conversation.

"Robert—Blue Eagle was his Indian name—was seven years my senior. He was a star athlete in high school. The girls chased him, but he wanted no part of them. Our father had been a Code Talker in World War Two, and Blue Eagle wanted to set an example for his Navajo peers. He enlisted in the Marines," her tone saddened, "but was killed in 1968 during the Tết offensive at Huế."

"Trời ơi!" (My God!) Lan empathized with her loss but was pleased her story might have encouraged Belynda to share hers. "We have both lost brothers. It is good we have become friends."

Belynda smiled. "You've got that right. Please, go on."

Lan did, telling Belynda how she had helped Kannon uncover the truth about what happened during the war. "In doing so, I grew to care about him." She left out the part about how her passion ignited, so much so that she and Kannon had made love on the ground of her cousin's home in backcountry Việt Nam.

"Wow! I'm sure there's more," Belynda said, grabbing

another sandwich.

"There is." Lan paused to take a sip of tea. "I have a nephew. His name is Đăng Đạo. Chấn was his birth father but never got to know his son."

"Why? Pray tell."

"He was kidnapped as an infant and corrupted by the vilest man on earth, who embroiled Đăng Đạo in drug smuggling. He was eventually *transferred* to the United States, where he became a gang leader."

"Another wow!"

Lan told Belynda about Kannon's and Đăng Đạo's near-lethal confrontation in New Mexico six years ago, and how, out of respect for Kannon's feelings, she had never met her nephew in person. Lan smiled, remembering Đăng Đạo's call one year ago, saying, "I'm no longer in the gang business and have reformed."

"Wow, wow, wow! Do you want to see him?"

"Yes. Kannon even suggested it."

Belynda finished her tea, so Lan refilled both cups.

"Just curious, do you know what happened to the 'most vile man on earth?'"

"I do."

"And?"

Belynda rocked while Lan recounted about her abduction in South Việt Nam, about being held captive in an underground chamber, and how she and Kannon killed the man who had taken her.

Belynda stopped rocking and arched her eyebrows.

"Holy shit!"

Thirteen

Based upon Belynda's reaction, Lan felt validated as a unique human being who had gone to Naraka—one of the Mahayana versions of Buddhist hell—and returned. So had her friend. Lan realized there was no reason to hold anything back, that she had overcome her reticence.

"Not only have I lost a brother, years earlier I also lost my parents and sister. None of them will experience the joy of knowing my son."

"I understand. That's sad." Belynda wrinkled her brow and leaned forward, touching Lan's arm. "You have been through so much. I sense much tension in your body. Is something else going on?"

Lan's lips quivered. Her cheeks flushed.

"I am lonely. Kannon and I do not talk about relational or emotional issues. We rarely touch."

"I know. You can't have physical intimacy when there's no emotional intimacy."

"Yes." Belynda got it. "This past weekend, instead of *being* with me, he rode to Lost Maples and met this crazy veteran who threatened our family. And now Kannon is away on a business trip."

"You're feeling abandoned."

"Yes."

"Are you worried about this *crazy* man?"

"No . . . well, yes, a little."

"Just checking. Your biggest worry is your relationship."

Lan nodded.

"So much trauma. Have you or Kannon been diagnosed with PTSD?"

Lan arched her eyebrows. "Both of us. Kannon feels he is no longer vulnerable to triggers."

"Is he?"

"My husband is addicted to action."

"There are ways to get past that," Belynda said. "But maybe he's further along in recovery than you think."

"I hope so."

"One thing for sure," Belynda said, refilling her teacup, "you're feeling isolated and stuck."

"It is like a stalemate. I am not sure Kannon really knows me or his son. The distance between us is increasing. Lately, his words sound hollow and leave me with an empty feeling. But if I cannot work this out with Kannon, I will have nothing."

"Oh, my God. You're one of the most intelligent and beautiful women I've ever met. You have yourself. You have your son, who I want to meet. And you have me."

Lan broke into tears.

Belynda rose and approached. She placed her cheek against Lan's and hugged her. "You also have a rich tradition few can match or understand. I see why you feel lonely."

"Listening to you gives me courage."

Belynda patted Lan on the shoulder, then returned to her own rocker and sat. "You are growing. You want more out of your life. This is your chance to take charge."

Lan let her eyes wander. "Even if it means separating from Kannon?"

Belynda offered a grim smile. "Do you love him?"

"Yes."

"Then why separate? But that's your decision. You could stay with me for a few days if you want. But first, have you two had the all-nighter discussion?"

Lan shook her head.

"Have the discussion with your husband."

"I may have to club him over the head."

"If necessary." Belynda giggled. "Just remember to separate your personal issues from couple issues."

"I understand. I am not certain Kannon does."

"There's always more therapy."

"I will try the all-nighter first. If—"

Derrick stormed through the hacienda door like a baby water buffalo, cutting off his mother.

"*Mẹ*," he said.

"The Vietnamese word for Mother," Lan said. She welcomed

him onto her lap and hugged him. "Hi, little one. Meet my friend."

"Yá'át'ééh," Belynda said. "That means, 'It is good.'"

"Yes, it is good."

Derrick nestled his face against Lan's shoulder.

"Go play now," she said, cupping his cheeks. "My friend and I are visiting." Her son jumped down, his long chestnut-colored hair flying in the breeze as he scampered toward the swing set.

"Mama Lan. Watch me."

She and Belynda turned simultaneously to see her son dangling from a horizontal bar, using only one leg to anchor. His t-shirt drooped and exposed his belly. "Derrick, use both legs, please," Lan said. Then to Belynda, "He scares me. I love him more than I thought possible, but he is much to look after."

"He's strong and agile, an angel, full of spirit and feeling. A future artist. He'll be fine."

A warm glow filled Lan's body.

"Has he started school?" Belynda asked.

"Derrick attends a Montessori school for the gifted."

"I'm not surprised."

"He learned to read early and has been accumulating books," something she had lacked as a child in her native Việt Nam. "Kannon said he would have to build another room just to house them all."

Belynda smiled at this.

"I wanted to have another child, a daughter." Lan looked away. "But I cannot."

"You need to resolve that, too."

"I know."

"Look! I have something to show you." Belynda reached into her canvas bag. Her brown eyes danced while she unwound khaki-colored wax paper, revealing small wooden figures that clacked against each other. The sound reminded Lan of a bamboo stick dance.

"These belonged to my great-great-grandfather," Belynda said, rising from the rocker. She placed the figurines on the hand-polished walnut table. Little wooden dolls, the tallest probably less than eight inches high, lay in a family-like array. "We call them curing dolls."

The breeze rustled the oaks, delighting Lan with the sound,

and she thanked Buddha for this Dine'é woman, who often brought icons such as these to class and discussed their origin and meaning.

"Curing dolls are to be used only once, then abandoned," Belynda added, stepping back from the table.

"They lose their power?" Lan asked.

"Not to worry," Belynda said. "These are virgin dolls and have never been used in a healing ceremony."

Lan leaned in for a closer look. "They are beautiful. May I touch them?"

"Certainly." Belynda returned to her rocker. The swish of her skirt sounded like the rustling of an áo dài in an evening breeze.

The dolls were pale, pasty like the moon. Choosing the second largest, one she assumed represented the mother, Lan turned it over in her hand, noticing how rough and primitive the carving appeared. There were tiny holes in the dolls. She pointed to one and looked to Belynda for an answer.

"These holes correlate to an injury or illness believed to have been caused by a forbidden act—one not in harmony with nature. The healer would place a shell bead or turquoise nugget in the hole to affect the cure."

"Fascinating," Lan said. She set the doll down and examined the other two.

A loud reverberation startled Lan. Belynda greeted the noise with arched eyebrows.

"It is a motorcycle," Lan said. "I am not expecting anyone."

"Mama Lan? Is that Daddy K?" Derrick hit the ground on both feet.

"No, honey. He is traveling by plane. Remember?"

Derrick stuck out his lower lip.

Lan started for the front yard. She motioned for Belynda to join her. Out front, the rider dismounted and approached.

"Good afternoon, ladies."

The scruffy-looking man cast a thin shadow across the lawn.

"I'm looking for Kannon Ballard."

Lan shuddered.

Wearing Army boots, crisp jeans, and a fatigue shirt, the man fit Kannon's given description of the individual encountered at Lost

Maples. "You must be Streak."

"Got that right."

She turned to Belynda, whose parted lips and furrowed brow spoke volumes. "The crazy veteran?" she mouthed.

Lan nodded.

Like a wisp, Derrick appeared. "Who is he, Mama Lan?"

"An old *friend* of your father's," Lan said. "What do you want?" she asked Streak.

"Nice-looking spread you got here." Streak's eyes focused on Derrick. "That your boy?"

"Yes," Lan said through clenched teeth. "Sir. I have to ask you to leave."

"Not until I talk to Kannon."

"My husband does not want to talk to you." Wishing she had her snub-nosed .38 handy, Lan did not want the man to know Kannon was not home.

"Belynda, please take my son inside the house."

"Sure. Come on, little warrior."

"What's wrong, Mama Lan?"

"Just go with Belynda."

While her friend ushered Derrick inside, Lan glared at Streak. "You are not welcome here."

"Your husband must not be home." The man narrowed his eyes into slits. "Else he would've already come outside."

"Go," Lan said.

"Aren't you afraid, you and the boy, at being alone?" His cheek bulged grotesquely. He turned his head to one side and spat an ugly substance to the ground.

Lan crossed her arms.

Belynda returned and took a stance beside her.

"Listen, creep. You don't want to mess with two strong women," Belynda said.

Lan welcomed her friend's harsh tone.

"What's the matter, bitch? Your panties riding high?" The creep hooked his thumbs on his belt.

"I bet yours are pink," Belynda said, a smirk on her face.

Lan's cellphone rang. She retrieved it from her pants pocket and flipped the phone open. The caller ID showed Stefan—Kannon's grown son from his earlier marriage—on the call. "Stefan, call—"

Streak snatched the phone from her hand and flung it into the cactus garden.

"Asshole!" Lan yelled. The next thing she knew, Belynda held a pistol in her hand.

"Nice little nine-millimeter you've got there," Streak said mockingly. "Don't you know you're not supposed to draw a weapon unless you plan to use it?"

Streak flinched as a bullet whizzed past and buried itself in the lawn.

"Calm down, ladies. You've made your point. I'm leaving. Just tell Kannon the CIA is interested in his connection to a rightwing militia group. And ICE might question how you got into this country, little lady. Wouldn't want to see your boy's mama deported now, would we?"

Lan slapped him. His face turned crimson. He took a step forward but stopped when Belynda brandished her pistol.

"You'll be seeing me again." Streak mounted his motorcycle and rode away.

Lan loosened her collar and watched Streak exit, wishing him to crash and burn. She could not believe what just happened. It was like removing a specious mask, only to reveal a horrible reality lying underneath. Her fears magnified—especially the not-so-veiled threat to her and her son. Moreover, would ICE pursue and question her entry into America? And what was this talk about a militia?

Lips compressed, Lan marched to the cactus garden and scooped up her cellphone. Belynda grabbed Lan's arm and led her inside. They made their way into the den and sat on the sofa.

"I think you have more to say," Belynda said.

Her body shaking, Lan wept.

Kannon, you promised!

* * *

After being comforted by Belynda, Lan brewed more tea. She returned Stefan's follow-up call to tell him she was okay. But she was not. She was shaken, worried, and angry. Lan also tried several times to reach Kannon, but he never answered, which frustrated her more.

"He is ignoring me," Lan said.

"I hope not," Belynda said. "Regardless, I think you should call the sheriff."

Lan shook her head. "Doing so might cause more trouble." She rose from the sofa, entered the kitchen, and grabbed the fresh pot of tea. Back in the den, she took Belynda's hand. "Come. Let us return to the patio."

She led Belynda down the hall past Derrick's room. He was building a rocket with his old-fashioned erector set.

Once outside, Lan refreshed their cups. They resumed sitting in the cedar rockers next to the table on which sat the three curing dolls.

Derrick bolted outside. "Mama Lan, what was that loud noise?"

The gunshot?

"Our guest's car backfired, honey," Lan said, casting a glance at Belynda.

Her answer seemed to satisfy Derrick, who headed toward his sandbox.

"Maybe your husband hasn't answered because he's in flight," Belynda said.

Lan glanced at her watch. "That is possible."

"Streak's a disgusting man," Belynda said. "He should be buried up to the neck near an anthill."

"Or tossed into a Việt Cộng punji stake pit." Lan blushed at the ugliness of her thought.

"I don't mean to pry . . . but was Streak correct? Are you in the country illegally?" Belynda ran her finger around the lip of her teacup.

Her friend's tone was not judgmental but compassionate. Lan was not used to such directness, but she trusted the woman. "I *bought* my visa while in Việt Nam and worked my way into America. After Kannon and I reunited, he sponsored me, then we married. I think my papers are in order, but I am concerned if the authorities ever question me closely."

"You're not a citizen?"

Lan shook her head. "I have the Green Card and have been a

permanent resident for over three years. A year ago, Kannon and I filed this form—N-400, I think it was—for my naturalized citizenship. It has not been granted."

"I wouldn't worry. Those things take time. I imagine they're swamped with applications."

"I hope that is the only problem."

"Mama Lan!"

Lan turned. Derrick had abandoned his sand fort and was playing on the monkey bars. She winced when he flipped off the top horizontal bar. Fortunately, he landed on his feet. He ran to Belynda, hugged her leg, and then disappeared inside the house.

"My." Belynda broke into a wide smile. "What a treat."

"He is full of surprises," Lan said.

Belynda set her teacup on the table. She reached for the smallest curing doll and handed it to Lan. "As we Dine'é say, you are out of harmony with nature."

Lan took hold expectantly. Tiny sticks encircled the small doll's waist. "What are these?"

"Prayer sticks . . . tied on with strips of corn husks." Belynda reached into her canvas shoulder bag and withdrew a pouch. She untied the drawstring and poured out a multitude of turquoise bits.

Lan caressed the smallest rough-hewn figure.

"To restore harmony and to heal." Belynda raised her teacup in a toast. "The turquoise nuggets must be placed in the holes where healing is needed."

"Oh, thank you." Lan clicked her cup against Belynda's.

These will enhance my mantras.

* * *

After seeing Belynda out the front door, Lan walked through their oak-paneled den, her heels echoing across the hardwood floor like water dripping on cavern stone. She looked in on Derrick once more, then returned to the patio to meditate, carrying her revolver.

Her sixth summer in America had passed and, except for the lower humidity, the heat was as oppressive as in her native Sài Gòn. At least South Việt Nam did not have thorny fat-eared cacti or slithering snakes that rattled. The isolation of her Texas Hill Country home, where cicadas droned in their musical scale, was closing in.

95

She wished she shared Belynda's confidence about restoring harmony. But living in a new country—with a young son and no family other than a distant nephew—was overwhelming. Could Navajo curing dolls heal hers and Kannon's relationship? Protect their son?

She picked up the female doll and placed a turquoise bit in its empty heart.

Fourteen

On Tuesday afternoon, as the Boeing 737 descended to Austin-Bergstrom International Airport, Kannon wrapped up his notes. He was more than satisfied with SyncTrak's planning session. Product development was moving forward, and they had revised and polished the company's marketing plan. Most importantly, a new round of venture capital was being put in place for the LLC. The sought-after equity positions for Roger and him were all but locked in.

The reigning directors had also flattered Kannon by offering him the open seat on the board. Not wanting the liability exposure directors were saddled with these days, he turned it down, preferring his role as adviser and consultant.

The 737 hit the tarmac with a jolt, wheels bouncing and screeching before settling into a steady rhythm. The landing jarred his thoughts back to the home front. Not only had he and Lan not spoken during his two nights away, he hadn't even checked voicemail. His marital concerns loomed large. No single issue seemed critical in the relationship, but it had become flat, platonic. Affection was wanting and sex infrequent.

Child-rearing? They didn't always agree on "best practices," but he couldn't recall any harsh disagreements. Often these past few weeks, though, Lan's facial expressions trailed far away. Maybe she was going through a mid-life crisis, questioning everything, including him.

Was she still bothered by her inability to bear another child? She'd always wanted a daughter, but whenever he brought up the subject of adoption, she became reticent.

Perhaps she was thinking about her lost love, the young Vietnamese scholar who had been working on his doctorate in history before succumbing to pancreatic cancer, facts not disclosed until after she had tied the knot with Kannon. Was she lamenting what might've been?

He'd asked only once. "The past is past," is all she had said. Was it?

Another issue receiving scant attention was faith. Perhaps his Christianity and her Buddhism constituted an unspoken breach. Yet, both had experienced their state of hell, a common bond in Kannon's mind. Her Mahayana Buddhism—of the Greater Wheel School—alluded to all things being temporal and that each individual's reality was an illusion. Her being kidnapped and confiscated in an underground cage at the mercy of a madman six years ago was not illusory. It kind of meshed with his experience as a Christian. Nowhere in the New Testament was he aware of any scripture addressing how to cope with the aftermath of being a combat veteran.

Still, Mahayana Buddhism advocated its Eightfold Path about doing the right things while Christianity championed its Ten Commandments and Golden Rule. Add Buddhism's Ten Fetters and Christianity's seven deadly sins, which equate to similar beliefs at the crux, and maybe they had more in common there than he realized.

Also, on the positive side, his and Lan's financial position was solid. Kannon no longer drank scotch but did allow himself an occasional beer or a glass of wine. The consulting work was going well, and the relationship with his older son was much improved. Still, unsettling feelings plagued him like corrosives attacked iron.

The plane reached the gate. After hustling off and entering the passageway to the terminal, Kannon activated his cellphone and accessed voicemail. The first was from Lan.

Tên khốn—he didn't know what that meant, but based on her tone, it wasn't good. "Streak was here. He threatened us."

His lungs constricted. It was like trying to breathe through a cloud of volcanic ash. He pressed Lan's speed code. "I'm sorry," he blurted.

"Kannon, I am angry."

No kidding.

Her voice crackling with tension, Lan filled details into the gaps from her voicemail, including how grateful she was for Belynda's support.

Kannon could barely swallow. He should've been there.

"Don't worry. Your papers are in order, and nothing will happen to you or Derrick."

Lan responded with an exasperated sigh. Then, "What is this

about a militia?"

Shit!

"For Christ's sake, Lan, I'm a retired CPA, not a member of any militia!" His loud tone attracted attention from fellow travelers. He softened his voice. "I'm on my way home. We'll talk then."

"Hurry," she said.

They rang off.

Kannon couldn't believe Streak had threatened to report Lan to Immigration and Customs Enforcement. What a bastard! Hell, from what he had read, ICE, even though hamstrung and inconsistent, was capable of destroying families. If Lan ever was investigated, he hoped his military service as well their marriage would more than compensate for the way she entered the country. The issue might become moot, though, if his marriage didn't survive.

The militia threat bothered him a lot more. He reflected on Streak's comment at the Black Forest Restaurant. "You don't know who you're dealing with."

Oh, man, had his family become a target?

Kannon speed-walked past the various food and merchandise vendors and caught a shuttle to the parking area. By the time he reached his Cherokee, the sky was overcast and the atmosphere was saturated with the fresh smell of ozone. He slipped behind the wheel, jammed the gearshift lever into first, and sped out of the parking lot.

Rain was falling by the time he reached home and found Lan sitting in her leather recliner, an afghan in her lap. A thin column of fragrant smoke rose from a bronzed Buddha incense burner. The smell was sweet, sandalwood, one of Lan's favorites, yet the look on her face was anything but sweet. They exchanged courteous but strained hellos.

Kannon sat opposite her in a pigskin-covered straight back chair.

"Are you all right?" he asked.

She nodded.

"This happened after Roger and Karen left?"

"Yes."

He wished his brother had stayed on, but there was no way he could've known.

"How's Derrick?"

"In his room building a space station with Legos. He is okay."

After a quick greeting with his son, Kannon returned to the den. "I don't blame you for being upset. I am too."

Lan cut her eyes toward him and rehashed Streak's verbal assault and Belynda's actions.

"She shot at him?"

"A warning. I would have done the same if I had had my revolver."

No doubt, Kannon thought. He'd suggested she keep it handy. Maybe it was just as well. Hers might have been more than a warning shot.

"Streak also said," Lan added, "'You'll be seeing me again.'"

Kannon swore. *I should've beat the shit out of him at the Black Forest Restaurant.* "I'll file a criminal complaint."

Lan shook her head.

"Why not?" Kannon asked.

"There are too many unknowns and uncertainties. I am not sure we can trust the authorities."

"Lan, this is America, not Communist Việt Nam." Although her concerns were not entirely unfounded.

She sighed. "We have always handled our troubles on our own."

True.

"Still, I will think about it."

"Fair enough."

Kannon noticed three primitive figures lying on an end table. Lan reached over and clutched the middle-sized one.

"What are those?"

"Navajo curing dolls," she said. "The holes represent wounds. Filling the cavities with bits of turquoise enables healing."

Interesting, Kannon thought. "Belynda is a Navajo? She brought you those?"

"Yes."

"Which hole represents Streak?"

Lan compressed her lips and fixed him with a look that could immobilize a badger. She flipped the doll over and pointed to a tiny nugget squarely planted in one of the cavities of the right butt cheek. Then Kannon noticed another bit of turquoise on the other butt cheek.

Does that one represent me?

"I want to discuss us," Lan said.

"Okay."

"I am out of harmony."

If she is out of harmony, so am I.

"I'm listening."

"This Streak business makes things worse. I was already confused, and now our family faces danger. This strains our relationship even more."

"I didn't know Streak was psychotic."

Lan's pupils dilated, appearing like black saucers. "I understand, and we must keep the Streak issue separate. This is about you and me, not Streak."

"Lay it on the table," Kannon said.

"You find ways to avoid intimacy." Lan crossed her legs, rustling her black silk pants and white áo dài.

"I don't mean to."

An imperceptible shake of her head suggested he'd struck a sour chord. "Whenever I have tried to get close to you, you decide to smoke your pipe and read a book or go ride your motorcycle."

Unfortunately, it had become a natural reaction for him.

"And your consulting work often takes you out of town."

"You want me to quit consulting?" Kannon leaned forward. The pigskin chair squeaked. "Lan, I need the mental challenge. It keeps my mind sharp."

"Austin has numerous high-tech companies, which need consultants like you."

"True. But—"

"Let me finish!" Lan said, dismissing what would've been a defensive comment. "Your brother has connections. Have you and Roger considered investing in a local company?"

"Not really. SyncTrak—"

"Wait!" Lan wrung her hands. "It is happening again. We are drifting away from the real subject. You are not hearing me."

Kannon flared his hands palms up.

"Intimacy," Lan said.

Intimacy.

Kannon rocked the pig chair on its legs, which clip-clopped on the tile, sounding like a discordant pendulum. "I thought that suggesting you contact your nephew showed caring."

"Distraction, diversion, manipulation . . . whatever you want to call it. Suggesting I contact Đăng Đạo was a nice idea but for the wrong reason."

Got it.

His intention, while initially lodged in a good-idea category, now belonged elsewhere.

"Emotional connection, Kannon." She touched her heart. "In fairness, it is not all you. I lost the world I knew and my new one is jeopardized."

"I understand," Kannon said. Well, some of it. She wasn't just talking about affection and sex.

"Do you?" Her face softened, but he could tell she was still walking up the mountain. "I would not feel as bad if things were better between us." She paused. "Are you happy with the way things are?"

A softball-sized lump stuck in his throat. "Not really."

"If not for Derrick?" she said, her voice trailing off.

Kannon gripped the sides of his chair. "If not for Derrick . . . what?"

"Anger is not helpful."

"All right. I get it. You're upset and unhappy."

She faced him with narrowed eyes. Her lips parted, forming an *O*, but no words emerged. What else could he say? It was hard not to press. Stifling his urge, though, was doubly difficult. Shaken, angry from his encounter with Streak, Kannon grew more unnerved by Lan's open-ended statement, "If not for Derrick."

"Look. It's natural to miss your first family and homeland," Kannon said. "I can't imagine the depth of those losses. But I've been wondering. Have you been thinking about the man you were engaged—?"

"Oh, my God!" Lan said, bringing her hand to her mouth. "I cannot believe you brought this up."

Kannon lowered his gaze. His slide was gaining momentum,

and he couldn't help but accelerate it. Self-destruction on the upswing. As if Lan had come to America focused on her former fiancé, who long ago had died in South Việt Nam. Could he dig the hole any deeper?

"I'm sorry. That was a stupid thing to say."

Lan buried her hands beneath the afghan and bundled it against her chin.

"What do you want, Lan?"

She raised her head and stared him straight in the eye.

"I would like to take Derrick and spend a few days with Belynda in Austin."

"I thought you wanted to go to BookLitls this weekend."

"Now is not the right time."

"Christ! You're talking about a separation."

"A temporary one. This will give you time to sort out what you want."

"I know what I want. It's you, here."

"Kannon—"

Lan's cell chimed. She set the curing dolls aside.

"It is Belynda. I must speak to her." Cellphone plastered to her ear, Lan rose, swept through the swinging kitchen door, which swung back and forth . . . back and forth.

The den, with its stone fireplace and oak paneling, might just as well be a scene in a still-life painting. Cold, lifeless, and filled with tension. As Kannon rose, sudden dizziness nearly toppled him to the floor. He inhaled deeply and steadied himself.

The disconnect.

He, a stranger in his own home, a stranger to himself, could touch the physicality of her being but not treasure it, sense Lan's humanity but not grasp it, understand the concept of a relationship but not fulfill it.

Self-doubt triggered his downward spiral. What he had said was stupid, yeah. Unfortunately, he'd traveled down this path before. *Déjà vu.*

Fifteen

Tubing a placid section of the Llano River, Streak wished its smooth waters would wash away his screwups. It was Wednesday, the day after the confrontation at Kannon's home. Fear and desperation had fueled his actions, but threatening Ballard's wife and kid accomplished zero, zilch.

Not the brightest thing to do!

Streak paddled his inner tube in wide circles, keeping his sparse campsite and motorcycle in view. After restocking his beer cooler at a convenience store, He'd ridden here and stumbled across this tube wedged among reeds along the bank. Now, he was waiting to hear from Sindy Zeller, his seductress and alleged CIA agent.

To Streak's understanding, the CIA wasn't supposed to operate in the United States . . . unless the organization suspected nexus between a domestic entity and a hostile foreign government.

Since several of Border Slot's militia operated overseas, that link might justify the CIA's involvement. Also, he wondered whether the CIA had been given looser reins due to increased terrorism. And wasn't the CIA supposed to request the FBI's help in domestic matters?

Unless, and his intuition spoke loud, Zeller wasn't CIA but conducting a rogue operation. If so, why? Funded how? If she wasn't rogue but real, the country needed to be protected from the CIA.

If the Viper bitch wasn't an agent, what was he going to do—report her to the FBI? Inform them that a shady woman posing as a CIA operative used sex to entice him to transport stinger missiles across an international border?

What Streak had been enjoying was pretending to implement the undercover wire operation. "Still trying to create the right timing," he'd told Zeller, and continued to tell her. The failure to get money from Kannon was messing things up. How much longer could he keep stalling?

A strong wind bent the pecan and sycamore trees that shaded his secluded campsite on the riverbank. Skyward, a red-tail hawk soared with the thermals. For a moment, Streak imagined himself back in the Bitterroots.

A water moccasin slithered into the water—a viper, like Sindy Zeller. He yanked on the string tied to the inflatable cooler and pulled it close. Inside the cooler were cigarettes, three beers, the slingshot, and his prized World War II vintage 9mm Luger—a war trophy his father had confiscated from a dead Nazi. The irony of piloting for a militia group that worshipped Hitler didn't escape Streak.

Grabbing the slingshot and one steel pellet, he waited to see if the snake would expose its head like a rising periscope. Ten seconds later and twenty-five feet away, the viper complied. Drawing a bead, Streak took a full breath, let out half to steady himself, and released the taut draw. When the pellet struck, the water moccasin's head smacked the surface. Ripples rolled outward as if Streak had slapped the water with the palm of his hand.

Satisfied, Streak tossed the slingshot back into the storage container. As he reached for a cigarette, his satellite phone rang. First, he lit the cigarette, snatched a beer and twisted off the top, then placed the beer between his legs. Finally, he whipped the sat from its waterproof pouch and answered.

"Yeah."

"You're not fulfilling your end of the bargain. I'm sure a respectable character like yourself would never try to flee the country."

Zeller the Viper.

"I'm not running. Besides, how could I without a valid passport? I'm still trying to get the leaders together. It's hard to pin these guys down."

"I can imagine, especially since you're floating on an innertube on the Llano River."

Streak's beer slipped through his legs and hit the water. He snatched it up. He scanned both riverbanks, couldn't see shit.

"How are you tracking me?"

"Need to know basis."

Think fast. Leverage Zeller's fanaticism and divert pressure onto Kannon.

"Then know this. The leaders have scheduled a Friday meeting in Texas. They're flying commercial and gave me permission for a motorcycle side trip before joining them."

"Why haven't you kept me informed?"

"To spare you the details. None of this means shit unless I pull it off."

"The meeting? That wouldn't be at Kannon Ballard's residence, would it?"

I'm fucked.

"What of it!" Streak said.

"He's a talented and resourceful man," Zeller droned on. "As a former chief financial officer and current consultant, he has a great cover. A perfect fit."

This is my chance. Play it right. I reached out to Kannon, and he told me to fuck off. Hell, I owe him nothing. So, what are my options? Blackmail him using his wife's questionable status when entering the country? Sell him out to the Militia?

"You there?" Zeller piped in.

"Hang on a minute." He wedged the satphone in his crotch and paddled to a cluttered sandbar. Clambering off the tube, he brought the phone to his ear.

"Right. A perfect fit. Kannon Ballard launders the money."

"We'll need evidence."

Evidence? There is no fucking evidence.

"I'll wire up for the meeting."

"Why are they including you?"

"Because I'm a better pilot, and I can plan the flight paths for upcoming missions." Streak flicked a cigarette butt into the river. "Once I get this done, I'm clear, right?"

"Clean slate once indictments are handed down. You were never in the militia."

"And expunge my earlier conviction?"

"Yes."

"And witness protection?"

"I'll give it strong consideration."

"You already stiffed me on the fifteen-thousand-dollar cashier's check. Why should I believe you'd offer witness protection now?"

"The money promise was a lure."

106

"You played me."

"Listen, you idiot. I'm running out of patience. You have until Friday to expose the militia and get evidence on Ballard. Get it done." She ended the call.

Streak grabbed his Luger and symbolically executed Zeller. But he'd played her well, he thought, buying himself more time. Time to come up with another angle to wrangle money from Kannon. Could he devise a triple cross—Border Slot, Kannon Ballard, and Zeller?

If not—he kicked sand at a turtle inching its way toward the water—he'd be caught between the Viper's fangs and Crandle's killing range.

A skunk's putrid odor whiffed past. Scudding clouds darkened the sky, and the water rippled in the breeze. Streak lit another cigarette, then plopped the innertube back on the river, creating a hollow echo. He leaped from the sandbar and flopped on the tube. With his free index finger, he made rapid circles in the river water, creating a tiny whirlpool.

How in hell was she tracking him?

He idled there a moment, then paddled to the bank to break camp. After getting dressed, he ran his fingers over the V-Rod. Streak clenched his jaw. No damn tracking device. How was he going to rid himself of the tail?

To calm down, he opened a fringed leather saddlebag and retrieved his chewing tobacco. He pinched a plug and stuffed it into his mouth, then mounted the bike and switched on the ignition. The twin cylinders rumbled to life.

At the intersection of his self-made trail and a paved farm-to-market road, he stopped to let an old Camaro pass. *Come on, lady. Move it!* The driver was Asian. Filipino, Korean, Vietnamese, or Chinese? He still couldn't tell the difference.

Her head barely reached the top of the steering wheel, but it was high enough for Streak to notice the funny look she gave him. He shrugged it off, but something about her oval-shaped face and the vehicle seemed familiar. Where? When? It didn't matter. He had someone else on his mind.

Kannon Ballard.

Sixteen

Tuesday, 20 October 2009, Kalispell, Montana

Whitehead approached the Flathead County Library in Kalispell. If not for the green awning and sentry-like lampposts, the blocky structure might be mistaken for a monastery. Entering the parking garage, he pulled his late-model black pickup into an available space on the first floor and exited.

Inside the library, Whitehead strode across the gray-carpeted ground floor and signed on to a public computer. After lengthy discussions with OT via satellite phone yesterday, he wanted to see what information the Internet offered regarding EMP weapons. He Googled, clicked on articles, and read. It turned out OT's input was more informative.

He thought about the upcoming EMP weapons briefing and wondered whether Crandle was sandbagging him. Did the Commander know far more about electronics and the Internet than he let on? No telling what secrets the man stored in his compartmentalized mind.

Nevertheless, Whitehead's mixed feelings about using electromagnetic pulse weapons hadn't diminished. His hesitation had much to do with the prodding by his adoptive Nez Percé parents regarding education.

Whitehead sat back, picturing the look of disapproval on their faces. When faced with dilemmas like this, he often went into the forest to seek out the answer.

Meanwhile, he decided to check out Sindy Zeller and Kannon Ballard. He Googled. No hits on Zeller, but several hits on Ballard popped onto the screen, which surprised him. He hadn't expected to find anything. Reading and growing more interested, Whitehead studied a photo of Ballard. Here was a guy who had returned to Việt Nam, killed his Việt Cộng nemesis, then returned to the United States, where he allegedly eliminated his former U.S. commander. More than one blogger had labeled Ballard's commander a traitor.

Another link caught Whitehead's attention. He clicked onto

the trail and discovered that Kannon Ballard was a consultant for SyncTrak, which manufactured GPSs and other electronic items like cellphones and tracking devices.

Interesting.

Despite no mention on the web of law enforcement connections, Whitehead questioned whether this Ballard character might be a cop of some sort, perhaps undercover. He recalled his and Bull's examination of Streak's address book, which contained Kannon's name as well as Sindy Zeller's. As for the *C*, dot, and *A*, if Streak's scribbles referenced the CIA, did that link Kannon Ballard to the Feds?

Jesus! Border Slot's personnel and grid coordinates could already be in the hands of the Feds. Crandle's going to kill me.

His sense of urgency escalated along with his heartbeat.

Hooah!

* * *

On Wednesday afternoon, 21 October, in a clearing adjacent to the Border Slot barracks, Crandle stood behind the podium on a raised platform. Directly to his front lay an array of hand-polished redwood stools encircling a crackling fire. Each man had sanded and polished one to his liking.

The weather was chilly, but not a cloud in the sky. Woodpeckers tapped for insects and squirrels foraged for acorns. Pungent smoke from burning wood blended with the aroma from cigars, creating a robust odor.

"Let's go, troops, get a move on," Crandle barked, after glancing at his notes.

His militiamen were casually dressed because the upcoming EMP mission demanded nondescript clothing. Even Crandle wore jeans and a flannel shirt.

Whitehead sidled alongside Crandle as the other militiamen took their seats. Brick, outfitted with a red, white, and blue bandanna, approached carrying a bone in his mouth. The German Shepherd placed his bone at the foot of his stool—crafted by his handler—then leaped on top and assumed a dog's version of "Attention!"

At 1300 hours, with Wagner's *Tristan and Iseult* playing in the background, Crandle began. "To the men of Border Slot Militia."

"Hooah!" The collective retort echoed off the cliff.

All rendered crisp salutes.

"Soon, we will undertake a different type of mission." Crandle leaned over and thumped a large, leather-belted suitcase to his right. "This will escalate Border Slot's *White Might* movement."

"What's in there? A nuclear bomb?" Hatfield asked.

To heighten their anticipation, Crandle delayed his response by lighting a cigar. Puffing on it, he looked at the ground, scanned the sky. And then he was ready. "It's a different kind of bomb. With it, we're going to paralyze a city, send it back to the dark ages."

Wide eyes and open mouths met his statement.

"We got, what, twelve men," Badger said. "It must be a small city." He laughed. A couple of the others joined in.

"The Commander is deadly serious," Whitehead added.

Brick barked.

"The target's large enough to get the nation's attention," Crandle said. "It's our turn to show the Feds how to grab land."

"What kind of bomb is it?" Nolan asked. "Improvised explosive device?"

"If not a dirty nuke, is it biological or chemical?" Badger asked.

"None of the above," Crandle said.

"You've got us, Commander," Porter said. "What the hell is it?"

"Electromagnetic pulse weapons."

"What the hell are those?" Nolan sounded more disappointed than curious.

"Think what lightning strikes can do to electrical circuits." Crandle waved his cigar at the men. "We have the capability not only to imitate but to magnify exponentially the impact of lightning."

Nolan scratched his head. "How?"

"EMP weapons are capable of delivering the equivalent of hundreds to thousands of lightning strikes, all concentrated to one area. There's a front-door impact and a back-door impact. And I'm not talking about sex."

Muffled laughter . . .

Whitehead jumped in. "A front-door effect sends ramped-up

electrical current into antennas or antenna-like objects and destroys dependent electronics. Back-door effects relate to large currents spiking through fixed electrical wiring and cables."

"A domino effect," Porter said.

"Like a string of firecrackers," Whitehead added. "A long string."

"I get it," Nolan said.

"Incredible," Badger said, chewing on an unlit cigar.

"This will be first of many attacks on the infrastructure of the United States." Crandle stepped from the podium and poked the fire. "Get this through your thick skulls. We can knock out power for weeks, months, even longer. We can fry anything electrical, burn computer chips. The Internet will go down. Airline reservation systems, banking institutions, the IRS, will be kaput. Gas stations won't be able to pump. Cellphone service . . . kaput. Vehicles will conk out. Food and ice will become harder to get. Chaos. Riots. Killing. The average citizen will be fucked."

"Shit, man, I like watching TV." Bull, head down, legs thrust apart, leaned forward and rested his wrists on his thighs as if taking a crap.

"How'd you get hold of EMP weapons?" Hatfield asked.

"That's on a need-to-know basis . . . and you don't need to know."

"Does it slaughter people?" Wolfhound asked.

"No."

"How come it doesn't kill?" Smitty asked.

"It just doesn't." Crandle glared at Smitty, who hung his head.

"How we supposed to get around?" Garrett asked.

"What about medical care?" another one asked.

"And banks!"

"No more porn on the Internet."

"Shit! No bars. How I'm gonna watch football?" McAfee asked.

Did Whitehead just nod at that comment about missing football games?

Perched on the edge of their stools, the militiamen continued muttering fear-based comments and questions—inappropriate for survivalists. Crandle was getting pissed but ignored them for now.

Instead, he scowled at Whitehead. Why wasn't his guy stifling the discontent? Maybe he wasn't one hundred percent into this thing. He walked over to him.

"Get control of these guys."

"Yes, sir."

His response carried little conviction.

Slowly, Whitehead walked to the podium and cocked a finger at the militiamen. "Settle down."

They did, which reinforced to Crandle how much the men respected Whitehead.

Placing his fists on his hips, Crandle shot a withering look at the men, then again at his second-in-command. He'd have Whitehead give the rest of the presentation. See how much he'd studied. Test his buy-in.

"Whitehead, as long as you're up there, why don't you proceed with the briefing."

His second-in-command didn't hesitate. He lifted the suitcase and placed it on the podium. After unbuckling the leather straps, he opened the case and grabbed hold of the bloated, two-foot-long cylinder.

"Hold it high," Crandle told him.

"One of many," Whitehead said.

"Looks like a regular bomb," Timmons said.

"It's the internal components that matter. A flux compression generator, a powerful battery, magnet, copper coil, and an internal explosive switch used to detonate the bomb are encased inside this shell." Whitehead didn't use notes. "While we want you to have a working knowledge of the components, you are to familiarize yourself with handling the bombs, how and where to place the weapons, and means of detonation."

Wolfhound raised his hand. "And it'll do all the stuff the Commander said it would?"

"That and more."

"Wouldn't the city dudes be able to reroute power from other stations?" Porter asked.

Whitehead shook his head. "The transmission equipment at

the local power stations will literally melt and need to be replaced, which takes time. Sizeable replacement generators are huge, difficult to transport, and in short supply. Some may have to be rebuilt on-station."

"Wow!" Nolan said.

"We'll have made our point," Whitehead added. "Plant the seeds of doubt and fear will follow. Folks will think—if it happened there, it could happen here."

Crandle clucked his tongue. Good job, he thought. It was time for him to step back in.

"Whitehead and I have prepared a proforma plan of attack. Here's an envelope for each of you. Inside you'll find team assignments and instructions covering your responsibilities, including placement and detonation of the bombs."

"What's the target?" Hatfield seemed restless to go, like a racehorse at the starting gate.

"And the date?" Wolfhound asked.

Crandle and Whitehead exchanged looks. They'd planned the attack to begin at 0130 hours on Tuesday, the twenty-seventh, but, fearing a leak, thought it best not to reveal the time or objective until game day. Security personnel placed around electrical substations was something they didn't need.

"We'll disclose that and more detail later." Crandle handed out the envelopes. "Study the contents. Commit to memory. You'll be tested." The men's faces displayed focus and intensity. "And men, nothing you've heard today is to be mentioned to anyone else." Crandle raked his finger across his throat.

"Slice and dice," Whitehead said.

No one laughed. All militiamen understood the reference to the training field.

"Before we say the pledge," Crandle said, feeling good about the preop meeting, "let's pray good fortune accompanies Whitehead and Bull on their forthcoming mission."

"Yeah, we know about their objective." Porter rose, walked to Bull, and clapped him on the shoulder. "You're going to bring our friend Streak back to the range."

"Roger that," Whitehead said.

113

"That's enough." Crandle stuck out his chest with satisfaction. He called the men to attention. "Let's recite the pledge."

I pledge allegiance to the Border Slot Militia and to the cause of the Posse Comitatus. As one chosen by God, I will exert selfless and extreme effort to restore power to His people by eliminating the illegal government and its tax schemes. I pledge to rid the world of those who should rot in hell. It is my purpose, no matter how difficult the conditions, no matter if I must sacrifice my life, to obey God's will and preserve White Might.

"White Might is Right! White Might is Right! White Might is Right! Hooah!"

After the men dispersed, Crandle addressed Whitehead. "The more I think about this Kannon Ballard and the possible, no, probable, reference to the CIA, I get so damn pissed I could bite a rattlesnake in two."

Seventeen

Thursday, 22 October 2009, Texas Hill Country

Kannon walked into the living room, acutely aware his last two days had been spent walking on eggshells. With Lan and Derrick at Belynda's, the place no longer felt like home.

He laid eyes on Lan's piano, wondering if he would ever hear her play again. She had seemed happier, no, satisfied, when playing. Maybe if she . . . stop it! He worried that at this sensitive time Lan would interpret any suggestion of his to be another attempt to manipulate her, like what had happened when he brought up Đăng Đạo.

She'd be right.

To occupy his mind, he'd read a lot, devouring Allen Wheelis's *The Quest for Identity*—again. Every time Kannon thought he'd locked in on his, it seemed to slip away.

He also read from Lan's favorite book of poetry. The author, Kannon read, was Hồ Xuân Hùòng, who created her work over two hundred years ago. Hùòng was a concubine and feared retribution if the real meaning of her poems—about men viewing women as sexual objects and oppressing them—came to the fore. She *disguised* her defiant poems, which, ostensibly, were about nature and compassion, by utilizing the art of double entendre.

It would help, Kannon thought, if he could understand the translations without having to refer to scholarly interpretations. Regardless, he concluded: *Lan probably feels I treat her as an object.*

The wall clock in the den chimed 1100 hours. Lan was due to return around noon. Although they had mutually agreed Derrick would stay on with Belynda a while longer, he'd miss his little guy. Not only that, Kannon wasn't sure whether Lan was returning for more discussion or for packing her bags.

Kannon's stomach growled. Not having eaten, he entered the kitchen, opened the refrigerator door, and grabbed a covered dish. At the breakfast table, he removed the plastic wrap, then forked a piece of roast beef. Brought it to his mouth. Hesitated. Set the fork down. If

Lan chose separation or divorce, it would result in his worst nightmare coming true—and a second failed marriage.

He left the kitchen. The hollow echo of his heels clacking across the Mexican tile floor reminded him of walking inside a mausoleum.

A pirated Disney figure crafted in Sài Gòn lay on his son's bed. How Derrick managed to sleep with it brought a tight smile. Scattered Legos lay across his son's worktable. He hoped, no prayed, that their marital situation wouldn't result in alternate weekends or a shared custody arrangement.

In a divorce, the woman usually got the house, but Kannon sensed Lan wouldn't want it. In her mind, this was his land, his home. He couldn't imagine its emptiness without his young son, much less this house without the flavor of his wife.

Christ! What if she decided to return to Việt Nam?

Stop it. You're driving yourself crazy.

Outside, stepping along the flagstone path, he brushed aside bougainvillea and rose vines clinging to trellises. At the rear patio, empty teacups sat on the table, along with the chessboard and game pieces Kannon had neglected to put away because he wanted to preserve the most recent visuals of his wife and son.

The familiar sound of Lan's chugging Volkswagen reached his ears. Kannon hustled to the driveway to greet her. As she parked, he straightened his spine. The car door popped open, and he offered his hand. She took it.

"Hi," he said. Wearing blue shorts and a yellow V-neck T, she looked great. "I'm glad you're here. I hope the time away has been good for you."

Lan shrugged as if to confirm his anxiety that what he said didn't matter. Not the response he wanted. When she started to walk away, he grasped her elbow. She stopped and turned.

"I want to go inside and freshen up," she said. "I'll meet you in the den."

Kannon released his grip.

Inside, she headed for the bathroom, he for the wet bar. Beer, wine, liquor? None of the above. He grabbed a pitcher, filled it with chilled water, and carried it along with two glasses into the den, where he placed them on a coffee table.

Lan entered and stopped underneath the ceiling fan, its base pitching slightly off-center, which pretty much depicted Kannon's state of mind. He poured two glasses of water and handed one to Lan, who wore her favorite scent of jasmine.

Each took a chair, he the proverbial pigskin and she the straight back. Too formal, he worried, thinking she would've chosen her recliner.

Lan sipped from her glass.

"I miss Derrick. How is he?"

"He is having a great time learning about Native American lore," Lan said.

"Good."

"He misses you, too."

"And I've missed you," Kannon said.

"I know." Her glistening eyes and moist lips belied any hint of arrogance and instead suggested warmth and understanding.

"I need to get some things off my chest," he said.

"I will listen."

"I don't know if there's anything I can say that will encourage you to stay," he said, "but I screwed up the other night. Suggesting you meet with Đăng Đạo was selfish. And I wish I'd stayed with you and not gone to Lost Maples."

"I appreciate what you say, but it is important to me you think before taking those actions, not after."

"I understand."

Kannon took a drink of water and then set down his glass. Time to bring up the poetry book.

"I've been reading from *Spring Essence*," Kannon said.

Lan's eyes widened, then she morphed into a closed-lipped smile.

"Do you see *me* in some of those poems?" she asked.

"Enough to realize you probably feel confined or objectified. Do you?"

"Yes, I have tried to tell you. Which is one reason I wanted you to read the book."

Touché! The barb stung, but it wasn't poisonous.

"As I have said before, it is not all you." Lan brushed the hair out of her eyes. "But I need you to let me be me. Encourage me to grow. And, as I said, I want you to think before acting."

"I'll try harder."

"I want you to do more than try," Lan said. "I want you to commit never to do those types of things again."

"Christ, Lan. I'm not perfect." Kannon gazed at the wagon wheel chandelier, wishing it would spin and spit out the right answer. Where was a shrink when you needed one?

"I do not expect you to be. Commit is a stronger word than try."

Kannon took a deep breath. "Okay, I commit," *to try harder*. "All right."

Kannon shifted his position. "I realize how much I've missed talking with you . . . along with affection and sex."

"So have I."

"You have?"

"Of course." Lan breathed deep and released a stream of air, seemingly charged with reproach. "You understand, though, I need to feel emotionally close first."

Why did God make men and women so different?

"As I said before you left for San Jose, it seems business ventures, motorcycles, and books come before me. I want us to spend more time together." Lan rose from the chair, walked toward the mirrored glass, and checked her reflection, then returned to her seat. "Another thing . . . and this is hard for me to say." She pursed her lips. "I have gained weight since Derrick was born. I have wondered if I am still attractive to you."

Kannon's mouth fell open. Why would she think that?

"You have not answered my question," Lan said. She pulled a purple silk handkerchief from her pocket and dabbed her cheeks. "Your silence says enough."

"Not true, Lan. I thought it was the other way around. After Derrick was born, it seemed all you did was pay attention to him."

Her expression softened.

Kannon continued. "Ever since you arrived in this country, all I've wanted to do is build a life with you. But since Derrick was born, it's like he's become a barrier between us. You asked if it bothers me you've gained weight. No, it's not even noticeable. You're a beautiful and sensual woman. I desire you."

Lan cocked her eyebrows. "You do?"

"Yes." Kannon focused on finding the right words. "For the first few years, every time I wanted to touch you in bed, he was there. Finally, I stopped trying. After he stopped sleeping with us, well, it had become a habit, our not talking or touching." Was any of this getting through?

Lan smiled sheepishly. "You are right. I have doted on Derrick and neglected you. The worst thing for me is we stopped sharing thoughts and feelings. I lost my connection with you."

"You're right. I've become detached and neglected you as well." Shuffling his feet, Kannon lowered his gaze, then lifted it and stared into her eyes. "And I think I get it, the emotional bond thing."

"I do not want to leave, Kannon. You must know, though, your recent actions have hurt."

"Yeah. I've done dumb stuff." *Got to cut that down.* "I'm sorry. I love you, Lan, and want you to stay."

"I need you to trust my love."

"I do, and I will."

Lan sighed. "I am in my forties . . . my first marriage, my first child, my only child. A gift I never thought I would have. When Derrick entered the world, I wanted to give him everything I had—to give my son enough love so he would never hate, no matter what happened." She bit her lip. "I have not been a wife to you."

"And I haven't been a husband to you. You're a bright, beautiful woman. I want you."

"Prove it."

Her cheeks glowed. He met her eyes.

Kannon had never seen her more beautiful. Lan's copper-colored skin radiated desire, and he wanted to feel her body next to his. It reminded him of his reaction when first seeing her in Việt Nam, the captivating eyes, the arresting tone of her voice, her fragrance. And now, as the ceiling fan wafted Lan's redolent perfume into his core, he felt enveloped in an aromatic vortex of wildflowers and spice and jasmine. His hands trembled as he reached for her waist. She let him pull her close but kept her arms to her sides.

Kannon tightened his embrace. Lan responded, then backed away. She walked to the sofa and motioned for him to join her. Together they sat, close, touching.

"If we are to mend," Lan said, "there is one other thing I want us to do."

He leaned toward her.

"I would like to go to counseling," she said. "How do you feel about it?"

"You mean together?"

"Yes. I have tried to be what I thought you wanted me to be. I must find me. We must find us."

Kannon exhaled. He'd undergone the counseling bit before. Could he do it with Lan? Obviously, it was something she wanted, and it was apparent he needed more work.

"All right," he said. "Let's do it."

She squeezed his thigh and beamed. He almost melted from her smile.

"Is there anything else you want to discuss?" he asked.

"Not now. This talk has been good for us."

"I agree."

"We must communicate like this more often." Lan wore the expression of a shy schoolgirl. "Let us toast with a glass of wine."

"Sounds nice."

Rising, Kannon strode to the wet bar and selected a bottle of Pinot Noir, an offering from the Laurel Vineyard in Oregon. Working the corkscrew, he opened the wine and poured two glasses, using the Waterford Crystal he'd inherited from his mother.

Lan stood, switched off the table lamp, and walked to the view window. "Do you remember when first we watched the moon together?"

Kannon approached her side and placed a wineglass in her hand. Waning twilight illuminated the low horizon and framed a quarter moon. "Yes, I remember."

Using her free hand, she took his and squeezed it. They toasted to the time they had shared a cocktail on the roof of the Rex Hotel in Sài Gòn. He slipped his arm around her waist and pulled her close.

She nuzzled against his shoulder, then turned and faced him. Tilting her head, Lan kissed him. Soft and gentle, her full lips tasted rich. The sensual rustling of her silk áo dài against his denim jeans excited him more.

Lan leaned back. "It has been a while since KannonRod has spoken."

Kannon smiled at her lyrical expression. "I hope he hasn't forgotten how."

"I will help him speak." Lan led Kannon down the hallway to their bedroom.

They set their wine glasses on the nightstand. While Lan repositioned the pillows, Kannon flung back the bedspread and top sheet, which ruffled the muslin canopy above their brass-framed bed. He took off his jeans and denim shirt and then lay on the smooth, clean cotton sheet.

Fully clothed, she joined him, resting her head on the pillows and placing one leg at a provocative angle. Clasping a glass of wine, she took a sip, then leaned forward and placed her lips on his, trickling the Pinot Noir into his mouth. He swallowed hard, began stroking her thigh. She feathered the hair on his chest with her fingers. The tingling sensation he had missed and longed for returned. For several minutes they lay side by side, not talking, but sharing wine and touching.

Kannon walked his fingers from her thigh to her breast and caressed the silk around her nipple. It became erect. He squeezed harder. Lan moaned and darted her tongue inside his mouth, probing deeply, then teasingly, pulled away.

"You want me to stop?" he asked.

"No. I want more, with music. Put on *Carmina Burana.*"

"Great idea." The scenic cantata piece resonated with sexual tension.

Taking the glass from her hand, Kannon placed it on the table and got up. At the stereo system they'd purchased for the bedroom, he flipped through CD cases until finding the one she wanted. He placed it in the carrier, set the repeat control, and increased the volume.

Before getting back into bed, he took off his shorts. Lan removed her áo dài, exposing her dark-like-chocolate areolas and firm

121

nipples, which crowned full rounded breasts the color of caramel. Next, she slipped off her black silk slacks, propped her head on an elbow, and placed the soles of her feet flat on the bed—legs splayed in invitation—her peach-colored skin gleaming in the dim light.

This is like seeing her for the first time.

Caressing her inner thigh again, he brought his lips close and kissed her soft skin, sensing deepening fragrances released by body heat. Lan put her hands behind her head and quivered. Flicking his tongue, he moved higher and higher up her thighs. She arched her back, giving him room to remove her panties. While he continued flicking his tongue along her creamy flesh, she undulated her pelvis and moaned.

Lan removed one arm from behind her neck, placed it around his, and guided him to her sweet spot. There, she smelled natural, as of the earth, and he stayed with her until she came, her body throbbing in a crescendo from *Carmina Burana.*

Afterward, she pulled his face to hers and kissed him fully on the mouth as if sharing all of each other.

"I love your scent," he said.

All the while the music played and the tension stayed.

Gently, she pushed away and looked into his eyes. Her mouth opened in a teasing smile. "There are other things we could do."

"What did you have in mind?"

"I'll demonstrate."

Lan rolled him onto his back and began stroking his penis. She brushed her lips down his chest, going lower, lower, until her lips and hand became like one.

When he was about to come, she let him go, then rose to kneel above him. Lan opened her thighs and straddled KannonRod, then lowered her body and enveloped him. She wriggled side to side, then undulated in cadence with the musical rhythm. Matching her movements, he ejaculated, as full and as satisfying as he'd ever experienced. He lay at rest, feeling spent but whole.

Lan, keeping him inside her, leaned forward and cradled his neck. "We have joined once more."

Eighteen

After making love last night, Lan awoke Friday morning entwined with her husband like tendrils of a vine. His body smelled musky, earthy, reminding her of when they first made love at her cousin's farm in Việt Nam. Feeling close, she wondered how they could have ever drifted apart and vowed not to let the distance return.

She kissed Kannon on the cheek. When he didn't stir, Lan rolled off his body and, as she did five mornings a week, slid to the floor. She assumed the lotus position to stretch and to meditate. Savoring new life, Lan focused on a single magenta-hued violet streaming from a porcelain vase. Like the flower, she and Kannon were again an open blossom producing sweet nectar.

Shutting her eyes, Lan found her vision of the Texas Hill Country, its small towns and country sounds no longer desolate but rich with songbirds clinging to swaying branches of cottonwood trees, warbling songs of aliveness and hope. Their music mixed with her life force and spread throughout her body. For the next fifteen minutes, she lost herself in dreams for Derrick's future and in wishes for herself and with her husband.

Lan broke her trance and stared at Kannon, who, if true to past days, already would have risen and begun his five-mile run. Grateful for his presence, she nonetheless sensed a slight disturbance, for even though his face appeared serene, she knew that restlessness and a quest for adventure simmered in his blood. She prayed no provocation would misguide his passion. Let him direct it to her and their son.

* * *

Kannon awoke, last night's loving warmth foremost on his mind. Hearing the soft slap of bare skin on a yoga mat, he rolled to Lan's side of the bed. She was on the floor, exercising.

"Good morning. How would you like to finish your workout up here?"

"It is a pleasure to be greeted this way," Lan said, as she stood. She hopped on the bed and lay beside him. "I did not realize how much I have needed you. There is a glow to our world."

"You speak like a poet."

"Feeling seen and being heard releases my song."

What a song.

* * *

After an hour of snuggling, Kannon became restless. Besides, he needed to use the bathroom. When he returned, "I'd like to see Derrick."

"I called Belynda while you were sleeping. He is on his way."

Kannon arched his eyebrows.

"I wanted to surprise you," Lan said, emitting a slight frown.

He started to say, "Why didn't you . . ." Don't go there. Not now. They were a family again. Instead, "Thank you."

The doorbell rang.

"I will get it." Lan hopped out of bed and slipped on sweats. "You are to spend quality time with Derrick."

Kannon nodded and gave her a broad smile. He crawled out of bed and donned a casual athletic outfit. Just as he was tying his shoelaces, Derrick entered, carrying his football. His son began tossing it into the air, watching it spin until it dropped into his arms. He wore a mischievous smile but didn't say anything, just stared at his dad.

"Okay, sport, I'm ready." Kannon intercepted one of Derrick's tosses. "I'll join you in the front yard."

"Yea, Daddy K." Derrick turned to leave.

Kannon stopped him. "Did you have a good time at Belynda's?"

"Yeah, Dad. She's really cool." Derrick launched out of the bedroom.

Why hadn't Lan insisted on his meeting Belynda? he wondered. It left him unsettled.

* * *

Mid-afternoon found Kannon, Lan, and their son adjourned to the back patio, she in a cedar rocker, while Kannon was toweling off after tossing the football with Derrick. The weather was balmy, branches on the trees motionless. A tinge of ozone hung in the air, suggesting the possibility of light rain.

"You need anything?" Kannon asked Lan.

She shook her head.

"I'm going to catch up on the news." Kannon entered his study, retrieved his laptop, and returned to the patio. While waiting for the computer to power up, he stole a look at two of the most important people in his life. Derrick was sitting on Lan's lap, an impatient look on his face, as she brushed his jet-black hair, tinged with a streak of chestnut.

As if sensing his stare, Lan turned and met his gaze. With one foot propped on the chair, the other resting on the wooden deck, she seemed relaxed, a sign of belonging. This was how it was supposed to be, he thought, yet, the longer he watched her, the more he wondered if you ever really knew another person.

Derrick hopped down and scampered toward the monkey bars, immediately disheveling his hair.

The computer beeped its readiness. Kannon connected to the Internet and clicked on *The Wall Street Journal*. Bypassing the headline articles, he surfed the editorial page. A missive about the continuing risk from third-world terrorists using dirty nuclear, biological, and chemical weapons caught his eye.

"Humph. It seems we'll always have something to worry about," he mumbled, thinking about Streak and the *Posse Comitatus*.

"Kannon! Where have you gone?" Lan's resonant voice clipped through the air. "I do not want to lose you again."

"I'm not lost."

"Share what you are reading." Lan reached into her incense bin and grabbed a stick of sage.

"Just reviewing SyncTrak's most recent financials." A lie seemed appropriate here.

"Can you not find something more pleasant?" She lit the incense, then stuffed the fragrant wand inside a pewter Buddha, one of several burners she kept nearby. As the pungent aroma poured from Buddha's mouth, nose, and ears, she waved the smoke to her nostrils and breathed deep. "Read the Austin American-Statesman and see if you can find something pleasant we can do with family and friends."

"Good idea. Give me a minute." Kannon tapped on the keyboard. "How about taking in a magic show?"

"Oh. I would enjoy going."

"A magician will be performing Saturday night at the Artist Palace. It's near Round Rock. The Pigeonaire he calls himself. He's also a hypnotist."

"Wonderful," she said, beaming. "I know where that place is. Belynda pointed it out to me. Is it all right to invite her? She lives nearby."

Kannon raised his eyebrows.

"You do not mind, do you?"

"No, that's fine." Relief was a better word, relief that Lan was willing to share her new friend instead of walling her off as his first wife had done upon acquiring a new girlfriend. Kannon just hoped Belynda wasn't a radical feminist.

"Invite Stefan. You have wanted to see him."

"I'll give it a shot. How about Roger and Karen?"

Lan nodded.

"I'll see about tickets. Then we'll call everyone." Kannon tapped on the keyboard. After finding out tickets were available, he placed calls to his brother and sister-in-law, who were a go, and then to his grown son, Stefan.

"Late notice, Dad."

"I know. But we'd love to see you."

"Let me check my schedule," Stefan said. "I'll call you back."

"Good enough."

"By the way, how's the budding scholar and athlete?"

"Derrick's doing great."

"Belynda gives a thumbs-up," Lan said, after placing her call.

After Kannon purchased the tickets, including one for Stefan, just in case, he clicked off and switched to SyncTrak's website. He entered the password to access the company's secure data system. He downloaded and scrutinized the unit- and dollar-volume sales reports, which included explanatory footnotes. The tracking units—designed to monitor felons and sexual predators—were selling and performing well. But there was no update on the progress of the company's implantable tracking device. One focus group deemed the prototype far too invasive.

* * *

That evening, Kannon entered the kitchen amid a sensory

array of scents wafting from noodle soup, sticky rice that always settled his stomach, and smells of roasting pork. A medley of grilled vegetables popping and sizzling on the stove completed this traditional Vietnamese dinner. His mouth watered.

They were just sitting down to eat when the landline rang.

"Maybe it's Stefan," Kannon said, tossing his napkin on the table. But Lan beat him to the phone.

"Yes?" She listened a moment, then compressed her lips as if not liking what she heard. "The call is for you," she said, cradling the cordless to her chest. "A woman."

Kannon shrugged and took the phone. "Who is this?"

"Sindy Zeller. I'm with the CIA." Hers was a raspy voice.

"What do you want?" He ground his teeth, not liking this.

"Your cooperation."

"On what?"

"Your friend, Streak, and his . . . your . . . militia connection."

The blood drained from Kannon's face. "He's not a friend. And I have no militia connection."

"I beg to differ. Cooperate, else I'll have your wife deported."

"No way. Her naturalized citizenship application is on the up and up."

Did Zeller know Lan had bought her way into this country?

"I'll put your ass in jail."

"Don't threaten me. I've done nothing wrong." *Wait a minute. This doesn't make sense. The CIA wouldn't call, they would appear.*

"What is going on?" Eyes wide, Lan wrung her hands.

Kannon held up a finger. "I don't know who you are," he said to Zeller, "but this is bullshit. Don't harass my family." He slammed the phone down on the counter, startling Derrick. His eyes clouded up.

"Sorry, son. It was one of those pushy marketing calls. Why don't you take your supper into the den and watch television?"

"All right, Daddy K."

Lan waited until their son left the room. "I say again, to use your vernacular, what is going on?" Her ruby-red lips remained parted. She wore such an imploring look of angst he wanted to meld with her and float away on a cloud, ignoring the potential implications from that phone call.

"It's nothing," he said, taking her hands. "I'll handle it."

"Kannon!"

Rats skittered inside his stomach. He swallowed to stem the rising bile. He'd served his country honorably, lifted himself above false accusations made by his old commander in Việt Nam, and fought the depression that haunted him for years. So why couldn't folks let things be? He took a deep breath and collected himself. "The woman said she was with the CIA."

Lan's face turned white. "The Central Intelligence Agency?"

"Yes."

"Was it about my citizenship application? Does the government want to deport—"

"You won't be investigated or deported."

"I have been in this country, my new country, six years now," she said. "I married *you*. I should already be a naturalized citizen. Why would the CIA question my status now?"

"That's just it. The CIA wouldn't. ICE would."

Lan sucked in a deep breath and exhaled.

"The whole immigration thing's a fishing expedition," Kannon said, sounding words of comfort, if only to himself, but knowing his tone lacked conviction.

Lan drilled Kannon with her deep-set, piercing dark eyes. "There must be more to this. Did she mention a militia?"

He stared at their dinners turning cold. "Yeah."

"Goddamnit." Lan folded into a chair.

Christ. She had never used that word, at least in his presence. One thing for sure, their marital interlude of reconciliation and tranquility was disrupted.

He gripped Lan's shoulders. "It'll be okay."

Wearing a mournful look, she nodded toward the den. "Derrick's crying."

"I'll check on him."

Inside the den, tears streamed from his son's eyes.

"Is Mama Lan in trouble?"

"No, Derrick. She's A-Okay." He knelt and hugged his boy.

Deep inside, the rustling of combat-induced adrenaline stirred.

Nineteen

Saturday at 0300 hours, Whitehead maneuvered his black four-wheel-drive pickup behind a grove of cedar trees and cut the engine, just one mile beyond Kannon Ballard's drive. Stepping outside the vehicle, he breathed in a lungful of refreshing Texas Hill Country air. He and Bull had driven straight through from Border Slot, Montana, stopping only for gas and snacks. As far as Whitehead was concerned, the newbie could walk back to the compound. Neither had slept. Both were cranky, and Bull's rancid farts made the journey all but insufferable.

"Think we'll find Streak here?" Bull asked for the umpteenth time.

"We'd better," Whitehead said, reflecting on Streak's address book. "Crandle won't rest until we find him." His Commander insisted on bringing Streak back alive to face the deadly training range. An order was an order. Otherwise, when Whitehead found Streak, he'd kill the bastard.

Whitehead was convinced by now that Streak posed a considerable threat. More troubling was the possible reference in Streak's address book to the CIA. Was he involved with the Feds? If so, why hadn't the Feds already come down on Border Slot?

Mad at himself for trusting Streak, Whitehead grabbed his pack. "Let's kit up."

Each pack included third-generation Armasight N-15 night vision devices, handheld radios, water, satellite phones, and an all-purpose pocket tool. Whitehead slipped a distance counter to his belt and holstered a silenced Army Colt .45.

"I need a handgun," Bull said.

"Perform well, and I'll issue one when we get back." Despite Crandle's fawning over Bull, Whitehead held misgivings. Bull might prove to be trigger happy.

"Okay." Bull shrugged. "I got my special weapon."

Whitehead sighed. "What?"

Reaching behind his back, Bull withdrew a weird-looking contraption from a large paddle-type holster. "Made this myself.

Holster and blade."

"What the hell is it?"

"I took some glass discs and used a carbide bit to drill a hole through the one-inch-thick glass core, then slipped the disc on this two-part tension rod that acts as an axle—"

"Two-part axle?"

Whitehead studied the odd-shaped device. The disc was sandwiched in the center of the axle between two hubs. He thumbed the disc. It spun freely.

"It's nothing but a pizza cutter on steroids," he said.

"Until I cock my arm and thrust it forward. At the point of release, I press this pin and the two middle ends of the axle retract. The disc releases and becomes a spinning missile."

"The weapon's a hybrid between a slingshot and a tomahawk." Whitehead turned it over and further examined it. "It's a Sling-Hawk."

"Like the name," Bull said, grinning like an apprentice making a point to his master.

Bull gripped the device as he might a tomahawk hilt and demonstrated a throw in slow motion.

"It's all about coordination and timing," Whitehead said.

"Yeah."

"You've tested this?"

"It works."

Whitehead couldn't imagine it being accurate. The release and timing would have to be spot on. Then Bull did just that, stuck a disc in the middle of a tree trunk twenty feet away.

"Damn impressive," Whitehead said. "Wouldn't want to be on the receiving end."

Bull nodded and holstered his hybrid weapon.

"Move out," Whitehead said, wondering how Bull had time to develop the crazy thing. Sure, they had a machine shop but . . .

The air was fresh and crisp, the sky purplish black. A waxing crescent moon was in its daylight phase and down for the night, an easy read for Whitehead due to his Nez Percé adoptive parents' teachings.

They crossed the highway. Whitehead paused to adjust his

night-vision goggles as Bull cut the strands on the barbed-wire fence that surrounded the property.

They weaved through the slit fence.

"I want to get a feel for the topography," Whitehead said.

For the next thirty minutes, they reconnoitered the fenced-in property. It consisted of rolling hills dotted with oak and cedar trees. Ancient cypress trunks bordered a dry streambed. A nice place to live, Whitehead thought.

They completed circling the perimeter. Based on his years studying terrain, along with calculations from the distance counter, Whitehead estimated the plot to be nearly fifteen acres, less than half the size of their compound. Still, you could garrison a battalion here. Without neighbors nearby, the expanse made it easier to maintain concealment.

"Now what?" Bull asked.

"Follow me."

Paralleling the driveway, he led Bull to the edge of a tree line. Whitehead pointed toward a rise to the south. They retreated into the woods and hiked until reaching the apex, which afforded an unobstructed frontal view of Ballard's ranch-style house.

They were roughly fifty yards distant. Except for an armadillo rooting behind them, nothing stirred. Whitehead peered through his night vision device, which rendered a greenish, funereal perspective of the home.

"How long we gonna stay here?" Bull demanded.

"As long as necessary," Whitehead said, gnashing his teeth. But yes, surveillance could be boring as hell.

"What if Ballard and Streak have already hooked up and gone to the Feds?"

"It's possible."

Whitehead shed his pack. Bull followed suit. They crept forward twenty-five yards and found concealment behind tended Ligustrum bushes. Whitehead parted the low branches and glassed the house through his NVD. Just as he fixated on unlit floodlights mounted beneath the eaves, a gust of wind rustled tree branches. The lamps flared on. Momentarily blinded, Whitehead removed the night goggles and rubbed his eyes.

"Infrared motion sensors," Bull said.

"Uh-huh."

The wind subsided.

Some night bird, apparently seeing its reflection, flew into the window, making a racket. Thirty seconds later, the floodlights faded out. The porch light flicked on. Soon, a woman emerged from the porch. Barefooted, she crossed the lawn.

"Whoa, Mama!" Bull whispered, observing through his night device. "Is she Ballard's bitch?"

"Shh." Whitehead repositioned his NVD.

Wearing only a bra and panties, she carried a stepladder. Whitehead watched her parade toward the largest window. *Oh, man. What a body!*

The woman positioned the stepladder, then climbed it and reached for the flood lamp. Panties growing taut against her butt cheeks, she removed the bulb and stepped down. After closing the ladder, she carried it back inside the house.

The activated floodlights also must've triggered an interior alert, Whitehead surmised, which raised a big question. Would she parade around like that if Streak were around?

He tapped Bull on the shoulder and gestured toward the stashed packs.

Once they reached it, "My dick got hard," Bull said. "Let's break in—"

"Goddamnit! Concentrate on the mission." At least Bull's reaction answered one question. The way he paraded naked around the barracks Whitehead thought he might be gay. Hell, on second thought, this weird dude might be bisexual—something to keep in mind when reporting to Crandle.

"What's the woman's appearance tell you, Bull?"

"She wants my dick."

Whitehead ignored the comment. "If Streak's here, I don't think Ballard would want his woman prancing around half-naked."

"Maybe they're having an orgy."

"Get your mind out of the gutter," Whitehead said, jabbing a finger into Bull's chest.

"Hey, man, don't you never touch me like that."

132

Whitehead narrowed his eyes.

"Just follow orders." He worried about the man's discipline and decision making. He was right not to have issued Bull a handgun.

"What the fuck we doing here, anyway?" Bull asked. "There's no damn Streak. No V-Rod. No nothing, except the hot chick."

"We wait." Whitehead pushed the sleeve back on his field jacket. His watch showed 0358 hours. "If Streak doesn't show by dawn, we'll clear out."

"It's a waste of time," Bull said.

"I'm not interested in your opinion."

I'll be pissed if this turns out to be a wild goose chase.

Whitehead's satphone vibrated. Crandle! He was tempted to let the call ride. Instead . . . "What's up, Commander?"

"How's it going?"

"We're in position, monitoring the house."

"Any sign of Streak?"

"Not yet."

"Keep after it." Crandle pause on his end of the call. "FYI, tonight I'm holding another briefing. Want to get the guys better schooled on EMP."

"Understood. Anything else?"

"Negative."

Just like that, Whitehead was fully drawn back in. Crandle's tone was easy, almost conciliatory. He determined to double down on capturing Streak and executing the EMP mission.

Nothing rustled now. No snakes or owls or armadillos or deer. Nothing showed—just a patch of light.

A patch of light?

Whitehead did a double take. There it was again, to his right, in the woods east of the house. "Maybe the night's not dead yet." He directed Bull toward the sighting.

Bull pumped his fist. "You think—?"

"Unless a deer is carrying a penlight, we might have an infiltrator."

"The hunt is on," Bull said.

"We'll circle to our right and get behind the dude," Whitehead said, wondering if there was more than one person.

"Seems like he or she would've heard us," Bull said.

"We were quiet. And whoever's out there might've just arrived." Whitehead paused. "Listen, if it is Streak, snatch, not kill. Anyone else, well, he's yours."

Bull removed his weapon and twirled the disc. "Why would anyone be hiding in Ballard's woods?"

"We'll find out," Whitehead said, wishing he'd already racked the slide of his Army Colt and chambered a round. To do so now would be a mistake. The sound would carry in the night.

Leading the way deeper into the brush, away from the house, he tracked the curvature of the long, winding drive. The terrain was gently rolling here and easy to navigate, nothing at all like working the steep valleys and ridges in the Bitterroots.

Starlight filtered through the trees and boosted the effectiveness of his night vision device. Whitehead led Bull across Ballard's drive and into the east woods, then headed south toward the house.

"Look there," Whitehead said. "A footpath."

"Tire tracks. Wider than a bicycle's," Bull said.

Whitehead pressed a finger to his lips and proceeded along the dirt path. Thirty yards further, they came across a partially hidden motorcycle, its nose pointed toward the entry drive.

"Streak's?" Bull whispered.

Whitehead nodded. "He's been here a while. Must've been asleep." He pulled out his two-way radio and motioned for Bull to do the same. "Tune to channel thirteen, then flatten yourself in that narrow depression. Any questions?"

"What if he shows up here?"

"Stay hidden. Press the Push-to-Talk switch once. It'll transmit a static alert."

Bull nodded.

Radio in hand, Whitehead handed his pack to Bull and took off. Avoiding fallen leaves and branches, he threaded his way through the brush, hoping he'd find it was Streak holding that penlight.

Like stalking bear on a bow hunt, except with heightened adrenaline. Nothing compares to the thrill of man hunting man.

Twenty

Just beyond the eastern tree line bordering Kannon's landscaping, Streak aimed a penlight at the ground. Where were his glasses? Placing the penlight in his mouth, he knelt and groped among the fallen leaves. He found the specs, wiped them clean with his handkerchief, and slipped the wire-framed glasses back on.

His breathing was rapid. He had difficulty swallowing.

Having lingered in place since seven the previous evening, Streak debated how best to approach Ballard. He had called once from his satphone but hung up when Kannon's wife answered. Exhausted, he'd fallen asleep on his poncho liner and woke up at 0400, just minutes ago.

Streak thought about his most recent screwups. The botched "financial deal" with Zeller accelerated his tailspin. She was either a fraud or jacking him around big time. Whichever, he couldn't trust her. She'd screwed him three times. First, sexual. Second, a worthless cashier's check. Third, the piddling cash advance.

Settle down, he told himself. All he needed was Ballard's money. Since his time on the innertube, he'd decided to play nice and apologize. At dawn, he'd ride to Kannon's front door, knock, and make his pitch.

If unsuccessful, he'd fall back on the triple cross idea. Blackmail Kannon Ballard over the firefight in New Mexico and Lan's illegal entry into America. If Ballard didn't pay up, rat him out to the Feds as an active militia member. Also, to buy time, screw Sindy Zeller by feeding her false information about Border Slot. Once he'd fled the country and felt safe, expose the militia for what it was. If all failed, stage a bungee jump with no cord.

Dawn couldn't come soon enough. Streak started toward his V-Rod, which he'd parked on a dirt trail about seventy yards away.

Tree branches rasped in the wind, sending a shiver as if he shouldn't be here. It wasn't the cooler air or the black night or Kannon's land but something else, like unseen eyes probing through thickets of oak, hickory, and cedar.

Having been a chopper pilot in 'Nam, Streak had never

participated on nighttime ground maneuvers. But he'd overheard surviving grunts talk, sensing a foreign presence, eyes like lasers drilling into their chests, as Việt Cộng armed with AK47s and rocket-propelled grenades watched U.S. combat troops enter the killing zone.

Quickening his pace, Streak no longer viewed the twigs and leaves as obstacles to be avoided. Instead, they were aggravating nuisances. Anxious to get the hell out of there, he stomped on the undergrowth as if by sounding out the ghosts would disappear.

A deer startled him as it thrashed through the brush. Maybe that was all he sensed, a deer lurking nearby. Streak wished he had a night vision device.

The wind strengthened and whipped his jacket, sending another shiver throughout his body. The breeze carried a congealed scent of animals, birds, and humus.

He zipped up but failed to erase the chill.

Plodding forward, Streak worked his way across terrain contoured like terraced fields. The ground fell sharply away to his front. He snagged his foot on a low-lying vine that sent him sprawling.

"Damnit!"

He landed on his side, the side that held his holstered 9mm Luger, and bruised his hip. The fall also took his wind. When he stood, his hip stiffened like a tightly wound spring.

After catching his breath, Streak withdrew his father's vintage Luger, brushed it free of debris, and slipped it back inside the holster, then resumed the trek.

Cresting the next rise, he paused abruptly, thinking he'd heard the rustling of leaves. Nothing. He took a couple more steps. High above, oak branches exploded.

Hoo! Hoo! Hoooooo!

"Jesus!" Streak almost shit his pants.

Fucking owls.

His chest constricted. Labored breathing reminded him of horrid dreams whereby his legs turned to lead and he was unable to escape his demons. Fortunately, the tree limbs settled, and Streak managed a chuckle. There was no way Crandle or Whitehead could've tracked him here. The only critters in the Texas Hill Country were wildlife.

For comfort, Streak rehashed the steps he'd taken to conceal his escape—the half-eaten sandwich and open beer left in his cabin, the written note about his mom, the few possessions intentionally left behind.

Oh, my God! My address book. Out of habit, he'd left it tucked away in a cutout of *Street without Joy.* Kannon's name, Zeller's, and a reference to the CIA were the only entries not crossed out. Had the militia found the book, figured out the connection?

Goosebumps peppered his arms and neck. How could he have been so stupid!

Please come the dawn!

A few steps farther, Streak heard a sharp crack, as if someone had stepped on a branch—someone other than him.

"How's it going, Streak?"

Whitehead emerged from behind a tree. Streak swore as he fumbled for his Luger.

"Don't even think about it." Whitehead clamped a vice-like grip around Streak's wrist. Also, his Colt .45 was aimed squarely at his forehead. Maintaining eye contact, Crandle's guerrilla plucked Streak's Luger from its holster. He breached the slide to see if a round was chambered, then released the magazine and tossed both into the woods.

"You're done," Whitehead said.

The wind howled. Demonic figures swirled close in his living hell.

"Just shoot me," Streak said.

"Too easy," Whitehead said. "Crandle wants to see you. But it's not to fly the Jolly Green Giant."

In the pale of night, Whitehead loomed larger than ever, his facial features locked in control mode, his handlebar mustache swooping above his lip, its ends mirroring miniature twin scythes.

"I was coming back. Honest. Told you guys I needed to take care of my mom."

"At Ballard's home?" Whitehead swiveled his head in a mocking scan. "I don't see your mother." Whitehead uncorked a short right that knocked Streak on his ass. "You're full of shit. Let's try that again."

Holding his aching jaw, Streak scrambled to his feet. "Ballard's a threat to Border Slot. I was going to—"

"Not buying it, Streak. I think you're working with the Feds."

"Then why would I be in the woods? Clearing a minefield?"

"No. I think you want Ballard's help but don't have the guts to ask him." Whitehead waved Streak's address book in front of him. "You've got a reference to the CIA here. Is he a Fed?"

"I don't know what you're talking about."

Whitehead gut-punched him. Struggling to breathe, Streak doubled over and knelt to the ground for support.

"For God's sake, Whitehead," Streak said in gasps. "I haven't told the Feds zilch."

Whitehead grabbed Streak's collar and yanked him erect. Breaking into a wicked grin, Whitehead brought up his two-way radio and pressed the push-to-talk switch.

The action unnerved Streak further. Whitehead wasn't alone.

"Got him, Bull. Heading back."

Shit! I remember him from training.

"Move it." Whitehead motioned with his .45.

"Fuck you."

Streak's head snapped back in blinding pain as Whitehead raked the front sight of his weapon across his forehead. Then followed a blow across the bridge of his nose, which sent arc lights bursting through his skull. Unthinking, he brought his hand up to his nose for protection, causing more pain. Blood gushed from his nostrils.

Eyes watering, Streak reached for his handkerchief. Whitehead just kept that shit-eating grin on his face and motioned him forward.

"Why are you doing this?" The words came out muddied, bloodied. Streak considered running. Shooting in darkness wasn't easy. Except that Whitehead had the unique gift of night eyes as well as the aid of an infrared tracking dot from his .45.

He tried to make sense of his scrambled thoughts. *If only I can regain some control.*

"I'm coming into some money," he said. "It's all yours. I won't say anything. Just leave me alone."

"Shut up!" Whitehead planted a boot on Streak's ass.

All Streak could think of was variations of "wished he'd done this or that." Wished he'd funneled correct information about the militia group to Sindy Zeller, rogue agent or not. Wished he'd approached Kannon gently and begged for money. Now it was too late.

They reached his V-Rod.

"Here's Bull," Whitehead said.

The goon looks like a buffed Charles Manson.

"Ah, the coward," Bull said.

"I'm not a—"

Bull kicked him in the nuts. Streak collapsed to the ground. Bull stomped on his head and drove his bloodied face into the dirt.

"That's enough," Whitehead said.

"Get up," Bull said.

Streak rose to his knees and heaved the rising bile from his esophagus. Still shaking, he stood, but buckling knees toppled him again. "Water . . ."

"Forget it, Scum," Whitehead said.

In the pale light, the men's eyes poured on him like black fire. The corners of their lips curled sadistically.

Bull held a weird-looking tool or weapon . . . a spinning disc mounted between the forks of a spindle.

"It's my Sling-Hawk," Bull said.

"What's that remind you of!" Whitehead added. "You're going to be sliced to pieces."

Streak pissed his pants. The training field. He'd flown Border Slot candidates into remote mountain locations and witnessed Crandle's murderous onslaughts from those modified skeet launchers and flying discs. He'd rather get shot in the back.

"Sick bastards," Streak stammered. His arms grew as heavy as if he were portaging a canoe.

Whitehead shrugged and stuffed a plug of tobacco into his mouth, offered one to Bull.

"Obliged," Bull said.

"I'm going for the pickup," Whitehead said, "so we can load the motorcycle. It's too loud to start here. Might wake the Ballards. Guard our friend." He figured that was a chore Bull could handle.

Bull nodded.

"What about the Ballard douche and his wife?"

"I'll call Crandle," Whitehead said over his shoulder. "See what he wants us to do."

Streak watched Whitehead trail away.

"It's you and me," Bull said, tapping Streak's forehead with his stupid contraption.

Each tap raised a bloody welt. Each tap heightened Streak's fear.

"Why don't you just take my cycle and ride off?" Streak asked.

"I've got other plans," Bull said, standing nose to nose.

His sharp, uneven teeth looked like jagged glass embedded atop a rock wall. His breath smelled like sewage.

"Straddle the motorcycle, faggot. Grab those handlebars. Place your feet on the rear footpegs." Bull removed his pistol belt and laid it on the motorcycle seat.

Streak fought his nausea and stumbled toward the V-Rod. Swinging his leg over the saddle, he heard the ratcheting of Bull's zipper as the militiaman dropped his pants.

Twenty-One

Standing alongside the V-Rod, Bull mashed Streak's chest against the gas tank. The pain from his raked forehead, broken nose, and aching jaw morphed into a sea of fear.

Bull cut Streak's belt in half, then peeled away the rear of his jeans and underwear as if he were filleting a salmon. Keeping pressure on Streak's waist, Bull moved to the tail end of the bike and spat on Streak's ass.

"No!" Streak screamed, unable to counter Bull's strength.

His forehead crammed against the bike's cold instrument cluster, Streak compelled himself to think.

Key
Ignition
Motorcycle
Horse
Buck

The ignition slot was located on the right side of the V-Rod below the seat, just behind the rear cylinder. And he'd left the key in the slot.

Twisting his arm until it seemed like it might snap in two, Streak groped for the ignition slot and found it. He turned the key.

"I'm gonna mount you, motherfucker," Bull said, grunting like a hog.

The rear of the V-Rod compressed as Bull climbed on back. Streak squeezed the clutch and with his right forefinger hit the starter button mounted on the handlebar. The headlight flicked on as sixty-nine inches of displacement exploded in a loud, throaty rumble.

"Yo! What the fuck—"

Streak twisted the throttle and released the clutch, cutting short Bull's curse. Rear wheel spinning, the motorcycle found traction and shot forward like a bull out of a chute.

"Shut it down!" Bull said.

Streak goosed the throttle to max. When the front wheel lifted, Bull lost his grip. He somersaulted off the V-Rod and hit the turf.

The motorcycle settled on both wheels. Still in first gear,

Streak reached the drive and attempted a too-quick counter-steer right. He lost control of the V-Rod and bit it. Panicked, he stood and stared at Bull, who was cursing and scrambling to his feet some twenty feet away.

An accelerating engine caught Streak's attention. He turned. The silhouetted form of a large pickup truck—one he recognized—barreled down the drive. "Oh, no! Not now!" Streak mouthed, thinking he was about to make good his escape attempt.

Streak jerked his head toward Bull, who'd fastened his jeans. The wannabe rapist reached inside his jacket and withdrew his weird weapon. As he cocked his arm and let loose, Streak dove behind the downed motorcycle. The disc struck and buried itself halfway into the squat sport windshield. Another disc ricocheted off the fork, just below the headlight.

Streak grabbed his slingshot from his back pocket. He snatched a marble-sized pebble off the ground.

Bull threw down his weapon and charged.

Using his V-Rod as a shield, Streak rose to his knees. He retracted the strong elastic band, took sight, and released. The missile rocketed forward and struck Bull on his forehead.

"Son of a bitch!" Bull shouted as he went down.

A cloud of dust rose as the pickup braked and skidded, ramming into a tree. The V-Rod lay on its left side, with the engine still thumping. Streak rushed to it and squatted with his back to the bike. The heat from the rear cylinder burned his bare butt. Palms facing backward, he grabbed the engine frame and, by extending his legs while bracing the ground, raised the motorcycle.

The pickup's door flung open.

Streak turned, swung his leg over the saddle, and rolled on the throttle.

"Don't do it!" Whitehead yelled.

Streak careened down the drive toward Kannon's house. A three-shot burst rang out, but the rounds whistled past.

Continuing in first gear, Streak raced the tachometer needle beyond redline, maintaining speed until Kannon's house came into view. He slalomed into a right turn and accelerated along the front sidewalk. Braking late, Streak slammed against the front door, which shook upon impact.

* * *

Whitehead couldn't tell if he'd scored a hit. Running, he fired two more shots as Streak raced around a bend toward Ballard's house. The sound of the V-Rod's engine trailing away suggested the bike was moving forward.

To be sure, Whitehead sprinted up the driveway until Ballard's house came into view. *Damn drive must be a half-mile long.*

He stopped and gaped in disbelief as the motorcycle plowed into the front door. "Wham!"

Streak lay beside the bike within the porch. Was he incapacitated?

Near success was turning into a disaster. Whitehead had a choice—pursue or exfiltrate—but time was short. First, he needed to account for Bull. Had Streak overpowered him? Not possible, he thought.

Whitehead raced back to where the footpath intersected the driveway. There was Bull, scrambling to his feet. Whitehead grabbed him by the collar and yanked him erect. "What the hell happened?"

"He got away," Bull said, rubbing his forehead.

"I see that! How?"

"Said he had to take a crap."

"You let him get out of sight?"

Bull shrugged. "Watching someone take a crap is not in my job description."

"You stupid fuck. You've failed the mission." Whitehead scrutinized Bull from head to toe. "Where's your pistol belt?"

"Yonder."

Whitehead followed Bull's outstretched arm and saw the pistol belt lying on the ground.

"Explain that."

Bull shifted his stance. When he did, it became apparent his zipper was undone.

"You were raping him?"

"No, man. Taking a piss."

Still gripping Bull's collar, Whitehead scowled.

Four inches shorter than Whitehead's six feet, Bull

143

nevertheless presented an intimidating presence. He wrestled free of Whitehead's grip and twisted his mouth into a snarl. His bulging forearms stretched the fabric of his camouflage fatigues.

"Get off my back," Bull said. "This mission sucked from the start. And like I said before, don't hit or grab me."

"Enough!" Whitehead kneed Bull in the balls. The FNG didn't anticipate the hit and doubled over. A swift uppercut sent Bull sprawling.

"Do I have your attention now?"

Gasping for breath, Bull couldn't answer. He tried to stand and failed there, too. Remembering the kick that demolished Streak's cabin door, Whitehead assumed a ready stance.

Bull rose to one knee. Whitehead twisted his body, tensed his right arm, unleashed, and whipped the point of his elbow to strike Bull on the left side of his forehead. He went down again. Whitehead waited. Once more, Bull rose to one knee. Whitehead grabbed him beneath the armpits and hoisted him upright against a tree. He rammed a short left into Bull's midsection, which doubled him over. Next, he struck another uppercut into the FNG's jaw. His head snapped back against the tree trunk. Blood trickled down his face.

"You've . . ." Bull's breaths were coming in hard. "You've made your point."

"We're clear?"

Bull fumbled for a handkerchief and put it to his nose. "Yeah. I messed up."

"This isn't over," Whitehead grunted. "Get in the truck. We're going to make a house call."

A wailing siren pierced the quiet. It appeared to be coming from Ballard's house. Of course, he'd have a security system. No doubt the county sheriff had been alerted and was on his way.

Frowning, Whitehead said, "Time to abort and regroup. Can't chance discovery, we've got to get the hell out of here."

The pickup started right up. Whitehead rammed the gearshift into reverse and backed out. Tires screeching, he sped down the drive and hooked a right on the highway toward Llano.

Bull grabbed his canteen and took a couple of swigs. "You're a tough motherfucker."

144

Whitehead didn't respond. Instead, wanting visual contact with Bull in this ongoing confrontation, he flicked on the overhead light. He noticed two contusions on Bull's forehead. He had only struck him there once. "How'd you get that second bruise?"

"Must've landed on a rock when I fell," Bull said, averting his eyes.

The response didn't ring true, but he'd pull it out of him. "You've jeopardized your role in Border Slot Militia. In the army, you'd be court-martialed."

"Give me another chance. I'll make good."

"We'll see." Whitehead couldn't believe how screwed up this mission had become. Crandle was going to be furious, especially after Whitehead told him via the sat call that they had Streak.

Whitehead's resentment at Crandle's orders escalated: "Take Bull," which he'd not wanted to do in the first place.

Regardless, the Commander would hold Whitehead responsible, and he held no intention of failing again.

Twenty-Two

Kannon, standing at cliff's edge, peered at the Class Five rapids roaring through the narrow canyon. The sound was intoxicating, like that from a C-130 turboprop. He spread his arms, inhaled, exhaled, and jumped. Soaring below the canyon rim, he arched his back and glided toward the churning river. As he neared the waterway, the river transformed into asphalt, and he found himself riding a motorcycle, leaning hard—

Incoming!

He woke with a start. An escalating rumble emanated from an approaching motorcycle—high revs, far beyond the redline. A loud thud shook the front door.

"What the hell?" The tremor caused him angst . . . the startled response thing.

He tossed aside the book he'd been reading before falling asleep and reached for his .40-caliber Sig Sauer attached to the back of the headboard. He removed the keyed safety lock from the trigger housing, retracted the slide, and chambered a round.

Lan, who lay beside him, squirmed. "What is happening?" She stretched for the bedside lamp and turned it on.

"You heard it too?" Kannon asked.

"Yes."

Lan usually adjusted slowly to the waking world. Not this time. She bounded from bed, clad only in panties.

"I hope another owl has not flown into the bay window," she said. "One did earlier this evening."

"It did?"

"I went outside and unscrewed the bulb so the window would not reflect a glare and fool another owl into thinking its reflection was a mate."

"Dressed like that?"

"No. I also wore a bra."

"That's not safe, Lan. I wish you would've told me."

"I did not want to wake you."

He let her comment go.

"Anyway, that thump was too loud for an owl. It interrupted my dream."

Kannon headed for the security console mounted on the wall rib separating the master bath from Lan's walk-in closet. The LCD displayed 0437. The monitor showed no interior intrusion, but he tripped the alarm, activating the external siren to alert the security-monitoring service. All the while, an engine kept thumping, sounding almost as if it were inside the house.

"I'm going outside," Kannon said. "Grab your .38 and go to Derrick's room."

"All right."

He waited until she retrieved her loaded revolver from behind the headboard and removed its safety lock. With Lan behind him, he led the way, pausing while she opened Derrick's door and slipped inside.

"Be careful," she said.

Kannon hustled through the den, past framed photographs and large woven tapestries from Việt Nam. Reaching the foyer, he made a mental note to add a motion sensor to the front door. Standing to one side, Kannon leaned forward and opened the palm-sized observation panel. He peered through the convex glass. "What the hell!"

A motorcycle, engine rumbling, was propped against one wall of the limestone-structured front portico. A crumpled rider lay beside the bike, his hands plastered to his ears, apparently to lessen the impact from the blaring house alarm.

Semiautomatic in hand, Kannon released the chain, unlocked the door, and squeezed his way around the damaged cycle. It was a V-Rod, the one Streak had ridden to Lost Maples, the one that had been parked outside the Black Forest Restaurant in Fredericksburg. Only now, the motorcycle's left side was bashed in, and a strange-looking round disc lay embedded in the sport windshield.

Streak's eyes held the startled expression of a wounded soldier. "Help me."

Keeping his pistol at the ready, Kannon hit the V-Rod's kill switch. "What the hell's going on?"

"I've screwed up. Big time." Streak rose to one knee.

147

"You've got nerve, showing up after threatening my wife and kid. I don't care what kind of trouble you're in."

"I'm desperate. I don't know what to do," Streak said.

"Doesn't matter. Turn around your beat-up piece of shit and ride out of here."

Streak rose and clutched Kannon's arm. "Listen, man—"

"Out," Kannon said, feeling jittery. "Lan," he hollered, "shut off the alarm."

A moment later, the earsplitting noise stopped.

"Kannon?"

He turned to see a robed-clad Lan standing in the foyer. Shoulders hunched, she tightened her belt. "Is everything all right?"

"It will be," Kannon said, "as soon as this asshole leaves."

"Authorities are coming," Lan said.

Kannon pivoted toward Streak. "You heard her. Sheriff's department is on its way."

Streak pleaded with his eyes.

Kannon shook his head.

Streak opened his mouth, tried to speak, but no words came out.

Should Kannon hold Streak for the authorities or just get him the hell gone? Damn, there'd been too much trouble. Yet, Streak was a fellow vet. The leave-no-man-behind mantra swam through his mind, stoking a fiery return to the war, stoking bad memories. And he didn't want to go there. Enough was enough.

"We're done, Streak."

The expression of disbelief on Streak's face was as if he'd received a death sentence.

Streak turned and showed his backside when attempting to manhandle the motorcycle. Kannon blanched. Ripped denim flapped in the wind. Streak's bare ass was exposed, blistered, as if from a burn. Blood oozed from who knew where. He grasped Streak's shoulder and spun him around. It was then Kannon noticed the bruised face and grisly welts.

"Good God, man. Who did this to you?"

"The sons-of-bitches who assaulted me. They . . . they may still be out there."

Holding his Sig, Kannon stepped beyond the portico into the still night and stared down his drive. Crisp autumn air permeated the early morning darkness. The quiet seemed unnatural.

He panned a one-hundred-eighty-degree scan but detected no movement in the crystal-clear night. Should he wait for the sheriff's department or make his own recon? Stay put, Kannon decided.

The distant wail of a siren reached his ears. It was hard to tell how far away it was because sound traveled far in a still night. "You hear it, right?" Kannon said, nodding toward the driveway. "You can tell them your story."

"God, no. Please, Kannon." He winced. "Don't tell them about me. I told you. I've got a record."

It was apparent Streak was in a lot of pain, physically and mentally. Kannon pursed his lips. Despite Lan's wishes, he'd become involved. And Streak's predicament tugged at his heart. He remembered giving aid to a wounded Việt Cộng trapped in concertina wire. Hell, when a man was down, he was down. Why kick him again? Besides, Streak was in no position to ride.

"All right," Kannon said. "Let's get your bike out of sight."

Streak sighed a measure of relief. Kannon wheeled the motorcycle to the attached garage entrance, punched in the code to raise the overhead door, and sequestered the V-Rod inside.

"Just beyond the Cherokee," Kannon said, pointing, "there's a utility bath. Some first aid supplies. Take a good, long hot shower. I'll bring you some fresh clothes. They'll be large but better than what you've got." Kannon paused at the door leading into the house. "Come in when you're finished."

Streak headed for the shower, then stopped and turned, torment etched on his face. "What are you going to tell the authorities?"

I don't have a clue. Worse, what am I going to tell Lan?

Twenty-Three

What was he going to tell either one of them? *We have a problem with trespassers. Post a guard. Lan, your husband's gone crazy and should be institutionalized.* Why did he have such a hard time saying no!

Shaking his head, Kannon exited through the garage side door and walked around front. He knelt and examined the damage done by Streak's motorcycle. It had struck the hinged side of the door, which bowed the hinges. The door frame and lock assembly were stressed too. He figured he could fix the door and frame with a hammer and screwdriver, nails and extra-large screws, and a chisel—until everything could be replaced.

He backed away and strode to the front yard, where again he stared down the drive. Were Streak's assailants still out there? The siren sounded closer, louder. Whoever it was, the siren and house alarm may have scared them off. Regardless, there was no way he was going to leave Lan and Derrick alone in this situation.

Let the sheriff's department handle it.

He walked inside and entered the kitchen. Lan, sitting at the breakfast table and twirling an empty coffee cup, arched her eyebrows. "I hear water running."

Kannon nodded, aware his harboring Streak could further damage the glow from his and Lan's recent lovemaking.

"He is here? In the bath?" Lan rose from her chair. "I cannot believe—"

"You should see him, Lan. He's beat to shit. I couldn't just throw him out."

"I know your heart, Kannon. You did not intend for this to happen. But it has. And having Streak in our shower is not acceptable."

"I'm thinking it through."

Hands on her hips, Lan narrowed her eyes. "Kannon . . ."

"After Streak showers," Kannon said, tugging on the end of his mustache, "he and I are going to have a long talk. I'll get to the heart of the matter."

"I think you should deliver him to the authorities," Lan said. "That will settle matters."

"I'm not so sure, Lan. It's not that simple." This was no random attack, Kannon figured, but a continuation of Streak's running away from a dangerous group of men. "I want to assess the total risk."

Lan folded her arms, stared him down. "Until this is settled, perhaps I should take Derrick away again."

No! was his first thought. But maybe Lan was right. She was tough and could handle any danger from staying home. But Derrick was young and naïve. He needed protection. Still, Kannon didn't want them to leave home again.

The shrieking siren dropped octaves and wound down.

"Let's discuss this later," Kannon said.

"Of course." Lan turned and left the room.

Kannon marched to the front door, which stood partially ajar. He dragged it open and was greeted by flashing red and blue lights.

"Detective Clarke, Patrol Division," the deputy said. "You folks all right?" The portico's overhead light bathed the bare-headed Clarke in glazed incandescence, rendered psychedelic by the blinking lights from the deputy's cruiser.

"Yes. Thanks for coming."

"You've had a break-in." The hulking man looked formidable but spoke in a genial tone. His face hidden in silhouette, Clarke wore starched Khaki pants and shirt. An embroidered shoulder patch graced his upper sleeve. Cuffs, nightstick, and a semiautomatic attached to his satin-black pistol belt added authority.

"Attempted break-in," Kannon said. "My wife and I were awakened by a loud noise. As you can see, it looks like someone tried to bash in the front door. It rattled the house. Unusual here in the country, so we called it in."

Another deputy opened the cruiser's passenger door and exited. Clarke motioned him over. "Deputy Tabor, meet Kannon Ballard."

Kannon offered his hand, but the greeting was cut short.

"Take a look around the house," Clarke told Tabor as he knelt at the door. He pulled a penlight flash from his shirt pocket and examined the bottom panels. "There's a tire tread impression here."

Kannon stiffened, hoping the observation wouldn't lead to questions probing more than he wanted to share. Then Kannon noticed a pool of liquid on the tiled base of the portico. He shrunk back, hoping Clarke wouldn't notice the spill.

He did. The detective stooped and dipped his finger into the pooled liquid. Took a whiff. Rising, Clarke brushed a hand across his shiny scalp. "The tread impression's too wide for a bicycle. Based on this oil spill, I'd say some idiot crashed his motorcycle into the door." Clarke looked at Kannon. "You hear anything?"

Kannon shook his head. "My wife and I woke up in a fog. All we heard was a loud crash. Come to think of it, there was a rumbling sound, like from an engine. Assuming the guy rode off, our security alarm may have drowned out other sounds."

"Maybe," Clarke said. He cast a wary eye. "A trail of drops leads . . ." he splayed his flash.

"Looks like the oil trail disappears in the grass," Kannon said. Please don't be traceable to the garage.

"Reckon so," Clarke said. "Tire imprints on the lawn, too. One coming and one going."

"We've had trouble with dirt bikers in the past," Kannon lied. "Riding through the woods, but never this close."

"Un-huh." Clarke faced Kannon. "Noticed broken glass, spilled oil, scraped tree trunks, and blood on your drive leading in."

Kannon shook his head. "None of that stuff was our doing."

Wrong answer, he thought.

Just then, Lan came outside with Derrick in tow. "He wants to see a real police car," she said.

Excellent timing.

Clarke smiled. "Hello, young man."

Derrick slunk behind Momma Lan.

"Maybe high schoolers tripped out on drugs or booze got out of control," Kannon said, his palms sweaty.

"Been some of that," Clarke acknowledged.

Deputy Tabor reappeared, having completed his round.

"See anything?" asked Clarke.

"Nada," the deputy said.

"I'd like to know what happened on the drive, though," Kannon said.

Don't overplay your hand, idiot.

"Well, whoever did it has skedaddled," Detective Clarke said. "Hope we don't find 'em splattered alongside the highway. Keep your eyes open. Call if you see anything else."

"Much obliged," Kannon said.

Derrick came to his side, tugged at his jeans. "I want to hear the siren."

Clarke grinned and offered a salute. As he drove off, the deputy honored Derrick's wish. His son broke into a broad smile.

His family reentered the house. Kannon trudged through the kitchen to the garage and gathered the tools necessary to repair the door and frame.

As he was kneeling at the front door, he heard Lan say, "I want you to stay in your room." That meant she was headed his way.

"Okay, let me have it," Kannon said.

"I want Streak out of our house."

"I understand, Lan, but . . ." Hoping for leverage, Kannon described in more detail the attack on Streak and again brought up the leave-no-man-behind mantra. He realized this was a mistake as soon as the words left his mouth.

Lan glowered. "I do not care about leaving no man—"

Kannon held up his hand. "You're right. I'm sorry. Our family comes first. But Streak's here." *And his attackers know where we live.* "After getting to the root of this, I might help him out."

Lan cocked her head, not a good sign. "How?"

"Money. Get him out of our lives forever," Kannon said.

"Money? Are you kidding me?"

Lan was doing an excellent job learning American clichés. "How much?" she asked.

Kannon fidgeted. "I don't know for sure. Maybe fifteen to twenty-five grand."

Eyes wide open, Lan's mouth formed an *O*, but she remained silent.

"We can afford it," Kannon said. Whatever action he took might not be enough to distance his family from further trouble.

153

Lan shook her head. "I understand you feel Streak saved your life, but this is going too far. War is war, Kannon. You know that better than I do. Why do you feel so obligated?"

"Because America has abandoned us and treated its combat vets like shit."

"And you do not want to abandon Streak." Lan sighed. "Do what you must. But I will feel safer and more comfortable if Derrick and I stay away a few days."

"I get it." With a lump in his throat, he asked, "Do you still want to go to the Pigeonaire's Magika?"

"Yes."

"All right," Kannon said. "After the show, you and Derrick can go home with Roger and Karen. I'll call—"

"It is better I stay with Belynda."

Kannon started to object but saw the resolute glare in Lan's eyes. Instead, he frowned and muttered, "Okay."

Twenty-Four

Later Saturday morning, after giving up on repair efforts, he'd nailed the front door shut, including reinforcing it with a tilted chair against the door handle and wedging a two-by-four between the top half of the door and the opposite wall.

Feeling deflated about Streak's reappearance, Kannon opened the fridge and grabbed some leftover roast beef and a couple of Dr. Peppers. Hungry, he tossed a loaf of bread, plasticware, and paper plates on the kitchen table. Streak must be famished too. Kannon believed in feeding *prisoners*.

Streak entered, wearing over-fitted jeans and a flannel shirt, clean but looking drawn and haggard. The pant legs were rolled up, and his shirt sleeves were cuffed. Bruises covered his pummeled face, which looked as emaciated as a tortured POW's. Bent wire-rimmed glasses perched on the bridge of his nose accented his decrepit look.

"You need a doctor," Kannon said.

"A doc would ask questions."

"You're probably right. At least eat something. You'll feel better."

Streak sat at the table, but his eyes trailed far off. "I don't have much of an appetite."

Kannon grabbed a seat for himself. "You're obviously involved in something dangerous and dirty, if not evil. And you've jeopardized my family. I should kick your ass." Except it appeared Streak's ass didn't need any more kicking. "You want my help, come clean!"

"Mind telling me first what went on between you and the deputy?" Streak said, his brow furrowed.

"Didn't mention you. You're clear."

Streak closed his eyes and tilted his head back, let out a big sigh. "Thank you."

"Doesn't mean it's a permanent fix," Kannon said. "Depends on how this conversation turns out and other external factors yet to raise their ugly heads, like whether the sheriff's department probes deeper. You get the drift, right?"

Streak frowned and nodded at the same time.

"Talk . . . now!"

Streak, shoulders drooping, hesitated, averting his eyes as if reluctant to give up the truth.

"I'm waiting," Kannon said.

"All right, the attack . . . it happened on your land, about a hundred yards in from the highway."

Kannon paid rapt attention to Streak's story. Repulsed at the attempted rape, he said, "What the hell were you doing on my property?"

"Working up the nerve to contact you again?"

"In the middle of the night?"

Streak shook his head. "Morning."

"You know your attackers, don't you?"

Streak took a deep breath. His battered face looked like a bleached canvas with rotten tomatoes stuck to it. "Yeah, I know who they are."

Kannon thought about the inscription on Streak's knife he'd taken at the Black Forest Restaurant in Fredericksburg. "Are they terrorists?"

"Home-grown variety."

"Rightwing, you mean?" Kannon slapped two slices of beef on the bread, added mayo and lettuce, and took a bite.

"They call themselves the Border Slot Militia," Streak said. "Their slogan is: *White Might is Right*. They're worse than bad."

"Describe these guys."

Between gulps of soda, Streak described two men, each a mercenary, one tall, the other short, built like a five-foot eight-inch fireplug. "They're dressed in camouflaged fatigues. The taller one has brown hair and a handlebar mustache. Chews Redman. The short guy, Bull, is new, built like a Bullmastiff. He's the one—"

"I get it," Kannon said. He considered forwarding these descriptions to Clarke, saying an anonymous tipster passed them on. As if the detective would buy it. "How in the hell did you get mixed up with a militia group?"

"After the Việt Nam war, I held various jobs—mechanic's work at rural airfields, piloting crop dusters, driving a combine at wheat harvests—but I was depressed. Thought myself a failure."

"Because?" Kannon wondered if Streak had ever heard of therapy or antidepressants.

"A month after I provided fire support at your outpost, I was shot down, crashed my chopper, which was never recovered." Streak reached for a piece of meat. "The only survivor, I was medevaced out and my commander . . ."

"Your commander, what?"

"He . . . he didn't believe I'd been shot down. Called it pilot error. And—"

"Were you?"

"Yes. But I had no witnesses, so he stripped my wings."

Everything about Streak seemed shaky. This story fit the fantasy mold, but what he described was possible. Still, that was no justification for what he was doing now.

"I say again. How did you get caught up with a militia group?"

"I latched on to what I thought was a great opportunity," Streak said, nibbling on a slice of beef, "maintaining and flying an old Jolly Green Giant helicopter to transport civilian parties into the wilderness for hunting, rafting, and skiing trips."

"Sounds plausible," Kannon said, rocking his soda bottle on the tabletop. "I'm guessing it never happened."

"At first, I thought we were legit. We took groups out, but I soon realized they were tactical training sessions for recent grads who were on the verge of being farmed out."

"You mean like escape and evasion, shit like that?"

"Yeah." Streak sipped from his Dr. Pepper, then shook his head. "The clincher . . . you read about the body found in one of the geysers a couple of years ago?"

"Can't say that I did."

"Long story short. One night we loaded up—me, Whitehead, Crandle, plus three more of his men—and picked up this other guy. I thought that was strange. This poor bastard, a stranger, didn't look like a militiaman. Crandle had me fly to this one geyser in Yellowstone he'd picked out. 'Hover,' he tells me. Next thing I know that poor sucker is dangling from a rope, headfirst. The geyser erupts, dousing him with hot steam and sulfurous gas before he's cut loose and dropped into the pool. Boiled alive."

"Poor bastard."

"Yeah."

Streak painstakingly explained about the razor-sharp killer discs. "There's a *practice* range at the compound, used for setup training, but marginal trainees are whisked off to remote plateaus in the mountains to undergo the real thing."

"Jeez," Kannon said, after listening to more sordid details.

"Crandle keeps a core group of graduates at Border Slot. They don't think of themselves as mercenaries but as God's *Chosen Ones*."

Kannon's neck and arms prickled. It was hard to believe something as bizarre as razor-sharp discs and a killing range could be real. Then he remembered seeing a disc embedded in Streak's windshield.

Kannon leaned back and stared at the ceiling. "These guys want to unravel the United States."

"Not just the U.S. The whole world."

Survival of the fittest. So, what's new here?

"Did you undergo the range?"

Streak shook his head. "Helicopter pilots like me are in short supply."

You mean stupid helicopter pilots.

"How did the two militiamen track you to my house?"

"They must have found my address book," Streak said, hanging his head.

"Careless," Kannon said.

"It was in my footlocker, hidden in a cutout of a novel. In my haste, I forgot about it. Yours was one of only two names not crossed out. Whitehead found it."

Kannon's muscles tensed. He wanted to knock the crap out of Streak. "What else does the militia know about me?"

"I don't know. Maybe nothing."

"That's not reassuring. They damn sure know where I live."

Streak's shoulders sagged, now a routine action.

"How organized are these guys?" Kannon asked.

"There's no coordinated national movement. Different militia groups operate in separate cells. They're all paranoid."

"You said Crandle contracts out militiamen. To whom?"

"Overseas and domestic rightwing groups, drug cartels, any group that can pay for a quality mercenary."

The situation was worse than he'd imagined. "What else haven't you told me?"

"Crandle wants to up the ante," Streak said, making eye contact. "You know anything about electromagnetic pulse weapons?"

"I'm familiar with the concept. I don't know if anyone has employed EMP weapons effectively . . . except in movies. So, we're talking about knocking out electrical grids, computer and communication systems, financial networks."

"Correct."

Kannon grimaced. By tying knots in the cyberspace network, terrorists could wreak havoc upon the developed world's sophisticated streams of data flow. Successful employment of electromagnetic pulse weapons coupled with biowarfare and dirty bombs would return the world to the dark ages—such thoughts sent chills racing down Kannon's spine, concerns he didn't need to share with Lan.

"None of this sounds good," Kannon said.

"No, it doesn't." Streak removed his glasses and pinched the bridge of his nose.

"Too much has happened too fast." Kannon hadn't had enough time to assimilate it all. Maybe he'd made a mistake diverting Detective Clarke's attention from Streak toward a random, attempted break-in.

"There's more," Streak said.

"Of course, there is," Kannon said, glaring.

"Crandle and Whitehead think I've contacted the Feds."

"The Feds as in CIA?"

Streak nodded.

The comment jarred him. Kannon thought about the phone call from Sindy Zeller, claiming to be CIA. What was it Streak said? Two names were not crossed out. The possible connection was haunting.

"What was the other name in your address book?"

Streak seemed surprised by the question. "Sindy Zeller."

"Son of a bitch. You've not only got a militia on my ass, but the CIA too."

"You know about her?" Streak appeared dumbstruck.

"Afraid so."

"How?"

"She called, threatening us about Lan's immigration status."

"Oh, my God. I didn't reveal . . ." Streak averted his eyes. "What can I say! I've screwed everything up."

"Why didn't you tell me all this at Lost Maples?"

"Would it have made a difference?"

"It might have, damnit." Kannon raked his chair back and stood. The chair back smacked on the floor.

"I'm sorry for exposing you," Streak said, his lips trembling. "I never should've called."

"A little late for remorse. The last thing I want is to get involved with a militia, much less the Feds and this Zeller bitch."

Streak, too, stood, hooked his thumbs over his pockets. "Sindy Zeller approached me at a bar in Missoula . . ."

Streak revealed how in his desperation to get away from the militia he had bought into the charms of Ms. Zeller and, during a night of torrid sex, *volunteered* to transport "custom motorcycles" from Canada, which he figured to be illegal contraband because of the money involved. He hadn't cared what the hell he was hauling if he got laid and paid.

"Good grief, Streak. Stinger missiles, a certified check requiring a counter-signature, it appears Zeller has resources."

"I'm not so sure. The check required Zeller's signature. Not only that, she'd also promised an additional sixty thousand when I delivered the crates to her in Missoula. It was there Zeller changed the deal, threatening my arrest and life in jail if I didn't go undercover."

"Sixty grand?" Kannon arched his eyebrows. "She's playing you big time, Streak."

"Yeah. And if Zeller *does* put me in jail, Crandle's reach would rip me apart."

"And may rip apart my family as well," Kannon said.

Streak didn't respond.

"Zeller apparently had you pegged, knew somehow of your connection to Border Slot. Got any idea how she latched onto you?"

"I wish I did."

"How did she find out you were a pilot?"

"I don't know," Streak said.

"But you and Zeller talk."

"At her choosing. Her call number is blocked."

As it was when she called here.

"The only way she'd know about me," Kannon said, "is because of you."

"Zeller thinks you're the money man for the militia."

"Why?"

"Because that's what I told her."

Kannon balled his fist, cocked his arm, and struck Streak on the chin, knocking him to the floor.

"I deserved that." Streak made no effort to get up.

Tempted to continue pounding Streak, Kannon sent a twin-dagger look instead. "You were trying to shift blame—"

"In my desperation, yeah."

The kitchen door leading to the den swung open, and Lan entered. "Kannon, what have you done?"

What is going on is I lost control.

"I overreacted."

Lan raked her hair in frustration. "You promised no more fighting."

I've promised lots of things.

"I want him gone this afternoon," Lan said, pointing at Streak.

"I know," Kannon said. "You don't need to tell me again."

Streak buried his head in his hands.

Lan gave one last glare and left the room.

Kannon massaged his knuckles. He hadn't hit anyone in a long time. His adrenaline drained, he drew in steady breaths. Desperation led to more desperation, which led to more desperation, ad infinitum. Kannon realized he wasn't going to accomplish anything by violence. What's done was done. He needed to tone it down.

He reached down and offered Streak a hand.

"Let's settle this and get you out of here, or Lan will be on my ass," Kannon said. "So, Zeller shafted you on the certified check?"

"Yeah."

"And she's following you somehow," Kannon said.

Streak shrugged.

He couldn't just boot Streak out. To do so would leave too many unanswered questions, leave too uncertain the future. "Sit," Kannon told Streak. He grabbed one of those store-bought icepacks from the freezer and two Ba Mui Bas from the fridge. "Remember this brand?"

"I remember. It's a good beer."

Kannon slapped the icepack on the table, then flicked off the bottle caps with an opener and thrust a bottle in front of Streak.

"Thanks." Streak accepted the beer. Before drinking, he removed his glasses and placed the cold pack against his nose.

Kannon sighed. "Zeller's flaky. Are you sure she's CIA?"

"She had credentials." Streak removed the icepack to sip on his beer, then said, "But hell, I don't know if they were valid."

"I get that," Kannon took a swig, then leaned back in his chair and clasped his hands behind his neck. "I thought it odd Zeller contacted us by phone instead of a personal visit. I think she's a fraud." Or severely mixed up. He brought the front legs of his chair back to the floor with a thud. "Regardless of who she is or what her motives are, I think she's stuck you with a tracking device."

"I looked for one but never found anything."

"What about your phone?"

"It's never been out of my hands."

"Did you use the chopper to deliver the Stingers to Zeller?"

"No. I was suspicious. If Zeller's play was a sting, I didn't want to risk losing the chopper. Instead, I offloaded the crates into a rental truck and used it to deliver the merchandise."

"Something's missing," Kannon said. "I'm curious and have to know. Run me through the steps you took."

Whitehead scratched his head. "My memory is fuzzy. Got a pencil and paper?"

"Yeah." Kannon left the kitchen and returned from his study with a pad and pencil. "Let's go to the garage. I want you to write down the progression of events while I examine your motorcycle."

Twenty-Five

Once inside the garage, Kannon turned on the overhead lights. After placing Streak on a stool in front of a worktable, he grabbed a fluorescent work light, lay flat on his back, and scooted close to Streak's banged-up V-Rod. It was a tight fit. Kannon played the light across the undercarriage, into the nooks and crannies, but failed to detect a tracker.

Meanwhile, Streak scribbled vigorously. Eraser fragments littered the floor around the stool. Mumbled cursing accompanied his mistakes.

Kannon set the work light aside, closed his eyes, and imagined himself an archeologist exploring artifacts in a darkened tomb. Lightly running his fingers over the unseen, he examined the undercarriage for an object that wasn't an integral part of the motorcycle. Amid the grime and grease, he located a device lodged into a gap behind the radiator and the bottom of the oil sump.

"I found something," Kannon said. "It's about the size of a thumb drive."

"Yeah?"

Kannon opened his eyes to see Streak kneeling beside the motorcycle. "Get me a flathead screwdriver hanging on the tool rack behind the VW."

Moving fast for a man in his condition, Streak returned with the tool in seconds. Kannon took the screwdriver and pried the head underneath one end of the object, then wiggled it loose. As he figured, a tracker had been mounted with industrial-strength double-sided tape. Kannon worked his way free of the bike, stood, and wiped his hands and the device with a damp rag.

"Why are you smiling?" Streak asked, wide-eyed. "I thought you'd be mad as hell."

"You're looking at SyncTrak's second-generation MoblTrac7," Kannon said.

"I'll be damned," Streak said. "That's how Zeller tagged me."

"Yeah, well, assuming it was Zeller and not Border Slot."

Streak shook his head. "Crandle and Whitehead had no reason

to suspect I'd bail. And I was privy to most everything going on. Never heard anyone mention the use of tracking devices."

Kannon thought about this.

"Maybe it wasn't Border Slot. Regardless, this unit can be pinged by a tracker cellphone to acquire the target's coordinates."

"Is there a way to backtrack to the cellphone number?"

"Good question," Kannon said. "I'd have to send it to the lab for analysis. However, it'd probably trace to a restricted number or burner cellphone."

"Makes sense."

"The unit has a serial number. I'll find out who bought this baby." The irony of SyncTrak's involvement didn't escape him. Or was it serendipitous? Regardless, finding the tracker gave him a tangible fragment in an otherwise amorphous situation. "Take a seat and finish your write-up. I'm going to get my laptop."

Walking toward the study, Kannon heard notes from some classical piece Lan was playing on her piano. First time he'd heard her play in years, probably to take her mind off Streak. Well, whatever it took.

Upon return to the garage, he booted up the computer, then, using his secure code, logged into SyncTrak. Accessing the sales database, he plugged in the tracking device's serial number and the name Modesto Poblete popped up.

"This sale, like the majority of our transactions, was conducted online." Kannon slid the laptop in front of Streak. "Does Modesto Poblete mean anything to you?"

Streak set his scribbling aside and stared at the computer screen. "Nah. But I see Moblete used a P.O. Box as an address."

"My bad," Kannon said. Memo to file—no more shipping to PO Boxes. "I was hoping to find Zeller's name on the buy list."

"No such luck?"

"No."

Kannon signed on to a fee-based search engine.

"A few M. Pobletes showed up but no Modesto. I'm not sure it's worth the time to try and track her down."

"Even if Poblete points toward Zeller, what good would it do?" Streak asked, leaning away from the laptop.

"Possibly to gain leverage," Kannon said. "Find out who she is, whose side she's on."

Streak removed his glasses and applied the icepack again. "Wish I could think of a way to disassociate you from all this."

Again, too little too late.

"Let me see your timetable," Kannon said. He gulped down some now lukewarm soda as he started reading the document. After completing the first read, he read it once more, slowly, and highlighted Streak's key points.

- Saturday p.m. 3 October: Met Zeller in Missoula. Screwed her. She screwed me.
- Sunday early a.m. 4 October: Signed binding documents under duress.
- Saturday 10 October: Dropped off V-Rod in Kalispell for new tires. Rented a truck and stashed it at a private airfield. Returned to Border Slot in Willys Jeep.
- Monday a.m. 12 October: Flew Jolly Green Giant to Calgary. Loaded "motorcycles." A certified check for 15 grand—worthless, required Zeller's signature.
- Monday p.m. 12 October: Returned to Kalispell. Landed on a private airstrip. Used pallet jack to transfer merchandise from chopper to truck. Drove to Missoula.
- Monday p.m. late: Delivered contraband to Zeller's rendezvous point on Mullan Road west of Missoula. Arrested for transporting stinger missiles. Instead of jail, Zeller offered me a deal to go undercover (wanted me to wear a wire) and nail Border Slot Militia. Promised to sign check(s) only if I "delivered" Border Slot personnel.
- Monday p.m. later: Tired! Dropped off the rental truck at U-Haul in Missoula. Hopped a flight to a Kalispell private airfield. Flew chopper back to Border slot.
- Tuesday early a.m. 13 October: You and I talked on the phone. Agreed to meet at Los Maples.
- Wednesday a.m. 14 October: Picked up V-Rod with new tires. Trailered bike to Whitefish. Garaged Jeep

there. Took off on my motorcycle.

- Saturday a.m. 17 October: met you at the park.

After studying Streak's timetable a third time, Kannon set the paper down.

"I agree with you. I don't think Border Slot is the tracker. The Feds, or whoever, say, Zeller, couldn't track the rental truck past Missoula. She also didn't know the location of the helicopter."

"Right."

"I'm guessing your V-Rod got tagged at the motorcycle shop in Kalispell, and she thought you'd ride back to Border Slot, revealing the militia's location."

"Zeller probably didn't know about the Willys and that I could switch vehicles," Streak rubbed his chin. "Could they have bugged my phone?"

"You use a satphone, right?"

"Right."

"They're easier to intercept." Kannon thought about *Big Brother's* listening capabilities.

"Maybe it's both," Streak chipped in.

Kannon reexamined the sequence of events with Streak at Lost Maples—their first encounter, reminiscences, the deteriorating dialogue, the request for money, rejection and confrontation, fellow picnickers, the mockingbird, the flat tire . . . the lady!

"You know, after you flattened my tire, an Asian woman in an old Camaro showed up, offered to help me. She said something about being careful who I associate with."

"Meaning me."

"Yeah. At first, I thought she'd witnessed the whole fiasco."

Streak furrowed his brow. "What color was the car?"

"Blue, light blue."

"I saw a Camaro with a similar description when leaving the park." Streak slapped his forehead. "Good grief. I saw it again at the Llano River. This time I got a look at the driver."

"Asian woman?" Kannon said, recalling the image of the Lost Maples' lady.

"Yep."

"Short, plump, round face, with dark, long hair? And her nose, her nose—"

"Looked as if it had been pinched in a vise," Streak said, completing Kannon's sentence.

"She may be our Modesto Poblete. Whoever this person is, she probably works for Sindy Zeller."

Streak clasped his hands behind his head and stared at the ground. "I'm so screwed."

Kannon was feeling further drawn in.

"Zeller's authenticity continues to nag at me. It's not that difficult to fabricate forged documents or credentials. And most anyone could acquire a tracking device. At one point, I was going to suggest you turn yourself over to Zeller, but the more I think about her actions—along with the rundown Camaro, which doesn't fit my image of Federal assets—more than ever I'm thinking she's a fraud."

"Who do you think she might be?" Streak asked.

"I don't know." If she wasn't a Fed, the concern about his aiding and abetting Streak's escape from the law dropped from high risk to low. "Christ! I just had a thought."

"What?"

"Suppose Zeller belongs to a rival militia group."

"Jesus," Streak said.

"Which could explain their misfires and/or lack of funding resources . . . and inability to locate Border Slot's headquarters."

"Scary thought." Streak's knuckles turned white. "Those guys with Zeller during the missile handoff . . . they wore no insignia."

"Or . . . relatives from a fallen militia candidate might hold a grudge against Crandle. Lord knows, from what you've told me, any number of people would want him whacked."

"The latter seems probable."

"I agree," Kannon said. "Zeller may be in this for revenge." He drank from his beer and studied Streak.

There was a far-away look in Streak's eyes as if he had no place to go. Even if he was able to leave the country, would Border Slot be far behind? Kannon sensed the depth of Streak's helplessness, and he didn't want to throw his ass to the wind.

Loyalty! How do you put a price on loyalty?

Streak had already exposed Kannon and his family to a predatory militia group, which probably couldn't be reversed. His family's safety was paramount. The problem was how to protect it. He wasn't sure what to defend against. Was there an out?

Money seemed the only option.

Lan might go ballistic. Having lived dirt poor most of her life, she constantly worried about it, whether it was Derrick's college education or Kannon's ongoing investments and consultancy for SyncTrak. But no other options seemed plausible. Payoff. Buy distance.

"I've made up my mind. Your presence endangers my family. I will not get further involved. We can't have any more contact."

"But—"

"No buts."

Streak's shoulders drooped. He held the dejected look of a person condemned to death. Kannon hurt for him.

Streak scooted back his chair and stood. "I'll be leaving then."

"I haven't finished," Kannon said, grasping Streak's shoulder.

"What more can you say?"

"We were comrades once, close friends in OCS. You saved my life. You've been through a lot. I won't leave you high and dry. You think twenty-five thousand bucks will help you obtain a new identity and clear the country?"

"Yeah." Streak's face flushed.

"How did you come up with that number?"

"Well . . ." Streak clasped his fists as would a child. "I've seen Crandle and Whitehead negotiate package deals. Driver's licenses, social security cards, education, work history, passports, and transportation costs. Even more for entering a country with no extradition treaty. Start-up expenses—"

"Christ. I'm not setting you up in business."

"I understand." Streak leaned forward. "Just enough to cover expenses—"

"All right. I'll *loan* you the twenty-five thousand. I'll download a pro forma promissory note, write it up, and we'll execute the document tonight. I'm in good standing with my bank. You can cash it there."

Streak's eyes moistened.

It took Kannon only a few minutes to craft a simple loan document, which of course, he never expected to be repaid.

"Can you ride?" he asked Streak.

"Yes." Streak wore a smile of gratitude. "You've got time to get some sleep and attend the magic show your wife mentioned."

Kannon nodded.

"I won't bother you again," Streak said.

"No. You won't."

They rolled Streak's V-Rod out onto the driveway. The bike looked ugly in its battered state, but the engine fired up right away.

A hole opened in Kannon's heart as he watched Streak ride down the drive and out of sight. So far, he'd lost someone thought to be a friend, lied to Detective Clarke, told a possible CIA agent to fuck off, and appeared on a militant rightwing group's radar.

Good job!

He reentered the house. Lan, sitting in bed, was reading. An unfinished glass of wine sat on her bedside table, as did the three Navajo curing dolls. Her arms and skin above her breasts were exposed, and the smell of Cinnabar was prominent, a taunting allure. He wanted her, but it wouldn't happen.

A packed suitcase stood at the foot of the bed. Later tonight, after the magic show, she and Derrick would return to Belynda's. He prayed for their safety and quick return.

Meanwhile, he . . . he would be alone with his angst.

169

Twenty-Six

On Saturday evening, Lan and Derrick—luggage included—joined Kannon as they piled into their cherry-red Cherokee Jeep and headed for Austin to see the Pigeonaire's Magika. En route, they would pick up Belynda Blu. Stefan was flying in from Dallas to rendezvous at the performance site. Brother Roger and his wife would join them there.

It was pleasant out. Kannon lowered his window to inhale the sweet smell of freshly cut hay. An armadillo waddled alongside Highway 29, its armored shell reflecting waning rays of twilight. Nearby, a farmer worked at clearing a field clotted with mesquite and cedar stumps, while another man was driving a combine on cleared acreage.

The magic show might provide a welcome diversion, albeit in Kannon's eyes one far too short. As agreed, after the show, Lan and Derrick would spend time with Belynda until Kannon was satisfied the Streak fiasco had settled down.

"I'm going to miss you guys," Kannon said.

"We will be fine," Lan said. "Spending time with Belynda will be good for all of us."

How so? Kannon wondered.

"I will get to see the Navajo lady?" Derrick asked.

Lan turned in her seat. "Yes. And your big brother, Stefan, too."

"Yay."

Kannon smiled. Though twenty-four years apart in age and exhibiting myriad personality differences, his two sons had taken to each other like soulmates. For that, he was grateful. He hoped neither would ever have to face war or its aftermath, or become embittered like his OCS classmate, or, at times, like himself.

Wanting to talk to Lan, Kannon adjusted the rearview mirror until he could see Derrick's reflection. "Son, why don't you listen to the music your momma recorded for you." Otherwise, Derrick would *soak up their words like a sponge.*

"Okay, Daddy K."

After Derrick inserted the earbuds connected to his iPod, Kannon turned to Lan. "Hope I did the right thing about Streak."

"I do too." Lan lowered her visor and popped open the vanity mirror. The lighted reflection showed drawn cheeks and eyes void of luster. She snapped the visor shut and folded her hands in her lap. "Do you really believe Streak will not bother us anymore?"

"I expect him to present the check and promissory note early Monday. I've already left a message with Chuck to honor the presented instrument and to draw the funds from our account—and deliver them to Streak in whatever form of currency he wants."

"What if authorities examine the promissory note and investigate the connection between you two and this militia?"

"The note's documentation states the money's for professional services rendered, with no monthly payments, interest to accrue at three percent, and P and I due in ten years, which should avoid any compulsory reporting for cash transactions under the Bank Secrecy Act. Also, in the scheme of things, it's a small transaction, not likely to come up in an audit."

"I am not thinking about an audit. I am thinking about Sindy Zeller, her hunt for the militia, and her challenging my immigration status."

All valid concerns.

Kannon had considered contacting the CIA to verify Zeller's status but concluded doing so would only raise red flags.

"Don't worry. Zeller's a fraud," he said. "Think of her like she's spam, you know, a caller or emailer threatening litigation if you don't respond to or click on a web link, which leads to malicious software or worse, stolen identity."

Lan frowned. "And the militia group?"

"They want Streak, not me." Regardless, Kannon planned to enhance their home security system, installing video cameras around the house as well as placing surveillance cameras in trees bordering the drive. As a last resort, the idea of selling out and moving away had entered his mind.

"Okay," Lan said, crossing her legs. "In the future, please screen all your calls."

They rounded a curve, and the Cherokee's headlights lit up a

171

deer poised on the shoulder. Kannon flicked his high beam to low and eased past. He checked the rearview mirror to see whether the deer had tried to dash across. It did but didn't make it. Another vehicle, horn blaring, rammed the animal and trucked on. Since Lan hadn't seen the deer accident, Kannon chose not to reveal it.

Kannon glanced again into the rearview and tightened his grip on the steering wheel. The driver behind was closing distance and flashing a single headlight. At first, he thought the source came from a motorcycle, then realized it was from a pickup with one headlight out. Cop? Local constable? Neither, Kannon thought. There was no siren or red and blue lights—just a prick behind the wheel.

Or Border Slot? No way, Kannon thought. Regardless, he accelerated, and the trailing vehicle receded into the background. Letting out a deep breath, he drummed his fingers on the steering wheel, then turned southeast on US 183.

Kannon sighed. Hating to admit it, he was anxious about meeting Belynda. After all, this was the woman who'd planted the seed in Lan's psyche about "taking a break from the marriage."

Well, as it's turning out, we are *taking a break from the marriage, albeit for reasons of safety, right? No concerns about the relationship, right? One night of delicious makeup sex cures all, right?*

Separating was the right thing to do, though. Still, injecting new folks into Kannon's narrow mix of friends was like throwing an unknown ingredient into a pot of stew. It changed the chemistry and the flavor. He might like the result . . . or not.

As if reading his mind, Lan said, "I need you to respect how important Belynda is to me. Other than our being minorities, we have much in common."

"I understand."

Lan turned toward him, eyebrows lifted, lips slightly parted. "Do strong women scare you?"

"No." *Yes!*

"I love you, Kannon. Once this settles down, we will begin our couple's therapy."

"Okay. And I love you, too."

He wasn't sure what bothered him most, the Streak-militia

debacle or the tug on his marriage. His first wife had outgrown him, lapped him, actually, and he feared it happening again. It was all about owning up and expressing feelings with the right words and the right actions. Did he have the capacity to do so?

Before turning off the roadway, Kannon glanced in the side mirror to see whether any headlights were in view. In the distance, yes. Feeling paranoid, he slowed down, turned off the car lights, and, without braking or using a turn signal, careened left onto a twisting artery. He let the Jeep roll forward. The blinking one-eyed vehicle drove past.

"What are you doing?" Lan asked.

"Wrong turn."

Lan rolled her eyes.

Kannon flicked the lights back on, did a U-turn, and returned to the main highway. He drove two miles before Lan directed him to turn into an isolated development outside Leander.

After crossing a dry creek bed, he noticed an oval house marker strung on a tree limb. The sign was painted light teal with luminescent dark blue letters scripting the name Belynda Blu.

Kannon steered onto her shale-lined drive and fronted a well-lit, flat-roofed bungalow painted a vivid purple and yellow. The grounds, illuminated like a Christmas tree, revealed native grasses, cedar, and colorful Texas perennials dispersed among rocks and cacti.

"I love her home," Lan said, smiling, as the Jeep drew to a halt.

The scene reminded him of a children's fantasy movie.

"You will like her."

"Yeah, right," Kannon mumbled, fending off Lan's attempted reassurance.

As Lan opened her door and stepped from the Cherokee, Belynda Blu emerged from the house. Shapely, roughly five feet six, she wore a short khaki skirt and watermelon-colored shirt. An attractive woman, her hair was Navajo black, her skin the color of henna. Pearl-white teeth brightened a sharp, angular face.

"Belynda, thank you so much for letting Derrick and me stay with you after the show," Lan said.

His wife appeared transformed. The worry lines lifted from

her face, and her cheeks shone full and bright. Even Lan's clothes seemed brighter. Having eschewed her usual áo dài, she was wearing a full-flowing, mid-calf mauve skirt and ruffled blouse the color of goldenrod. Both women outmatched his starched blue jeans, western-styled khaki shirt, and denim jacket.

Kannon exited the Jeep. Derrick, who was wearing jeans, beaded moccasins, and a bright green shirt, unbuckled his seat belt and, carrying a juice pack, hopped out too.

"*Yá'át'ééh,*" Derrick said in a soft voice.

"What?" Kannon asked.

Both women laughed.

"*Yá'át'ééh* is 'hello' in Navajo," Lan said.

Belynda knelt and hugged Kannon's little guy. "I have something for you." She produced a multicolored Native American headband and placed it around Derrick's head.

Derrick beamed with pride and hustled back to the Cherokee.

Rising, Belynda spoke to Kannon in a deep-throated, sexy voice. "I've heard a lot about you."

Which is what worries me.

Belynda was measuring him, filling in the tally sheet, and he didn't want to know his score. While he didn't detect a frosty manner, her expression seemed a tad "holier-than-thou."

"It's my pleasure to meet you," Kannon said. "Lan speaks highly—."

"Come on, Daddy K. Let's go."

Timely interruption . . . "Everybody ready?"

Kannon opened the Jeep's rear door for Belynda and the passenger door for Lan, then ensured that Derrick was buckled in properly. He walked to the driver's side and slid behind the wheel.

"Daddy K? Does the magician make people disappear?"

"Turns 'em into bats."

"Mama Lan!"

"Daddy is teasing, honey."

His son mumbled something unintelligible. Kannon turned for a quick look. Derrick, wearing the headband, held a pinched straw between his teeth, which looked like mirrored white picket fences, absent a plank or two.

As Kannon started the engine, a dark-colored pickup, parked about fifty yards away, revved its engine and pulled away from the shoulder. "Son of a bitch."

It faced the other direction, so Kannon couldn't tell whether it was the one-eyed deer killer.

"Son of a bitch," Derrick echoed.

Uh oh.

Belynda remained silent.

"You may not use bad words, young man," Lan said.

Her stern tone cut like a hot blade. Kannon pictured Derrick's lower lip quivering. She didn't need to spank their son, just a glare would do.

And Kannon was next.

"Can you not respond without cursing?" She gave him the look, one capable of shattering a windshield.

"Won't happen again," he said.

Was his imagination getting the better of him? Like during the War, at night, when swaying palm fronds cast shadows too easily interpreted as belonging to the Việt Cộng. Startled responses and adrenaline flow were native to him since Việt Nam. Which was why he possessed a concealed handgun permit. Which was why he carried a 9mm Sig P238 inside his jacket pocket.

Just stay alert, he reminded himself.

Ten minutes later, Kannon spotted a sign for the Pigeonaire's Magika. It was located between Leander and Round Rock, off State 1431. He turned onto a narrow, asphalt-topped entryway, which gave way to a crushed-stone parking lot, its spaces delineated by uneven rows of gnarled cedar trees. Their spindly wind-blown leaves flitted in irregular patterns like butterflies.

Kannon threaded the Cherokee through the sentinel-like grove and found a parking space. The adults piled out. Derrick unbuckled his seat restraint and bolted through the open rear door toward Stefan, his proxy twin, who, along with Roger and Karen, was waiting at the edge of the parking lot.

"How're you doing, dude?" Stefan asked.

"I'm cool, man." They high-fived and fist-bumped.

"Good to see you, Dad." Stefan embraced Kannon, a welcome

indication they'd closed the distance that had existed between them for too many years.

"You look great." Kannon stepped away but held his son's shoulders. They were firm, solid, like the rest of his body, even though you couldn't tell because of the loose-fitting jeans and bulky ice-blue pullover. "And this is Lan's friend—"

"Belynda," she said. "My goodness, Stefan, you look just like your father. Even your mustache is shaped the same way."

"I'm Karen," Roger's wife said. "Fortunately, Stefan doesn't emulate all his father's traits."

Kannon frowned at his sister-in-law, who smoothed her amber-tinged sweater layered over a green turtleneck.

"Just teasing, sweetie." She pinched him on the cheek.

"Be nice, or I won't let you sit next to Derrick," Kannon said.

"And you must be Kannon's brother," Belynda said.

"Yes," Roger said. Wearing his familiar garb with wool pants and brown tweed sport coat, his brother looked every bit like a Professor Emeritus of Accounting.

"Don't let his apparel fool you," Karen said. "At heart, he's a ham, always seeking the center of attention."

"Probably to counter his boring profession," Kannon added.

Roger ignored Kannon's attempt at humor.

Striding through the parking lot, his brother slowed his pace and grabbed Kannon's arm so that they lagged behind the others. "Who's the awesome-looking woman . . . she with the beautiful brown eyes?"

"I'm shocked," Kannon said with a mocking tone in his voice, "that you can still notice."

"You're never too married to look. Just don't touch. That's my motto."

"She's a looker, I'll admit."

"Her skin's like Lan's, creamy, ageless," Roger said, out of Karen's earshot.

Kannon pursed his lips, stared at his brother. "She's arrogant."

"Oh?"

"Her expression when she sized me up, like she found me

lacking, condescending attitude, you know."

"You mean, like, she's better than you."

"Yeah. Kinda."

Roger gave him a bemused look. "All women are better than you."

"Cute."

"Belynda is encouraging Lan to assert herself more, expand her life's aura, those sorts of things."

"And express her feelings?"

Kannon nodded.

"Blasphemous," Roger said.

"No, no, I understand it's a good thing, but—"

"You need to stretch. It's not like relationships are your strong suit."

"Yeah, yeah."

"I know you, brother," Roger said, pulling Kannon aside. "Something else is going on."

Kannon stared at the ground, then at his brother. "We've had some trouble . . ."

He told Roger about Streak, the SyncTrak tracking device found on the motorcycle, the payoff, and the militia. "As for Sindy Zeller . . ." Kannon stated his case.

"Got it," Roger said, unbuttoning his sport coat. "You think she's a fraud."

"Yep."

"Sounds like you could use your own militia," Roger added.

"Hey, you guys," Belynda said. "You three look like triplets. Line up for a pic."

Twenty-Seven

Like a modified barn, the Pigeonaire's Magika theater had a pitched, wood-shingled roof that swept down like a parapet and extended three feet beyond the open-air side walls to shield attendees from wind and rain. If the weather turned really nasty, accordion-style partitions would slide from recessed housings and enclose the sides.

ELECTRICALLY OPERATED WITH MANUAL OVERRIDES—a well-placed sign displayed.

No security, Kannon noticed, thinking about the pickup parked near Belynda's home and the trailing headlight beforehand. He touched his handgun inside his jacket pocket for reassurance.

After showing their tickets to the attendant, he and Roger herded their crew through the old-fashioned turnstile and entered the theater. They scuffed across a barn-wood floor constructed from five-inch-wide planks with pew-like benches anchored to the floorboards. A balcony, supported by rough-pine posts, sat above the horseshoe-shaped seating arena and provided five additional bench rows. Seats were numbered. The theater accommodated one hundred customers to watch performers on an oval stage.

A cool country breeze circulated through the arena, scattering promotional flyers lying on a table. Ignoring the clutter, Kannon scanned the theatergoers for rugged, out-of-place faces and suspicious bulges in jackets and pants. No suspicious stares targeted Kannon's party, but weapons could be easily concealed inside—

"Cool place," Roger said, distracting him.

"Smells musty. Reminds me of a horse corral."

"Better watch where you step," Stefan said.

"I'd worry more about your father's bullshit than the kind you step in," Roger said.

"Ha!" Kannon mustered a smile but couldn't shake the angst. Derrick, who had been clinging like a magnet to Stefan, broke loose, as a six-year-old boy would when distracted by an object of interest, in this case, an early Halloween display. "Get back here!" Kannon hollered. He chased after him and grabbed his boy by the arm.

"Ow!" Derrick's lower lip trembled.

"Sorry," Kannon said. "Just don't run off."

"Kannon . . ." Lan shot him a look of disapproval.

The theater was packed. Their seats were located on Bench G, numbers one through seven. Programs lay on each seat. Leaning toward Roger, Kannon whispered, "I'm going to take a quick look around. Keep an eye on Derrick."

"Okay," Roger said. "I understand."

A couple of minutes later, Kannon returned, shaking his head.

"Sure you're not being paranoid?" Roger asked. "Anyway, you're carrying, right?"

Kannon nodded, wishing he could shake the feeling of being followed. "Switch with me. I'll take the aisle seat."

"I don't see how you can sit down, Dad, with all the starch in your jeans," Stefan said.

Kannon forced a chuckle.

"Try to relax," Roger said, sliding one seat over.

"Okay. Will do." Kannon glanced at Lan, who was giggling with the other two women fawning over Derrick. Despite her laughter, his wife's face showed taut worry lines.

Shake it off, Kannon. Enjoy the moment with family and friends.

Shifting focus, he listened to his brother and son. Stefan had abandoned the prosecutorial world to establish his law firm and was telling Roger ". . . I help aging entrepreneurs prepare for the disposition of their companies."

Roger, the retired accounting professor emeritus, countered by discussing the tax advantages of electing S-corporation status for shareholders in small corporations.

Lights flashed, the signal for silence. The accordion walls slid from their recessed housings, enclosing the arena. Kannon unsnapped his top shirt button and waved the program as a fan.

The curtain drew back and the squatty Pigeonaire, dressed like "Dracula," made his appearance to scattered applause. A spotlight lit up the magician's face. Ragged mustache hairs extended below his lower lip like stringy tobacco leaves hanging from a fence rail. Thick, coal-black eyebrows arched above angular eye sockets.

"Welcome to the secret world of prestidigitation and

hypnotism." The performer bowed at the waist, then straightened to welcome a female assistant dressed like a waif. "Many have entered my domain," he continued, speaking as if he had a mouthful of sand, "but not all have returned."

Stage floods switched on. The entertainer tipped his top hat. Three pigeons took flight—much to Derrick's delight—and circled the stage before disappearing behind a canvas backdrop.

"Surrender yourselves to my magic," he garbled, "and you will become as free as my flying pigeons." With that, the Pigeonaire spread his arms. Two more pigeons emerged from his coat sleeves and became airborne.

Lighting techs tracked the birds. One, disoriented, flew a haphazard pattern, only to plow into a ceiling fan above the front row.

Thunk!

Feathers fluttering, the bird dropped into a woman's lap. She screamed and flung the carcass at the magician's feet.

Lan brought her hand to her mouth. Roger and Stefan shook their heads.

"What happened?" asked Derrick, standing on his seat.

"A creature has been hurt."

"Poor bird," Belynda added.

The lights came on.

"Cleanup center stage." The startled performer scooped up the pigeon and handed it to his horrified assistant, who immediately dropped the dead pigeon. "There will be a short intermission."

During the timeout, a few patrons, disgusted looks on their faces, stalked out of the theater. Most remained in their seats. As the clamor settled down, Kannon glanced at Stefan, who appeared to be enamored with Belynda, sitting to his right. She leaned into his son's shoulder and asked, "Do you have other family?"

"Uh . . . no. I've never been married." Stefan shot Kannon a quizzical look as if asking, "What's the deal here?"

Belynda turned to Lan, so Kannon leaned across Roger and whispered to his son. "Graduated in the top ten percent of your Columbia Law School class, huh? Let's see how smart you are in handling this case."

Stefan's face turned crimson. "How old is she?" he mouthed.

180

Kannon shrugged.

Stefan frowned.

The lights dimmed. The show resumed.

The Pigeonaire's sleight-of-hand trick produced a baby rabbit from behind his ear. Next, the magician manipulated props for a classic levitation act. His female aide, lying supine on a gurney, rose and floated, remaining suspended. The magician passed a hoop over his assistant's body from head to toe. She then descended to the gurney amid enthusiastic applause.

"I want a volunteer from the audience," the performer said.

Roger raised his hand. He had always been active in school plays and local theater, Kannon recalled, which belied the standard image of an accounting professor.

"He's a wannabe entertainer," Karen said.

Roger rose and loped to the stage, towering over the magician.

Two suspended microphones descended from the rafters. The pasty-faced Pigeonaire switched off his clipped microphone.

"This ought to be good," Kannon said, smiling. The knots in his neck loosened a bit.

"What's your name?" the magician asked.

"They call me Mr. Ballard."

The magician pulled a wallet from inside his cape and opened it. "Congratulations, you correctly identified yourself." He handed the wallet back to Roger, who, with raised eyebrows, examined it himself to ensure the wallet was his, and intact, then stuffed it in his coat pocket.

"Clever," Kannon said.

"Ever been hypnotized?" the Pigeonaire asked.

As Roger shook his head, the magician proffered a spinning wheel and a pocket watch with a chain. "Staring at this wheel only makes you dizzy. And trying to read the time from a rocking timepiece makes you nauseous." He threw them both offstage. "You look intelligent," he said to Roger. "What's your profession?"

"Retired professor."

The magician turned to the audience. "Would you like to see an intelligent man act like an idiot?"

The audience erupted. "Yeah, yeah!"

"This is fun. I cannot wait to see what happens next," Lan said.

The assistant brought a stool and directed Roger to sit, facing the audience. "You are a professor of—?"

"Tax and economics."

"Professor Emeritus," Kannon shouted.

"Ooh, how exciting," the magician said, his jowl elongating like a clown's.

The audience laughed, and Roger, good-naturedly, laughed along with them. The lights dimmed. At stage center, a single large candle appeared to ignite spontaneously.

"Listen to my voice. Stare at the candle. Sleep." The Pigeonaire rattled off commands, his tone a monotonous drone.

Roger seemed transfixed by the candle. Soon, he was gone, zoned into another dimension.

"You are a ballerina. Dance."

The distinguished professor emeritus from the University of Texas bounded from the stool, reached into his rear pants pocket, retrieved his handkerchief, and stuffed it down his crotch. Then he raised his hands overhead.

"What's he doing? Stefan said.

"It's called the fifth position," Belynda said.

"How's he know what to do?" Stefan asked.

"We attend the ballet," Karen said.

"And that's a pirouette he's attempting, I think," Belynda continued. "Now it's an arabesque, and oh, my, a cabriole."

"Looks like he's trying to kick a chicken through a fence," Kannon said, wondering whether Belynda might have been a ballerina. "I hope the magician doesn't have him strip to his underwear. That would be grotesque."

"I'll never go to the ballet again," Karen said.

"Look! He's performing a demi-pointe." Belynda sniggered.

"He can't be faking," Kannon said. "No one can dance that badly."

"Dad! Eyes right," Stefan shouted.

Kannon turned his head, saw the silhouette of a man holding a semiautomatic standing against the wall. An explosion ripped through the closed theater. Another. And another. Kannon flinched, slapped his hands over his ears. Flash-bang grenades, he realized. Then a sharp report. More gunshots followed—muzzle flashes. Roger, who had been leaning forward, fell face down on the stage floor.

"My God, Roger's been hit." Kannon reached for his weapon but thought the better of it. He might be mistaken for the shooter.

Smoke grenades popped, obstructing visibility. He couldn't see the shooter.

"Roger!" Karen's contorted mouth expressed her horror.

The crowd erupted in hysterics, the tension as thick and suffocating as the smoke filling the arena. Stunned patrons either collapsed or pushed and shoved as they stumbled over each other trying to escape.

Oh, man, Roger could be bleeding to death, or already dead.

"Drop low and stay calm!" Kannon shouted. "Get the damn walls open." He might as well have been hollering into a barrel.

Kannon leaned toward Lan and handed her his handkerchief. She hunkered down at bench level, clutching Derrick to her breast. Stefan had his arm draped around Belynda. Both were kneeling, while Karen, upright, frantically tried to work her way toward the stage.

The sickly-sweet stench of smoke was overpowering. Gasping and coughing intermingled with jumbled screams. More rapid-fire shots from a semiautomatic ripped through the air. Amid the chaos, Kannon stood on a bench and tried to see the stage through the haze. "Stefan! Call nine-one-one. Then see if you can get those damn partitions open."

"On my way."

Kannon looked at Lan. She gripped his arm. "Go," she said. "We will be all right." He stared at Derrick's tender head buried in his mother's chest. His little body was shaking. Kannon leaned forward and kissed his young son on the back of his head. "Be right back, partner. Hold tight to Momma."

"Grab ahold of my belt and follow me," Kannon said to Karen.

Staying low, he crab-walked forward, Karen trailing behind, clutching his belt. The noxious fumes were nauseating. Shallow inhalations of smoke burned Kannon's throat and lungs. His eyes watered and his nose ran. He untucked his shirt and held the front tail over his nose as he wedged into the aisle cluttered with screaming patrons charging in both directions trying to escape.

A shattering crack of glass erupted, eliciting more screams. Slowly, the side walls began retracting. Cylindrical ceiling lights came on and gleamed dimly. With the receding walls and the large overhead fans whirling at high speed, the air in the arena began to clear. Kannon reached the stage and scaled it. Karen followed.

The Pigeonaire and his assistant were nowhere in sight, but Roger was, motionless, lying in a pool of blood. The man crouching at his brother's side gaped at Kannon. "No pulse."

Kannon double-checked. The man was right. No pulse.

Karen brushed Kannon aside and cradled her husband's head.

Kannon stood in disbelief. Roger was his brother, often a mentor, and a man he'd grown to love as a friend. A man respected and looked up to by all his family, peers, and countless students. He couldn't be dead. Not Roger.

Why was it then he sensed his brother's soul leaving his body?

Karen hadn't grasped the finality of the situation. After making sure the airway was clear, she placed one hand over Roger's heart and with the other pinched his nose closed. She tried to breathe into her husband the breath of life, then fingered his wrist as if his heart still beat. "It's faint, but pumping."

"Karen—" *There is no pulse.*

She stared at Kannon, her eyes wide, her face rigid in a dark look of horror. He met his sister-in-law's gape. Her almond-shaped eyes were smudged with mascara, which also ran down her cheeks, and her lips were quivering. He saw what she didn't grasp. A clean round hole spotted Roger's right temple. Scattered brain matter splotched the floor.

Kannon shook his head and squeezed Karen's shoulder. She pushed his hand away. He understood Karen now realized Roger was gone. He was her man, her friend, her lover, and she claimed the right to be alone with him at the end.

A high-pitched wail reached his ears.

"My son! My son!"

It was Lan's voice. Her tone shredded Kannon's brain as would a band saw.

Twenty-Eight

Kannon leaped from the stage, his heart thumping in his throat. Had something happened to Derrick?

He bullied his way down the aisle, barging past anyone in his way. Seemingly nonsensical words scratched through the fog of confusion. The smoke had mostly cleared, but a pungent stink hung in the dense air, burning his lungs. Reaching the exit, he emerged into a smoggy night clogged with people scrambling in all directions.

"Lan! Where are you?" Her screams rose above the cacophony, but he couldn't determine her location.

"Dad! Over here!"

Kannon stumbled into Stefan. Lan and Belynda were standing alongside. All three looked bewildered.

"Where's Derrick?"

"They took him! They took our son." Lan pounded on his chest, tears pouring down her rage-flushed cheeks. Her intense, desperate tone, the strength behind her driving fists, scared the hell out of him. She might as well have reached in and yanked out his heart. Kannon looked from Lan to Belynda, back to Lan. Their clothes were disheveled. Both women's faces appeared bruised under the diffused outdoor light.

"Are you badly hurt?" he asked, holding Lan by her shoulders, all the while scanning the crowd for signs of Derrick.

"It does not matter. We need to find our son."

"Lan and Belynda were lying on the ground by the time I got outside," Stefan interjected. He sounded defensive as if Kannon might hold him responsible.

"It's not your fault." But who was responsible? Streak? The militia? Himself? "Stefan, did you see anything?"

"No. I was helping the manager retract the walls."

Shit. If only he had told Stefan to stay with Lan, this probably wouldn't have happened.

"Lan and I had just reached the exit and could only see a few feet," Belynda said, wiping tears from her face. "Two men came out of nowhere. One struck Lan on her chin and snatched Derrick while she was falling. The other one knocked me to the ground."

Kannon's stomach knotted. Lan's chin was already turning purple. Belynda appeared shaken but unhurt. His brother shot, Lan attacked, and Derrick missing . . . all within minutes.

"No one could see a damned thing," Belynda added, brushing a wisp of hair from her face, "too much smoke."

Not what Kannon wanted to hear, but it didn't surprise him. His eyes darted about the crushed-stone parking lot. Every dark-headed young boy looked like Derrick.

"Where is my boy? Where is my boy?" Lan shouted to the stunned crowd. No one responded.

"Stefan. Call nine-one-one again. See what the hell's keeping the police. Then circle back to the stage. Karen needs support."

"Okay, Dad."

Belynda, huddling close, cut her eyes from Kannon to Lan, as if uncertain what to do.

"Stay with Lan," Kannon told her "I—"

"Sir."

A tall young man approached Kannon. Sweat dripped from his stained shirt. His cheeks were taut, and his eyes, like smoldering embers, brimmed red from the smoke.

"Sir, my name is Sasha," he said, gasping for breath. "I'm the director of the Pigeonaire's Magika. I was upstairs in the balcony monitoring the show when all this started. One of the patrons told me your son is missing."

"Yes! Tell me what you saw."

"When the man collapsed on stage, I assumed he'd been shot, but I didn't see who might've done it. Fighting the smoke, I ran to the controls to retract the side-sliding walls—"

"For God's sake, man, get to the point!" Kannon realized he'd upset the kid. "Sorry, go on."

"I glanced through an upper window and noticed a couple of guys running away," Sasha added. "One of them was holding what might've been a young boy."

"Which direction?"

"Across the parking lot into the cedar grove," Sasha said, pointing east. "I lost sight of them in the trees."

"Lan—"

"Go," she said as if anticipating Kannon's decision.

Just as he turned to sprint after the attackers, shrieking sirens assailed his eardrums. Two Williamson County Sheriff's Department vehicles, as well as an ambulance, arrived, followed by two fire trucks. The county cruisers skidded to a stop. Deputies emerged from their vehicles like bats winging from a cave.

"You guys tell the deputies what's happening," Kannon said over his shoulder.

"Hold it, sir."

One of the deputies.

"Come on." Kannon boiled in frustration. "Someone's taken our son." He pointed in the direction indicated by Sasha. "Surround the area. Set up roadblocks."

"We'll take care of the procedures, sir." The deputy's hand rested on the butt of his holstered pistol, while his partner moved toward Kannon. "I'm Sergeant Creighton, and this is Detective Hollister. Criminal Investigation Division. No one's going anywhere till we get a handle on what's happening."

Sergeant Creighton whipped out a cellphone, punched one number, and spoke into the device. Another deputy shouted into a bullhorn and told the remaining patrons to stay put. One cruiser blocked the parking lot exit, another the road leading into the theater. Several firefighters rushed inside the arena to investigate. The structure didn't appear to be on fire.

Kannon noticed Detective Hollister had taken a position between him and the woods.

"Two men grabbed our boy," Lan said, her voice raw with frustration.

"Where were you, ma'am?" the sergeant said to Belynda.

"With her . . . there!" Belynda pointed toward the theater's entrance.

"And you, sir?" the sergeant motioned another team to come forward.

"Inside the theater," Kannon shouted. "You're wasting time. My brother was shot. Our son—"

"Was taken from my arms," Lan interjected, looking

187

incredulous.

"You're sure about this?" Creighton intervened. "Your boy was taken? He didn't wander off somewhere, go to the restroom?"

In this melee?

"No!" Lan said.

Creighton directed the third team of deputies to enter the arena, coordinate with the firefighters, and assess the situation.

Fuck this.

Kannon pivoted, tore off in the direction indicated by Sasha, but Hollister leg-whipped him and sent Kannon flying to the ground. The deputy planted his knee in Kannon's back, grabbed his right arm, and twisted it behind him. "I'll slap the cuffs on you if you don't settle down."

"For Christ's sake."

"I've already placed Unit Five on the other side of the ridge," Creighton said. "You'll likely get yourself killed if you go charging around."

The deputy was right. Kannon knew better than to go off half-cocked. He was letting his emotions get the better of him and never would have led a combat patrol that way. It was a good way to find yourself targeted in the crosshairs of an AK47.

"Okay, I'm cool," he said. "I'll cooperate." Sergeant Creighton released his grip and helped him up. Kannon's jacket was unfastened. Pieces of crushed stone clung to his sweat-drenched shirt. The deputy brushed them off . . . and noticed the bulge.

"Sir, are you carrying?"

Shit! He'd forgotten about the 9mil inside his jacket. "I have a concealed-carry permit, Officer."

"Using your left hand, remove your wallet and show the license."

Kannon did.

"You're rattled, sir. Don't need to be carrying right now. Reach inside your jacket and remove your weapon. Two fingers."

Acknowledging the futility of resistance, Kannon merely said, "All right."

The circle of onlookers swelled and edged closer.

"Lock him up," one of them said.

"Asshole," said another.

A woman spat on him.

"Step back," Creighton ordered the crowd.

Some did. Some didn't . . . but Kannon, Lan, and Belynda remained center attractions in this bizarre circus.

Where was Stefan?

"Hollister. See if Unit Five has located any suspects or witnesses across the ridge."

Creighton turned to the three of them. "We received several nine-one-ones. Most were about the disturbance here. Another reported seeing two men throw a child into a vehicle and speed off," he cocked his head to the right, "on the other side of the ridge there. We didn't know if there was a connection. It now appears there is."

Kannon had wondered how the sheriff's department knew to post a unit opposite the ridge, which lay beyond his vision. Now he understood.

"Did they get a license number or description of the car?" Lan asked.

"It was a late model pickup."

Damnit! Kannon remembered he'd cut off Streak from describing what the two militiamen were driving. Could it be the same vehicle, the single-headlight pickup truck he'd noticed earlier? If it was from Border Slot, Streak might've known the license plate number.

"Unit Five reports negative," Hollister said. "Whoever placed that nine-one-one call wasn't around. There's a service station at the corner. I've dispatched deputies to question attendants and customers there."

"Hope one of 'em speaks up," Creighton said under his breath. *For God's sake, please let there be witnesses.*

Another sheriff's cruiser drove up. Two additional deputies exited and headed their way.

Creighton motioned them over. Kannon assumed he was briefing them on the situation. Their conversation turned animated. What the hell were they talking about? Kannon moved in to listen, but the deputies waved him off. This was crap. God, he hoped those guys were competent. Regardless, he was already thinking about what he must do on his own.

Creighton borrowed the bullhorn and spoke to the crowd. "Folks, we'll want to talk to all of you. Please accompany these deputies," he nodded to the new guys, "to the illuminated corner of the parking lot."

The newly arrived deputies herded the others as instructed.

Another deputy brought Sasha and Belynda forward.

"Tell Sergeant Creighton what you told us," Kannon said. The kid's tendons in his neck were like corded rope, his muscles accentuated by a tight-fitting shirt.

Sasha raised his eyebrows as if to question who was in charge. Creighton nodded his okay and flipped to a blank page on an official-looking notebook. Sasha repeated what he'd told Kannon and Lan earlier, adding he saw the two men toss a young kid over a low picket fence, hurdle it, and then vanish inside a thick grove of cedar trees.

"Son," Creighton said, "Describe these men best you can."

As Sasha spoke, his eyes closed as if to recollect the images.

Lan, her face rigid, stared hard toward the cedars.

What thoughts were running through her mind? Was she cycling through the loss of her Vietnamese family, worrying in desperation whether her son might be added to the list? Was she blaming him?

"The air was clogged with smoke," Kannon heard Sasha saying. "One guy, the shorter one, was maybe five feet six to five feet eight, really stocky. His face looked kind of like a boxer's, you know, flattened nose and all."

"Hair?" Creighton said.

"Buzzcut."

"What about the other guy?" Creighton flipped to another page in his notebook.

"He had red hair . . . mustache. He was taller, probably over six feet. Oh, his cheek bulged out—"

"Like chewing tobacco? Gum?"

Sasha nodded. The kid seemed more collected and coherent now than when first describing the situation to Kannon. But he'd heard enough. Trembling, he leaned against a lamppost for support. The depiction of the two kidnappers' height and physique fit Streak's earlier descriptions of the Border Slot men called Whitehead and Bull.

"Can you describe what the two men were wearing?" Hollister asked.

"It happened so fast," Sasha said. "Both wore dark clothes, maybe green or black."

Hollister nodded. "Anything else?"

"No, sir," Sasha said.

"Both wore boots," Belynda interjected.

"Cowboy, combat?" said Creighton.

"I think . . . a lug-type sole," Belynda said.

Half the people in Texas wore boots, Kannon thought. But those guys were probably wearing combat boots. Belynda's observation was helpful, though. The type sole could help in tracking the kidnappers if that came into play.

"Dawkins and Heathcote are here," Hollister said, "from the service station."

"Unit Five," Creighton said to Kannon and Lan, and then to the newly arrived deputies, "Any luck at the service station?"

Wearing grim expressions, both shook their heads.

"From here the terrain slopes down to the road that borders the service station, roughly two hundred yards distant," a deputy from Unit Five said. "A well-worn trail zigzags through a wooded area. The ground is damp. Footprints everywhere."

"Lug-type?" asked Hollister.

"Couldn't tell. All meshed together," a Unit Five deputy said.

So much for a useful clue.

In tandem, the Unit Five men turned to go. One guy stopped after three paces and pivoted. "Sir, is this a NIMS situation?"

Kannon understood he was referring to the National Incident Management System established under the Department of Homeland Security.

Sergeant Creighton shook his head. "Not necessary, not yet."

How much time had passed since the shooting . . . twenty-five, thirty minutes? Maybe there was still time to locate Derrick before the bastards vacated the area. "If you'd get off your asses—"

The deputies glared at Kannon.

"Your tone is unnecessary, sir." Hollister's face reddened.

"It's not going to help get your son back. We're doing what we can. We'll keep you posted."

Kannon dug his fingernails into his palms. Aggravated, he didn't like being hamstrung by the County Sheriff's Department. But then Hollister placed his arm on his shoulder. The action comforted Kannon. It was unfair to judge these guys, deputy sheriffs just doing their jobs.

Still, based upon Streak's input about Border Slot, Kannon didn't think the sheriff's department had much chance of finding Derrick. Another thought made him feel worse. If only SyncTrak had developed a suitable tracking device for children. It was a bitter, haunting irony.

I need a plan.

Step one: Put a stop order on his twenty-five K check. Have his banker arrange to stall Streak until Kannon arrived. If necessary, he'd torture him to reveal more detail about the militia group, including its coordinates.

Step two: Prepare Lan to manage the home front.

"Get a description of the boy," Creighton told Hollister. "Then activate an Amber Alert. Ensure they notify the surrounding counties, especially Travis County since we're close to the county line."

"What else will be done?" Kannon asked Creighton.

"The Texas Department of Public Safety will issue the alert. We'll notify the FBI as well."

Kannon overheard Sergeant Creighton place a radio call to his Division Commander, probably to work the case up the chain to the Sheriff. If the Sheriff added two plus two—Detective Clarke's house call regarding Streak's "break-in" and Sergeant Creighton's investigation here—well, he hoped the Patrol Division and CID communicated like the myriad US intelligence agencies did—inefficiently.

In reality, he needed to allow for the likelihood that the sheriff's department would connect the dots and piece together the intrusion at Kannon's home with Derrick's disappearance.

Hollister took Lan aside and questioned her out of earshot. Kannon guessed their purpose was to see how the stories matched up. *Damn!* He should've warned her not to reveal anything about the assault on Streak, the Border Slot Militia, her threatened immigration status, much less mention Sindy Zeller, whoever she was. Those were connections he didn't want the authorities to know about just now. If anything, revealing all that crap would hinder, not help, in Derrick's recovery.

Sounds drifted past. Somehow, through the miasma, Kannon deciphered his wife's words. "Derrick is about forty inches tall, has on a cowboy outfit like my husband's, and his hair is curly and black, with a streak of brown. Oh, and his skin color is just like mine. Here is a photograph."

"That's good, ma'am. Thank you. What does your son call you?" Creighton asked.

"Mama Lan."

"And your husband?"

"Daddy K."

Sergeant Creighton spoke into his shoulder-mounted radio mic, grew silent, cocked an ear to listen, and then faced Kannon. "They're bringing out your brother, sir."

Spinning around, Kannon saw two EMTs wheeling a gurney out the front entrance and across the parking lot. It was something he didn't want to see. Stefan preceded the stretcher, with Karen at his side. Her face was so wretched in pain Kannon barely recognized her.

Roger's body was encased in a body bag.

The rear doors of the EMS vehicle opened, and EMTs rolled the gurney inside. Karen was the only other person allowed to accompany Roger. As the horror of his brother's death and Derrick's abduction sank in, Kannon deflated. It was as if a giant vacuum had sucked all the oxygen from the atmosphere.

I'm responsible for this. Derrick. Lan's incredible suffering. A dead brother. Karen, now a widow.

Kannon's eyes locked onto the emergency unit departing the area. Inside was his brother's lifeless body. Inside was a grieving widow who must be asking herself a thousand questions. How in hell would he answer them? Once again, even though he had started out trying to renew a friendship, he saw his life and those lives closest to him blown apart.

Step three: Get the hell out of Dodge.

Twenty-Nine

Lan, now free of Hollister, reached Kannon's side. She seemed stoic until she noticed the gurney and Kannon told her who was on it.

"Oh, my God. Why would anyone shoot Roger?" Lan asked, slumping against him.

"I think the militia believed it was me on the stage," Kannon said, pulling her close.

A double loss, Kannon thought. Lan looked up to Roger as if he were her big brother. He was gone and there was nothing Kannon could do about it. How much more could she take? How much more could he take?

Hold it together, Kannon. Focus on finding Derrick.

"And our boy," Lan clutched the lapels of Kannon's jeans jacket, "what will they do to our boy?"

"I don't know." Ransom, revenge, slavery—these were the horrible fears running through his mind. "But I will get him back."

"You must." She relaxed her grip.

Kannon whispered to Lan about handling the home front because he planned not to be there when the authorities arrived to set up a command post.

Sergeant Creighton and Detective Hollister, who had been conversing with Stefan and Belynda, returned. "Sir, ma'am. Do you know why anyone would want to harm your family? Kill your brother? Take your son?" It was Hollister who spoke.

Kannon clenched his jaw. If he answered differently than Lan had, they would both find themselves at sheriff headquarters replying to a barrage of unwanted questions. Kannon didn't like the possible consequences. "The only thing I can think of," he said to the deputies, "is we're relatively wealthy. Maybe this is a ransom deal."

Creighton's brow furrowed.

Hollister spoke again. "You're sure? No enemies from the past? Soured business deals?"

Kannon hesitated before answering. "None I can think of."

"Scorned exes? Affairs?" Creighton's brow remained

furrowed.

"Come on," Lan said. "We are a loving family. There has been no unfaithfulness. You are wasting time—"

"They need to do this, honey," Kannon said, wanting to reassure her.

"I don't believe this was a random attack," Creighton said. "If you've answered our questions honestly, I believe the perps targeted you guys . . . for ransom I suspect."

Or revenge.

"We'll want to monitor your cell and landline calls," Creighton continued, "in case the abductors call."

"Of course." Kannon expected they would set up a task force, with the FBI at the helm, using his house as the listening post. What the authorities didn't need to know about was his satellite phone.

Hollister took Creighton by the arm. The two of them stepped away, but not so far Kannon couldn't overhear the conversation. "It doesn't make sense," Hollister said. "This was no simple kidnapping. If so, why kill the guy on the stage? He posed no harm."

"I agree," Creighton said.

"Stefan Ballard and Belynda Blu said the brothers looked alike." Hollister doffed his cap. "What if this was a case of mistaken identity?"

"Or worse," Creighton motioned toward Kannon. "What if one brother had reason to kill the other!"

The conversation trailed off. Did the deputies want him to overhear this? Kannon perceived the focus shifting to a different track. He whispered to Lan, "When Hollister questioned you a while ago, what did he ask?"

Lan recited the same basic questions the deputies had asked him. Understandable. After all, who were the most likely suspects in a child's disappearance? Family. Her answers had been similar to Kannon's. Were they easier on her because she was the mother? If so, maybe it was because they believed Kannon had orchestrated the whole thing. In a bizarre sort of way—agreeing to help Streak—he had.

"They're muddying the water," Kannon said to Lan while eyeballing Creighton and Hollister.

"I do not think it can get any muddier."

Several theatergoers, all ambulatory, were being herded toward ambulances, likely due to smoke inhalation. Stefan and Belynda, each leaning against a cedar tree and holding a bottle of water, wore perplexed looks, made macabre by the flashing red and blue lights cast by the patrol cars. Kannon motioned for them to come forward.

"This is a nightmare," Stefan said.

"How could this happen here?" Lan stepped away from Kannon, her look of anguish deepening his agony. "I wish I had never come to America."

Kannon gaped at her, stunned. He never would've expected her to react like this.

"Lan, you don't mean that," Belynda said.

In Việt Nam, he had seen Lan remain calm while under fire. But now her son was missing. Kannon grasped his wife's shoulders and spoke in a soft but firm voice. "Get hold of yourself."

Lan gripped his upper arms, her nails digging in like pincers. Her eyes widened as if expecting an explanation. Kannon wished he could give her one.

"I am sorry," she said in a choked voice. "I did not mean what I said . . . about coming to America."

"I know you didn't."

"If anyone can find Derrick, it is you."

"And I will."

Belynda steered Lan by the elbow to a nearby wooden bench.

Speaking to Stefan, Kannon said, "This is all my fault. I triggered this disaster by setting in motion a stream of uncontrollable events."

"Self-recrimination isn't going to do any good now, Dad."

"I know. It's just . . . if only I hadn't gone to Lost Maples."

"Belynda told me about it," Stefan said, cuffing Kannon on the shoulder. "You had no idea."

"No." Kannon stared at Stefan, whose eyes were still bloodshot from the smoke. "But my effort resulted in some vicious bastards abducting my son and killing my brother."

"From what Belynda told me, there's a lot more to this story than what you've told the deputies," Stefan said.

"The less you know, the better." Kannon turned away and approached Creighton and Hollister. "Since things have calmed down a bit, would you mind returning my pistol?"

The two deputies stared at each other. It was like they were conversing through telepathy. "All right," Creighton finally said. "Can't see any harm in it.?"

Hollister frowned.

Kannon took the pistol and slipped it inside his jacket. "Thanks."

The two women returned as the deputies moved away. Lan took Kannon's hand in hers. "I know you are hurting too."

"The anguish on your face says it all," Belynda added.

Kannon's jaw quivered, but he managed to hold back the tears.

"Dad, you need to take charge as you have in the past."

Kannon tapped his temple. "A plan is forming. I'm—"

"Call my nephew," Lan said unexpectedly.

"Do you think Đăng Đạo will help?"

"I do," Lan said. The lines in her face softened a bit.

Stefan looked puzzled. "The guy who put a bullet in your shoulder? The gang leader?"

Lan shook her head. "Đăng Đạo is no longer a gang leader. He has come clean."

Kannon gazed skyward. Clusters of stars shone through the thinned-out smoke. A banana-clipped moon glowed like polished brass.

My nephew by marriage and a former adversary could soon become my comrade. If Đăng Đạo agrees to help, he would be a tremendous asset.

As his thoughts shifted into combat mode, Kannon resolved to put aside their differences.

Step four: Assemble a team.

Thirty

Saturday Night, 24 October 2009, Border Slot Montana

Crandle gathered his men around the campfire for an impromptu meeting. He handed out an ice-cold beer to each man, then bit off the end of a Rocky Patel Churchill cigar and lit it.

"You men been studying your instruction packets?"

"Yes, sir," Nolan said. The others nodded.

"Have you cashed out your institutional-based assets as instructed?" Crandle asked, puffing away.

The men exchanged guilty looks.

"This isn't bullshit. Get it done. ASAP."

Yes, sirs buzzed around like a daisy chain.

"Whitehead's going to test you on EMP weaponry when he returns," Crandle said.

"Have you heard from him, Commander?" Timmons asked.

"No sitrep yet," Crandle said.

"Sir, why not just write Streak off and get another pilot?" Garrett asked.

"Not enough time to break one in, and I have no intention to delay our EMP attack. If necessary, I'll fly the chopper for the airdrop segment."

Badger rose from his stool and belched. "About this airdrop, Commander, can you give us a little more detail on what to expect?"

"Garrett will assist me on the airdrop."

"Damn, Garrett, you been hiding this from us?" Nolan asked.

Crandle nodded to Garett, who said, "All I can tell you is that a device much larger than the one Whitehead demonstrated at our meeting last Wednesday will be released from the chopper. It will be detonated using an altitude-based timing trigger. The destruction zone will be greater."

"What kind of guidance system?" Badger asked.

"Good question," Crandle answered. "We'll integrate GPS coordinates with a laser-guided delivery system."

"Then, why the ground assaults?" Hatfield asked.

"Because I want men on the ground to report on the weapons' impact. Also, in case something goes awry with the airdrop, we'll still have the attacks on the power stations. All bases covered."

"Simultaneous assaults?" Porter asked.

"No," Crandle said. "Ground attack first . . . to determine what's taken out from the initial blasts. The airdrop will occur ten minutes later."

"Wow," said Badger.

"Synchronization is critical," Crandle added. "Another thing," he said, tapping his wristwatch, "use manually wound watches. Any other questions?"

"Got one," McAfee said. "What if electronic equipment isn't operating or is turned off during the attack? Will that gear be affected?"

"Should," Crandle said. "The jacked-up power melts telephone lines, surges through electrical lines, resulting in fried circuits, computers, auto engines, communication systems. The damage to electronics may be irreparable, whether they're on or off."

They repeated the Border Slot Pledge. Then, "Dismissed," Crandle said.

Crandle returned to his cabin, entered the bedroom, and locked the door. Inside his ham shack, he activated his radio set and accessed several channels for any street-based intelligence that might indicate his operation was in harm's way. No negative intel was transmitted.

Bored, he opened his wall safe and counted his money. It was all there—one million bucks. Crandle decided to perform a status check on his underground command bunker complex. Only Whitehead knew of its existence.

Hurrying along the tunnel, Crandle considered moving the vault from the armory to the bunker. His fifteen million might be safer there.

Thirty-One

Saturday Night, 24 October 2009, Northwest of Austin, Texas Hill Country

Keeping Border Slot's pickup within sight, Streak shifted into fourth gear and twisted the throttle on his battered V-Rod. Twenty minutes had passed since Whitehead and Bull snatched Kannon's boy.

The skies were clear, the pavement dry. Amid traffic in the dark, Streak counted on it being difficult for the militiamen to tell who, if anyone, was following.

Streak patted his inside jacket pocket, which burned from Kannon's twenty-five K check. Unable to cash it till the banks opened Monday morning, it would've been easier for him to lay low, but he wanted payback against Whitehead and Bull, along with saving Kannon's kid.

If the opportunity arose—he was carrying his Luger recovered from the attempted rape site—he'd kill the two militiamen, stash the boy in a safe place, like a church, cash Kannon's check, and run.

After crashing into Kannon's front door, Streak had hoped the deputies' arrival with lights flashing and sirens blaring would've scared off the two militiamen. But those guys didn't scare easily. Instead, they were the type to execute a strategic withdrawal, only to regroup, which was why he had camped across the highway from Kannon's place and kept watch.

Later, having observed Kannon's Cherokee pull out from his drive, only to be followed by a one-beamed pickup truck, Streak saw trouble brewing. With no time to pack, he'd jacked his scoot into action and joined the pursuit. When he attempted to overtake both vehicles and warn Kannon, the Border Slot vehicle smacked into a deer. Avoiding the carcass, Streak nearly high-sided into a crash and backed away.

When Kannon stopped to pick up the woman—the same one who had confronted him at Ballard's residence—Streak figured the militiamen were huddling nearby. Not only fearful of being caught

200

again, Streak also didn't want to trigger a firefight. So, he'd kept trailing them, only to park alongside the same road as Whitehead's truck. By the time he worked up the nerve to ride to the theater and alert Kannon, the V-Rod wouldn't start. Minutes later, explosions blasted into the night. He finally got the bike running and was about to ride off when he saw the two militiamen crash through the brush carrying Kannon's kid.

Now, Border Slot's pickup turned onto Highway 183, heading north. Streak downshifted and did the same, not knowing how familiar the militiamen were with the territory. The vehicle kept within the speed limits, avoiding attention. At a stoplight, Streak maintained distance and positioned his bike to the right rear of an eighteen-wheeler. Taking advantage of the break, he removed a handkerchief from his pocket and used it to wipe his glasses, then tied the bandana around his neck.

He altered his riding position, trying to lessen the pressure on his butt. The muffler burn hurt like hell.

The light changed. Streak eased into first gear, using the truck for concealment. The farther he traveled from city lights, the stars shone brighter, and the air turned colder. His hair streamed in the wind, and his cheeks stung from the chill.

Streak glanced at the gas gauge. The needle edged near empty. He hoped they would stop before he ran out. Come on, guys, stop, he implored to God, if there was a God.

Guilt, wherever it was coming from, kept nipping at his conscience. He couldn't imagine the horror the kidnapped boy was feeling, much less the angst Kannon and his wife were suffering.

They passed through upscale Cedar Park and newly revitalized Leander. Running through the gears to maintain pace, Streak shifted into fifth. Up ahead, the eighteen-wheeler slowed as several vehicles exited from Highway 183 and traffic continued to thin out. Streak changed lane position and eased past the slow-moving truck.

Would Whitehead or Bull notice the single trailing headlight and become suspicious? Streak wondered whether they were heading toward the Fort Hood area, where he knew Whitehead maintained contact with a small nest of disaffected U.S. Army veterans.

Border Slot was composed of desperate men who had crossed beyond the line of reason and become vessels of destruction. On the surface, there appeared to be no rhyme or reason to their butchery. But, like all terrorist organizations, their objective was not to build or revolutionize, but to destroy, instilling fear and chaos. One effective method of ensuring compliance among its members was to assassinate family and associates of any would-be defector.

I am a defector. Kannon and his son are by default acceptable collateral damage to Border Slot.

Streak tapped the fuel gauge, hoping the needle was stuck and that a tap would advance the indicator. No luck. In the distance, brake lights flashed as the militants veered northwest onto Highway 29, away from Fort Hood, toward Burnet, and picked up speed. My God, were they returning to Kannon's place?

Streak eyeballed his instrument panel. The low fuel light lit up.

Estimating fuel to last for only another twenty to thirty miles, Streak began losing hope. He could overtake the pair, but then what? You can't curb a pickup with a motorcycle. And having to maintain throttle control with his right hand, he couldn't shoot accurately with his left. It was too awkward. Besides, the kid might die in a crash.

Whitehead and Bull passed Kannon's drive. Thirteen miles later, they turned north again onto an unpaved farm-to-market road. Streak downshifted and widened the distance. When he could no longer see their taillights, he turned onto the same rural road. Were they going to Ft. Hood after all?

The temperature dropped noticeably, and the sweet smell of cottonwoods indicated a nearby creek. Bordered by mesquite trees, the backroad was composed of deep, fine-grained sand, mud, and ruts. Not good.

The road forked. Unsure which prong to follow, Streak counter-steered to the right. The V-Rod wobbled but stayed upright.

His headlight beam picked up a settling dust plume. He stood on the footpegs to increase traction and twisted the throttle to increase speed, but the pickup remained out of sight. Regardless, it would soon become evident to Whitehead and Bull, if it wasn't already, someone was tailing them. Maybe they had already careened to a stop and set up an ambush. Streak wished he had rigged a switch to turn off the permanent-running headlight.

Clouds gathered overhead. Streak gnashed his teeth, frustrated for having a depleted satphone, which was difficult to charge without power during a night in the woods.

The porous sand clogging the road deepened. A gust of wind whipped up fine-grained grit and irritated his eyes. Five minutes later, slip-sliding at thirty miles per hour, he still hadn't sighted the vehicle. Even the dust plume was gone. Maintaining his stance on the footpegs while gripping the throttle, Streak grabbed his handkerchief with his left hand and tried to wipe the grit out of his eyes.

"Ow!" Instead, he'd rubbed grit into one eye and knocked off his glasses. Now the damn engine was sputtering, losing power. The front wheel slithered violently. A panic-squeeze on the front brake lever sent him vaulting over the handlebars.

He landed hard. The V-Rod flopped to the ground, its powerful engine convulsing its last.

Streak swore.

Encrusted with sand, he lay on his back in the road and gasped for breath. His head hurt, but the loamy surface had cushioned his fall. He didn't think any bones were broken.

If I could just do something right.

Above, the gathering clouds, backlit by moonlight, raced across the sky. Streak lay still a few more moments, then rolled over and attempted to stand. Colors whirled in his head like spinning kaleidoscopes. Refracted starlight danced like discordant lasers until the shimmering stars faded to black.

Thirty-Two

Hearing unintelligible words, Streak opened his eyes and rolled to his side. Two ill-defined hunks hovered above him. *It can't be!* His leg muscles spasmed. His throat constricted. Whitehead and Bull stared down, ready to masticate his body into human chum. Was he in the middle of Crandle's death field?

A hand grasped his shoulder.

"Get off me!" Streak shouted.

"Hey, buddy," one guy said. "Are you all right?"

"Chill, man. We're trying to help you," said a second voice.

"What?" Streak shook his head, blinked. No one was yelling or kicking the crap out of him. No one was shoving him over the seat of a motorcycle.

Men, vegetation, and mechanical shapes slowly came into focus. These guys weren't militiamen.

Thank God.

Streak shuddered again, this time from the chill of a strong wind that roiled the sandy road and buffeted the oaks and cottonwoods. The breeze also carried a smell like rotting garbage.

Jesus. It was himself, unwashed and covered with grime.

"Have some water," one of the guys said, extending a canteen. The other dude handed over Streak's glasses, still intact. After slipping them on, he dug his elbow into the gritty road surface and rose to his knees. His right side hurt. His head spun like a kid's after riding a tilt-a-whirl. Accepting the canteen, Streak unscrewed the cap and tilted the container to his lips.

"Small sips," said one of the guys.

Streak nodded. He drank slowly, then gathered his strength and stood. "Man, this tastes good." He took several more swallows and then returned the canteen. "Thanks."

"No problem."

The two young men helped steady him. Freshly shaven, they looked like twins—ruddy, in their late teens or early twenties. The twins, standing over six feet tall, wore military-style haircuts. Each was bulked up. They carried a seasoned air that belied their years.

Streak wondered if the twins were serving in the Army or Marines.

"What day is it?" Streak asked, brushing himself off.

"Early Sunday morning," one of 'em said, his hand supporting Streak.

"Man, I've been out all night?"

"If you crashed last night, yeah. You're lucky this road is lightly traveled, else you'd likely have tread marks across your body."

"You got that right." Streak observed the twins' padded riding gear, the type dirt bikers wore. One suit was white with blue lightning flashes slashed across the front, while the other's outfit blazed green and gold. Nearby was their pickup, with dirt bikes racked in the cargo bed.

"What happened?" Blue on White asked.

"Don't know, exactly. I was looking for a couple of buddies of mine who're camping." Streak shuffled his feet as in "Aw, shucks."

"I must've taken the wrong road."

"Not the brightest thing to do at night," Green and Gold said. "Ever think about wearing a helmet?"

"I am now."

Heavy gray clouds patched a bluish sky. Purple haze shaded the eastern horizon, and a rippling creek ran alongside a stand of cottonwoods.

"Your motorcycle's beat to shit," Green and Gold said.

His V-Rod lay crapped on its side like a dead horse.

"Let's check this baby out," Blue on White said, heading toward the downed cycle. The twins righted the V-Rod and propped the six-hundred-pounder on its side stand. They examined the forks, the steering column, the undercarriage, and how well the tires beaded to their rims. "Lots of dings, no structural damage though."

"That's a relief." Streak asked for the canteen again and drank some more water. The remaining cobwebs washed out of his head. "How about the radiator?"

Green and Gold knelt, probed, gave a thumbs-up. "Let's see if you've got power."

His brother found the key in its slot on the right side below the seat, gave the key a turn, and pushed the starter. "You have power. No gas."

"I ran out just as I hit deep sand on the curve."

"We've got two full Jerry cans," Blue on White said. "You know, the ones with the donkey-dick spouts. A couple of gallons should get you going." The twin jogged to the pickup.

"Much obliged," Streak said. The use of military jargon for five-gallon containers brought a much-needed smile.

After gassing up the V-Rod, Blue on White put the bike in neutral, again turned the key, and hit the ignition switch. The motorcycle sputtered to life and settled into a resonant, ear-catching, rumble.

"Are you okay to ride?" Green and Gold asked.

Streak flexed his arms and legs, rotated his neck side-to-side. At least all his bones were in place. "I am."

"Then you're good to go."

"Thanks again." Streak straddled the seat and watched as the twins got in their pickup and drove off.

Up the road, the tree line gave way to scrub brush and wispy mesquite. Then the meandering route lost itself in the rolling hills. It was in that direction a young boy was being transported to hell, either in the Ft. Hood area or at Border Slot. Streak could etch another failure on his hitching post.

The temperature was dropping. It looked like rain.

Appropriate, he thought, for a thunderstorm to fall on his wretched soul. Ten miles down the road raindrops blotted his glasses. The air grew heavier, as did the weight of his conscience.

I tried to save the boy. Nothing more I can do. All I need now is to wait another day, cash Kannon's check.

Streak shifted into gear and turned toward Austin. He needed to find a place to hole up for the night before going to the bank the next morning. Riding on, he reached an intersection, catching pavement just as thunder cracked and lightning flashed. Streak tightened his grip on the handlebars. Blood rushed to his face, and he rode with downcast eyes, unable to shake off the guilt. He deserved every punishment Heaven could throw.

Another flash of lightning . . . the strike cleaved loose a new fear. What if Kannon put a stop order on the check?

Thirty-Three

Streak decided he needed a place to think. Years ago, when married, he and his wife had visited a lush park in Austin. What was the name of that place? He drummed his fingers on the handgrips. Steady rain hammered the pavement. Despite the outward appearance of his motorcycle, its parts were holding firm and the engine was running smoothly. Thanks to Kannon, he needn't worry about a tracking device stuck to the bottom of his mount.

His mind closed on the name. Barton Springs, yeah, that was it, an excellent place to hash it out.

He pulled over to the shoulder and stopped. Trying to shield himself from the crappy conditions, Streak reached back and opened the right saddlebag. He retrieved an Austin area map and examined it. Located between Lake Austin and Town Lake, Barton Springs lay south of the road bisecting Zilker Park. He put away the map and headed in that direction. Since it was Sunday, traffic was light. Even better, the rain had stopped.

At I-35, he raced south, then traveled tree-lined avenues until reaching Barton Springs Road. At the park entrance, he forked over the admission fee. Inside the park, a miniature train filled with kids and doting parents rolled along the narrow rails. Picnickers were sprawled on blankets next to baskets of food. Yips and yells echoed off the limestone cliff bordering one side of the Barton Springs pool, which maintained a constant sixty-eight-degree temperature due to its underground source.

Spying a concession stand, Streak sauntered over and purchased a sandwich and drink. He sat on a bench among spreading oaks and pecan trees. As he munched on a ham and cheese sandwich and sipped from his can of Coke, words of "Push me again, daddy," emanated from the playground.

The sensory input drew Streak back to his childhood home in Wallins Creek, Kentucky, a small, safe harbor town alongside the Cumberland River. Buried in nostalgia, he bowed his head and thought about the two young men who had stopped to help him earlier this morning. A feeling of warmth flowed through him.

There are good people in the world, and I haven't been one of them.

Sounds of laughter caught his attention. Little boys and girls wearing coats ran across the open ground, chasing each other, playing tag, giggling. Streak watched as one boy separated from the pack and raced toward him.

"Hi, mister," the kid said.

"Back to you," Streak said.

The kid stuffed his hands into his pockets. "Why are you sitting by yourself? Don't you have a family?"

The question stung. *Got no family. Got no friends.*

"Raul! Come back here. You know you're not supposed to talk to strangers."

Streak looked up. Must be the boy's mother, he thought. Yeah, he was a stranger all right, a stranger to himself.

The boy started to leave but stopped and removed his fisted right hand from his pants pocket. Approaching Streak, he slowly unclenched and revealed one red melting "M & M."

"Would you like it?" the boy said.

Despite himself, Streak smiled. He took the "M & M" and placed it in his mouth. "Thank you."

The boy turned and ran off, but his youthful innocence stayed with Streak. He had found his answer. Sick of his cowardice, he wanted his humanity back.

Thirty-Four

Sunday, 25 October 2009, One Day Post Kidnapping, Texas Hill Country

Steady rainfall fell from a military-gray sky and pinged the windshield during Kannon's drive home. The temperature was forty-two degrees, unusually cold for this time of year. His palms were moist, his heartbeat rapid, as if piranha were snapping at his core. Kannon wished the last twenty-four hours could be erased. Roger's death. Derrick's kidnapping. Would Lan ever forgive him for what was happening to their son?

Kannon stole another glance at his wife, who lay collapsed in the passenger seat like a crumpled doll. She had been that way since they had been turned away at the medical examiner's office in Travis County where an autopsy on Roger's body was scheduled.

Clearly exhausted, Lan had agreed to pop a mild sedative. And he was tired too, too tired to turn off the unpleasant encounter with Karen outside the MEO.

"I don't want you here, anyway," his sister-in-law had said, pouring salt on his wounds. At first, he thought Karen just wanted to be alone with her deceased husband. Yet, when Kannon again tried to console her, she held up her palm. "I don't need your *help*." As he turned to go, she added, "Trouble follows you, Kannon."

Her words, spoken in a slicing tone, cut like a hot knife and couldn't be unheard. Nor could the image of Karen's face be unseen. She had aged ten years. The depth of his sister-in-law's grief was beyond his comprehension. There was nothing Kannon could do or say to apologize even partially for his death.

Lan stirred, stretched. "I am not sure what is worse, the nightmares or the reality." She grabbed a handkerchief from her purse, moistened it from a water bottle, and dabbed her cheeks.

"Both are horrible." Kannon stole a glance at her drawn face. "Are you sure you can handle the authorities alone?"

Lan released a sigh, not one of resignation but frustration. "I will not be alone. Belynda will be with me."

Understanding her friend's presence would comfort Lan, Kannon worried Belynda might inadvertently reveal details that would prompt the sheriff's department or the FBI to push the investigation in a direction he didn't want it to go.

"I'd like for Stefan to stay here too."

Lan nodded.

Kannon had already asked him. Stefan readily agreed.

"We need to work together," he said, "and keep our stories straight."

Lan didn't respond, which pained him. Instead, her eyes glazed into that thousand-yard stare, the kind veterans often displayed after prolonged exposure to combat. He, too, was hurting and wanted her forgiveness, but now was not the time to ask.

Focus! Focus! Focus!

Initial steps of their on-the-fly plan were already in place. Lan had contacted Đăng Đạo. He wasted little time in offering his assistance and was due in from Albuquerque at 0900 tomorrow.

Also, last night, he had left a message on his banker friend's voicemail to stall Streak if he arrived ahead of Kannon. Call it kidnapping if you want, but he planned on drafting Streak to the rescue team. First round, second pick.

The rain intensified. Fallen leaves streamed in the wind as Kannon turned onto their half-mile-long driveway. A downed limb stretched across the drive and cracked beneath the slow-rolling Jeep.

Drumming his fingers on the steering wheel, Kannon returned his thoughts to the allegedly reformed gang leader who had once threatened to kill him, a man used to running his own show. Yet, Đăng Đạo's willingness to jump into a maelstrom likely to escalate in volatility wasn't surprising. Not only was Lan's nephew a man of action, there was also the family bond, a strong and honored trait among Vietnamese. After all, Đăng Đạo and Derrick were first cousins.

Time was critical. The plan needed to be honed using sound strategy and effective tactics—along with options allowing for as many unanticipated consequences as possible—all the while being mindful that best-laid military plans change after the first shot was fired.

Kannon stopped in front of their garage and punched the remote switch. Leaving the engine running, he got out, walked through the garage, and propped open the door leading to the kitchen. He returned to the Jeep. Pelted by the rain, he carried Lan inside and laid her on their bed. Her chest rose and fell in a deep, regular rhythm, but the expression on her face was anything but peaceful. Her skin was tightly drawn and wax-like in appearance, her facial expression one of near death.

He grabbed the woven afghan from the foot of the bed and draped it over her. She immediately curled into a fetal position.

Rest, baby, and come back. I need you.

Just as he turned to leave, she murmured, "I will manage the home front, including the authorities."

Her words a salve, Kannon sighed in relief. "I know you will."

* * *

After parking the Cherokee in the garage, Kannon walked to the backyard, hoping the cold would sharpen his senses. The wind lashed at his hair. Large, frosty raindrops stung his face.

He stared at Derrick's playthings, the climbing bars, the sandbox, his Tonka trucks. But the play area was bereft of Derrick's beautiful presence, his laughter, his hugs and squeals and kisses, his quick mind.

Stooping, he picked up a toy bulldozer, then collapsed to his knees, crying as he'd not allowed himself to do before. His chest heaved in hulking, ragged surges. He fell to the ground and lay on his side. Heavy raindrops whacked his jeans jacket, sounding like thumping mortar rounds popping from distant tubes.

Thirty-Five

Shivering, Kannon stirred from his stupor. His clothes were soaked and plastered to his body. The last thing he needed was to become hypothermic. He rose and stumbled toward the house, his joints stilt-like.

Inside, the silence bit sharp and deep. Moving as quickly as possible, he entered the bedroom. Lan lay just as he'd left her, with the afghan pulled to her shoulders. Softly, Kannon touched her neck. Her pulse pumped in a low rhythm. The waxy look was gone as some color had returned to her cheeks.

Then in a move Kannon knew was crazy, he checked Derrick's room. It was empty, of course, the bed untouched, a twisted verification his son was gone. Getting those bedcovers mussed again was up to him.

After a hot shower, he dressed in sweats, snatched a bag of pretzels and a Dr. Pepper from the kitchen, then went to his study. He sat at the desk and turned on the lamp. Its soft light delineated wall-mounted photographs as well as sundry icons positioned on the maple bookshelves—memories of life, his life. One item, a gift from Stefan, was a cocktail glass inscribed with the words *Forever Empty*, a reminder of his vow to avoid drinking scotch. Another was the gilded shadowbox frame that held his military decorations.

His eyes zeroed in on a portrait collage of Derrick, the most recent shots taken when celebrating his sixth birthday with friends from the Montessori school. He was dressed in a little blue blazer, knotted Mickey Mouse tie, and his first pair of full-length trousers. His eyes were lit up by a broad, missing-tooth smile, and he was holding out a bowl for more ice cream, the Chomper incident long since passed.

Kannon shook off his melancholy, opened the Dr. Pepper, and ripped open the bag of pretzels. He grabbed his satellite phone and keyed the number he wanted, vowing no source would be off limits in his search.

Sindy Zeller didn't answer, which Kannon expected. He left a straightforward message. *I'm not part of any militia. My six-year-old son's been kidnapped, probably by Border Slot. I don't know who the fuck you are, but I'm damn sure you're not CIA. Regardless, you must have information about this group. I need support and action. Now!*

An unidentified call came in. "Yeah?"

"It's me, Streak."

Kannon crushed the bag of pretzels. "You sleazy bastard. My son—"

"I know, man. I was there."

"What the hell are you talking about?"

"After leaving your place Saturday morning, I set up shop across the road."

"Because you had no place to go and couldn't cash my check until Monday."

"Right. I started thinking about why Whitehead and Bull had bailed from your property the other night. It's not like them to back off. Even from sheriff deputies. I figured they withdrew because they didn't want confrontation just then, and . . . they didn't have me."

The Việt Cộng tactic of one step back, two steps forward, Kannon thought. "You're telling me you had no part in this."

"Hell, no!"

"You know they killed my brother?"

"Oh, Jesus."

"I'm going after them. I don't want any apologies. You know Border Slot militia. You know the terrain. I demand you help—"

"I'm in," Streak said.

"Where are you?"

"Motel. Near Zilker Park."

Kannon paused, sipped from his Cola, wondering why Streak had changed his tune.

"Keep the room. We'll use it as a meeting place. I'm picking up a guy at the airport tomorrow at zero nine hundred and will bring him there."

"Okay."

"Why in God's name didn't you call when you saw Whitehead and Bull following us?"

"The battery on my satphone was dead." After a moment of silence, "I never thought they'd stoop so low as to kidnap your son, much less kill your brother."

"What did you think they were going to do?"

Streak sighed.

"I don't know."

"We've been down this road before. What else haven't you told me?"

Streak recited the rest of his most recent incidents—following the bastards out of town, crashing his motorcycle on a sandy road, being befriended by a couple of dirt bikers, and how later during the day he had experienced an epiphany at Zilker Park.

"Has Border Slot kidnapped children before?"

"Not that I'm aware of."

"You think revenge is the reason they took Derrick?"

"Partly," Streak said. "There's always the possibility of—"

"Child slavery!" Kannon blurted. "But you do think they're taking him to Border Slot?"

Streak paused, then said in a raspy tone, "I do."

I need a plane.

"We don't have much time," Kannon said. "Can you fly fixed wing?"

"Instrument qualified," Streak said.

"Okay. I have a rancher friend who owns a Cessna 208 Caravan. I'll call him to see if it's available."

"Sounds good."

"I'll call you shortly," Kannon said.

After clicking off, he tugged on his ear, which ached from pressing the phone tightly against it.

A harsh reality surfaced. What better way to strike against society than to kidnap a kid from a typical, traditional home and convert him into a militant! It reminded Kannon of the stories he'd read about early American Indians capturing young boys and either killing them or turning them into one of their own. In one sense, he hoped to hear from the militia—for them to be *normal* kidnappers—demanding a ransom.

Thirty-Six

Sitting at his desk, Kannon called Tucker, the guy who owned the Caravan. The call went into voicemail. Kannon left a message: "An old Army buddy, a pilot, showed up unexpectedly and wants to fly me to an impromptu game hunt in Montana. Is your plane available?"

How many lies will I tell? How far will I go to reclaim my son?

Disappointed at having to leave a voicemail, he made just-in-case arrangements for Monday afternoon with a local company flying out of Bergstrom.

Hearing a rustling behind him, Kannon swiveled in his desk chair. Lan had showered and slipped on a lemon-colored áo dài over black silk pants. She also carried the baby Navajo curing doll gifted by Belynda.

He rose and embraced her. The warmth from Lan's body spread throughout his, but her tears belied her colorful apparel. "How're you feeling?" he asked.

"I feel like my heart has been pierced by punji stakes."

"I know." For him, the sky had turned to lead and was crushing his heart and soul.

"I am still a bit groggy," she added. "What have you been doing?"

"I've been on the phone . . ." This was going to be tough.

"And?"

"Streak called. He's switched sides."

Lan pushed away to arm's length, tilted her head back, and stared at Kannon as if he were crazy. Shaking her head, she stumbled to a corner chair and collapsed into it. The leather creaked even from her slight weight.

"Streak is going to help?"

Her statement was more of disbelief than a question. Kannon flared his palms in defense. He reiterated the conversation between him and Streak. "He knows the territory. And his knowledge—"

"I get it," Lan said. She bristled like a porcupine. "I just do not want him in this house."

215

"He won't be."

His cell dinged. "Private line," caller ID read. Kannon pursed his lips. "This might be the Zeller bitch."

"Mr. Ballard. This is Sergeant Creighton. Anything new at your end?"

Inevitable, Kannon knew. He put the call on speaker so Lan could listen in.

"No," Kannon lied.

"We've assembled a team. It's headed your way," Creighton said. "ETA, two hours."

"Understood. See you soon." He looked at Lan. "I've got to leave. Creighton's interested in me, not you. If I'm not here, he can't question me. And you won't know where I'll be."

"I understand."

"They'll question you hard. Maybe even take you in." Kannon toyed with the crunched bag of pretzels.

Lan gripped the armrests on the leather chair.

"They'll place a listening device on our landline, probably tap your cell too."

Lan bit her lip, nodded.

"Just maintain your stoic demeanor. And you'll have Belynda and Stefan."

"I am glad to have both." Lan twisted in the chair as if she were trying to pop her back.

Kannon preferred his older son not to be in the limelight, but his presence would provide another safety net for Lan, giving Kannon comfort if nothing else. His son could do his legal work anywhere, so long as he had his laptop.

When Lan faced him again, her lips trembled.

"What is it? My leaving?" Kannon asked.

"It is Derrick," she almost screamed.

Of course it is, you idiot.

"Lan, we—Đăng Đạo, Streak, and I—will get our son back."

She remained still, staring daggers but saying nothing. Kannon rose from his desk chair, walked over, and took her hand. She rose to face him.

"I love you, Lan. You and Derrick are the most important

people in the world to me." *And of course, Stefan.* "Everything I do, everything I touch, everything I see and feel, has you in it. You bring out the life in me."

Lan gave him a tight squeeze, one he vowed to remember, and then she stepped back. She turned to leave the study but stopped at the doorway and turned. "Deputy Creighton does not believe us, does he?"

"He's an officer of the law and has a job to do."

"Answer my question."

"Sergeant Creighton believes we know more than we are telling. It's part of the investigative process for law officers to keep an open mind."

"What do I say to him?" Lan asked, smoothing her áo dài.

They started laying out a plan, rehearsing her spiel as if preparing for a play.

"Push Creighton about the FBI's participation," Kannon said.

She looked puzzled.

"The FBI pursues kidnappings across state lines. It might enhance our credibility—that neither one of us was involved in Derrick's disappearance." Figuring at best he had only one or two days to recover his son, if he failed, well . . .

"I will pursue the issue," Lan said.

"Good."

The doorbell rang.

Kannon double-timed to the front door and peered through the peephole. It was Stefan.

"Come around through the garage," Kannon hollered since the damaged door was nailed shut.

They met there. His son was wearing blue corduroy pants, a bright yellow oxford shirt, a half-inch-wide belt, and polished brown loafers with royal blue socks. His cheeks were flushed from the cold, probably from driving with the top down. Kannon gripped him by the shoulders and drew him close.

"How're you holding up, Dad?"

"All right. Thanks again for coming. It means a lot."

They entered the den where Lan joined them.

"Hello," she said, hugging him. "I am glad you are here. With you and Belynda, I will need no one else." She broke the embrace and pursed her lips as if daring anyone to disagree. No one did.

Kannon brought Stefan up to date while Lan entered the kitchen. Soon, the aroma of almond- and spice-flavored coffee filtered into the den. Lan brought out the steaming brew on a silver platter in her special Sài Gòn cups.

They sat around the coffee table.

"Lan and I have just started preparing a game plan," Kannon said.

Eyeing the steam escaping from his cup, Stefan compressed his lips and arched his eyebrows as if querulous.

"Something's on your mind," Kannon said. "Say your piece."

"Dad, this is nuts." He shoved his cup aside. "You should come clean with everything you know. Inform the police, the FBI, and anyone else who might help."

Kannon shook his head. "I don't trust them, Stefan. Based upon what Streak has told me about these guys, and the way the Feds have botched this type of operation in the past—think Ruby Ridge and Waco—we're better off with a quick strike."

It was Stefan's turn to shake his head. "Dad, I know your MO is to handle this on your own—"

"I'm going, son."

Stefan sighed. "I hope your will is up to date."

"That's uncalled for," Kannon said, surprised by the hostility.

"It's how I feel, Dad. I've already lost an uncle, and maybe a step-brother, I don't want to lose my father too." Then Stefan turned to Lan. "Do you know what you're getting into?"

"I am willing to risk all. We are a family. I am ready for my husband to do whatever is necessary to get Derrick back." Lan's dark, deep-set eyes fixed on Stefan like twin torpedoes aimed for mid-ship.

"You're both crazy." Stefan folded his arms and leaned back in the chair. "However, add another crazy man to the team. I'm going with you."

"The hell you are," Kannon said.

"So you say." Stefan didn't shrink. "I can help."

Kannon gritted his teeth. At times, dealing with his stubborn son was difficult. In one sense, he wished Stefan could join them. He was strong, athletic, and capable, but never had been exposed to combat. Why expose him to those horrors? Kannon didn't want to lead Stefan down that path, didn't want him to find the combat high, didn't want to expose him to the danger of crossing over, becoming sub-human and unable to return to normalcy.

Besides, Kannon's loosely conceived plan for rescuing Derrick bordered on criminality. Nope, no way was he going to drag Stefan into this . . . except to corroborate his lies.

Christ! I'm exposing all of them to obstruction of justice. Dismiss the angst, Kannon. Dismiss the angst. I can do this.

"Son, it's not going to happen. You're an asset in almost any circumstance, but your presence would affect my concentration. I can't afford any distractions."

"You are strong, Stefan, like your father," Lan interjected, "but we need you here."

Stefan slumped. The light faded from his eyes. His reaction reminded Kannon when he had been rebuked for wanting to lead a combat mission while still too green around the gills.

"I know you're disappointed, Stefan. I understand," Kannon said, gripping his shoulder, "but I want you to maintain a low profile. Your purpose is to support Lan and act as a liaison."

Stefan folded his arms across his chest.

"All right, Dad."

A grudging response in both tone and body position, for sure.

Creighton will check Lan's call history, maybe Belynda's too, and their service providers, hopefully not Stefan's.

"What are you thinking?" Lan asked.

"Contact me only in an emergency. Use Stefan. At my satellite phone number. Memorize it and delete the number from your contact list. I'll leave my cell in the study." *I'm likely to be out of cell range, anyway.* "If Creighton or Hollister arrives with a warrant to search the house, he'll find it and ask where I am. Tell whomever I had to run to the nearest drugstore to get some things for Lan and must have forgotten the phone. You expect me back any minute."

"Got it."

"Clue in Belynda when she gets here."

She nodded.

"If any calls are made, Dad, regardless of source, they'll still be able to ping you if they want. With GPS-enabled tracking, the authorities could triangulate an approximate location."

"You're right, of course." Kannon emitted a wry smile. He had something else up his sleeve.

"Won't the deputies question why you're not here to take any ransom calls, Dad?"

"Remember. I'll be back any minute. Lan can handle it in my absence."

"You will call and update us," Lan demanded, her lips pinched and eyes like lasers.

"Of course, and," Kannon emphasized, "all of you must plead ignorance to my plans."

"Plausible deniability," Stefan the lawyer mumbled. "All right. I'll be your liaison." He cocked his head toward his dad. "Any chance Border Slot might show up again?"

"I don't think so, not with the sheriff and FBI here." Kannon prayed this would play out to be true.

"Okay," Stefan said.

"Just in case," Kannon said, "I'll provide you with a handgun."

"I already have one." A gleam appeared in his son's eyes.

"I'm not surprised," Kannon said, knowing Stefan possessed a concealed license permit. "Just don't be reckless."

"Pot calling the kettle, Dad."

Reluctantly, Kannon nodded and stood. "I'm going to pack my gear. Stefan, why don't you join me in my study!"

As he turned to leave, Lan grabbed his arm. "What do you want us to do about Roger's funeral?"

"Play it by ear. Karen will talk to you two. It's me, she hates." A lump nearly closed his throat. "I'll say goodbye to Roger my way."

Kannon headed for the study. Stefan followed.

"Have a seat." Stefan sat on a tractor seat affixed to an old refurbished churning vat. Kannon rummaged in his left-hand bottom desk drawer and withdrew a paperback-sized padded envelope.

"This is a prepaid cellphone, a SyncTrak prototype we plan to release in two thousand ten. Charge it. Make a couple of test calls.

220

It'll be our secret."

"A burner," Stefan said. "Got it."

After Stefan left, Kannon walked to his bedroom. As he filled a backpack with cold-weather gear, he considered the enormity of the upcoming task. He was planning a blind operation, one based upon soft intelligence. Was Derrick being held at the militia compound? Was he even alive?

He shook his head to wrestle away any doubt. After adding two Sig Sauer semiautomatics—a .40 caliber and the pocket-sized 9mm to his gear—he lugged the backpack to his study.

Next, Kannon went through a mental checklist. Wanting to do some map study, he opened his laptop, logged on, and got a feel for the layout of Montana. It was a big state, but not as big as Texas. Border Slot could be anywhere, but, based on what little information Streak had given, he focused on the northwestern portion, figuring the mountains and forests would be a good place to lodge a terrorist group masquerading as a hunting guides operation. He memorized the locations of small towns ranging from Missoula to Kalispell to Whitefish and further north to Yaak, a place he'd once ridden through on one of his motorcycle journeys.

He logged off and stuffed the laptop and a portable printer into his pack. He also replaced the cracked pipe stem he'd bitten through when meeting up with Streak at Lost Maples. He added the Meerschaum pipe and Mark Twain-branded tobacco to the mix. The addictive tug from tobacco triggered thoughts of a higher high. Combat was a surreal dimension. Did he crave the thrill of going to any length to initiate another adrenaline-induced fix? Was there an atavistic gene—a combat gene—which, once activated, couldn't be shut down?

Maybe, but his goal was to save his family. In doing so, he was putting everyone at risk. They all could wind up in prison. God, was he doing the right thing?

Kannon reentered the den. A thermos of coffee was waiting for him to take on the road. After hugging Stefan, he stood before Lan. She embraced him, then stepped back and placed her warm, moist palms on his cheeks.

"Bring him back."

Thirty-Seven

Monday, 26 October 2009, Kootenai National Forest, Montana

"Snow's coming," Crandle said, eyeing the thickening nimbostratus clouds. The near-freezing wind exhilarated him, like a plunge into fifty-degree water.

"Reckon so." Whitehead, who had just returned with Bull from Texas, was squatting on his haunches, fiddling with a handmade arrow.

The two of them were bow-hunting in the Percell Mountains, northwest of Yaak and Border Slot, an isolated area near the state's 545-mile, mostly unmanned border with Canada. Hoping the physical exertion would diminish his building anger and frustration over the botched op, Crandle counted on the wild-game hunt to settle them both down. He also wanted to kill a moose to provide meat in anticipation of tomorrow's banquet.

With Bull doing the driving, his second-in-command had slept much of the way during the thirty-hour grueling drive from Texas to Border Slot. So, he was reasonably alert.

They had reached their drop-off point in a tandem military-styled Gator with a modified box bed to hold big game. Neither of them had spoken a word while tracking the narrow logging road through pristine evergreens and sloshing across frothy streams, which allowed Crandle thinking time on how best to handle Whitehead.

Unfortunately, the silence heightened the palpable tension between them. Only after vacating the Gator and trekking on foot did the thaw begin. Crandle needed to be careful. He didn't want to demoralize Whitehead because the EMP blasts were to take place in less than eighteen hours.

A gusty headwind flipped up the bill on Crandle's cap, so he pulled the bill down and looked up range, returning his attention to the hunt. He blew into the call horn. A low guttural rasp spread across the forested mountain slope. He handed the horn to Whitehead, then rattled dry branches and pawed the ground to enhance the lure.

"I want a sitrep," Crandle said.

"We had Streak in our hands, Commander, literally had him in our hands. We captured him in the woods surrounding Ballard's house. I told Bull to guard Streak while I went to get my pickup. Just as I returned, Streak escaped on that damn motorcycle of his."

Crandle's face grew hot. "And?"

"I fired several rounds."

"Hit him?"

Whitehead shook his head.

"I'm surprised you missed."

"You try hitting a moving target at night with a pistol at thirty yards," Whitehead shot back.

"You went after him, right?"

"Streak headed straight for Ballard's. We'd lost the element of surprise. Sirens were blaring—"

"You let him escape."

"No, damnit. Bull let him escape. The FNG . . ." Whitehead strung out the letters like he was stretching rubber. "He lost focus, tried to rape Streak."

"He what?"

"You heard me. The guy's a pervert."

"Why didn't you stop it?"

"Told you. I'd gone for the truck so we could haul Streak's motorcycle back here."

"You shouldn't have lost sight of him."

"Commander—"

"Shut up a minute. I need to think." No way could Bull be a faggot, Crandle thought. If so, OT would've mentioned it. "Why didn't you send Bull to get the pickup?"

Whitehead lowered his head.

"Sure, in hindsight—"

"Hindsight, blindsight! You drove Streak to Ballard through your collective fuck-ups."

Whitehead twisted his handlebar mustache.

"You were in charge. I hold you responsible."

"That's not fair, Commander. Bull's hard to control, even after I beat the shit out of him."

"Is that how he got the lump on his forehead?"

"That and Streak nailing him earlier with his slingshot."

"You're shittin' me."

"Nope. That's what bought Streak time to escape."

"Unbelievable." Crandle stopped and pulled a clipped cigar from his inside coat pocket. Shielding himself from the wind, he struck a match and lit up. He inhaled and held in the smoke a moment before exhaling.

"There was no way to assess the situation inside Ballard's house," Whitehead said.

"You're being defensive," Crandle shot back.

"I couldn't ignore the screaming alarms. We couldn't afford any contact with law enforcement."

"Okay, I get that."

Crandle heard a grating, raking sound up ahead. He peered intently into the timberland ahead but couldn't see anything. More thrashing . . . rutting season was essentially over, but maybe this was a horny bull still on the prowl. "You hear it too, right?"

"It's the rasping of antlers against a tree trunk. Get ready."

Crandle placed his cigar on a slab of granite. Withdrawing a heavy arrow from his quiver, he nocked it to the string of his longbow.

"There . . . to the right," Whitehead said, rising.

Crandle followed Whitehead's outstretched arm. Mesmerized, he watched a Bull Moose lumber into view. Its shoulders were broad and thick, with a pronounced hump, and its paddle rack was as wide as a Ram truck's grill. The moose's dewlap extended several inches below his neck.

From their observation spot on a rocky promontory, the forty-yard distance to the target was unobstructed. The wind blew in their favor, fanning the moose's musky scent toward them. Crandle lightly ran his fingers over his bow. Few men were strong enough to pull and hold a seventy-pound-draw. He could. No one else in the militia, not even Whitehead, could match him.

"The stout gentleman wants more pussy," Crandle whispered.

"Still trying to prove his manhood," Whitehead said, without humor.

Crandle took a deep breath and drew back. Expelling the first breath, he sucked in another, exhaled half of it, and let the arrow fly.

It was a clean release. The broadhead-tipped arrow cut through the cold air and embedded deeply into the bull's chest, likely puncturing its lungs and heart. Bugling in rage, the moose thrashed off into the evergreens.

"Good shot." Whitehead hoisted the supply pack. "He won't get far."

Crandle nodded, then bent over and picked up his quiver.

"You've picked up the Nez Percé flair for a shoot."

"Yep," Crandle said, picking up his cigar. "But you're the tracker. Let's find this big boy before the wolves do."

The wind howled, driving snowflakes as Whitehead led off. The ground was soft, like melted tundra. A crisp, mint-fresh forest odor permeated the sheltered area. Reaching the target area, Whitehead pointed out a blood trail that led into a large cluster of sharp-needled spruce. They continued tracking beneath a thick canopy of needled fir and spruce that kept the snowfall from reaching the forest floor.

Crandle used his height advantage to peer past Whitehead's shoulder. Despite his aggravation, he marveled at Whitehead's ability. If there was a blood trail, Crandle couldn't follow it. Broken branches? Scraped bark? He didn't notice those either.

The terrain turned rocky at timberline. Had he missed the kill? Crandle worried the moose might still be running. As they trekked forward, Whitehead told him about following Ballard and his family to a magic show in Austin, hoping Streak might be with them.

"Was he?" Crandle puffed on his cigar.

"I'm not sure."

Crandle sighed.

"How could you not be sure? You either saw him, or you didn't."

"All right, I didn't get a visual."

"I guess this was Bull's fault too," Crandle said, blowing smoke at his number two's face.

His second-in-command exhaled a deep, frosty breath. "We were looking for Streak in the crowd attending the magic show when the magician asked for a volunteer to undergo hypnosis. The guy who went on stage looked like Kannon Ballard. He even said, 'They call me Doctor Ballard.' Bull says he has to piss. Then I realized the man said doctor. Nothing in my research on Kannon Ballard indicated he had a doctoral degree. I figured the man was a brother or something. Next thing I know, flash-bangs and smoke grenades go off inside the arena."

Crandle grimaced.

"You might as well have jumped up and down waving a flag yelling, we're the Border Slot Militia."

"It gets worse. Bull shoots the hypnotized guy on the stage, thinking it's Kannon Ballard."

"Again, unbelievable," Crandle said. "Are you sure it wasn't Kannon Ballard?"

"It was his brother. Confirmed. Just before we snatched the kid, I overheard the mother say her brother-in-law had been shot."

What a cluster fuck!

"Do you know anything about this Kannon Ballard?"

Whitehead provided Ballard's background from soldiering, marriage, consulting, his return to Việt Nam, and the gun battle in the Sangre de Cristos.

"How'd you find out all this shit?"

"At the library in Kalispell. Looked him up on the Internet after researching EMP shit."

The kind of information that would no longer be electronically available if the electronic missions prove successful. It doesn't matter, Crandle thought, he could live with it.

"Ballard's a decorated combat vet," Whitehead added. "As you know, Streak flew choppers in 'Nam. They knew each other."

Crandle shook his head. "Streak. Smeek. Your whole operation stinks of clouded judgment and incompetence. Streak and Ballard are real problems and must be eliminated."

Whitehead didn't respond.

Despite his intentions, Crandle realized he was demoralizing Whitehead.

Thirty-Eight

Crandle chewed the end of his cigar. None of this, the mountain scenery, the physical exertion, his thrill at shooting a moose, quashed his anger and frustration. Instead, the more Whitehead revealed, the more agitated he became. Maybe his number two wasn't the right man to carry on Border Slot. Perhaps he was giving his second-in-command too much slack. His son Patterson, if he were alive, would've never allowed such lapses. Why couldn't Whitehead measure up to his expectations?

His Number Two squatted to study the ground, then pressed on, following a trail Crandle couldn't track if his life depended on it. The two of them became engulfed in another stand of evergreens and lost sight of the timberline.

They crossed a wide stream trickling through the conifers. Crandle stooped and sipped from the frigid waters. A moment later, the trees thinned out, revealing granite outcrops dusted with fresh snowfall atop yellowed remnants from prior years' accumulation. Downslope, leafless aspens stood like disjointed skeletons.

"Let's see if I've got this straight," Crandle said. "Bull shoots Ballard's brother by mistake. You compound the issue by kidnapping a fucking kid. If I were Kannon Ballard, I'd be squawking. Now we've got multiple threats out there. Streak. Ballard. The FBI. Every law enforcement agency in the land could be on our tail."

"Streak's got a record, remember! He's also up to his neck in our shit. He can't afford to go to the FBI or any other authority."

"He could ask for a plea deal—"

"He knows we'd get him in prison. We've done it to others before."

True.

Crandle drew on his cigar. "Okay. That adds credibility. But I got one question. Why the hell didn't you drop the freakin' kid?"

"It was an intuitive decision."

"What do you mean?"

"It gives us leverage."

"How?"

"Well, number one, money, of course—"

"Just another link for the Feds to find us," Crandle said.

Whitehead bared his teeth, a flexed arrow between his hands. "Let me finish. We don't know what, if anything, Streak told Ballard. So, number two, we can use the kid as bait to get Ballard to flesh out Streak."

Crandle planted his hands on his hips. "Maybe."

"I'd rank it higher than maybe."

Crandle didn't respond.

Whitehead did an about face and again headed out beneath the pervasive blackened clouds. Abruptly, he halted, and Crandle almost bumped into him. "There's your fucking moose."

"Hooah!" Crandle mouthed.

Lying on its side, its chest no longer heaving, was a Western Canada bull moose, a species not often seen in northern Montana. Crandle put its weight at half a ton or more.

"Let's get this animal skinned and sliced, prime pieces only, so Anh can start roasting. Leave the rest for the wolves." Anh excelled at making wild game tender. Crandle supposed it was something she'd learned in Việt Nam or at the Thai refugee camp.

Whitehead set down the arrow he'd been flexing and popped a fresh chew of tobacco into his mouth. He emptied the supply pack and arranged the gear on the ground.

Each of them donned leather gloves in preparation to field dress the animal. His number two wielded a long-bladed knife with a hefty hilt to whack off the moose's head. Next, he lopped off the hooves. Together, after tying its hind legs, they rigged a pulley system and strung up the moose to drain its blood. Crandle opened the chest cavity and removed the entrails while Whitehead began peeling the hide.

"There's more to support my reasoning about Ballard," Whitehead said.

"Let's hear it."

"Ballard handled that Việt Nam business on his own, right?"

"So you said."

"He's a lone wolf. Ballard won't rely on the Feds."

"That's a big assumption," Crandle said, flaring his nostrils.

"I think Ballard will come after the kid on his own."

"How would he find us?"

"Streak's info!"

"It's possible." Thinking more about this, Crandle said, "You may be right. Streak doesn't have the guts to come back. But Ballard, yeah. He could very well be on his way here now. Kill two birds with one stone."

Crandle stared at the blood draining from the downed moose. Despite the loose ends Whitehead left in Texas, his logic might be valid. The kid could be used as leverage to get Kannon Ballard to do just about anything he wanted, even *encourage* him to assist with the technical side of future operations.

As for ransom . . . his Militia could always use more money. Most likely, though, Ballard's phone line would be tapped, and he didn't want to give the FBI a link. Still, it was an option.

Another idea was forming, one which might allow Bull to earn redemption. Based upon what Whitehead had told him, Crandle was beginning to question his decision to promise Bull a role in Border Slot if he passed the final training exercise, which he had. Crandle feared by ditching him now OT might get pissed and disrupt the flow of EMP weaponry. He couldn't afford that. Need to keep OT close. Solution? Give Bull a solo assignment.

"You've made a good point," Crandle said.

"We'll remain on high alert," Whitehead said, smiling.

"Right." Crandle darted a steely glare at Whitehead. "Let's talk more about the kid. He looks different."

"He is different."

"What do you know about the peckerhead's mother?"

"Ballard's wife is Vietnamese."

"His bitch is a slant-eye?"

"So what? You're fucking one."

The hair on the back of Crandle's neck bristled as he hacked at one of the moose's forelegs. "The kid's a mutant."

"He's not a mutant."

Crandle propped on one knee and pointed his bloodied knife at Whitehead. "I know what you said about using the kid as leverage, but we don't have to keep him alive."

229

"Ballard won't cooperate without living proof," Whitehead said.

"Another point taken." Crandle shook his head. "Still—"

"I don't want to kill the kid." Whitehead locked eyes on his. "Think of the son you lost . . . the dreams you had for him. This boy can be trained."

"I've told you . . . no one but me brings up Patterson." Whitehead's words planted a pang in his gut. Was Number Two screwing with him?

"Anh could help raise him." Whitehead stood with his thumbs hooked on belt loops.

"You're pouring it on, aren't you! Leave Anh out of this. She has enough to do."

"Just a thought."

"What is this with you about Anh? You got a thing for her? You wanna poke my snatch?"

"No. It's just . . . well, you treat her like shit." Whitehead spat out a wad of gummy tobacco juice.

"That's none of your damn business. You want a punch, find one. Your job is to handle the militiamen. If you ever want to run Border Slot, you've got to stay focused on missions."

"Understood."

"Let's finish our business here and then head back to the compound for the final briefing on tonight's EMP mission."

Whitehead nodded, then stooped to pick up the arrow he'd set down earlier.

"Another thing," Crandle said, about to unload the idea that had popped into his mind earlier. "I don't just want Kannon Ballard. I want the rest of his clan neutralized."

"I'll work out a plan."

"Already got one. I'll send Bull back to Texas. Cover all the bases."

"Alone?"

"You got it."

Whitehead's eyes bulged as if he'd been scalped. "You haven't listened to a damn word I've said. Bull's a screaming SNAFU-guy. He's a danger on any operation, as part of a unit or solo.

What's he got on you?"

Crandle glared and moved nose-to-nose with Whitehead. "I've made a decision. As of now, Bull reports directly to me."

"Can't you see what you're doing!" Whitehead said. "I know you're high on the guy, but if any other militiaman screwed up that bad, I'd have killed him. You're the one endangering Border Slot if you send Bull solo."

Crandle clamped down on his anger.

"That boy is tenacious, tough, and ruthless. I'll talk to him. He can handle it. I don't want you thinking about anything but the mission, wiping out Kalispell's electrical grid." He jabbed a finger into Whitehead's chest. "Don't fuck it up."

Whitehead's jaws twitched. "Thanks for the vote of confidence."

"Can the sarcasm," Crandle said. "You're not irreplaceable."

"Try running the militia without me."

Crandle fumed but let it ride. He turned back toward the moose. All its blood had drained.

"Anything else we need to talk about?"

"Yeah! Ax Bull."

Goddamnit!

"Let it go, Whitehead, let it go!"

"No can do! You've always told me to speak up, Commander. I'm speaking up. You're wrong."

"Let me sum this up for you," Crandle said, his blood boiling. "Ballard and Streak come? We're ready. Slam dunk capture. If they don't, Bull nabs both and brings them to Border Slot. Kills the rest of Ballard's family and anyone else who's there."

"Big mistake. It's at least a two-man mission."

"You're insubordinate . . . *again.*" Crandle tapped his bloodied blade on Whitehead's shoulder.

Whitehead shoved the blade away. "You're pushing it, Commander."

Crandle slapped him.

Whitehead let loose a war cry and broke in two the arrow he'd been holding. He dropped the pieces at Crandle's feet.

"Don't pull your Nez Percé crap." Crandle hoped his flinch

had gone unnoticed.

Whitehead crouched and retrieved his long knife. He scraped both sides of the blade on the hide to rid the blood and then flashed the knife at Crandle. "I could gut you and hang up your carcass to bleed out like this moose."

The war cry, the threat, chilled Crandle. Had he gone too far?

Whitehead rammed his knife into its scabbard and slung his bow over his shoulder. He hoisted his pack, turned, and jogged eastward through the clearing and into the forest.

"You'll be back," Crandle hollered. "You've got no place else to go."

Thirty-Nine

Once obscured within the forest, Whitehead stopped running. He laid down his bow, stripped off his pack, and removed his canteen from its canvas pouch. He splashed water over his face and then shook his head like a dog shedding water.

Crandle, blowing smoke in his face, belittling him, challenging his leadership ability—never had anyone treated him with such disrespect, even the military.

Still, threatening Crandle might've pushed the Commander over the edge. Whitehead wished he hadn't gotten defensive and lost control, maybe jeopardized his goal of eventually running the Militia. Those were the reasons Special Forces kicked him out of training.

Whitehead gathered his gear and resumed his pace, sidestepping rocks and brushing past needled evergreens. He was in his element. As usual in conflicts of this magnitude, he sought his answers in nature.

Thirty minutes later, he reached a clearing glazed with melting ice. Stopping, he slouched against a granite shelf and scooted to the ground. He rested his arms across his knees and watched as a light wind feathered the leaves on the forest floor. The tart smell from spruce and fir filled his nostrils. Overhead, the scree of a soaring hawk pierced the silence. Being alone, immersed in nature's elements, further calmed him. His smoldering rage began to subside.

Whitehead rose and straightened. He removed his jacket and fatigue shirt, then replaced his wet T-shirt with a dry one so he wouldn't get chilled.

After donning his outer layers, he took off again, concentrating on the barren aspen trees populating a mountain slope. Sheathed in white bark, the *eyes of the aspen* spoke prominently. "The trees' iconic symbols result from broken limbs," his father had taught, "and are to be read with reverence. They have one root system. They are family."

Whitehead stared at one eye now, framed on top with a half-clipped eyebrow. Its drooping pupil brought silent tears as he mourned the senseless murder of his Nez Percé parents. They were peaceful and worshipped nature. Given his circumstances, would they understand his life path? Would they forgive him for washing out of Special Forces, discarding a life that might have provided better opportunities?

He proceeded from tree to tree, searching for eyes that spoke to him. Some were newer, fresher, and not yet adequately seasoned to read with certainty. Others, just the opposite. One eye was owl-like, jagged and worn, but also elegant. It was as if this one had been observing life's cycles for decades, gaining wisdom, which only the passage of time could grant.

He happened upon a third aspen eye, defined by a thick, dark brow. Fully furrowed, the brow protruded beyond the pupil. This nearly scabbed-over icon admonished and shamed him, not only for his insubordinate behavior but for losing Streak and mishandling Bull.

I shouldn't have walked away. If I'd stayed, though, I might've done something more destructive.

Whitehead moved on. A fourth eye beckoned.

Its eyebrow was cocked as if to imply thought. The eye itself was clear and defined, stirring him to reconsider his thought processes at Ballard's premises. His motivation that night was to avoid confrontation with the sheriff's department. He wanted Streak, if for nothing else than to resolve the matter and focus on Border Slot's mission. So maybe he'd been wrong not to have stormed Ballard's house. That would've prevented the subsequent fiasco at the magic show. Yet, Streak could've already moved on. Or maybe not.

Following the family into Austin the next night had been for the sole purpose of finding Streak, their AWOL pilot. And then the fucked-up shooting. Bull had been positioned on the other side of the theater and when questioned later, said he thought the man on stage was Kannon Ballard because he had identified himself as Dr. Ballard.

"It was too good of an opportunity to pass up," Bull had said.

Whitehead admitted that the three men in Ballard's party looked alike, but it was then he remembered there was no reference to Kannon Ballard having a doctorate. So, mistaken identity. Nevertheless, a no-kill order was in place.

What could he have done to prevent the debacle? The order

had been made clear. He'd expected Bull to follow it, especially after the beating given him. Maybe the whack from Streak's slingshot had further muddled his thinking. No, it was rage, perversion, and the inability to follow orders. Impulse drove Bull. Despite the FNG's cleverness in developing the Sling-Hawk, his recklessness was unacceptable. He'd warned Crandle, damnit. Regardless, the ultimate disposition belonged to his boss.

As for the boy . . . on their sprint to the SUV, Whitehead at first wanted to release him but thought it dangerous because the kid might identify them. He quickly decided that was moot because Streak probably would've already described him and Bull to Ballard. Thus, the idea about using the kid to leverage Kannon into revealing Streak's whereabouts had formed. Also, there loomed the ransom option.

Suggesting Crandle treat the kid as his own was an afterthought, albeit a bad one. But he wasn't giving up.

The wind picked up. Sleet skittered down the fir and spruce, plucking their needles. He reached for the tobacco tin in his back pocket, pried off the top, and pinched another chew to plug into his mouth.

A good buzz.

He pulled a pair of binoculars from his pack and scanned the area. Upslope, two grayish-brown wolves loped across the snow, heading in the direction from which Whitehead had come. They couldn't detect the smell of Crandle's butchered moose this far away, but their presence reminded him of Lobo, the handle Crandle had assigned to the wolf that often tracked the Commander's hunting forays, hoping for scraps from the kills.

What was Crandle doing? Whitehead wondered. Was he still in the field, or had he returned to the compound?

Checking his compass, he changed direction. He encountered an aspen trunk with two eyes and a curved line underneath. It resembled a smiling face. Whitehead smiled back. The aspen eyes had spoken.

Forty

Monday, 26 October 2009, Nondescript Motel, Austin, Texas

Kannon steered the Cherokee into a rest stop. He had left home at 2345 hours, wearing jeans and a Route 66-emblazoned sweatshirt. His loaded backpack sat in the rear.

Despite ingesting caffeine, he couldn't stay awake. It was only half-past midnight, and Đăng Đạo's plane wasn't due in until 0900. Too much time to kill.

He picked up his satphone and keyed the number for the burner phone now in Stefan's hands. "What's going on?"

"Creighton's due any minute," Stefan said.

"Glad I got out in time. Any word from the FBI?"

"Not yet." Stefan paused. "Lan and I ran through the game plan again."

"Good. How's she doing?"

"Okay. My stepmom's a tough lady."

Yes, she is.

"No ransom call from Border Slot, I take it."

"Nada."

Kannon frowned, surprised at his dejection, which struck like a hammer. He'd been holding onto a kernel of hope that a simple ransom call would get his son back.

"Keep me posted," Kannon said.

"Will do. What's next?"

"The less you know, the better."

They clicked off.

Still no word about the Cessna. A long day lay ahead. Kannon closed his eyes, worrying about what would happen if Creighton collared Stefan's burner phone.

* * *

Kannon woke at 0700. After grabbing breakfast at a nearby IHOP, he headed for the Austin-Bergstrom International Airport. When his satphone vibrated, his heartbeat ratcheted up. No caller ID.

Please be about the Cessna.

236

"Ballard!"

"Sindy Zeller here."

Shit!

"Wait one." He put the phone on speaker and set it on the passenger seat. "You got my message?"

"I listened to it. You're in a shitload of trouble, Mr. Ballard."

"Who the hell are you, Zeller?"

"I'm someone you don't want to screw—"

"I'm not interested in screwing you, Ms. Zeller. Streak already took care of that. I want my son back. And you have information about this militia group."

"Maybe I do. Maybe I don't."

"Lady . . . my son is a vulnerable and scared six-year-old boy who's in extreme danger! But you don't give a shit, do you?"

"It's out of my hands. Besides, you got yourself into this mess."

"You are one cold bitch," Kannon shot back. "Have you no compassion?"

"As for your wife, Cô Võ Thị Lan," Zeller continued, ignoring his question, "her mode of entry into America is questionable. If you don't cooperate, I'll slap you in jail and ship her tight ass back to her home country so fast it'll make your head swim."

"Just try it, Zeller." Kannon white-knuckled the steering wheel. "Besides, if you are who you say you are, you're aware of my war record. I'm a patriot. I deserve respect."

"Your past doesn't mean shit."

Spoken like a real asshole. Streak's bitch-factor evaluation is understated. I need a different angle.

Kannon thought of the short, plump Asian woman who'd observed them at Lost Maples, the same one Streak noticed at the Llano River. "I'm sure you're familiar with the name Modesto Poblete?"

Zeller didn't boomerang an immediate reply.

"Since you guys lost your tracking device," Kannon added, "I guess Modesto's unemployed at the moment."

A deep breath sailed from the other end of the line. "Well done, Mr. Ballard." Another pause. "You do know, by harboring

Streak, you're aiding and abetting a member of a militant group whose avowed purpose is to overthrow the United States Government."

"I'm not harboring anyone."

"Yes, you are. My job is intelligence, and I'm great at it."

Kannon clucked his tongue. "You're not that good, Ms. Zeller. I don't believe you're involved in intelligence. In fact, you demonstrate a noticeable lack of it, or else you'd know Streak wants out of the militia. And, if you had a shred of humanity, you'd be concerned with my son's kidnapping."

"Not my area of expertise."

Exasperated, Kannon spoke through gritted teeth.

"Just what the hell do you want, Zeller?"

"I want the Border Slot Militia." She clicked off.

* * *

Kannon didn't know what to make of the conversation, but it was 0845, time to pick up Lan's nephew. He found a vacant slot at the curb by the passenger exit and wedged the Cherokee into it. Leaving the engine running, he got out and propped his elbows on the open door.

As he waited for Đăng Đạo, his bowels tightened like hardening lava. Even though he agreed wholeheartedly with his and Lan's decision to recruit her nephew, he was the guy who'd sworn to kill Kannon if ever they reencountered each other. Now, supposedly, they were on the same side of the fence.

During their encounter in the Sangre de Christo Mountains in '02, Đăng Đạo wasn't even aware he had an Aunt Lan. Using computer-enhanced photographs, Kannon had been able to demonstrate familial resemblance to Đăng Đạo by displaying shots of both his birth father and Lan, which apparently instilled enough doubt for him to consider it. But it had taken a while to convince Đăng Đạo, who was then on the wrong side of the law.

Now, at thirty-nine years old, there he was, all five-foot five-inches of him, wearing pressed chinos, a bright green polo, penny loafers, and shouldering a military-style duffle. Thick black hair extended to his shoulders. Moon-shaped glasses perched on the bridge of his nose added a dignified look. No one looking at him would surmise his curriculum vitae included a double major in linguistics and computer science, along with an MBA. Đăng Đạo also appeared fit. After all, he was a ninja.

"I don't see a weapon in your hand," Kannon said. An electric jolt arced through his old shoulder wound, a reminder of their shared past.

"I have no desire to shoot you." A thin smile crossed Đăng Đạo's face.

"Appreciate that."

"You have married my aunt and fathered a son. We are a family now. I want to bring to justice those who took my little cousin."

A surge of compassion swept over Kannon. "I'm grateful you've agreed to help," he said, extending his hand.

Đăng Đạo shook it, then placed his other hand on top of their clasped hands, a Vietnamese custom to display warmth.

"Let's go. It's time to meet the other guy."

"I am ready," Đăng Đạo said.

Though Đăng Đạo spoke in a thick, measured accent, his usage of the English language was excellent. It intrigued Kannon how Vietnamese bilinguists could switch from their indigenous rising and falling, singsong language to flatter tones when speaking English.

Yet, a nearly imperceptible quaver marked Đăng Đạo's otherwise flat tone. Did it carry anxiety, or hostility?

Forty-One

Monday, 26 October 2009, Ballard Residence, Texas Hill Country

"I am glad both of you are here," Lan said, arranging the three curing dolls on the hacienda-style coffee table. She placed two sage incense cones in holders, one a chubby Buddha, the other a mockup of an adobe lodge. After lighting the cones, she cast a thankful glance at Belynda and Stefan sitting on the sofa.

Belynda's hair was tied in a ponytail and cascaded past her shoulders. She wore a long, flowing white dress with embroidered sandstone icons in varying reddish hues. Lan recognized the images from framed photographs adorning her friend's classroom walls.

"I'd run through a gauntlet for you," Belynda said.

Outfitted in tight-fitting clothes that accented his sculpted physique, her stepson was another matter. Lan wondered whether he was trying to impress Belynda. If so, she would not blame him. But his demeanor appeared sullen. Something was on his mind, and she thought she knew what it was.

Returning her attention to the incense, Lan fanned the aromatic sage to her nostrils. It helped steady her.

"Stefan, you carry the same leadership traits as your father. I know you would rather be with him, but he is experienced in combat. You are not." She prayed Kannon's mission would not result in violence. Under the circumstances, though, reality probably dictated otherwise. "I hope you never engage in fighting."

Stefan's cheekbones relaxed. His demeanor softened. "I understand."

"Good."

Wearing her most comfortable baggy pants and a bulky sweater, Lan leaned over and grabbed the wooden doll with the prayer sticks tied around its waist. Did this *child doll* carry the sticks because *he* was weighted by the sins of his parents?

"Is he a Buddhist icon?" Stefan asked.

Lan shook her head.

"Native American," Belynda said. "When a Navajo is in

discord with nature and commits a forbidden act, it causes an injury or illness to his body and soul." She went on to explain the purpose of placing turquoise bits in the holes.

"But Lan and Derrick are innocent," Stefan said. "Neither has done anything to—"

Belynda patted him on the knee. "I know. Our purpose is to keep everyone's hearts and spirits strong."

Lan stuck a turquoise nugget in a hole below *Derrick's* heart and reached for another—

A staccato knock sounded. Lan flinched and dropped the doll. Her nerve endings twitched like tiny fishes in flooded rice paddies.

"And now a new scene begins," she said, annoyed by the prospect of another inquisition.

"I'll get it," Stefan said, starting toward the door.

"No. I will." Lan gestured for him to sit down.

She picked up the dropped doll, then walked to the front door.

"You have to come around back," she said as loud as she could.

Moments later, two deputies, the stout Sergeant Creighton and the taller Detective Hollister, stood at the patio door. Wearing clean, pressed uniforms, neither man carried an ounce of flab. The slender Hollister's dark hair was closely cropped. A clipped mustache framed his upper lip. Creighton was clean-shaven, with medium length blond hair. It was their grim expressions, though, that concerned her. If they believed her story, their expressions should show compassion.

Creighton spoke. "Time to get down to business, ma'am."

"I understand it is necessary, though I am not used to all the ways in my new country."

The deputies exchanged glances. "In all due respect, lady, this ain't your country," Hollister said. "We're officers of the law and can come any damn time we please."

"Tone it down," Creighton said to Hollister.

Lan glared at the two, wishing she could spit fire. Instead, her task was to win them over and give Kannon time. "Come in." She led them into the den. "You remember Belynda and Stefan?"

"Of course."

"Please take a seat." Lan motioned to a couple of straight-backed chairs, which had been Stefan's idea.

"We'll stand," Creighton said.

You can stand on your heads for all I care, Lan thought, as she took a seat at Belynda's left on the sofa. Stefan sat on the far right. The three of them now faced the deputies.

At least they did not arrive with a warrant.

"Where's your husband?" Sergeant Creighton asked.

"He should return any moment. He has gone to a drugstore to pick up something I need."

"At this hour!" Detective Hollister said. "What, for God's sake?"

"Tampons," answered Lan.

Hollister blushed. Creighton shook his head. "All right, ma'am. He needs to be here. Call him."

Lan puffed her cheeks and glowered. Kannon did not want her calling from her cellphone. But this was an emergency. Orders. Then she remembered he had left his cellphone here. She snatched her cell off the coffee table and keyed her husband's quick dial, which she knew would roll into voicemail.

Everyone heard it ring.

Creighton and Hollister frowned.

"He must have forgotten it in his haste," Lan said.

"We'd like to believe your story, ma'am," Creighton said. "But your husband's not here, and he doesn't have his phone. Put yourself in my shoes. Doesn't that seem a bit strange?"

"For God's sake, there's enough stress here without you two adding to it," Belynda said.

"Why isn't the FBI here?" Stefan asked.

"I'll call them if necessary," Creighton said.

"You see, folks. We're just not buying your story," Detective Hollister added. "Tells me you're not expecting a ransom call. Him not here and with no phone and all."

"How would you read it?" Creighton asked. "Seems to me your husband's on the run . . . or tackling the kidnapping on his own."

"Big risk," Hollister added, "taking the law into his own hands."

Lan rubbed the back of her neck. This was not going well.

"That's not true," she said. Lan made a point of checking her watch. "Kannon should be back by now. What if the men who took Derrick grabbed my husband?"

The deputies looked skeptical.

"Mine if I check your phone?" Creighton reached out his hand.

Lan looked to Stefan for guidance. He nodded. She handed it over.

Creighton took the phone and examined the call list. He pinched a small notebook from his shirt pocket and placed a tick mark beside an entry.

Belynda, meanwhile, using tweezers, started doctoring cavities in the largest curing doll with bits of turquoise. Creighton seemed mystified.

"What are you doing?" Creighton asked Belynda, as he returned Lan's cell.

"Some sort of voodoo?" Hollister asked.

"I'm a full-blooded Navajo," Belynda said. "These are curing dolls, icons of our heritage. Placing turquoise in these holes fosters healing."

"Yeah, whatever!" Hollister smirked.

"I beg your pardon," Belynda said. "Are you demeaning my culture?"

Creighton let out a loud, exasperated breath. "No, ma'am."

"I don't appreciate it." Belynda straightened and crossed her legs, exposing a little thigh. "Don't you have phones to tap?"

Hollister glowered. "Watch your tone, lady."

"Why? Are you going to arrest me for swearing?"

Lan allowed herself an inner smile.

"It doesn't matter what he thinks," Stefan said.

"It's not just about the Navajo," Belynda said. "It's about the dignity of humanity."

Stefan stood, crossed his arms. "Come on, officers. You haven't even asked about my little brother. Don't you care?"

"We do care, son . . . for the child." Hollister softened his expression a bit.

"Ladies, I apologize for my partner's rude comments. But most kidnappings involve a family member." Creighton pursed his lips and winked at Lan. "It seems the circumstances here suggest a strong possibility a family member is involved."

"My husband and I were at the magic show!" Lan said, rising from the sofa. "How could we have kidnapped our son?" She began wondering if the deputies were prejudiced against the Vietnamese and the Dine'é People.

"I know." Creighton shifted his stance. "But it could've been arranged. No ransom calls, right?"

"No calls," Stefan chipped in. "As Belynda said, we thought you were here to tap the phones, not harass my stepmom."

Lan allowed another inner smile. This was the first time she had ever heard Stefan refer to her that way. She said to the deputies, "Do either of you have children? Losing one is like the devil reaching in and stealing your heart."

"I do," Creighton said, locking eyes with Lan. "I believe your son is missing, but your husband is missing too."

"I am insulted," she said, using her most indignant tone.

Belynda filled another hole in the feminine curing doll. Stefan placed a turquoise chip on the child icon's forehead.

"Let's stay on course here," Creighton said. "As I said, a child's disappearance is often traced to a relative, usually one parent or the other . . . sometimes both."

"You're pathetic idiots," Belynda said. "You have no grounds for those statements. All you're doing is upsetting her."

"I'll ignore that for now, Miss *Belyndaaa*, but watch your attitude."

Belynda turned purple at Hollister's response. "For the deputies' ignorance . . ." She placed another nugget.

Stefan motioned palms down toward the floor. Belynda winked at him.

Creighton addressed Lan.

"Why don't you tell us about the troubles going on between you and your husband?"

Lan folded her arms. Good God! She and Kannon were considered suspects.

Forty-Two

After Creighton had asked what troubles were going on between Kannon and herself, Lan wanted to clock the deputy on the head, but she needed to remain calm. Unfortunately, her mind and body were in disconnect mode. Besides that, due to her warm, clammy palms, she fretted she might be running a slight fever.

Her confidence ebbing, she stared at Creighton, then at Belynda, who rose from the sofa and came to her side. Lan felt tempted to reveal the whole story—how she had met Kannon in Việt Nam, how much they had been through together, about the militia, Sindy Zeller, and Streak—because continuing this charade might well implicate her friend and stepson.

Belynda could plead ignorance, but not Stefan. Lan wished she knew more about American law.

"Your questions are shocking. They frighten me," Lan said to Creighton.

"Answer the question, Mrs. Ballard."

"Why are you doing this? My husband and I have a strong love for each other. I came to America because of my love for Kannon and because I was carrying his child."

"Whom you refuse to search for," Belynda said to Creighton, shaking her head as if in disgust.

The deputy didn't respond.

Creighton walked to the window, opened the blinds, and peered out as if looking for her husband coming up the drive. Frowning, he returned and confronted Lan. "First scenario, your husband is responsible for the child's disappearance, and you either knew about it or, worse yet, are a participant. Is the child dead, Mrs. Ballard? Do you and your husband have an insurance policy on him? Do y'all need the insurance money?"

Holding an intense look, the deputy flipped his notepad open and shut, open and shut. Lan dug her nails into her palms to keep from screaming out loud. Belynda's mouth was agape.

"Second scenario," Hollister said, holding his chin high, "Mr. Ballard has turned Rambo and has set out to rescue the boy himself."

245

Lan stiffened.

"Which would be stupid," Hollister added.

"Third scenario," Creighton's turn again, "variation of number one. Mr. Ballard does, in fact, resent your presence, and the child's. He arranged for his kidnapping without your knowledge and by choice has left the building, as they say—"

"My husband would never harm either one of us. And he would not abandon me."

"Fourth scenario, Mrs. Ballard, is a variation of number three. Your husband's having an affair, maybe with your dead brother-in-law's wife." Creighton looked smug.

Could either three or four be remotely possible? No way!

"Ridiculous," Lan snapped.

"The grieving widow has not responded to our calls," Hollister said.

"Karen just lost . . ." Lan shook her head. "You are confusing me. It is none of those scenarios."

"If you're involved, Mrs. Ballard, which door is it?"

"None of the above."

Creighton jumped in. "If you're not involved, ma'am, which do you think more likely, number three or four?"

"You're twisting this around," Belynda said.

Lan turned her back to Hollister and stared straight into Creighton's eyes, then stepped away from both deputies. She gripped the child doll tighter. "My husband would not betray me."

Fighting to control her emotions, which, if she let go, Lan realized, would explode in a mixture of frustration, anger, and fear. Instead, "I became a mother at forty-one. We cherish our son. We cherish each other."

"It used to be," Belynda said, leaning forward, "that in America you're innocent until proven guilty."

"As their lawyer," Stefan said, "I find your line of questioning unreasonable and badgering. My father is not involved. A third party kidnapped Derrick."

Creighton and Hollister ignored him.

"You're saying you and your husband don't fly off the handle?" Hollister said.

Lan looked to Belynda for an interpretation.

"He means arguments," Belynda said.

"Of course, we have arguments. But they are not—"

"Severe," Creighton said. "We hear it all the time." He wrote another note, closed the pad, then looked up.

Lan's armpits were wet, and her mouth was dry. She, Belynda, and Stefan might well as be characters in an American version of Kafka's *The Trial*. Yet, it was a trial of their own making.

"My husband must be on his way back. What if he was in an accident?" Lan stated, her eyes wide.

"That would be convenient, wouldn't it, Mrs. Ballard," Creighton said.

They were challenging everything she, Belynda, or Stefan said. "This is callous."

"You are either incredibly naïve or a poor liar, Mrs. Ballard. I tend to believe you are more naïve than a liar," Creighton said. "Your responses and body language don't suggest you're lying."

Oh, but I am.

"Stop it," Belynda said. "You guys are unbelievable. You're as bad as the Nazis."

"Lady, we'll haul your ass in for obstruction of justice," Hollister said, gesturing as if he was about to slap cuffs on Belynda.

"Justice . . ." Stefan said. "Let's calm down. My little brother is missing. Your job is to find him, not make his mother feel worse."

"Maybe you're involved in this, too." Creighton clenched his teeth and glared at Stefan.

"Oh, come on!" Her stepson shook his head and frowned.

Justice. Lan's heart and mind were already filled with torment. How could she make room for this added fury and frustration? She started to feel a twinge of anger toward Kannon. Maybe he was wrong. Perhaps they should have told the authorities everything. Still tempted to do so, she stared at Stefan, but was met with a subtle shake of the head, which Lan interpreted as, "Stay the course." The action reminded her of what this was all about—delay and divert.

"What about the FBI?" Stefan asked again.

No response.

Creighton motioned for Hollister to come close. They exchanged whispers for what seemed like an eternity.

Lan peeked at the wall-mounted clock, which chimed two-thirty. It could be hours before Kannon and Đăng Đạo took flight. If only she could talk to them, but that was impossible with the deputies here. Instead, she knelt by the coffee table and placed two turquoise nuggets into the male doll.

When she rose, Stefan embraced her. "You're doing great," he said.

"Yes, you are," Belynda added.

"Am I?" Lan asked. "This is hard. The deputies are harsher than they were at the Magika."

"I know. Just hang in there," Stefan said.

"They do not believe me," Lan said.

No one said anything. The silence settled in her stomach like a chunk of steel. Feeling both anxious and sad, Lan traveled back in time to her brother's sickbed, the revelation about his son who came to be known as Đăng Đạo, and Kannon's first appearance at her family home on Sài Gòn's Bùi Viện Street . . . and the love they found.

Stefan grabbed Lan's forearm and spoke softly in her ear. "I'm going to call Dad."

Lan nodded and squeezed his hand, but just as Stefan turned to go, Creighton and Hollister returned and converged on them.

"After I use the bathroom—if you do not mind—I will brew some tea," Lan said.

"Then we can commence the vigil," Belynda said.

"I'll be back in a moment." Stefan turned toward his father's study.

"Hold on, everyone," Creighton said. "Stay put." He winked at Hollister. "We've decided on a change of venue."

"What do you mean?" Lan asked.

"While you're in the bathroom, leave a note for Mr. Ballard, tell him that you have decided to take a ride in the squad car," Hollister said with a smirk.

"I'm under arrest?" Lan's face turned blood red. "You cannot do this."

"Person of interest," Creighton said. "We don't need to arrest you or issue a warrant. All we need is probable cause."

"Who's going to monitor the phones?" Stefan's knuckles turned white.

Hollister turned to Lan. "Reroute the landline to your cell."

Lan pouted but did as she was told.

"You're not taking her anywhere." Stefan's tone was belligerent.

"Yes, we are," Creighton said, glaring at her stepson. "You're out of your league, son. You're a civil lawyer, not criminal. We checked."

"Why?" Lan's knees were shaking. "I need to be here for my son."

"Not happening," Hollister said. "We have new information."

"Oh, my God." *What new information?* Dizzy, unable to think straight, Lan collapsed against Belynda.

"I may be a civil lawyer," Stefan said, looking at Lan and Belynda, "but I know their intimidating approach is SOP for certain officers of the law. They could be bluffing, trying to force from you false confessions."

"Like a toxic laxative," Belynda added, "reaming your bowels when there's nothing left to be reamed."

"Good one," Stefan said. He added. "Belynda and I will follow you to the sheriff's department, Lan."

Forty-Three

Kannon steered into the parking lot of the nondescript motel in Austin. The air smelled like wet copper. Scudding clouds painted the sky in dark sepia tones, offset by champagne-hued shafts of light streaming to the ground. Cedar and oak trees stood like sentinels silhouetted against the dusk-like aura, belying the fact it was only 0930.

Kannon parked in front of room nine. Before getting out, he called Tucker. Still no answer, no word on the Cessna.

"Grab your bundle," Kannon said, as they exited the Cherokee.

Đăng Đạo toted his military duffle and Kannon his backpack. Two retro metal chairs with heart-shaped backs bordered the doorway to the motel room. A potted plant beneath the single window desperately needed water.

Kannon knocked. Streak opened the door.

They stepped inside and set down their totes. The room contained a microwave, a small fridge, and a coffee maker, which Streak had drafted into action. An old-style percolator popped and sizzled, casting an enticing aroma that partially offset a men's locker-room smell. A bland Formica-topped table with four rickety chairs sat catty-corner to a king-sized bed.

Introductions were made. Streak extended his hand, but Đăng Đạo ignored it. Instead, with lips compressed, he put his hands together and bowed stiffly, as if to imply the man lacked merit. His unsmiling nephew continued to size up Streak, who wore black jeans, a pair of black Red Wing boots, and a red flannel shirt. From a wall hook hung a black Carhartt western-style jacket—a stark contrast to Đăng Đạo's preppy attire. Kannon didn't ask how he'd obtained the western clothes, because Streak appeared stupefied by Đăng Đạo's greeting.

"Aunt Lan has fully briefed me on your part in this disaster," Đăng Đạo said. The words sizzled from his nephew's mouth like the prolonged hiss of a pit viper.

Great start.

It didn't matter. Another issue took precedence.

All he had to do was take a veteran combat pilot defecting from a militia group and a well-educated Vietnamese ninja with a questionable background and meld them into a team. As simple as deciphering the tax code.

"Take a seat," Kannon said.

Attempting to ease the tension, Kannon detailed positive comments about Streak's background and current situation, then summarized Đăng Đạo's status for Streak. Kannon added, "His birth father was my interpreter in Việt Nam. At two years of age, Đăng Đạo was kidnapped by a Việt Cộng cell leader and educated in guerilla warfare."

"Intriguing!" Streak said, twitching his index and middle fingers back and forth.

"Let's get started." Kannon dug into his backpack to retrieve the laptop and portable printer. He powered them up, then connected to the motel's Wi-Fi. Đăng Đạo had also brought along a laptop and did the same. Kannon dug out his Meerschaum but didn't light up.

"Aunt Lan has told me a lot about you," Đăng Đạo said to Streak, as Kannon began filling coffee cups. "She said you are a Quisling."

Kannon nearly dropped the coffee pot. *Quisling, the Norwegian traitor who supported the Nazis during WW II.* Streak's mouth opened, but no words came out.

"I do not trust you, Streak Man." Đăng Đạo leaned forward, holding a coffee cup. "You assaulted my aunt Lan. You are the cause of my cousin's disappearance."

"I can't undo what's done," Streak said. He withdrew his slingshot from his back pocket, apparently drawing comfort from it. "I want to help."

"Lot of good that dumb slingshot will do in a firefight." Đăng Đạo's lips tightened.

"Hey!" Streak brandished his homemade weapon at Lan's nephew. "You don't have to worry about me."

"I do worry," Đăng Đạo said. "I would not turn my back to you."

It was as if a tornado had scooped up his nephew and Streak

251

and spat them out at opposite poles. Streak glanced at Kannon as if wanting him to intervene. But Streak needed to hold his own, or Đăng Đạo would grind him to shreds.

"I don't trust you, either," Streak said, staring at the floor. "Your fucking people shot me down in 'Nam."

"Maybe if you were a better pilot—"

"I'm a damn good pilot!" Streak said.

"Im nào," Đăng Đạo said.

"In English, please." Kannon's scarred hand twitched. He massaged it.

"I told him to shut up." Đăng Đạo blew a wisp of hair away from his forehead.

"All right. Enough!" Kannon grew tired of the jaw-flapping between the two. The sought-for guarded, if not magical, truce wasn't happening. Still, he didn't want them glossing over their differences, because later, like the pricking of a festering wound, the slightest trigger could activate an unresolved conflict and destroy the team's focus. That could get them all killed. "We need to stay on track. I need you two to set aside all personal conflicts for the sake of Derrick's rescue. If you can't get along—"

"Kannon . . ." His name sailed on Streak's tremulous sigh. "I'm sorry for the harm I've caused your family. I'll do anything possible to help bring your son back."

Đăng Đạo arched his eyebrows.

"The past is past," as Lan had said. "To jell as a combat team requires months of training. We have maybe twelve hours to come together and develop a plan. Đăng Đạo, you either get on board, or I'll put your ass on a plane back to Albuquerque. And Streak, you're out of bargaining chips."

The two of them appeared as lifelike mannequins posed for an advertising stunt. Kannon wondered whether Đăng Đạo had been expressing his pain or empathizing over Lan's.

"You guys realize you share a common bond, right?" Kannon added.

"What?" Streak asked.

Đăng Đạo shrugged.

"Both of you have turned against violent, irrational leaders."

"Interesting point." Streak cast a questioning glance toward Đăng Đạo, who seemed to acknowledge the connection.

"Are you guys in?" Kannon squared his shoulders. "Or am I better off tackling this alone?"

"Không!"

That was the most emphatic (No) Kannon had ever heard. "Đăng Đạo, does that mean you're on board?"

"Vâng." Đăng Đạo said, nodding.

That's a yes. "Streak?"

"I'm in," he said.

A slight smile etched Đăng Đạo's face.

"All right," Kannon fired up his pipe, "we're good to go."

"What about the Cessna 208?" Streak asked.

"I'll try the guy again."

This time Tucker answered. "Yeah, it's available. Fueling it up now. Tell me about this pilot of yours."

"Flew gunships in 'Nam. Also qualified on fixed-wing aircraft."

"That's good enough for me, Kannon. I know you've been through a lot. Bring me some venison."

"Will do." To the others, "We've got a plane."

Kannon canceled the alternative plane reservation.

"Can you fly it?" Đăng Đạo rolled his eyes.

Kannon frowned at the scornful motion. His nephew mouthed an okay.

"Damn straight I can." Streak said.

Good. Streak was holding his ground. Like the spark of flint on stone, it reminded him of his classmate's performance in officer candidate school—the man he once knew.

"Streak. You told me your Jeep was in Whitefish, right?"

"Yep."

"Can we fly into there? It's obviously closer to Border Slot." Streak shook his head.

"Kalispell or Glacier are the closest airfields."

"Which is better?" Kannon rubbed his chin.

"Kalispell."

"Which means we have to find a way to get from Kalispell to

Whitefish," Kannon said. "Renting a car leaves a paper trail, and I don't want to do that. Do either of you have a false driver's license with a matching credit card?"

No one raised his hand.

"That's a problem." Kannon was surprised neither of them had a second identity.

"Not for me," Đăng Đạo said. "I will steal a car."

"Better we pay cash for a shuttle or a cab," Kannon said.

Đăng Đạo shrugged.

"Okay, then," Streak said. "I've got something to show you." He rose, went to the bedside table, and returned with a sheet of paper, which he slapped on the table. It was a hand-drawn map.

"Cool!"

The rough sketch included each building's floor plan, location of doors, windows, and outdoor landmarks such as meeting spaces and trails. Listed on a separate page were the militiamen's names as well as their physical descriptions—including those who had tattoos—along with quirks like sleeping habits, skill sets, and other strengths and weaknesses.

"Forty acres," Kannon muttered. "That's a good size spread."

"Most of the land is off to the right of the map. The chopper pad, obstacle course, firing range, my hut, and the workshop."

"Workshop?" That got Kannon's attention.

"Yeah, they got all kinds of machine tools in there. Can make almost anything." Streak paused. "And . . ."

"And what?"

"A practice killing range." Streak used hand quotes to emphasize *killing* and went on to describe it.

"Damn," Đăng Đạo said.

"What's the best way to infiltrate the compound?" Kannon asked.

"Well, the compound backs up to a sheer cliff," Streak said, "though there's a narrow trail behind Crandle's cabin."

"I see," Đăng Đạo said. "It leads to the armory."

"Right. An electrified fence surrounds the buildings. The front gate is charged too. Twenty-yard-wide minefields protect the side flanks."

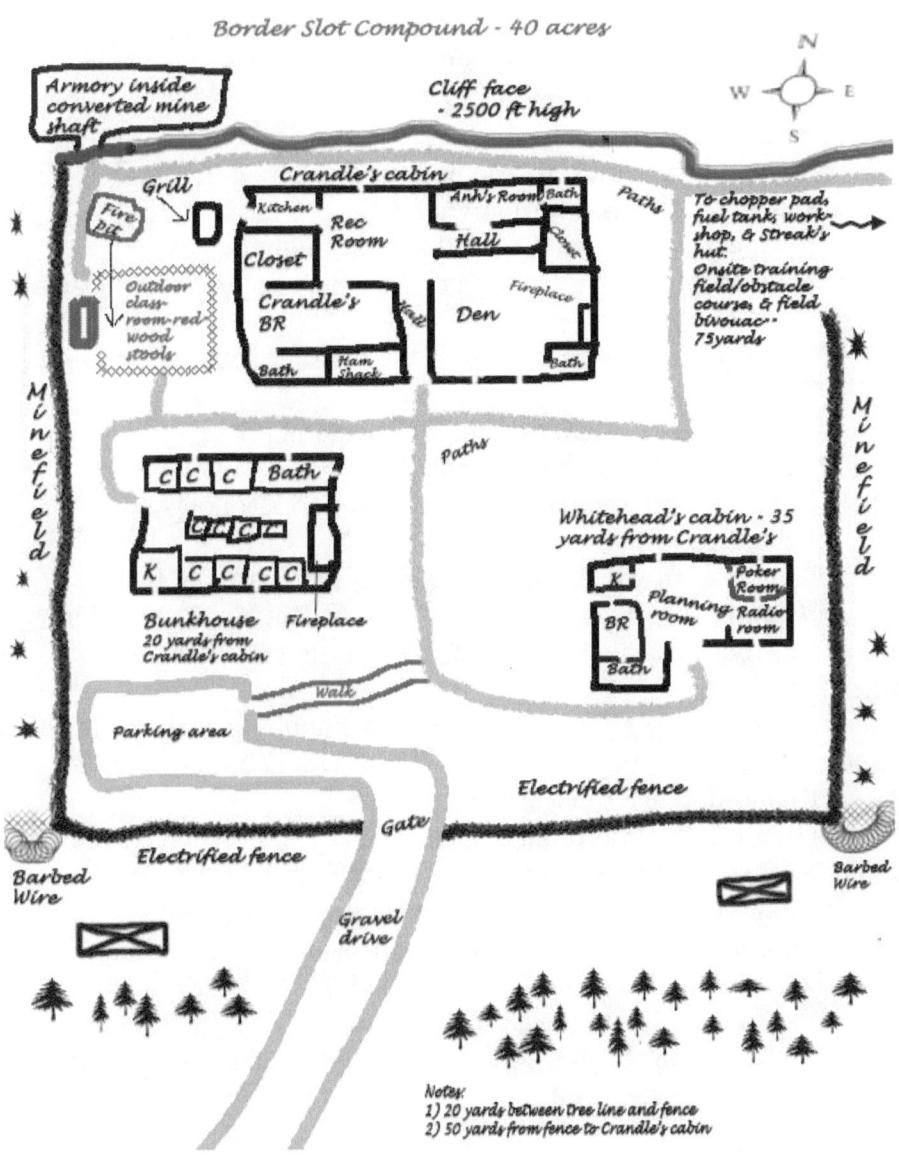

Border Slot Compound - 40 acres

"You don't know?" Đăng Đạo asked, rubbing his chin.

"I was told not to test it. I didn't."

"Understandable," Kannon said. "The asterisks at the sides of the map, those designate the mines?"

"Yes."

Kannon didn't think art loomed high in Streak's future, if he had one, but the map was informative.

"It appears, then, that a frontal assault might be best."

"Your map shows a front gate. Are there any others?" Đăng Đạo asked.

"No. The gate remains open in the daytime, but they close it at night."

"The gate . . . manual or remote?" Kannon asked.

"Remote, with manual override."

"I don't suppose you have a remote unit," Kannon said.

"I chunked it."

Đăng Đạo frowned. Streak cut his eyes toward the floor.

Oh, man, that could've come in handy. But Kannon couldn't place blame because he knew Streak never intended to return to Border Slot.

"If it's gone, it's gone," Kannon said, thumbing back and forth between the map and the list of militiamen. "What about sentries?"

"Random. I never discerned a pattern."

"Give me the coordinates," Đăng Đạo said. "I have special mapping software. I will Google Border Slot."

Streak voiced the coordinates. While Đăng Đạo keyed them in, Kannon tapped his fingers on the table waiting for an image to materialize.

Once it did, Kannon examined the aerial visual, getting a feel for the terrain, aching for his son. "Damnit!" He pounded the table, jostling the coffee pot.

Streak flinched.

"You are *seeing* him?" Đăng Đạo asked.

"Yeah." Kannon found it difficult to accept he might be looking down on Derrick. The thought made him sick with rage.

Đăng Đạo brought him back on track. He connected to Kannon's printer via wireless and printed three copies of various downloaded versions of the Border Slot area and adjacent terrain. Since the portable printer had copy capability, they made two copies of Streak's hand-drawn map.

"These Google maps give us a general idea," Kannon said, "but the details are too fuzzy to be useful in planning an op. Where can we get topographical maps at this late date?"

Pursing his lips, Đăng Đạo pulled out a satellite phone of his own and made a call. The conversation transpired in Vietnamese.

"What's up?" Kannon asked.

"Since we must land at my airstrip near Albuquerque to pick up supplies, I instructed my associates to obtain topo maps."

"Great if we can get them," Kannon said, closing his laptop. From an earlier conversation, he knew the *supplies* included a weapons cache. Was Đăng Đạo really reformed?

Memo to file: Follow up on Đăng Đạo's associates.

Forty-Four

Goose pimples prickled Kannon's arms and neck as he stood alongside Đăng Đạo at Tucker's private airstrip. The reddish bumps occurred more from longing for Lan's touch and compassion than from the cooler air. He prayed Sergeant Creighton wasn't causing her too much aggravation, further frazzling her nerves.

The air was nippy. Heavy clouds masked the sun, but no rain, for which Kannon was grateful. He peered at the sleek, gleaming Cessna 208 Caravan, which sat alone. The aircraft was a high-winged, single-engine turboprop with a fixed three-wheel landing gear, a large side cargo door, and room for nine passengers. The owner had removed the cargo belly pod to improve fuel efficiency, but there was still plenty of room for their gear.

"Cool. Very cool!" Streak said, after conducting both an internal and external flight check. "It's powered by a Pratt and Whitney PT6 and has a Garmin G1000 integrated avionics system."

That registered with what Tucker had told Kannon. The plane was wired so that passengers could plug into the avionics system.

"Hop aboard." Streak opened the left-side pilot's door and climbed inside.

Kannon and Đăng Đạo boarded the aircraft through its rear air-stair door on the opposite side of the cargo slot. They donned the communication headsets and plugged in.

"Let's get off the ground," Kannon said, rehearsing their transport plans: Fly to Albuquerque, refuel, fly to Kalispell, hire a cab to reach Streak's Willys at Whitefish, hit Border Slot, rescue Derrick, reverse scenario—sans cab—for escape and evasion. Simple, right?

After familiarizing himself with the controls, Streak started the Pratt and Whitney engine. The propeller spun alive. Soon, a steady drone permeated the cabin as the plane sped down the short runway.

Kannon prayed he was making the right moves. Since two-thirds of their airtime would take place at night, Streak would have to fly the aircraft using instruments. Any unforeseen circumstances causing interaction with the FAA would complicate matters, so they hadn't filed a formal flight plan. Another risk.

The flight plan called for refueling at a field-expedient airstrip east of Albuquerque, courtesy of Đăng Đạo.

Liftoff.

"I want to take another look at Streak's hand-drawn map and their *roster*," Đăng Đạo said, withdrawing his copies. Seconds later, his nephew looked at Kannon with a grim expression. "Anh is a Vietnamese name. Who is she? What is she doing there?"

"Fill us in, Streak," Kannon said.

"Anh is a Vietnamese refugee Crandle smuggled into the country. She cooks and cleans, as well as services the Commander." Streak pivoted in the pilot seat and mimicked quotation marks. "The only reason she's there is that she's got nowhere else to go, or any means to get there if she did."

"Sex slave," Đăng Đạo mumbled, between riveted lips.

"Crandle keeps her under wraps," Streak added. "Anh doesn't have a phone, and she's prohibited from leaving the compound."

"She is a prisoner," Đăng Đạo said, glowering. "Crandle is a Neanderthal."

Kannon touched his nephew's arm. "I'm sorry."

He expected this to come up, but with a little more tact. However, there was no use skirting the issue. "We'll rescue her as well."

His nephew nodded as Streak turned back to the controls. They lapsed into silence. A few minutes later . . .

"Brief me on what else you know," Đăng Đạo said to Kannon.

"The local authorities are concentrating their search in central Texas. Amber Alert hasn't come up with anything."

"Do you expect it to?"

"No."

"Once the cops realize you have disappeared," Đăng Đạo said, "they will expand the investigation into New Mexico and Oklahoma."

And probably into Mexico, Louisiana, and beyond. Kannon doubted their search would lead to Northwestern Montana and the Border Slot Militia—another reason for not filing a flight plan—unless Lan, Belynda, or Stefan let something slip.

"They must think it is you who took the boy," Đăng Đạo said.

"Or set out to rescue him," Streak interjected.

259

"Good point, Streak Man."

"The latter's more likely," Kannon said, thinking back to the magic show when he attempted to run after the kidnappers. For Đăng Đạo's benefit, he presented more detail—how Streak happened to pilot for the militia, the stinger missile sting, the planned use of EMP weaponry, and the spectral if ubiquitous presence of Sindy Zeller and her probable lackey, Modesto Poblete. Some of it his nephew already had heard from Lan, but not all. "I'm sure whoever shot Roger thought it was me."

Đăng Đạo nodded, then cocked his eyebrows. "EMP weapons. Missiles. Something else to worry about."

"Yeah." Kannon pegged Streak. "Anything I've left out?"

"Crandle's got a ham shack."

"I'm not surprised." With the right equipment and conditions, Crandle could maintain contacts worldwide. From what little Kannon knew about ham radio sets, their airwave frequencies weren't secure, unless operators communicated in code. "Do you know the frequency?"

"No. He keeps the room locked," Streak said

Đăng Đạo frowned. To Kannon, "We will discuss later, yes?"

"Yes."

"Before we land, I would like to learn more about my birth father."

"A pleasure. I wish you could've known him. Lan cared for Chấn till the end."

Đăng Đạo swallowed hard. Kannon cuffed him on the shoulder.

"In addition to being my interpreter, Chấn was my friend. I trusted him. He accompanied me on every operation, except one—"

"The one that drew you back to Việt Nam thirty years later?"

"Lan must've told you."

"She detailed the connection between you two."

"You mirror him. Chấn excelled in combat, in reading his people, and in navigating the land. Because of his agility, I called him the Deer Walker," Kannon said, smiling.

"Deer Walker," Đăng Đạo said.

His nephew listened intently to the rest of Kannon's

monologue, but it was hard to read his facial expression. Vietnamese were notorious for not letting their emotions show. It reminded him of Lan, who, behind an inscrutable face, often cached an explosive load of emotion. Kannon also realized his nephew never took notes about anything. *He must have an eidetic memory.*

"Deer Walker," Đăng Đạo repeated, then fell silent. He leaned back in his seat, perhaps reflecting on what might have been had he known his birth father. More and more, Kannon saw in his nephew the image of Chấn. He also believed Đăng Đạo intuitively understood the immense polar-opposite pressures his father had been under during the war.

"Đăng Đạo, about those associates you spoke to from the motel—"

"You have seen them before."

Kannon stared out the window. Watching the West Texas landscape pass underneath, he listened to the steady drone of the engine, allowing its sound to steady his frazzled nerves.

Forty-Five

Kannon woke just as the Cessna Caravan approached the refueling site east of Albuquerque. Even though they had gained an hour, the sun rode low, and orange bands cleaved the purplish horizon. A quarter moon hovered in the darkening sky, all of which reminded him of a setting he and Lan had shared atop the Rex Hotel in Sài Gòn.

How was she doing with Creighton? he wondered. Had they received a ransom call? Sighing, he activated his satellite phone for when they landed, then spoke through the intercom.

"How's it going, Streak?"

"Situation under control," he said. "Flying on instruments. The Garmin navigation system is slick."

"Good."

Đăng Đạo, who had fallen asleep, stirred.

"About time you woke up," Kannon said, still functioning on adrenaline.

"I have an internal clock." Đăng Đạo yawned, stretched, then glanced out the window. "There is the airstrip."

Kannon spotted the makeshift LZ. It was illuminated by candle-lanterns and sandwiched between treeless flat-top buttes squared off by sheer rock walls. The dirt airstrip looked smooth enough but emptied abruptly into a dry creek bed. At its edge, a windsock flapped lazily, indicating the approach to land must come from the opposite direction.

Streak turned the aircraft, then manipulated the rudder pedals and flaps and settled into a smooth glide path. The fixed landing struts held firm as the Cessna struck pay dirt, bounced, and bounced again before settling into a steady but bumpy taxiing.

Đăng Đạo leaned forward and pointed over Streak's shoulder.

"Đấy!" he said, using the Vietnamese word for there. "Take us into the clearing framed by the large grove of trees on the right."

As soon as the plane stopped, Kannon opened the side doors, jumped to the ground, and ran toward the nearest pile of rocks. He placed the satellite call to the burner phone with one hand while unzipping his fly with the other.

Fortunately, Stefan had set up voicemail. Unfortunately, his son didn't answer. Creighton wouldn't be at it this long, would he? Or had the deputy hauled his wife, Stefan, and Belynda to the station?

Drop the paranoia.

Kannon would have to trust the three of them were okay. He left an ASAP message for Stefan, then holstered his sat, finished his other business, and zipped up.

Returning to the plane, Kannon inhaled the dry, high desert air. After cruising for nearly four hours at three thousand feet—at a monotonous pace of two-hundred miles an hour—he was relieved to be on the ground.

A floodlight flicked on, revealing a mid-sized fuel tanker parked underneath a thick canopy of broadleaved cottonwoods. Inside the clearing, several tree stumps had been cut to ground level to make room for aircraft. The fuel truck, rusted and pitted, reminded Kannon of an abandoned boat in dry dock. Two Vietnamese men exited the truck.

"Lại đây," Đăng Đạo said in a strong voice.

Roughly interpreted to, "Get your ass over here," Kannon knew.

The two men double-timed to their leader, where they exchanged crisp salutes.

Former gang leader, indeed.

Đăng Đạo directed his men to help Streak pivot the plane around and position it to taxi out of the clearing.

The new guys' hard-bitten, focused expressions impressed Kannon. Both stood about five foot seven and wore pressed chinos and short-sleeved khaki shirts, which exposed baseball-sized deltoids. The only way he could tell them apart was that one sported a thin-banded mustache. Kannon figured they were brothers . . . and that he *had* seen them before.

"This is Quán and Kim," Đăng Đạo said.

The two men nodded and cast thin smiles at Kannon.

"It's nice to see you again," Kim, the one with the thin mustache, said. "You're a tough guy."

Kannon's first thought was to dive for cover. His underarms

became suddenly wet.

"Got the stuff?" Đăng Đạo asked his guys.

The question temporarily derailed Kannon's plunge into the past.

"Enough to topple a small government," Quán said.

Kim motioned the fuel tanker forward to position it for refueling the plane. Kannon followed Đăng Đạo and Streak to the rear of the tanker. The cargo bay contained a false metal door in the back. Behind it was a cavity full of AK47s, banana clips, ammunition, and grenades—frags, CS, flash-bangs, and white phosphorus. There were also boonie hats, compact high-intensity flashlights, Pulsar Edge GS night vision goggles, two-quart collapsible canteens filled with water, and additional supplies that could greatly aid their mission.

"Are you familiar with this weapon?" Đăng Đạo grabbed an AK and sharply executed the Manual of Arms.

"I am," Streak said. "The militiamen carry AKs. Usually, they're kept in the armory, but under certain conditions, Crandle's been known to issue them within the compound."

Though impressed with his counterpart's demonstration, Kannon hoped they wouldn't have to resort to automatic weapons. Đăng Đạo brought out three mobile GPS devices as well as three handheld field radios. Relatively light, they were AN/PRC-148s.

"Field-tested by your military in the Middle East," Đăng Đạo said. "They have an estimated range from three- to six-kilometers, depending on the weather and terrain obstacles."

"Got it," Kannon said. He examined one of the radios, running his hands over the push-to-talk switch, volume and preset frequency dials, and squelch tuning. "Fresh batteries?"

"Of course."

"We have to assume the militia is expecting us," Kannon said, staring at the equipment.

"Yeah," Streak said.

"Got plastic explosives?" Kannon asked. C-4 could be instrumental if they had to breach the electrified fence or any other Border Slot fortifications.

"You betcha," Kim said.

Quán produced six white bricks of the clay-like substance,

which could be molded into various shapes—plus blasting caps, timed fuses, electrical detonators, manual fuse igniters, and detonation cord. They could detonate electrically or non-electrically.

"Nobody can say you're not well-stocked." Kannon surmised Đăng Đạo could procure most any weapon he wanted.

Quán handed Đăng Đạo a Walther PPK, an effective weapon even though its slide assembly was stiff.

"Here is ammo for your two Sigs," Kim said.

Kannon accepted a box each of .40 caliber and 9mm shells. Streak selected a Beretta Tomcat and slipped it inside his jacket.

"What about topo maps?" Kannon asked. They'd help immensely when delving into more detailed planning.

Kim shook his head. "Sorry, I could not obtain the maps on short notice."

Kannon felt like another tire had gone flat.

Đăng Đạo shot Kim a withering look, then to Kannon, "If there is time, we will try to get them in Montana."

"Makes sense."

"For your stomach and spirit," Quán said, tapping Kannon on the arm. The Vietnamese man popped the lid off a large plastic bowl, revealing a generous portion of steaming spring rolls and rice cakes. "The *nắm tôm* sauce is a salted shrimp-paste and will also protect you from evil."

Arching his eyebrows, Kannon surmised the offering was an appeasement for their confrontation six years ago in the Sangre de Cristos.

"That's kind of you. All is forgiven."

"Likewise." Quán winked.

A revving engine diverted everyone's attention to the fuel tanker. He and Đăng Đạo stepped back as the unseen driver maneuvered the truck out of the hideaway. With the tanker gone, Kannon observed Quán and Kim leaning against separate tree trunks. Each man had his arms folded and one ankle crossed over the other.

They were brothers all right. Like being stabbed, the observation revived the sharp pain from Roger's death.

Focus, Kannon, focus.

Shifting thought back to Quán and Kim, Kannon found it hard

to imagine what kinds of activities comprised their day jobs. "Đăng Đạo, how do you keep these guys below the radar?"

"We fly above the radar now."

"About that?"

"As I told Aunt Lan, we are no longer a gang," Đăng Đạo said, buckling a pistol belt around his waist. "After the firefight in the Sangre de Cristos, I studied the photographs you gave me and thought hard about what you said. It struck me that the man who kidnapped and raised me was nothing like the inside of my heart."

"And you decided to go straight."

"It took a while."

"Above the radar—"

"We're private contractors, specializing in security. Like Blackwater, only much, much smaller. Most of our clients are Asian."

A born-again capitalist, Kannon thought. "Guess it adds a sense of legitimacy."

"It does." Đăng Đạo adjusted the fitting on his pistol belt. "I formed an LLC, of which I am president and chief executive officer."

"Fits with your MBA." Security firms were known to tread on the edge, though. He suspected Đăng Đạo's did as well. Yet, as Kannon continued filtering his nephew's words, a new idea formed. Quán and Kim could be useful.

"All right," Kannon said, opening the passenger door. "Let's pack and stack this gear so we can depart while there's a twinge of light." When finished, they rolled the plane to the airstrip.

"It's an atmospheric timeout," Streak said. "No wind."

Wanting to be sure nothing was left behind, Kannon returned to the tree-canopied clearing, which held the captured smells of sweet cottonwoods and the sickening odor from the truck's diesel fuel. Adding to the mix was the dust kicked up by Quán and Kim as they swept the area clean. Would Đăng Đạo agree to incorporate the brothers?

Returning to the airstrip, Kannon pulled out his satphone and punched the number for Stefan's burner. Same result. Had the militia come back and whacked everybody? That sucked. Doubt—one of Christianity's seven deadly sins—also made Buddha's list of the ten fetters.

I'm on a roll.

Seeing Đăng Đạo moving close, Kannon braced for a question he knew was coming.

"Did you reach Aunt Lan?"

Kannon shook his head.

"It will be all right," Đăng Đạo said. "Remember, we are a family of warriors."

"I have no problem remembering that."

"Ready for takeoff," Streak said, twirling the cowboy hat on his index finger.

"Okay." Kannon squared his shoulders. "Streak, I want you to hear this too. Đăng Đạo? How about we take Quán and Kim along to Montana?"

Dust particles reflected off Đăng Đạo's glasses in the waning light, which lit up the tight smile on his face.

Forty-Six

Monday, 26 October 2009, Kootenai National Forest & Border Slot Compound, Montana

After Whitehead disappeared within the wooded mountain slope, Crandle struck with his knife at the gutted carcass they had strung up. He was mad at himself for coming down so hard on his second-in-command. The idea of trailing him resurfaced, but Crandle decided against it. If Whitehead didn't want to be found, he wouldn't be found.

Taking a breather, he tossed his knife at a tree. The blade stuck. As its handle wavered back and forth, Crandle closed his eyes and, in a silent appeal, implored Whitehead to return. When he opened his eyes, he noticed a gray timber wolf loitering nearby. It seemed to be grinning. Crandle knew the animal because it had been cast from its pack a year ago. On its right side, the gray-furred loner wore a jagged scar on bare skin as proof of its exiled status.

"Hello, Lobo. You'd like to bite a chunk out of me, hey."

Crandle didn't try lassoing the animal, a game the two of them had played more than once. Instead, he pulled his semi-auto and fired a warning shot to scare him off. The wolf yelped and retreated into the woods.

He finished carving the choicest cuts with as much precision as possible. Even so, he left more of the meat than he usually would for Lobo. Next, he fashioned a travois from stout aspen branches and a poncho. He rubbed snow on the raw meat to help preserve it, wrapped the cuts in butcher paper, and placed all of it onto his rough-hewn sled. Crandle strung his lariat through the armholes in the poncho, slung the uncoiled rope around his chest, and began hauling his butchered kill downslope, backtracking through the trees and snow-covered granite.

After reaching the Gator, he hefted the packaged meat onto the rear cargo space, then opened his water bottle and drank from it.

The inclement weather held, but he knew it wouldn't drive Whitehead in. If his number two didn't return, Crandle would have to decide whether to carry out or to abort tonight's EMP mission. He didn't relish having to make that decision.

Crandle cranked up the ATV. Riding off, he thought about the timber wolf. Its presence reminded him of Jack London's *White Fang*. Fangs reminded him of snakes. Snakes reminded him of Streak, who had a coyote friend named Kannon Ballard. Damn them all.

Careening around aspen and evergreens, dropping into treeless depressions beneath dark-racing clouds, he also thought more about the kid Whitehead had dragged in. The boy was a half-breed, which led him to William Potter Gale and his contaminated blood. If Gale could disown the Jewish half of his lineage and become a principal proponent of the *Posse Comitatus* movement, then Crandle could train Whitehead's fledgling half-breed his way. It'd be a challenge to drill the brainwashing out of him. He'd teach the boy who his enemies were and to reject any other heritage that might run through his veins.

I could call him Patterson the second, or Patterson II. Crandle smiled at his creation. *Hell. I'll call him Patu. And Patu will not have a social security number or ever pay a cent to the IRS.*

* * *

After dropping off the wild game for Anh to marinate for tomorrow's celebratory feast, Crandle walked toward the bunkhouse. Hatfield and Badger were loitering outside, but he ignored their curious looks because he didn't want to entertain any questions concerning Whitehead's absence.

"Bull, get your ass out here."

The newbie emerged.

"To the armory," Crandle said.

"Yes, sir." Bull saluted. It pleased Crandle that Bull sported a shaved head, clean fatigues, and shined boots. He no longer resembled a snorting buffalo.

"What's up, Commander?"

"After Whitehead's report on the Texas operation, you're lucky to be still standing."

Hatfield and Badger snickered. Bull didn't. Instead, the FNG's face turned beet red.

"I can do better, Commander."

269

"Damn straight you will. You're going back to Texas."

Bull's lips curled into a smile as Crandle told him what he expected, then led the newbie along the trail leading to the armory.

"Wait outside," Crandle said, once they neared the converted mine shaft.

After unlocking the camouflaged entrance, Crandle entered the modified cavern chamber, which maintained a constant cool temperature. He flicked a switch. Lights, powered by solar panels, flickered on and illuminated stocked EMP devices and rows of assault rifles and handguns arrayed in military precision. The weapons were secured by tempered steel rods running through the trigger guards.

His central safe, also constructed from tempered steel, sat in a corner. Later, Crandle intended to move it to his adjacent bunker.

For now, he gathered the necessary equipment, then locked up the interior and exited the armory with a duffle. It contained Bull's assigned rifle and a semiautomatic pistol, threaded silencers, and extra capacity fully loaded magazines.

Once outside, Crandle handed over the duffle.

"Thirty miles down the road there's a two-thousand-one white Dodge Ram at a service station," Crandle told Bull. "A camper top covers the truck bed. Stash your weaponry out of sight. If word comes back to us that you got stopped, we'll say you stole the truck, but you'll never reach jail." Crandle demonstrated his customary finger across the throat motion. "Clear?"

"I understand, sir." Bull accepted the truck keys. His gnarled fingers reminded Crandle of tree roots.

"Nolan will take you there."

Bull nodded.

"You know what I want, right?"

"Yes, sir. Complete the Texas job. If Streak and Kannon Ballard are there, I'm to bring them back alive, but I heard talk one or more of those dudes could be on his way here—"

"So why go, you're thinking. I believe in covering all the bases. If they come here, I'll have men on alert. We'll get the sons-a-bitches. If not, it's your job to nail 'em."

"Sir, what if there are others at the residence?"

"Kill them."

Bull pawed the ground. "I will succeed, sir. I want to be part of this team."

"Carrying this off will help your case."

Bull snapped to attention. "Appreciate that, sir."

Maybe Whitehead's beating the crap out of him had an impact. "I like your new attitude."

Baring his teeth, Bull reached for his back pocket. He pulled out the Sling-Hawk he'd been demonstrating around the compound.

"Perhaps you'll get a chance to use it." OT's brazen brother reminded Crandle of himself when he was younger. Bull possessed the raw traits of a front-line warrior.

"Ballard could be a challenge. He's not afraid of a fight," Crandle added.

Bull licked his lips. The buttons on his fatigue shirt seemed ready to pop. "I'll make him eat shit, Commander."

Literally, Crandle thought. "One more thing. Here's five grand. Finish the job, bring Streak and Ballard back, there's another fifteen thousand in it for you."

"I'll earn it." Bull smiled.

"Now get the fuck out of here."

Bull took off at a run across the snow-clotted ground, lugging the weapons load toward Nolan in a waiting SUV.

I'll keep tabs on him. If Streak and Ballard aren't there, I'll let him destroy whoever and whatever is left.

* * *

Moderate snowfall fell around Crandle in the crisp air. A blustery wind swirled off the high cliff wall. The air smelled like diluted gun oil.

An eagle screeched, soared with the thermals. Circling lower, the predator cocked its head in its search for prey. The eagle dived. Sighting along the eagle's flight path, Crandle projected his vision to the killing zone. A rabbit, barely visible in the snow, hopped its last when the eagle's claws dug into its flesh.

Survival of the fittest.

It was now 1930 hours. Crandle's thoughts returned to Whitehead. The upcoming EMP mission wouldn't be complete without him. If he failed to show up at Border Slot by 2100, Crandle

271

would have to make a go or no-go decision. If he canceled the mission, what would he tell his men? He'd have to concoct a believable story, such as Whitehead had come down with a severe stomach virus. A temporary diversion, Crandle recognized, because eventually, he would have to fess up.

As for putting either Hatfield or Badger in charge of the ground op, Hatfield couldn't say five words without pissing off somebody. He'd probably get fragged. Badger wasn't as tough, but he was more personable. And he wasn't afraid to speak up. Neither guy had led a complicated mission before, though, and Crandle was reluctant to turn over control of the ground op to an unproven leader.

If Whitehead doesn't show, I'll abort the ground op but execute the airdrop.

Forty-Seven

Five hours till crunch time. The strike was to take place at 0130 hours. About to enter his cabin, Crandle stopped when he heard footsteps crunching along the gravel walk. Standing under the porch light, he peered through the cold, dusky gloom and scowled. It was Nolan, returning after dropping off Bull at the service station. *Damn. Why couldn't it have been Whitehead!*

"Well?" Crandle ran his hands through his buzz cut.

"Damned if that red pate of yours don't look bright under that light."

"Cut the crap. How'd it go?"

"Bull's hyped."

"He'll do all right." Crandle paused, glancing past Nolan, past any hope of Whitehead's return. "Tell the guys we'll have a briefing at twenty-one hundred hours."

"Is tonight the night, sir?"

"Roger that. No one's to leave the compound."

Nolan saluted.

Crandle waved him off and turned back to his cabin. Inside, his leather recliner creaked as he lowered himself into it and leaned back. A fire crackled in the fireplace, warming the den. The burning hickory gave off a sweet smell, as did the wood from the wood-burning stove in the kitchen. Outside, the wind swirled as the second significant snowfall of the season continued.

He bit off the end of a cigar and lit up. Crandle remembered one of several incidents that had toughened him up in his youth. As a six-year-old, he'd walked into his parents' bedroom to see his mom tied spread-eagled on her bed. He thought his father was hurting her, and so he'd jumped on his dad's back, right when Father Crandle was spewing white *juice* on his mother's face. His dad had taken a belt and beat the shit out of him, literally. As further punishment, for the next five weeks he had to cut clumps of hay with a straight razor sharpened on a stone.

In the long run, that occurrence with his mom helped him learn how to treat women, both his dead wife and now, Anh. He hollered

273

for her. "Anh! Get your ass into the den. Bring the boy."

The click from Anh's bedroom door opening reached his ears. Carrying Patu, she entered the den wearing loose-fitting lime-green pants and a bright orange blouse to hide her curves. The boy still looked pale, but better than yesterday.

"Fourteen hundred hours tomorrow afternoon," Crandle said. "You'll be ready."

"Yes, Commander." She set Patu down. "I will get up early and start the wood fire. When the coals are ready, I will take the cut meat from its wine bath and place it on the grill."

"Good. The banquet will celebrate the success of our first EMP attack. What do you think of that, Patu?"

"I don't know what you're talking about. So, I don't care."

"Don't look down at the floor when you talk to me. Look into my eyes. And you'll say, Sir, every time you address me. Understand?"

"Okay," Patu said.

Crandle grabbed the boy's arm and spun him around. Popped him hard on the rear, then spun the little shit around again. Patu's lips turned inward. His eyes reddened. Crandle was about to smack him again, but Anh stepped in and took Patu's hand.

"Say, 'Yes, sir,'" Anh told him.

"Yes, sir."

"That's better. Anh, fix me a bacon sandwich."

She started off with the boy.

"Leave him here."

Anh turned around, looked about to cry. "I am afraid you will hurt him."

"Don't go blubbering on me. This world is about survival. Life's not fair. If it was, do you think you'd have spent all those years in a refugee camp? What if I hadn't come along? Look at you now. You're free. You've got a roof over your head, food and clothes."

"He is not like you. Patu, as you call him, is a gentle boy. Even your voice scares him."

"Not for long. You don't make a boy tough by babying him. I'm going to teach him strength, how to survive." Like his father had done for him. Like he'd been doing with Patterson.

Anh shook her head.

"Disgusted, are you?" Crandle asked. "Keep flapping your lip and I'll turn you over to the boys. Now get in the fucking kitchen and make my sandwich."

Anh turned and stomped off without saying anything.

Women! They're all bitches.

If not for the men fighting and dying, none of 'em would have a decent place to live. Every bitch he ever knew claimed to be against war until her security was involved. And then it was: *Send the other mother's boy, not mine.* The hypocrisy sickened him.

Hearing the clang of iron on metal, Crandle chuckled. Anh was mad. He liked her that way, especially at night.

"Come 'ere, Patu."

The boy didn't move.

"Get the fuck over here, peckerhead."

Patu walked toward him, jerky and unsteady, like a wooden puppet.

Crandle leaned forward in the chair and picked up the kid. Patu tried to squirm away.

"Put me down, Sir."

"Spunky little bastard, aren't you? If you don't adapt here, you're not gonna make it. Understand? This is your home now."

"You're mean."

"Listen, boy. Don't confuse strength and power with meanness. The weak are jealous. They've lost the game and know it."

Patu's eyes grew round like bullet casings.

"Do ya know what spunk is, Patu?"

"No, sir."

"It's guts. Being tough."

Crandle set the boy down and reached into a canvas duffle. He pulled out two unopened boxes, Christmas gifts he had intended to give to Patterson all those years ago. The first contained a brand-new semiautomatic pellet rifle, the second, a repeating-shot pistol. Both were gas operated, and each fired .22-caliber pellets. "I'll teach you how to shoot these before moving on to real weapons. You'll learn how to ride. How to throw a lasso. How to throw a knife. How to live off the land."

275

"I know how to shoot . . . Sir." Patu stuck out his chest as he took the air pistol and pointed it toward Crandle. "Bang! You're dead."

"You little turd!" He raised his hand to slap some sense into the fucker when the front cabin door burst open.

"Whitehead!"

His second-in-command stood sculpted like a statue. Clumps of snow fell from his jacket onto the floor. Ice hung from his mustache, and his face was as red as the embers in the fireplace. But what caught Crandle's attention the most was that damn knife in his hand.

"Don't do anything stupid." Crandle locked his eyes on the gleaming silver blade.

The sound of Whitehead's canvas coat sleeve rasping against the canvas coat body ripped through the den as he whipped his arm forward. The knife whistled above Crandle's head.

"Are you crazy?"

"Settle down, Commander. I could've punctured your heart if I'd wanted." Whitehead shut the door behind him and moved opposite Crandle. "That's for the face slap."

Crandle's shoulders slumped. "I . . . I never should've done that."

"No. You shouldn't have."

"I'm sorry."

Whitehead smiled. "Apology accepted."

"Guess you've been in the woods all this time."

"Yep."

"Doing what?"

"Talking to the trees."

Ah, the aspen eyes. Whitehead had told him about those before. "What did they tell you?"

"Many eyes spoke to me." Whitehead shed his jacket. "They revealed understanding and guidance. The wisest one told me I belong at Border Slot."

How do you talk with fucking notches on a tree, much less believe what they say? It didn't matter. Crandle liked the answer.

"So, you're in?"

"I'm here to tackle the mission, Commander."

"You'll follow orders."

"Yes, Commander."

"Welcome back, Soldier. Anh, make that two bacon sandwiches," he hollered.

Whitehead closed the distance between them and reached out his hand. Crandle took it, thinking that the last several hours had passed about as fast as an inchworm climbing a hill.

Forty-Eight

After serving the two men their sandwiches, Anh, feeling an ache in her heart, sat Patu at the table. He still had not eaten. She wanted to get protein into him. Last night she had prepared a warm chicken broth, but he refused to touch it. Bewildered, she thought the boy must have been in shock. Not knowing what else to do, she had washed his face and put him in her bed while she slept on the floor. He did not look much better this afternoon.

She was glad about one thing, Whitehead's return. He was the only one who ever showed her any kindness, and she wanted to talk with him about this boy. But he was engaged with the Commander, who had been more antagonistic than usual during Whitehead's short absence.

She thought about tomorrow's celebration. She believed in doing her best and would prepare the finest meal possible. Besides, Whitehead had told her that moose meat was full of protein. She prayed that the boy would like it.

For now, though, "You must nourish your stomach, little one." She set a tuna sandwich on the kitchen table, which was a polished redwood slab supported by iron legs. It seemed every flat surface in the compound was made of redwood, including the stool the boy sat on.

Licking his lips, the dazed boy leaned forward, but then drew back and folded his arms. His gestures reminded Anh of the wounded young children who had entered the Thai refugee camp, hungry but reluctant to eat from the hands of strangers.

"I want my *Mẹ*," the boy said.

"You used the Vietnamese word for Mother," Anh said. His pronunciation, the sharp singsong drop in tone for the word, was distinct. She knelt by his side and took his hand. "*Bạn là tiếng Việt Nam?*" she asked. (You are Vietnamese?)

The boy's eyes grew wide. His lips trembled as he said, "Tôi là một nửa người Việt Nam." (I am half Vietnamese.) Then he added in English, "And half Caucasian."

This made sense. The boy's facial features, his eyes especially, looked like the eyes of a Caucasian. His hair, though, was long, thick, and black like hers, and he seemed to know her language well. A person to talk with, even a little one, in her native language, excited her.

Her elation vanished as fast as it had materialized. Why was he here? Anh worried because she knew what Commander Crandle thought about people unlike himself.

"*Tôi muốn biết tên của bạn,*" Anh said. If the boy told her his name, maybe she could encourage him to show more of himself.

"*Tên tôi là Derrick Austin Ballard.*"

"*Tôi là, Anh.*"

The Derrick boy raised his eyebrows a little. His eyes searched her face.

"*Derrick là một cái tên hay. Bạn là một cậu bé nhạy cảm và mạnh mẽ. Tôi muốn có một đứa con trai như bạn một ngày nào đó.* (Derrick is a good name. You are a sensitive and strong boy. I want to have a son like you someday.)

She hoped Derrick would like that she favored his name.

His cheeks puffed out and got red. Water filled his little eyes. Still kneeling, Anh put her arms around the boy and pulled him close to her breast. His small arms encircled her neck. Together they cried until their eyes were not so full. Then they both straightened and stared at each other.

Anh put the tip of her finger on his lower lip in the hope that he would smile. He did not. She decided to switch to English. "Were you taken from your *Mẹ?*"

He raised his eyebrows.

"Yes." He started to cry again.

"What sort of horrible men—?" She stopped herself, recalling stories told by an uncle about atrocities committed by the Việt Cộng. There must be horrible men everywhere. Would she ever find any good ones? She thought Whitehead might have been one once, but now doubted he was of a kind soul.

"I want to go home," the boy said.

"I know you do."

She wanted to take him with her and run away. But where? If only she could gain access to Commander Crandle's phone. Yet, she did not know what correct numbers to push, much less where the numbers would go. Maybe Derrick—

"Anh, bring Patu out here." Commander Crandle's voice boomed through the closed door.

Hearing his ugly tone reminded her of the roar of a cyclone. "Be strong, little one."

Carrying the boy's sandwich, Anh opened the kitchen door and led Derrick into the den. Whitehead was gone. She understood he was getting ready for tonight's big mission.

Even though it was cold outdoors, the den windows were open, and the aroma from the tub of claret wine drifted past. Although the smell was not unpleasant, it seemed incongruous in this wretched place, like a trickster riding a good wind.

"Come here, Patu," Crandle said.

"My name is Derrick."

Feeling her muscles tighten, Anh feared what the Commander might do if the boy did not behave.

"I want Mama Lan and Daddy K."

"Mama Lan . . ." The Commander smirked at Derrick. "Mama Lan does not want you. Neither does your daddy. You belong with us now."

"Stop! You are frightening him."

"Shut up, bitch."

Anh stepped forward and grasped Derrick by the shoulders.

Crandle scowled.

"You will not speak another word to him in Vietnamese. Do you understand? That's the part we're gonna eliminate. Right, Patu?"

"How did you—?"

"I listened at the door," Crandle bellowed.

Derrick's mouth was wide open, and his eyebrows were arched high. Anh knew he looked to her for help, but all she could do was hurt for him.

I will do what I can to protect you.

Crandle walked to the boy. Towering over him, the Commander slapped Derrick. The boy's cheek turned crimson, but he did not cry. Instead, he straightened his shoulders and stuck out his chest.

"My name is Derrick," he said again.

He already behaves like a soldier. Anh wondered what the boy's birth father was like, and if he was alive.

"Listen, you little shit. Your new name is Patu."

The boy pressed his lips together and remained defiant.

"Your parents died in a fire," Crandle said.

"No, they didn't. Two men took me from my *Mẹ*." Derrick spoke his words with force, but fear shone in his eyes.

Anh did not know if a fire disaster was true or not, but she did understand the Commander wanted to empty the boy of what made him strong. He intended to use his *kill toys* to corrupt this boy.

At the refugee camp, older women talked about how communists altered minds by continually speaking untruths. And she was witnessing it.

"I am your father, now," Commander Crandle said.

"No, you're not. My father is Daddy K."

Crandle jerked Derrick around and popped him on the rear. "You'll learn, you little fucker."

Anh clenched her fists. Blood rushed to her face. But she knew if she stepped in, the Commander would do worse.

I must wait for my time.

"See that sack?" Crandle said to Anh. "Be sure Patu wears his new clothes at the banquet tomorrow. Also, find an unfinished block of redwood and have the kid start sanding it."

Disturbed by Crandle's commands, she reached into the sack and pulled out a set of army clothes. "Where did you get these?"

"None of your damn business." Crandle paused. "Another thing. Teach him to salute."

Anh shook her head. She took Derrick's hand and led him back to her room. Still carrying the sandwich, she closed the door and sat on the bed. "You are brave, Derrick. But you must do as he says, or he will hurt you."

He shook his head. "He is a bad man." Water filled his eyes once more. "Why am I here? Where are my Mama Lan and Daddy K?"

"Listen to me." Anh leaned forward and cupped his cheeks. "I will do what I can to keep you safe. I do not want that man to hurt

281

you. Do you understand?"

"Yes."

"Every time he calls you Patu, I want you to say inside your head, *I am Derrick*."

"Why?" His eyes were innocent but questioning.

"This is a game you and I will play. Each of us will think good thoughts about who we are. If punished, we must remember to know the fight that comes from inside the head. Do you understand?"

"I think so."

"Will you play this game with me?"

"Yes, Miss Anh." Derrick leaned close. His little lips touched her cheek, which spread warmth throughout her body.

If his parents are gone . . .

"Will you eat now?"

The boy nodded. When he started on the tuna sandwich, Anh returned to the kitchen and got an apple and a red can of Coke from the refrigerator. At least Crandle was no longer inside the house. She wondered how it would feel to live in a place like this with a good man and a son.

After slicing the apple and placing the pieces on a plate, Anh returned to her room. She found Derrick sitting on a bench against the wall opposite the window. Handing him the apple slices and drink, she said, "Tell me good things about yourself."

Derrick's eyes brightened. "I go to Montessori school."

Between bites of apple and sips of Coke, the boy told her about school and that, yes, he liked it, including playing ball with his playmates. Missing them, he was also afraid he would get in trouble for being absent too long. Anh told him she did not think so. She listened as Derrick spoke about the land he lived on and about his Mama Lan and Daddy K.

Despite wishing you as my own, I hope your parents are alive.

"Those are all good things to remember when Commander Crandle is mean to you."

"Yes, Miss Anh."

"Can you think of anything else?"

"I like to play chess with my *Me*."

Derrick's eyes had brightened. His energy was growing.

That a young boy understood this complicated game surprised her. Feeling a glow herself, Anh stared at the wooden shelf that Whitehead had built for her. One thing that had been in her parents' possession sat in the middle of it. The chessboard was tattered, and the pieces were worn, yet playable

"Look here," she said, unfolding the board.

Derrick touched it with a gentle hand.

"This will be another secret in our game against the bad man."

"How?" he asked.

"This will be our *master* game. If," she did not want to say when, "the Commander is mean to you, think about your next move and how you might counter."

His lips formed in a tight smile, one an imp might make, and he twisted his small hands together. He was pleased.

The battle for control of the boy's brain was escalating.

Forty-Nine

Monday Evening Late, 26 October 2009, In Flight

Thirty minutes into their second leg, Kannon finished devouring his platter of spring rolls and rice cakes. The rest of his crew had consumed theirs as well.

Only a dim amber glow from the instrument panel provided illumination since the cabin lights had been turned off. Đăng Đạo occupied the seat to Kannon's left, while Kim kept Streak company from the copilot's seat. Quán, content to be alone, sat one row back.

"I hope Quán is right," Kannon said, brushing crumbs off his lap, "that the *nắm tôm* sauce will protect us from evil."

Đăng Đạo crumpled his Coke can. "You are replacing your God with *nắm tôm* sauce?"

Kannon didn't respond. Instead . . .

"Streak, earlier, you mentioned we're fighting headwinds. Are you sure we've got enough fuel?" he asked.

"It's roughly one thousand miles from Albuquerque to Whitefish as the crow flies," Streak added. "The twin fuel tanks hold 166 gallons each. We should have at least an additional range of two hundred miles if necessary."

Kannon glanced at Đăng Đạo, who was monitoring the conversation. "We will make it," his nephew said.

"What's our airspeed?" Kannon asked Streak.

"One hundred seventy-three knots."

It seems as if 675 horses would carry us faster, Kannon thought. *It's like we're plowing through molasses-laden air*. The possibility of running low on fuel added to his worries.

His desired reassurance that Lan, Stefan, and Belynda were okay hadn't come. Too many men in battle lost life or limb because of distractions over personal matters. He didn't want to become one of them. Likewise, he didn't want to cause harm to the guys through his missteps.

Kannon leaned back. He wanted to beam the team forward, hit the ground, and begin the operation. Ironically, five men comprised this team. In 'Nam, mobile advisory teams consisted of five personnel, including a medic.

This team lacked a medic. Kannon prayed they wouldn't need one. The team's makeup—three Vietnamese and two Americans—were combat tested. Of the five, Streak, surprisingly, seemed to be the most at ease, probably because in his mind there was nothing to lose.

Would he and Streak be agile enough to handle their part of the rescue? Not only were they older than the three Vietnamese, they also had been through a lot in the last four days. Sheer adrenaline was carrying them now. How long could it last?

At least Quán and Kim added youth and firepower. In their early thirties, the brothers, recruited directly from Việt Nam by Đăng Đạo, had resided in the States for eight years. Both spoke passable English and were much more affable than first appeared. Quán, whose right cheek was scared from just below his ear to the corner of his mouth, outranked the mustachioed Kim by two years. Now, though, Đăng Đạo's men were to march to a different drumbeat—Kannon's.

Questions! Would Streak and Đăng Đạo maintain their truce or try to kill each other? Would Quán and Kim stand firm if the team came under fire? Skilled fighters, yes, but how would they respond to his leadership?

And how would he handle the pressure?

His old shoulder wound ached. The scarred area on his right hand itched, and his body heat was rising. Kannon worried he might detonate a chunk of C-4 just by holding it against his chest. He looked over his shoulder to see Quán hunched forward like a silent overseer. Kim, in the copilot seat, seemed absorbed by the plane's instrument panel. Kannon hoped the brothers didn't feel his tension.

"You keep rubbing your hand," Đăng Đạo said. "Did you get that scar from the War?"

"Nervous habit. My son bit me. I ignored it. Got infected and left this ugly scar."

"Feisty kid."

Kannon hoped that feistiness would keep Derrick alive.

"After the bite, I started calling him Chomper. Lan got pissed, which led to an argument. She made Derrick repeat, 'Do not cắn,' (bite), twenty times."

Đăng Đạo laughed. *"Ngừng dáng lo ngai."*

Kannon arched his eyebrows. "And that means?"

"Stop worrying."

"I'm okay." Obviously, Đăng Đạo knew he was stressed.

Kannon leaned forward and addressed Streak. "Mind if I turn on the cabin lights?"

"Keep 'em dim," Streak said.

After switching on the lights, Kannon handed out copies of the Google maps and Streak's hand-drawn graphic to the brothers. "Study these."

"ETA?" Kannon asked Streak.

"Six hours."

"Give us a situation report on the militia personnel," Đăng Đạo said.

"Will do," Kannon said. "Streak, jump in any time."

"Roger."

Retaining their headsets, Kim crawled from the copilot's seat while Quán stepped forward from the row behind. Each knelt facing Kannon. It was good to see facial expressions.

"Duncan Crandle heads the militia group. He provides the seed money. A guy named Whitehead is the combat leader. He washed out of Special Forces but not because he lacks skills." Kannon provided more detail on each. After fielding questions, "Streak, tell us what you know about the other guys."

Streak provided a brief biography of the nine militiamen he was familiar with under Crandle's and Whitehead's command. The tenth, Bull, he didn't know much about, except that he was a sadistic pervert. He added, "McAfee's agile and is approximately two inches taller than Đăng Đạo. His face resembles an old catcher's mitt. Timmons is Kannon-sized and built like a football tight end. He's got smooth, pale skin, and piercing eyes. Most of them wear Nazi-style buzz cuts."

Đăng Đạo shook his head. *"Kẻ thua cuộc."*

"Translate," Kannon said.

"Losers," Đăng Đạo said, shrugging as if there were no room for discussion.

"Don't underestimate their leadership. According to Streak, in addition to being a top-notch combatant, Whitehead was raised by the Nez Percé and is an expert woodsman. We'll be in his element." Kannon scanned their faces to see if they were taking this seriously. Satisfied, he went on to describe Crandle's version of the *Posse Comitatus*, which extended to hatred of modernity and nonwhites.

"Your official government not much better," Kim said.

"We're not out to reform governments." Kannon's neck hairs stood on end. But he didn't want to waste time discussing the merits of capitalism versus communism. "It's my son we're after."

"Take back what is yours," Quán said, rubbing his scar on his right cheek. "Nothing more, nothing less."

Kannon finished the briefing by describing the launch machines and death discs, and what little he knew about Anh.

"Are you shittin' me?" Kim asked.

"Assholes." With thumb and forefinger, Kim formed a circle and plunged his other index finger into the hole like a dildo.

These guys were nothing if not graphic. Their eyes, though, spoke a universal language—hard, sharp, and determined—a buy-in, Kannon hoped. Quán's acerbic "nothing more, nothing less" comment seemed laced with defiance, an attitude Kannon needed to watch. What had happened that turned the shrimp paste gesture from salted to sour?

"We've run into militia types in western New Mexico, but nothing like what you described." Đăng Đạo presented two thumbs-down.

On with business. Kannon studied Streak's map, wishing he could reach inside the paper it was drawn on and grab Derrick.

"Where do you think your son might be held?" Quán's facial scar quivered when he spoke.

"In Crandle's cabin." Kannon drew an imaginary circle over it. "The cabin backs up against a cliff, front and side doors only, no back door."

"Crandle's got to have another way out," Đăng Đạo muttered.

"I agree," Kannon said.

"Border Slot's located in an old mining area," Streak said. "The mountain's riddled with tunnels and unmarked shafts. I've heard rumors of an escape tunnel."

287

"Entrance probably from main cabin but where exit?" Kim asked.

"Wish I knew the answer to both," Streak said.

"What about this Anh woman?" Quán asked, shifting from one knee to the other. "She might know."

"How we contact her?" Kim asked.

"There's no pattern to her movements," Streak chipped in. "And she doesn't have access to a phone."

Kannon pointed his finger at Anh's room on the map. "She could be tasked with watching Derrick."

If he's alive.

"Maybe there is a way we can reach Anh." Đăng Đạo winked at Kannon. "Her room is in the back, facing the cliff. The map shows a window in her room."

"A small one," Streak said, "but large enough for one of the brothers to squeeze through."

Kannon swapped gazes with the brothers. Neither offered any objection.

"The path behind Crandle's cabin will come in handy," Quán added.

Let's hope.

"Streak Man, how high is the cliff behind Crandle's house?" Đăng Đạo asked.

Streak pivoted in his seat. "Twenty-five hundred feet," he said, turning back to the instrument panel.

"About half a mile," Kannon muttered. He turned to Quán. "Wish we could get our hands on topo maps."

"Let me assure you," Streak said. "The contour lines are tight, tight, tight."

"As in sheer?"

"Roger."

"What's your thinking?" his nephew asked.

Kannon scanned the faces of the three Vietnamese. "Any of you guys ever paraglide?"

Kim cupped his hands in the form of a bird and initiated an imaginary flight. Đăng Đạo nodded and smiled. Kannon asked Streak, "Think it's possible?"

"I guess so," Streak said, without turning around. "An old logging road leads up there. It's not connected to Border Slot's compound. You could jump off the cliff and glide to the chopper pad. The thermals can be tricky. Just have to clear the trees."

And the cliff.

Kannon looked at the brothers. "Are you willing to give it a shot?"

"Let's do it," Quán said. His dark, intense eyes made it difficult to distinguish his irises from his pupils, much less read him.

Kim, who by now was perched on both knees, scrunched his shoulders and, this time, mimed a swooping flight.

"They are adrenaline junkies," Đăng Đạo said.

"Can you paraglide in the dark?" Kannon asked.

"Weather permitting, yes. Quán and Kim are pros. And," Đăng Đạo pointed to his eyes, "we have the Pulsar night goggles."

"Equipment," Kannon said. "Can we get it in Kalispell or Whitefish?"

"You betcha. I know for sure one of them in Kalispell carries paragliding equipment."

Kannon offered a gratuitous smile. Because he didn't plan to hit the militia compound until Tuesday night, there would be time in the morning to acquire the equipment—cash basis only.

"Okay, Kim paraglides, lands, and navigates to Anh's room to make contact," without scaring her to death. "If Derrick's present, we could extract both without resorting to violence."

"It would give us an advantage," Đăng Đạo said. He locked eyes with Kannon. "Even if we are successful, it does not resolve the issue of disposing of the militiamen."

"I realize that," Kannon said. "But I'd rather not resort to violence unless necessary. Get Derrick, then let the CIA or FBI or ATF take down Border Slot."

Đăng Đạo tapped Kannon on the shoulder. "You are naïve. We must destroy the whole militia. If not, and we are successful in rescuing your son, the group will hunt you down."

Kannon took a deep breath and exhaled. His nephew brought to the surface what he had been suppressing—the unpleasant thought of having to kill again. "As I said, only if necessary."

His nephew shook his head.

To be resolved, Kannon thought, but he liked the idea of being able to recon the militia compound from the top of a cliff.

"Streak Man, do any of those outfitters have connections to the Border Slot Militia?" Đăng Đạo wiped his glasses. Kannon wondered whether his nephew was trying to grind down the lenses.

"Shouldn't be a problem," Streak said. "The outfitters rent and sell outdoor gear all the time. And don't forget, the militia compound is a good hundred and fifty miles away."

Rubbing his chin, Kannon worried the purchase of a paraglider might raise suspicion. However, if they could pull it off tactically, advantage Team Kannon. Instead of breaking down into teams of two and three, by positioning one of the brothers to paraglide, Kannon could orchestrate a three-pronged approach instead of a two. He bet neither Crandle nor any of his men expected a visitor to drop from the sky.

"Turbulence coming up," Streak said.

Kim returned to the copilot's seat. Quán reclaimed his place one row back. The plane dipped and rose, dipped and rose. Kannon tightened his seat belt and worried: *Could Kim do it?*

Fifty

Monday, 2100 Hours, 26 October 2009, Border Slot Compound

Crandle stood in the clearing adjacent to the Border Slot barracks. He stepped onto the raised platform and motioned for Porter to increase the volume of Wagner's *Die Meistersinger*. He stuck out his chest as the lifting music trumpeted an Aryan victory over a beaten Jew—symbolic of his movement to restore *White Might*.

He studied the sky, grateful for the lessening snowfall, which bode well for the coming airdrop. Whitehead joined him on the podium. "Glad you're here," Crandle said, squeezing his second-in-command's shoulder.

"Glad to be here."

"Have you questioned the men on the EMP weaponry?"

"Yes, Commander. They're good to go."

"You're satisfied?"

"Stake my life on it."

"Good enough."

The rest of his men assembled, planting their butts on the hand-polished redwood stools that encircled a crackling fire. Anh deposited Patu on the unfinished block of redwood he'd been ordered to sand and polish. Dressed in army greens, black boots, and a green baseball cap, Patu looked bewildered. Crandle smirked. "Time for you to grow up, kid."

Anh stalked off. Despite her billowing clothes, lustful eyes followed her. *Don't worry, guys. I'll bring in a shitload of Asian whores.*

Crandle signaled Porter to lower the volume of the opera.

"Men, this is it," Crandle said. A hushed silence fell over the area as Crandle mind-rolled his long-range plan.

"Tonight, we begin in earnest. We will pull off a successful EMP strike. This will be a major step in advancing our movement."

"Hooah!"

"Initial target?" Wolfhound tossed a cigar butt into the fire.

"Kalispell."

291

Silence.

"Damn. My ex lives there," Badger said.

"Kiss her goodbye," Nolan said.

Chuckles.

"Clue 'em in, Whitehead."

"Logistics. At present, our air-assault capabilities are limited by our chopper's range. But, with Kalispell close by, we can more easily work out any kinks. Think of it like a preseason game."

"Sir, how are we going to extend our range for airdrops in the future?" Timmons asked.

"I'm working on getting us a C-130." The venerable four-engine turboprop transport had a two-thousand-mile range.

"What the hell we going to use for an airstrip?" McAfee asked.

"That's simple. We'll take over an airport."

"A future mission," Whitehead said.

"We'll escalate to larger cities," Crandle added. "Additionally, we'll be targeting hydroelectric stations and nuclear power plants. We'll hit at random, establishing no pattern. Create havoc. Military and police will be hampered due to malfunctioning electronics. Count on races consolidating their ranks and engaging in interracial warfare. Let the riots begin. Whites against niggers, slant-eyes, spics, wetbacks, ragheads, and misguided Shields of David."

"Anarchy!"

Whitehead stepped from behind the podium and strode among the men, patting them on the back. "We intend to create uncertainty. It'll put us in a position to hold cities for ransom. I'm a city government. Should I pay up? What happens if I don't? That sort of thing."

"Ransom financing will be astronomical," Crandle interjected. "Once a city pays off, we leave it alone . . . for a while. We'll EMP it later."

"Eventually, the need for a plane becomes irrelevant," Whitehead said. "Nothing will fly. And we'll be where we want to be. Ground zero."

"Hooah!"

"Here's a reminder of your squad assignments," Crandle said. "One: Whitehead, McAfee, and Wolfhound. Two: Badger, Hatfield, and Nolan. Three: Porter, Smitty, and Timmons. The third team will remain here in case Streak and Mr. Kannon Ballard appear."

"Women's work," Hatfield said, referencing Squad Three.

"Screw you!" Timmons said.

"What about Bull?" It was McAfee.

"On his way to Texas." Crandle noticed a frown on Whitehead's face. "In case Streak and Ballard don't show up here."

"What about the kid?" Timmons said.

"He'll be with me in the chopper. I'm afraid he'll overpower you if I leave him here."

Laughter.

"Early indoctrination. Good idea." Wolfhound reached over, took off Patu's cap and tousled his hair. "Say, Hooah!"

Patu shook off Wolfhound's hand.

Whitehead's frown deepened.

"Leave the little fucker to me." To Patu, "I might toss you from the chopper if you cause too much trouble, despite your leverage value."

"Fuck you," Patu said.

At least he shows gumption.

"Garrett will handle the drop from the bird," Crandle added. "Are you ready?"

"Yes, sir," Garrett said. "Between OT, Whitehead, and the drills, I know how to arm the weapon, set the altitude-based timed-release fuse, and when to let it fly."

"Good. Counting on you," Crandle added. "Whitehead . . ."

His second-in-command stepped up to the podium. "Remember, the two ground assaults—conducted by our EMP LightsOut Ground Squads—will take place at zero one-thirty, the air blast to take place ten minutes later. I'll lead the assault on the primary target, clearly marked on your maps, while Badger's squad destroys the secondary target."

"Wear gloves at all times when handling the bicycles and the EMP weapons, including the detonators and fuses," Crandle interjected. "The cylinders encasing the bombs won't disintegrate. Don't be signing the fucking bombs with your fingerprints. Everybody got that?"

"Hooah!"

"We'll communicate by radio until just before the blasts occur," Whitehead said, twisting his mustache.

"What if the radios don't work after the blasts?" Timmons asked.

"Wait five minutes. Turn them on again. If they don't operate, stick to the prearranged escape and evasion plan. And remember to use manually wound watches."

"Any more questions?" Crandle asked. "It's now or never." He squared his shoulders and placed his hands behind his back in the parade-rest position.

"You're sure these aren't nuclear?" Nolan asked, a stupid smile on his face.

"Yeah, right," Whitehead said, shaking his head. "We're going to nuke ourselves. Come on, Nolan."

"What if this damn EMP makes me sterile?" Hatfield asked.

"In your case, a blessing for mankind," McAfee jibed.

The militiamen laughed.

"Well, shit! It could happen."

"Might make you bionic," Porter said.

McAfee stood, grabbed his balls, and shot the finger.

Crandle chuckled.

"Flight time is approximately one hour, so be prepared for takeoff at twenty-three hundred. LightsOut teams will carry concealed side arms only. The compound guard squad will draw AKs."

"Time to get rolling," Whitehead said, bounding from the platform. "Wear civilian clothes."

"A final reminder," Crandle said, unleashing a genuine smile. "You signed on to Border Slot knowing you'd be taking risks. This is combat. You'll be rewarded for a successful op. Each squad member will receive a cool thirty thousand. Whitehead gets an extra bump."

Crandle stepped up again to address his trained warriors. "Who is best equipped to live off the land?"

"We are! White Might . . . Hooah!"

Fifty-One

Tuesday, at 0030 hours, west of Flathead Lake, just outside the national forest, and roughly ten miles south from the center of Kalispell, Crandle sat in the pilot's seat of the HH-3E and watched his EMP LightsOut teams pedal off on an old logging road. They wouldn't strike pavement until reaching the city. The middle cyclist in each squad carried an EMP weapon in an elongated backpack. The third militiaman carried the accessories, including a pair of short-handled bolt cutters. They were to rendezvous back here no later than 0300.

Patu sat in the copilot's seat, too small for the harness to be effective, but Crandle would rather have him bouncing around there than flopping helter-skelter in the back of the bird.

"How did you like your first chopper ride?" Garrett asked.

"I liked it."

"Look at that, Garrett. You got a smile from Patu."

"Lots of potential for that kid." Garrett hopped out of the helicopter and stared after the pedaling militiamen. "Think you gave them enough time to hit their objectives, Commander?"

Crandle checked his watch. "It's zero forty hours now. The logging roads, as well as the gravel ones, can be tough to ride. But they'll make it. Whitehead will notify us when in place."

"I'm amazed at the size of the bomb we're hauling in the chopper."

"Hits the scales at seven-hundred pounds."

Crandle disembarked, followed by Patu.

"Assuming everything goes according to plan, we'll take off at zero one-fifteen?" Garrett asked.

"Yep! Stop worrying."

Crandle stared idly at the Jolly Green Giant, thankful Whitehead had come around, thankful Border Slot was about to make history. "We'll hover at low altitude, observe the results of the ground blasts, then gain altitude for the airdrop."

"Yes, sir! I just hope to hell we're out of range when that baby blasts." Garrett paused, then, "Sir, what are we supposed to do if our chopper becomes disabled?"

"That's not gonna happen," Crandle said, wondering what he'd do if the bird failed? *Damn you, Streak. You're the only one who knows how to handle an emergency autorotation to get us safely on the ground.*

* * *

"This mountain bike vibrates like a jackhammer," Wolfhound said.

"Try transporting a bomb," McAfee added.

"It may be freezing, and snow may be falling, but I'm sweatin' like a pig on a skewer," McAfee said.

"This bouncing bomb's hammering my spine," Hatfield added.

Whitehead saw they were struggling. The jostling wasn't helping him, either. He vowed to develop a better transport system in Border Slot's workshop.

For now, he wished he'd brought along some relief for the acidic bubbles bursting inside his stomach. The discomfort had begun just before his return to the Commander's cabin. A lot depended on this op. If anything went wrong, Crandle would blame him. His career would be over . . . and probably his life.

"Let's stop and readjust our loads," Whitehead said. "Lower air pressures. It'll ease the jarring impact over this rough road. And don't grip the handlebars. Hold them loosely, and you'll have better control."

"Counterintuitive," Nolan said.

"Just do it."

Each man let some air out of their bicycle tires and readjusted their load. They remounted and rode off.

This mission reminded Whitehead when at age ten he had spent the summer with a friend in Missoula. One of their favorite pastimes was a night game whereby they tied garbage cans together and stretched the connecting rope taut across the street. During their manning of the trashcans, if one of them got *struck* by a car's headlight, rather, a battle tank's ray gun, game over.

This, though, is a real operation, with real ray guns. Gun and run. And it was game over if anyone got caught.

"Remember, guys. After triggering the electrical detonators, we separate and ride our assigned grids to survey the impact from the detonations. Escape and evasion are an individual's responsibility. Get caught, you're screwed. Talk, and you're dead." Whitehead hoped this message was locked in.

They reached the southern outskirts of Kalispell within the allotted time. They stopped at an all-night gas station close to the city airport and aired up their tires, drank water, and took a piss.

"Take a good look, men. If all goes well, this town will become incapacitated." Whitehead studied his crew. All wore streaks of sweat on their faces. "Keep your bicycle lights on," he reminded them. "If anyone asks, we're participating in a bicycle rally. Questions?"

There were none.

"Badger, you, Hatfield, and Nolan give us a five-minute head start, then head to your spot off Eighteenth Street and Fifth Avenue. I'll lead McAfee and Wolfhound to our staging location northeast of town."

* * *

Whitehead led his squad up South Main, turned east on Highway 35, and pedaled hard for roughly seven miles before sequestering the squad behind a hedge. His watch showed 0120. Traffic was nominal at this hour. In ten minutes, would the cars stop running? Lights stop shinning?

His objective differed from the more typical power relay station that Badger and his squad were to attack. Absent tall utility poles and the confluence of transmission lines, most of the equipment to power the city was housed in his squad's targeted one-story nondescript building, which was about as large as a mid-sized warehouse. There was no apparent security.

The three of them knelt to begin final preparation. Wolfhound extracted the EMP cylindrical bomb from McAfee's backpack. Whitehead ran his gloved hands over the cylinder. It was hard to imagine the catastrophic damage this baby was supposed to cause.

Whitehead verified their radio frequency. He pressed the push-to-talk switch.

"LightsOut Two. This is LightsOut One. Over."

297

"LightsOut Two, here. Read you loud and clear. Over."

"Are you in position?"

"Roger."

Good. Badger's squad was ready to go. Whitehead pulled out his satphone and called Crandle.

"LightsOut One to LightsOut Control. In position. Over."

"Roger. Understand the play will start on time. Out."

"Damn! You guys as nervous as I am?" Wolfhound asked.

Whitehead shook his head. But yeah, he was anxious as hell, even though there was no outside security present.

"Leave the bikes here." Clutching the bolt cutters, Whitehead rose and stepped from behind the hedge. The other two followed, carrying the bomb. Maneuvering behind the building to remain undetected, they reached the wooden enclosure housing the building's electrical junction box. Whitehead cut the lock and pried open the wooden access gate. They placed the bomb beneath the regular circuit box and set the time-delay fuse.

"Are you sure a five-minute delay is long enough?" McAfee asked.

"What! You're afraid the EMP is gonna melt your bicycle chain?"

McAfee frowned. "No, I'm afraid it's going to melt my balls."

Shaking his head, Whitehead activated the timer.

They raced back to the hedge. Whitehead caught his breath, then said. "You two mount up and hit your grid area. Stay out of trouble. Don't arouse suspicion. Observe, observe, before making your way back to the staging zone. I'm gonna stick around till it blows."

After McAfee and Wolfhound took off, Whitehead wheeled his bicycle from behind the hedge to better witness results. He propped the bike on its kickstand.

A few minutes later, his EMP device exploded, sounding no louder than a blown transformer. Did the ground tremor, or was it just his body shaking?

Streetlights went dark. Security lights no longer functioned. Cars in the vicinity seized up. He turned around and looked south in time to see a high, arcing green light fade from the sky in the direction of the relay station, the one with the poles and transmission lines. Evidence of the Badger team's strike . . . just like an aurora.

He turned on his radio, hoping it would function. It didn't. Neither did his satphone. Did any of the others? he wondered.

The bomb worked, though. The fucking EMP weapon worked!

Except for those watching late-night television, most residents probably wouldn't notice any difference till morning, Whitehead thought. *No alarms to wake 'em up.*

The Medical Center's lights were still on, though. Why? Was the hospital on a separate circuit? Whitehead couldn't be sure. Then he remembered reading about shielded cables and faraday cages. Was that it?

He heard a scattering of complaints from the street.

"What the hell's going on?"

"My car just stopped, man."

"It's an alien attack," said another.

A stranded driver standing beside his vehicle tried using his cellphone. Cursing, he kicked the front tire and threw down his phone. He stomped on it and walked off, angry as a wounded bear. Others appeared confused, didn't know what to do.

Yet, a few vehicles continued running, lights and all. Why?

A driver with a working van hollered to the stalled drivers to get their damn cars off the road.

Five minutes remained until Crandle executed the final part of their plan. Whitehead counted on the coming air assault to fry all vehicles.

He mounted his bicycle—its light no longer worked—and rode behind a dumpster to kill time. He worried. Their extraction counted on the helicopter not being disabled by the airburst. If that happened, each militiaman was responsible for finding his way back to Border Slot. And then what?

What if something did happen to Crandle? Like a second-string shortstop hoping for an injury to derail the starter, Whitehead couldn't help but think how he'd run the militia if Crandle became incapacitated.

Fifty-Two

"You see that, Garrett? No streetlights. I can't wait to hear the guys' reactions on the ground." Feeling jubilant, Crandle removed his right hand from the cyclic for a high-five.

"I sure as hell do, Commander. How about you, Patu? You've just witnessed history."

Patu, wearing a headset mashed to his ears by an elastic band, stood on the copilot's seat and peered below. "I like firecrackers better."

Crandle held the chopper steady at three thousand feet above the city, thankful no electronic pulses had rocketed upward and seared their bird's electronics. After hovering for another minute or two, he returned his attention to navigation. "We'll circle the city before climbing to drop altitude."

"Why are you going to bomb a city and hurt people?" Patu asked.

"Won't hurt people," Garrett said.

"I don't understand."

"You will," Garrett added.

Crandle smiled. Garrett was a solid militiaman who remained calm under pressure and who paid extraordinary attention to detail. He had the physique of a 1950s era high school halfback and demonstrated both mental and physical agility.

"See some moving lights down there," Garrett said.

Crandle followed Garrett's outstretched arm. The mobile lights appeared like flickering candles in a fog.

"There's also a light cluster around the hospital area. Why's that?" Garrett asked.

"I bet they have backup generators," Patu said.

Crandle arched his eyebrows. "How would you know that you little turd?"

"Daddy K explains things to me."

"Got to keep this kid," Garrett said.

We'll see. We'll also see how the air blast affects those remaining lights.

Five minutes later, nerves pulsing, Crandle piloted the HH-3E into hover position at an optimum altitude of ten thousand feet. According to his GPS, Kalispell lay directly below. Cloud cover obscured what, at best, would be a silhouetted image of the city.

Crandle's leg muscles almost cramped as he readied the bird for the drop. He was dealing with an unknown. Would the above-ground EMP blast spread upward and disable the chopper? He didn't want to lose the bird, but for damn sure he didn't want to lose his life in a crash. It was tough operating the bird single-handed, which again fueled his rage at Streak. He should be taking this risk.

Concentrate!

"Get ready, Garrett."

The hefty bomb rested on two old pairs of roller skates. Garrett slid open the right-side door. The Jolly Green Giant shook like a giant paint mixer, sounding like a clattering bucket of bolts. It continued to buck like a pissed-off horse. "Damnit, Garrett. Don't let the bomb fall out prematurely."

"Got it under control, sir."

Crandle inhaled deeply. Manipulating the collective at his left and cyclic to his center and using his feet to control the tail rotor pedals, he held the bird as steady as possible.

"Activate the time-delay fuse," Crandle he told Garrett.

"Done!"

Crandle tilted the bird to the right.

"Let it go!"

Garrett rolled the bomb out of the bay, roller skates and all. It fell toward earth, programmed to detonate at three thousand feet.

"Let's get the hell out," Garrett said.

Crandle rammed the cyclic forward to dip the nose of the Jolly Green Giant and pulled on the collective to gain speed. His abrupt handling of the control caused the bird to lurch.

"Damnit, Commander. Watch what you're doing."

When Crandle turned to assess Garrett's situation, he inadvertently pulled up on the collective again, causing the chopper to shift dramatically. At the same time, he pulled back on the cyclic. The bird nosed up.

Patu, once again standing on his seat, slid to the far right

301

before flipping over the back. His scream startled Crandle. His son, Patterson, might have screamed similarly in the crash that took his life.

"Grab him!"

Crandle heard shuffling and assumed Garrett was trying to grasp the boy to keep him from falling out the open side door.

"I've got him."

Crandle turned and saw Garrett clutching one of the boy's legs and drag him to safety. As the militiaman struggled to right himself and reseat Patu, Crandle reached over to help. He accidentally hit the cyclic again.

The bird tilted even more. Garrett went flying out of the helicopter, dangling at the end of the safety lanyard.

Frantically working the controls, Crandle stabilized the helicopter. Then the bird lurched as if a weight had been released.

"What happened?"

"The line broke," Patu said.

Crandle stared in disbelief at the plummeting Garrett before losing sight of him in the clouds. "That's on you, Patu."

* * *

Five minutes wound down to three, two, one. Whitehead looked toward the sky. He couldn't see anything but thought he heard the distant thumping of rotor blades. Had to be his imagination. The helicopter would have gained altitude by now and not be in hearing range.

Then he saw a bright flash, which expanded like ripples in a pond before disappearing. The following explosion sounded tremulously through the night like the soft thumps from a roman candle.

"Son of a bitch." Whitehead could only stare.

Cars stopped rolling. One stalled immediately to his front. Even in the dark, he saw shock register on the face of a middle-aged woman whose hands seemed frozen on the steering wheel.

Lights in the Medical Center extinguished, which meant medical devices weren't working either. Patients would die. Consequences he hadn't considered. A guilt-ridden shudder rattled his body.

Surely, the hospital would have backup generators. Wouldn't they? If so, would they work? Jesus! Does Crandle know what he's doing? Are we ready for this?

He pedaled southwest, toward the center of town. Interweaving between residential blocks, he noticed a few outside house lights still burning, the types sitting on a pole in the front yard. Gas fueled? Whitehead wondered.

He reached the Center Mall. Two men at a twenty-four-hour service station stood in front of gas pumps. The station was blacked out, but the two men continued punching buttons and squeezing handles.

"What's the matter?" Whitehead asked.

"I was pumping gas when suddenly everything stopped working," one of 'em said.

"Frustrating as all get-out," the other added.

Riding on, Whitehead encountered a guy at an ATM. He was swearing.

"I want my card back." He kept trying to peel the card out but couldn't get it. The next thing the guy did was get a crowbar from his car and whack the shit out of that ATM, trying to pry open the card slot.

Wow!

Ahead, on the main street, drivers stood outside their stalled vehicles. Others were locked inside. One driver crawled through an open window while another hacked at his driver's window with an emergency glass breaker.

Downside. Whitehead's radio still didn't work. It was fried, like everything else electrical or containing a chip. Frustrating! Eliminate ground assaults. Conduct future EMP attacks only from the air.

Whitehead pedaled back to the staging area.

Just before turning off South Main onto W Center Street, he noticed a set of headlights coming south. Would the vehicle stop running? he wondered. When it didn't, he figured it must have come from north of town. If so, that said something about the effective range of a post-electromagnetic detonation.

Regardless, the mission appeared to be a success, perhaps too much so. Just before Whitehead began his bicycle sprint back to the rendezvous site, a voice came out of the darkness.

"Hold it, Bub."

"What?"

"Police. I'm commandeering your bicycle." The *Uniform* accosting him stood about six feet tall, a bit pudgy, probably not in the best of shape.

"The hell you are."

"I've lost all communication. My vehicle's not running. I need your bike."

"No can do!" Whitehead noticed the officer's stalled police cruiser, driver's door open. They stood twenty feet apart. No one else was around. Or was there a partner lurking in the shadows?

"Sir! You don't understand. This is an emergency," the officer said.

"Officer. You don't understand. You're not getting this bicycle. I have an emergency of my own."

"Get off the bicycle now!" The officer moved forward, his hand on the butt of his service weapon, the other on what might be a taser.

This was not a situation Whitehead wanted to find himself in. Confrontation. Against someone in a profession he held in some respect. And the timing was tight. He needed to get the hell out of Kalispell. Meet up with his guys. He couldn't do it on foot.

His .45 was holstered in the pit of his back, underneath his fatigue jacket. If Whitehead reached for it, the officer had the advantage. No contest. Besides, he didn't want to kill the guy.

Disarm and disable!

"Get off your damn bicycle." The officer whipped out his taser.

Whitehead tensed, but nothing happened. The EMP pulse must have disabled the taser. When the officer went for his handgun, Whitehead splayed his hands. "No need for that, Officer. I'm just as spooked as you are. What's happening?"

"I think we're under attack." He kept his pistol holstered.

"Man, I hope not." Whitehead hopped off the bicycle and started to remove his jacket, wanting easier access to his weapon if the occasion necessitated it.

"Leave the jacket alone. Hands where I can see them."

"Chill, Officer. I'm hot from riding."

"All right. Go ahead."

Under the watchful, suspicious officer's eyes, Whitehead removed his jacket and lay it across the arrow-shaped seat.

"What are you doing out here?" the officer said.

"I was riding in a rally with some other guys. Then all the lights went out. The others rode to their homes to check things out. That's where I was heading when you stopped me." He started wheeling the bike backward toward the policeman.

"Say, I know you," the officer said.

"Name's Caruthers," Whitehead said.

"The hell it is. I remember you from high school."

"You're mistaken. Didn't go to high school here." Except Whitehead did remember him, from the wrestling team. His name was Jennings.

"Let's see an ID."

Whitehead stopped and leaned the bike against his leg. He again showed his hands. "Going to reach for my wallet." He withdrew it and handed the billfold over. When Jennings lowered his eyes to examine it, Whitehead rammed the rear wheel into the policeman's crotch.

"Oomph," went the officer. He reached for his semiautomatic.

Whitehead clocked him in the jaw and then lunged for the handgun with his other hand. Jennings was stronger than he'd anticipated. The officer reeled back but deflected Whitehead's grab for the service weapon. Both fell to the ground, the policeman on the bottom.

They grappled and barrel-rolled over the ground. Whitehead pinned the officer's hand with his knee to prevent him from drawing his service weapon. He managed to gain a chokehold, which caused Jennings to release his grip on the pistol butt and struggle against being strangled.

Again, the officer's strength surprised him. He wedged his arms between Whitehead's and ground his thumbs into the joint between Whitehead's thumbs and forefingers, which forced him to relax his hold.

Jennings landed a sharp blow to his face. As Whitehead's head snapped back, the officer flung him off his body. Upright, Whitehead whipped a quick kick to the officer's groin. Despite his pain, Jennings scrambled upright and drew his weapon, only to face Whitehead's already drawn Colt.

Whitehead fired. His high school classmate went down.

Fifty-Three

Tuesday, 0145 Hours, 27 October 2009, Flight Over Kalispell

They were flying beneath the cloud cover and had decent nighttime visibility, but Kannon couldn't see squat on the ground. If it were daylight, he would see the mountains and canyons below, areas he and his family should be vacationing in, areas that Derrick— *Oh, Christ.* The horrible pain of abandonment his son must be feeling, the pleading for his mother, anger at his father for not protecting him.

Stop dwelling on this shit.

Kannon checked his watch. By his reckoning, the Kalispell lights should be showing. "We should've begun our descent," he said to Đăng Đạo.

His nephew nodded toward the cockpit and said, "Our pilot looks concerned too."

Kannon followed his gaze. "We've been fighting headwinds all the way from Albuquerque. I'm worried about running out of fuel." As if they didn't have enough to worry about, he noticed Streak craning his neck to stare out the cockpit. "Streak, are you sure we're on course?"

"No city," Kim said, still occupying the copilot's seat.

Streak turned from the Garmin G1000 integrated avionics system and shot a perplexed look at Kannon. "You're not going to believe this . . . either the Garmin has gone haywire, or someone's moved the whole damn town."

"What the hell are you talking about?" Kannon's eyes darted from Streak to Đăng Đạo.

"The airstrip is located at the southern edge of Kalispell. It's supposed to be right in front of us," Streak said.

"Maybe I was right about Streak Man the first time," Đăng Đạo muttered, squeezing a full water bottle so hard the top popped off.

"We should be above the city right now," Streak said in a loud tone.

"With a population of twenty thousand plus, things should be

307

lit up," Kannon said.

"Fuel indicator lower than low," Kim said.

Shit!

Đăng Đạo twisted his body to look back at Quán, who had been snoring intermittently, and doused him with water. "Wake up!"

Mumbling something under his breath, Quán leaned forward. Yawning, he intertwined his fingers and extended his arms to stretch. His yawn morphed to shock at recognizing the alarm plastered on the other's faces. "What's up?"

"We're lost," Kannon said, figuring Streak had made a navigation error.

"And almost out of fuel," Đăng Đạo added.

"So much for the myth of *nắm tôm* sauce," Quán said, shaking his head.

"Definitely not a cure-all," Kannon said, with a backward glance.

They proceeded north. Streak strained toward the windshield as if ready to jump through it to get a better look. "Wait one. I see lights far ahead."

Kannon rose and peered forward. "Those aren't city lights."

"It's the Glacier Park International Airport," Streak said.

"Are you sure, Streak Man?"

"Hell, yes. I've flown in and out of there many times. I recognize the light pattern."

"Kalispell must be blacked out." Kannon drummed his fingers on the armrests. "Time to break radio silence."

"Agreed," his nephew said.

"I know the frequency from my helicopter flights." Streak activated voice transmission, using his familiar chopper call sign to maintain a semblance of protocol. "Glacier International, this is JGG73. Come in. Over."

"JGG73 this is—"

And then, nothing.

"Damn. It cut out."

Not good, Kannon thought. "Try again."

Streak repeated his call sign and transmitted again. He tensed forward, his arms rigid. "No comms!"

"The lights just went out!" Đăng Đạo said.

"Maybe the whole area's suffering from a power failure," Kannon said.

Kim turned and offered a thumbs-down. "Power grid sucks."

"Does the region not have backup generators?" Đăng Đạo asked.

Good question.

"What's the fuel gauge reading?"

"It's talking to me and I don't like what it's saying," Streak said.

"Can we make it to Glacier?"

"I hope so."

A feeble response, Kannon thought. Was that the best Streak could offer? "What's the altimeter reading?"

"Fifteen hundred feet." Streak's staccato tone spoke to his state of mind.

The engine coughed and sputtered.

"*Trời ơi.*" Đăng Đạo's tone carried fear. "We are out of gas."

"Scaring the shit out of me," Kim interjected. The brothers jabbered rapid-fire in their native language.

The engine continued to sputter.

"Switching back to the other fuel tank," Streak said.

"Should have done that earlier," Đăng Đạo said.

Kannon frowned. "He already did. There can't be much left in either tank."

Yet the engine caught rhythm and settled into a steady drone.

"Close call." Đăng Đạo muttered.

"We need to get this baby on the ground," Kannon said. "Try contacting the tower again."

"Glacier! This is JGG73 . . . Mayday! Mayday! Mayday!"

Again, the wait . . .

"No response," Streak said through clenched jaws.

The engine coughed. The propeller spun to a stop. Streak tried restarting the engine. No luck this time. The *nắm tôm* sauce Kannon consumed earlier lodged in his throat.

"*Chết tiệt!*"

Kannon didn't know what Đăng Đạo meant, but for sure he

wasn't happy. Neither was he. *Christ!* The Cessna had turned into a glider. Kannon's stomach churned, his feelings the same mix of excitement and fear he'd faced before commencing a combat op in 'Nam.

"What's the range without power?" Kannon asked.

"One or two miles," Streak said. "We're losing altitude fast."

The plane crabbed to starboard. Đăng Đạo clutched Kannon's arm. "What is happening?"

"Crosswinds," Streak said.

"Don't want to die this way," Quán said in a muffled tone far too calm for the circumstances.

"Parachutes, parachutes," Kim said, in a high-pitched, near-hysterical tone. "Should've brought parachutes."

It's a little late for that now. Worse, it's nighttime. Selecting a safe landing area will be difficult. What else can go wrong?

Kannon's sweat glands oozed a peculiar odor as self-condemnation flashed through his mind. If only he hadn't met Streak at Lost Maples. His brother Roger wouldn't be dead. Karen wouldn't be a widow. And Lan, Derrick, and Stefan wouldn't be in danger.

Circumstances like these lead men to prayer.

He prayed Streak's knowledge of the terrain would tip the scale in their favor. He didn't relish a crash landing with C-4 and ammo on board. "We're counting on you, Streak. Set her down best you can."

"Yeah, Streak Man," Đăng Đạo blurted. "You're back in 'Nam, returning to base after a resupply mission. Number one Vietnamese *cô* waiting for you, the mother of your *con trai.*"

Girlfriend and child, Kannon understood. He almost chuckled at his nephew's use of black humor to motivate their pilot. Yet, he couldn't help reflecting on Streak's chopper crash in Việt Nam during the war. *Was that going through Streak's head now?*

"Buckle in," Streak said, gripping the yoke.

The silenced Cessna continued crabbing northeast. Kannon didn't buckle up right away. Instead, perched at the edge of his seat, he stared at the altimeter. It read nine hundred fifty feet, then dropped to six hundred, then four. Streak needed at least a quarter mile stretch of land to set down—a road, pasture, anything flat—but the three-dimensional terrain display showed them hurtling toward hills and gullies. Even if Streak found a suitable flat strip, could he avoid power lines, trees, and rocks?

Kannon cast a glance at Đăng Đạo beside him. Braced in the crash position, Lan's nephew, his nephew, looked like a huge snail inside its shell. Turning in his seat, Kannon stared at Quán, who was leaning against the forward backrest, his hands clasped on the back of his head—palms flat and crossed. Up front, Kim clutched the copilot's control column as if it were a portal to safety.

Did the brothers have family members who cared? Kannon wondered. And Streak, so alone in the world, would he live to earn the redemption he sought?

The altimeter read three hundred feet, two hundred, and kept dropping. Kannon thought of the balsa wood gliders he'd played with during his childhood, gliders that often crashed.

He buckled in.

The plane banked left. The brothers chanted, perhaps a Buddhist mantra.

"This plane has turned into a flying coffin," Đăng Đạo said.

Kannon glanced out the window again, still couldn't see a damn thing. "Streak, any visuals?"

"Hold on," Streak said. "It's gonna get rough."

The Cessna rolled forty-five degrees to the left. Kannon, riveted to his seat, lurched against the cabin wall. *Christ almighty*! The plane rocked further left, nearly vertical to the horizon.

"Chết tiệt." Đăng Đạo said again.

Blood rushed to Kannon's head, his seatbelt barely constraining his body. The violent shift loosened the retaining straps on their gear stacked in the rear. Equipment bags flew about the cabin. The edge of one container smacked his shoulder and landed in his lap. Kim vomited, filling the cabin with a putrid smell. Kannon almost lost it himself. He regained focus to see Streak struggling to trim the plane. Loose equipment settled on the floor as the plane leveled out.

"What the hell's happening?" Kannon braced for the crash impact.

"Rocky cliffs and strong crosswinds," Streak said.

Kannon raised his head for another look at the three-dimensional display. As the altimeter reading edged downward, he made his count—five, four, three, two, one, zero. The glide path ended as the Caravan smacked down hard, lurched, and became airborne once more. It sailed maybe a hundred feet. Again, the wheels touched. "Let the fixed landing gear hold," Kannon muttered, shutting his eyes.

They stayed grounded, sort of, as the plane bobbled over rough terrain, much like a motorcycle hitting deep tractor ruts. Tree branches flashed past, slapped at the wings. Streak retracted the flaps as he braked. The landing struts gave way as the three wheels dug in. The plane bounded, dropped, then jerked to the right, accompanied by a ripping sound as the fuselage clawed over jagged rocks, nosed over, and flipped on its back.

Fifty-Four

Disoriented, Kannon opened his eyes, touched his limbs, and counted his fingers. All there.

I'm upside down.

Propping himself to keep from head-butting the ceiling, which was now the ground floor, he unbuckled his seatbelt and slowly twisted his body until he was upright but contorted.

"Is everyone in one piece?" Kannon asked.

"Okay here," Đăng Đạo said from his inverted position.

Streak groaned.

Alarmed, Kannon looked at his pilot, who was nearly doubled over in his seat. "Are you hurt?"

"Bruised my forehead, but I'm all right," Streak said, battling with his seatbelt.

Kim, who had already gotten loose, assisted Kannon in freeing Streak from the seatbelt constraints and reversing his body position.

"It was like being stuck in one of those inverted traction gadgets." Kim mimed holding a jar and turning it over.

Quán, apparently unhurt, stood beside Đăng Đạo. The shorter Vietnamese men held an advantage here—they didn't have to crouch as much.

Suddenly, the cabin lights flickered on, indicating functioning electronics.

"Kill the power. I don't want any beacons drawing the curious to the crash site," Kannon said, massaging his damaged shoulder, which had been aggravated by the dislodged container. He shook it off and checked his watch. It displayed zero two hundred.

Streak, too, grimaced as he gingerly touched his forehead before switching off the lights.

Đăng Đạo steadied himself on Kannon's other arm. *"Mượt,"* he said, frowning.

"What?" Kannon asked.

"Mượt. (Smooth.) I want the rest of this mission to go smoothly."

"So do I," Kannon said.

A clanging noise startled him. The passenger door shot open, courtesy of Kim's solid kick. The Vietnamese man inched his way back, motioning Kannon toward the exit. Crouching, he led the others out into a cold, dry night.

Above, stars shone. The quarter moon was visible. Wind gusts stirred up the sandy loam and carried the scent of freshly cut hay.

Kannon studied the guys. "Any bones broken?"

None were. At least everyone was alive and in one piece. But this was like being offloaded at the wrong landing zone. All Kannon had to do now was reorganize and establish control, not an easy task. He knelt and scooped up a handful of sand.

"Looks like we're in a dry riverbed," Kannon said.

"Higher ground to our right," Đăng Đạo said with a determined look.

"Roger that. Let's unload the gear."

"*Sẽ làm.*" (Will do.)

Quán returned to the downed craft and scavenged the equipment that had come loose during the crash. "Like a wolf foraging for food," he said, after distributing the found items. Then he and his brother—their muscled arms bulging against their short-sleeve khaki shirts—dived into the rear cargo area to unload the bulkier gear.

Kannon dug into his pack and withdrew a penlight. He approached Streak, who appeared woozy. Under the red-beamed glow, Kannon examined the wound. A dark, purplish knot protruded from Streak's forehead. Blood trickled from the injury, appearing black in the tinted light.

"Sit," Kannon said. "You need to clear the cobwebs. I'll get the icepack out of the cooler. Put it on that knot."

"Where you want the equipment?" Kim asked, his scarred cheek twitching in the dim moonlight.

Absent artificial illumination defiling the sky, Kannon didn't need night goggles for short-range vision. He spotted an area about twenty yards away, which looked like an oasis on a dry sea. "Stack it at the base of those trees." Then to Đăng Đạo, "Come on, let's recon."

They circled the plane. Oil drained onto the sandy ground, creating a stream of sludge. The nose wheel was gone. The right wing had sheared off at its mid-point. One of the prop's three blades was bent like an elbow, and Kannon found another impaled in the ground. The third blade was missing. The plane looked like a beached killer whale, belly-side up, and appeared to be a total loss. He would have to deal with it and the owner later, if there was going to be a *later*.

Now, though, the sickly-sweet odor of airplane fuel overcame the smell of hay and soured the air. Kannon fanned the fumes. "We were lucky we weren't blown to hell."

"A good sign," Đăng Đạo countered.

"Yeah. Let's make the most of it."

Before the brothers hauled the gear to the designated oasis, Kannon secured a mobile GPS from Đăng Đạo's cache. Once the brothers took off, he and his nephew vacated the crash site and clambered up the steep right bank to higher ground. From this vantage point, they discerned the path carved by the landing. Streak had steered the plane between two sharp, rugged rock walls, maybe fifty feet apart, before the terrain leveled out.

"Whoa," Kannon said. "A tight fit."

"Streak Man is a good pilot." His nephew speared the ground with his foot. "What do you think we should do?"

"Get a fix on where we are. Plan a route out." Kannon turned on the GPS. Fortunately, it activated. He studied the display. Using varying map scales, he alternated between topographical layouts and satellite views. "Jeez! This place is hard to get to."

"How hard?" Đăng Đạo asked.

Kannon tapped on the GPS. "As the crow flies, we're about eighteen miles northeast of Kalispell."

"The Jeep is garaged in Whitefish, right? How far away is it?"

Kannon again tapped furiously on the GPS.

"Seven and a half miles, slightly south of due west."

They descended to the riverbed. Scattered boulders and gouges along the plowed-up riverbed resembled a WWII-era antitank fortification.

The pair followed the impromptu landing strip back to the damaged Cessna. Kannon pointed to an outsized, defaced river rock. "Guess that's what ripped off the front wheel."

"And flipped the plane." Đăng Đạo walked off a few paces

and examined the mangled tricycle strut and wheel. He just shook his head.

Streak, with an oversized bandana securing the icepack to his forehead, apparently had shaken off his injury and was working with his global positioning device.

"You did good landing the plane, Streak Man," Đăng Đạo said.

Streak flashed a *V*.

Kannon patted Streak on the shoulder, then strode quickly toward the riverbed's left bank to check on Quán and Kim, who had finished laying out the equipment. "You guys okay?"

"My brother . . . too dumb to get hurt," Kim said, going into his pantomime routine.

Kannon assumed the gestures were intended to demonstrate that Quán possessed a pea-sized brain.

Quán pointed at his brother's groin. "I'm smart enough not to piss my pants."

Kim gave Quán a playful shove.

Ah, more black humor—the irreverent but time-honored means of coping used by military men under stress.

"Gather round," Kannon said, having collected his thoughts. "Let's establish Plan B."

Đăng Đạo trotted over. Streak followed. The five team members formed a circle.

"We've had a white knuckler for sure, but we're all in one piece." Kannon scanned the terrain, detecting ghostly mounds and dark shadows. "I'm concerned someone might've observed the crash."

"No sweat. We're pretty isolated," Streak said.

"Which isn't a bad thing, considering what we're carrying," Kannon said.

As was his custom, his nephew took out his handkerchief and cleaned his glasses. Sadly, it seemed that wiping their eyeglasses was the most common trait shared between Đăng Đạo and Streak.

Kannon snatched a weapons bag and winced as his shoulder complained.

"Follow me."

Fifty-Five

After hiking a hundred yards west, Kannon halted the team. "It's seven point five miles to Whitefish. I need a volunteer to jog into town and retrieve Streak's Willys."

"Does Crandle know about the Jeep?" Đăng Đạo asked. "What if he has someone watching?"

"I'm pretty sure he doesn't," Streak said.

"Pretty sure does not cut it," Đăng Đạo said.

"It's a chance we've got to take," Kannon said.

"You say it's a vintage World War Two-era Willys, right?" his nephew added.

"Right." Streak removed the icepack and tossed it to the ground, then wiped his glasses.

"I just thought of something," Kannon said. "The blackout! Damned weird. What if electromagnetic pulse weapons caused it?"

"I had not thought of that," Đăng Đạo said.

"Me either," Streak added.

"And the lights went out at Glacier," Kannon said. "We don't know about Whitefish."

"Maybe Streak's Willys not run," Kim said, making a slashing motion across his neck. "Did EMP cause plane crash?"

"*Tôi không biết.*" Quán said, meaning he didn't know.

Kannon shook his head. "If in range, an EMP strike would've instantly killed the engine. Also, we had functioning electronics after the crash."

"It makes sense. Our GPSs work. And vehicles—"

"No one knows the range of an attack like this," Streak said, interrupting Đăng Đạo.

"True," Kannon said.

"Then this Willys Jeep might be fried," Quán said.

"It's pre-computer age," Streak said. "No solenoid. Nothing to fry."

"The battery, plugs, condensers," Kannon said.

"An EMP weapon shouldn't . . . oh, right. And I've got the battery hooked up to a trickle charger."

317

"Who knows how long before power can be restored. Even then, the Willys might not run, but we'll need a vehicle." Kannon's mind tumbled over the possibilities. He couldn't come up with a good idea other than Đăng Đạo's earlier offer to steal one. Renting a vehicle was a last resort.

"We're wasting time speculating. Streak, what's the name of the outfit where your Willys is stored?" Streak gave it to him. Kannon produced his satellite phone and tapped in 411. He received a response and asked for the storage facility's number. He got it, dialed it, and listened to a voicemail. "Whitefish is alive. Streak, you in any condition to run?"

"Streak Man too old," Đăng Đạo added.

Kannon's max was five miles. He could probably gut it out, but the unfamiliar territory concerned him. Because of his knowledge of the area, Streak was the logical one to tag. What if someone in town with militia connections recognized him? A Vietnamese man with a history of clandestine operations might be the right ticket.

"Boss man is a good runner," Quán said.

Meaning Đăng Đạo.

A horse whinnied, reminding Kannon of the smell of hay he'd detected across the riverbed. The animal whinnied again. It didn't sound far away. Riding was faster than jogging, safer than filching a vehicle. "Can anyone ride bareback?"

"If I can ride a water buffalo, I can ride a horse," Đăng Đạo said.

"Get after it, then." Kannon hoped the horse was neither nag nor wild. "Careful, though, don't get chased by its irate owner wielding a shotgun."

His nephew motioned for Quán and Kim to come forward, then the three Vietnamese—NVDs positioned to slip over their eyes if necessary—headed for the area from which they believed the whinnying originated.

As they trotted off, Kannon reached into the cooler, pulled out two sodas, and handed one to Streak, who popped the top and drank. The wait began for what Kannon hoped to be the arrival of a manageable horse minus its owner in pursuit.

"I'm going to map a route for Đăng Đạo to follow into

Whitefish," Kannon said.

He reactivated his GPS. Five minutes later, he had completed the route, inputting waypoints as well as the destination. Then he checked his satphone for messages. There was one. He keyed to retrieve it and heard Stefan's voice. "Dad, I know you don't want to hear this, but Lan has been detained at the Williamson County Sheriff's office in Georgetown. She's not under arrest but is considered a person of interest. I'm trying to get her released."

Kannon swore. Another sickening knot in his gut.

The nightmare grows.

Stefan's message had come at 2200 hours last night. It was now 0300 the next morning. Kannon called.

"Hey, Dad."

"Got your update. Just what I didn't want to happen."

"I'm doing my best."

"I know that, son. Where are you?"

"Outside the sheriff's offices." A pause. "Your voice sounds croaky, Dad. Are you all right?"

Kannon wrestled with whether to mention the plane crash. *Negative.* "Yeah. Finish the briefing."

"Lan is still being questioned."

"Have you been in there with her?"

"I was for a few minutes, but Lan told me to leave and that she would call for me if necessary. Ditto for Belynda, who's with me."

Strong, stubborn woman, his wife.

"Sorry, Stefan, I should've known better than to ask. Any feel for the tone of the interrogations?"

"Cordial but firm," Stefan said. "They're pursuing several angles."

"What are they?"

"One, they're considering the possibility of a third-party kidnapping, but no leads have turned up."

"Because there aren't any," Kannon said.

"Two, you're playing the rogue lone wolf intent on rescuing Derrick."

"Well, they got that right. What about their other theories?"

"Are you ready for this? You, or you and Lan, arranged the

319

kidnapping and de . . ."

"Go on, say it."

". . . and death of your son for insurance money."

Idiots, Kannon thought. "There's no policy on Derrick, just on me, and Lan's the beneficiary to the tune of a million bucks." *Easily verified. And the way things are going, she could collect.* "What else?"

"You're having an affair with Roger's wife and arranged to have him killed so you could run off with her and your son—"

"And live happily ever after. Unbelievable. Surely Lan doesn't think—"

"She doesn't."

Kannon sighed. He glared at Streak, the man responsible standing beside him on an oasis in the middle of a dry riverbed. Get a grip, he told himself. *I'm responsible for this whole damn mess. But I've come too far to back out now.*

"Do you have a read for what Creighton and Hollister really believe?"

"Based on what they've learned about you, I'm guessing number two, Dad."

Kannon considered what more could be said or done. He needed to get Lan off the hook. But how? Zeller? If Zeller was who she claimed to be, she might help. If the move proved wrong, though, contacting her might wreck this mission and rip his family further apart.

Was it worth the risk? Zeller had played Streak by setting him up to be nailed for transporting illegal weapons. And it was a high probability she'd planted the SyncTrak tracking device on Streak's motorcycle, along with threatening Lan with deportation. The big question is: Why?

"Stefan?"

"Yeah?"

"Contact Zeller."

"Me! Why don't you call her?"

Kannon read uncertainty in Stefan's voice.

"Identify who you are. Maybe she'll be softer with you." Fat chance, Kannon thought.

"Dad! She threatened to have Lan deported, right?"

"Yeah, but Zeller knows where we live. She could've already picked Lan up if she wanted to. The bitch may be a CIA agent, but I believe she has an ulterior motive and is just trying to extract information."

"What do you think her motivation is?"

"I have no idea. But I don't see how calling her can make our situation any worse."

"Famous last words," Stefan said, regaining his confident voice. "How should I handle it?"

"Explain Lan's situation. Appeal to her good nature." If she has one.

"She's going to ask about you."

"You don't know where I am." Which was true. "I don't trust her enough to reveal everything."

"Give me her number."

Kannon did, then added to his son's To-Do list. "If things crater, call this guy." He gave Stefan the name. "He's a criminal attorney."

"Got it. I'll call her if necessary. Gotta go. Being paged."

The call terminated. Kannon gritted his teeth. He hoped he hadn't just directed Stefan into a major screwup.

"Bad news?" Streak asked.

"It could've been better. We've got a lot to do and a short time to do it in."

The hollow sound of horse hooves clip-clopping across rocks caught his ear. Soon, a silhouetted animal emerged, all three Vietnamese aboard. Kannon remembered the numbers of Vietnamese who could pile on a scooter or a three-wheeled Lambretta.

"What? You want more horses?" Đăng Đạo signaled for the two brothers to dismount from the sleek, black animal, which he controlled with a rope-fashioned bridle.

Now, along with other law-breaking incidents, Kannon could add horse theft. Was that still a hanging offense in Montana?

"One question," his nephew said. "What do I do with the horse once I get there?"

"Hitch it to Streak's garage," Kannon said. "Somehow we'll

notify the owner where to find his horse . . . unless someone has a better idea."

No one did.

Streak dug into his pocket for the keys to the garage and Jeep and offered them to Đăng Đạo. Kim handed over a waist pack, which included a radio and, most likely, a weapon.

"Let me see the route" Đăng Đạo said, leaning toward Kannon.

"This riverbed curves gently for two miles," Kannon said, holding the GPS in one hand while pointing southwest with the other. "Then it makes a sharp bend. An old forest service road runs adjacent to this arroyo after it turns south. They intersect here," he added, pointing to the spot on the GPS map.

He handed the device to Đăng Đạo. His nephew studied the screen and then placed the device inside the waist pack.

"We'll reconnect at the junction of the arroyo and the road I pointed out earlier," Kannon said. "Good luck." He slapped the horse on its rump. The horse jolted into a gallop as Đăng Đạo rode into the night, headed for Whitefish. *I hope this isn't the last I'll see of you, Nephew.*

"Quán, Kim, since we've got canteens, leave the cooler. They'll slow us down," Kannon said.

"Let's hump it," Quán said.

Stars were plentiful as they started off in the brisk air. They opted not to use their night vision devices unless necessary. The NVDs provided a narrow breadth of field and were cumbersome when navigating longer distances.

Following the riverbed, they marched like ghosts between the rocky bluffs that Streak had skillfully avoided. The air turned musty from rock dust and smelled like wet chalk. A stream trickled alongside the chasm wall before disappearing underground. Forty-five minutes later, after a few stumbles from traversing uneven terrain, they reached the arroyo's elbow.

"The road should just be over the right bank," Streak said.

The four of them clambered up and there it was.

"Wait one. I want to check the route." Kannon dug into his pack, grabbed his Pulsars, and slipped them on. He looked both north and south along the path. It was rocky and tight. Weeds had sprung up tall and ragged in both directions. "Appears to be in disuse," he said, replacing the night goggles in his pack.

They trekked along the deserted forest road until it intersected with the riverbed.

"And now we wait," Kim said.

Streak slumped to the ground, his head apparently bothering him. The brothers dropped their gear and squatted on the road's shoulder. Kannon peered into the distance, anxious to see Jeep headlights approaching.

"I hear something," Quán said.

"Helicopter," said Kim.

The staccato whump-whump-whump of whirling blades reached Kannon. Streak shook as if an earthquake were happening, then hugged the ground.

"What's wrong?" Kannon asked.

"I thought at first it was the militia bird," Streak said in a muffled voice. "But it's not."

"Get out of sight anyway."

They crouched beneath dark-shadowed evergreens. The reverberating sound made by the chopper took Kannon back to 'Nam, but he'd never been affected like Streak was just now. Was he crumbling under pressure, just not up to the task? Or was he experiencing pure fear?

Kannon remembered his exaggerated responses to triggers of war those many years ago. Then he thought about the killing range Streak had described and shuddered. Yeah, Crandle could instill that much terror in another man.

Fifty-Six

Once the chopper disappeared, Kannon focused on Streak. "Are you all right?"

"Clearing the cobwebs, as you say."

"After thinking about what you'd said about Crandle's killing field, I understand your reaction."

"Appreciate it."

"Good to see you regaining composure."

Now, where the hell was Đăng Đạo? Kannon looked at his watch again. It was 0430, one hour since his nephew had taken off on horseback. Had he reached Whitefish? Was he having trouble reading and locating the GPS coordinates for the rendezvous point?

Or worse?

Quán and Kim didn't appear concerned about Đăng Đạo's no-show. Instead, acting like noncommissioned officers, they hung together, amusing themselves by doing push-ups and throwing ninja stars at a dead tree trunk.

Kannon returned his thoughts to the blackout in Kalispell and, by possible extension, to Glacier. Were they on the same electrical grid? Was it an area-wide power outage? Or had Border Slot used their Jolly Green Giant to execute an EMP airburst? The concept of wiped-out electronics was mindboggling. The impact on humanity, the structure of this country, if not the world, would be unprecedented—a new age of darkness.

He asked Streak, "Assuming Border Slot had unleashed an EMP attack, what's the highest altitude a Jolly Green Giant could reach?"

"Ten, twelve thousand feet." Streak said, tenderly touching the knot on his forehead. "What are you thinking? I don't see how an EMP weapon could've been dropped accurately from a chopper."

"They might've used some sort of guidance system."

"I suppose so. My job would've been to pilot the helicopter, but I don't recall any discussion of EMP airdrops or guidance systems when I was around."

"Regardless, assuming there was an EMP attack, it gives us

another reason to stop these bastards."

"You got that right," Streak said.

Shivering in the deeper, penetrating wind-chill, Kannon slapped his arms against his chest. "My understanding is you could stand right next to an electronic bomb and your body not be affected."

"Except maybe your brain."

Kannon thought about that. He remembered the flap over prolonged proximity to cellphones and tower signals. Perhaps a powerful magnetic pulse could scramble a man's brains.

He rose and stomped his feet. The jolt ran up his body and hurt his teeth. *Come on, nephew.* Đăng Đạo had taken one of the PRC-148 radios as well as his satphone but had not responded to his attempt to reach him. Why? Would an EMP blast have enough lingering effect to disable a radio and satellite phone at some distance? Maybe the electromagnetic destruction had spread to Whitefish.

Craving a smoke, Kannon crouched behind some boulders to conceal the match and block the wind. He clamped the stem between his teeth and lit his pipe.

Once more, Kannon stared down the road. He was about to call the garage again when, finally, a flicker of headlights materialized out of the darkness.

The lights were distant and seemed to approach at a walker's pace. Crap, the vehicle might belong to authorities searching for the crash site, or for them. Kannon didn't want to risk flagging down the wrong party.

As the vehicle got closer, "Streak, could that be your Jeep?"

"Hard to tell. The headlights are close together, though, so, yeah, probably."

"Quán and Kim, *lại đây*."

The brothers pried their throwing stars out of the tree trunk and trotted over. The team peeled back into the woods, careful to maintain a field of vision. Huddling, they exhaled whitish vapors in the frigid air. As the vehicle got closer, Kannon averted his gaze to preserve his acclimated eyesight.

"It's my Willys," Streak said. "I'd recognize that clatter anywhere."

Kannon stepped onto the road and held up his hand. Đăng Đạo

cut the lights and killed the motor.

"I am grateful this clunker didn't break down," Đăng Đạo said.

Understandable. The vintage Willys looked as though it'd been salvaged from a junkyard. The station-wagon type, its sides were composed of faux wood. Peeling paint and multiple dents further marred the pitted metal bodywork. The side mirrors were missing, and the two front windows sported spiderweb cracks. But the side-mounted spare tire appeared serviceable.

Streak and the brothers gathered their gear and loaded it in the Jeep.

"Whitefish must've been spared the power outage."

Đăng Đạo nodded. "Streetlights and storefronts were lit up." His nephew opened the driver's door, and a jerry-rigged overhead light exposed a face flushed from the cold. Otherwise, his nephew wore his normal enigmatic expression.

Puffing on his pipe, Kannon drew his nephew aside. "Did anyone hassle you?"

Đăng Đạo shook his head.

"I don't understand why you didn't answer my calls?"

"Had my sat turned off." Đăng Đạo patted the PRC inside his pack.

"At least your GPS worked," Kannon said.

"Still, I was fortunate to find this road."

Kannon glanced at Streak and the brothers as they finished loading the Willys. Something didn't seem right. Something was out of whack. "Why did it take you so long?"

Đăng Đạo drew in a long breath and exhaled slowly. He locked his eyes on Kannon's. "I made a command decision."

"Which was?"

A rapid-fire exchange between Quán and Kim drew Kannon's attention away from his nephew. The brothers were examining a paraglider.

"Đăng Đạo—"

"From the wilderness store," his nephew said.

"In Whitefish?"

"Kalispell."

"You drove to Kalispell to secure paragliding equipment?"

Đăng Đạo nodded. "Nothing works in that place. No electricity, no alarms, people on the streets were *khùng*!"

Interpreting the comment, Kim circled his index finger alongside his temple, meaning crazy.

"What else did you notice?" Kannon asked.

"The air smelled bad."

"Fried electrical systems, I imagine."

Kim pinched his nose.

"Candlelight, lanterns . . . reminded me of old times," Đăng Đạo added.

"I think militia used bicycles for ground attack," Kim said. He mimed riding a bike.

Why not? If the Border Slot Militia delivered a land-based attack, maybe they had used bicycles for transport.

"Back to the paragliding equipment," Kannon said, "You broke in and helped yourself?"

"It was the best time to do it."

"You could've been shot."

His nephew shrugged.

"You ignored my calls, didn't you?"

"*Không.*"

The "No" was laced with anger, but Kannon couldn't let the issue slide.

"Đăng Đạo!"

His nephew didn't lower his head as if in shame. Instead, "All right. I ignored your calls because you would have told me not to enter Kalispell, much less steal the equipment."

Đăng Đạo reverted to drawing out words when he got heated. An uninformed person might think him slow. He was anything but. Still, "You disobeyed a command."

"*Nguyền rủa,*" Đăng Đạo said in a muffled voice as he walked off.

"What's that mean?"

"Nothing. It means nothing."

Yes, it did. His nephew's tone told him he'd been cussed out. Kannon snuffed his pipe and pocketed it. He was no longer cold.

327

In addition to stealing the paraglider, Đăng Đạo had also purloined topo maps, shooting gloves, caps, and face warmers, as well as down-filled sleeping bags—everything they needed. Kannon couldn't fault the initiative. He acknowledged his nephew saved them time and aided their rescue effort.

Still, Đăng Đạo's bent toward independence worried him. He couldn't afford for his nephew to cut his own orders. His actions reminded Kannon of senior, recalcitrant noncommissioned officers' ability to scrounge. If there was a demand and the item existed, they would find its source. Just as poignant, his nephew's stance and resolve reminded Kannon of the fierce look that Đăng Đạo's father had shown when the two of them fought together.

"We're in this together," Kannon said. "I need to be able to trust you."

"Jeep's loaded and ready to go," Streak said, holding open the driver's door.

Assuming the rescue of Derrick would prove successful, and they all survived, Kannon would have to compensate a plane owner, store owner, and rancher. His *expense account* was growing. Would there be more?

And so it goes.

Fifty-Seven

Streak pulled the choke, turned the key, and started the Jeep. Its two shifters—the long, beanpole-shaped primary lever and the shorter, four-wheel-drive stick—vibrated wildly as the Willys bounced along the forest service road. A probable three-hour drive from Whitefish to the top of the cliff overlooking Border Slot awaited them.

As Streak ran through the gears, Kannon recalled his grandfather's 1940s era black Chrysler, which also harbored a musty smell and featured a long shifter. Both vehicles lacked heaters. And it was cold.

A palpable tension permeated the Jeep. Riding shotgun, Kannon glanced behind him. Quán and Kim, sitting on the double-wide, cracked Naugahyde bench seat, were muttering in Vietnamese, while Đăng Đạo, balanced on the edge of the wooden jump seat, stared out the window.

The deafening silence put Kannon on edge. Was everyone undergoing a letdown after the adrenaline rush? Conceivably, no one's thinking was spot on. After all, they had survived a plane crash, scratched their way out of the wilderness, stolen a horse, and robbed a store—all connected to this rescue effort.

He faced forward, zipped up his parka, and considered what more if anything he needed to say to his nephew. It was only through loyalty and principle he exerted any authority over these guys. Would his leadership hold?

Maybe it was best to let things simmer down a bit. Place a restraining order on his ego. Stop being such a hardass. Admit that his nephew had procured everything they needed—the Willys, the paraglider, and accompanying gear. Kannon turned again and tapped his nephew on the knee.

"I was wrong. You were right, Đăng Đạo. You did great. We wouldn't be as far along as we are without you."

His nephew smiled. Quán and Kim gave a thumbs-up.

The ice was broken. Don't mush it up.

Kannon noticed a mom- and pop-type service station. "Let's

329

gas up."

"We are obviously beyond the effective range of the EMP attack," Đăng Đạo said.

"Roger that."

Filling up and buying snacks seemed to loosen further everyone's pent-up anxiety.

Kannon tracked their circuitous route on his GPS. They crossed several streams and paralleled an elongated lake. The population was scattered, and they encountered no other vehicles along the way.

"I want to be atop the cliff overlooking the militia compound by midmorning," he said.

* * *

Two and a half hours later, at a T-bone intersection, they came abreast of a fenced-in enclosure. Inside were three used cars, which led Kannon to think of muffler pipes and the best way to employ C-4 explosives. After considering using only stealth to rescue Derrick, Kannon realized he'd have to use explosives as a diversionary tactic—at a minimum. The main reason was that he couldn't figure any other way to breach the electrified front gate and fence.

"Bangalore torpedoes would be more effective than unshaped charges to blast holes in the gate and fence."

"Got that right," Đăng Đạo said.

"What're you going to use for canisters?" Streak asked.

"Muffler pipes," Kannon said.

"Good idea," Kim chipped in.

"We'll take a close look at these autos on the way back. See if we can salvage anything useful."

"Roger that."

At 0945, Kannon stood on the 2500-foot promontory above Border Slot, peering through binoculars at the militia layout. Cone-shaped firs and spruce shot up from the valley floor like pinnacles through a frigid mist, allowing a shrouded view of the pitched cabin roofs. Best he could tell, the Border Slot compound matched Streak's rough-scaled map.

Frustrated at being unable to see more detail, Kannon backed away from the cliff.

330

"Wish this damn ice fog would clear."

"It'll burn off." Streak turned up the collar on his parka.

"I'm not so sure," Kannon said, pointing north. Dark nimbostratus clouds covered the horizon. "If that storm system moves our way, this whole area could be engulfed in bad weather by noon."

"Hmm. Hadn't noticed," Streak said. "Snow clouds all right."

Kannon's watch showed 1000 hours, 0900 Central Time. "I'm going to make a sat call before the weather worsens."

"Good luck," Streak said.

Stefan answered on the second ring.

"Dad! I was just about to call you."

"What's the word?"

"Great news."

Kannon liked the sound of that.

"We're just leaving the courthouse. Here's Lan."

"Hi, *em bé*."

Tears misted in Kannon's eyes. He couldn't remember the last time Lan had called him that. She'd coined the Vietnamese word for baby into a term of endearment. "How're you doing?"

"I am tired and disgusted. Otherwise, I am fine."

"How about Belynda?"

"She showed her finger to Sergeant Creighton as we were leaving."

Kannon smiled. He was growing to like Belynda's fire. "Oh, man, do I miss you, Lan."

"I miss you, too, *em bé*. Where are you?"

"Freezing my ass off on top of a cliff."

He wanted to talk to her for hours. Would that opportunity ever come again? But he couldn't even spare minutes, just seconds. He was already feeling soft, losing his edge like he had when returning to combat in Việt Nam after a week's R and R in Taiwan.

Neither one of them mentioned Derrick. They didn't have to. Each knew what was at stake.

"Stefan needs to speak with you," Lan said. "I love you."

"I love you too." Kannon waited for Stefan to speak.

"Dad, wait a sec. Lan, why don't you and Brenda head for my Challenger? I'll be there in a moment."

Kannon assumed Stefan and Belynda must've followed the patrol unit in his son's car last night. When his son returned to the phone, "Was it Zeller?"

"Yeah, Dad. She must be legit. Sergeant Creighton and I were in the CID Commander's office when he got a phone call." Stefan chuckled. "You should've seen the look on his face when he said, 'Who the fuck is Sindy Zeller?'"

Yeah, who the fuck was Sindy Zeller? None of her actions made sense unless she was goading them into going after Border Slot. If so, why not employ CIA resources instead of manipulating him and Streak? But Lan got an Out-of-Jail-Free card because of Zeller. That mattered.

"Wait one, Stefan. I'm putting you on hold. I want Streak to hear this."

Kannon motioned Streak over, brought him up to date, then lifted the satellite phone back to his cheek for a low-volume conference call. Streak huddled close. "Stefan, how much do you think Zeller knows?"

"Hard to tell. She asked where you were. Told her I didn't know."

Kannon winked at Streak. "She believe you?"

"I don't think so. But she was receptive to Lan's situation. I wasn't privy to the conversation between Zeller and the CID Commander, but after the call, the CID told Creighton to get serious. He's sending out an experienced detective, Hamilton, I think his name is, to provide protection and monitor our phones."

"Good idea," Streak said. "Crandle doesn't know for sure where you are. It wouldn't surprise me if he sent another team to your home."

Kannon frowned as the weight of Streak's comments sank in. It brought to surface a concern that had been lurking in the back of his mind. What would keep Border Slot from returning?

"Dad?"

"Just thinking." Kannon massaged his hand. No way could he sandbag the deputy and not inform him about the possibility of Border Slot showing up again. "Emphasize to Hamilton he needs to stay on his toes. The kidnappers might make a return visit. Nothing more, nothing less. Got it?"

"Got it."

"Get my shotgun. You know how to use it."

"I'll be ready," Stefan said. "What do I tell Lan and Belynda?"

"Tell 'em everything. Lan won't be scared off. Belynda might, but based upon their relationship, I doubt it. Both women know how to use a weapon, right, Streak?"

The conscience-driven Streak broke into a sheepish grin.

"Anything else, son?"

"Nada."

"All right. Signing off. Good work, Stefan." To Streak, "What do you think?"

"I'm glad the women were released, but Zeller's still a bitch on steroids."

Based upon his voice only relationship with her so far, Kannon couldn't agree more, but his family safety was of primary concern. Stefan was good with a shotgun. Lan had combat experience. And an armed detective would be there. *Enough?*

Đăng Đạo approached. "Aunt Lan?"

"On the way home," Kannon said.

His nephew gestured a thumbs-up. Then they returned their attention to the brothers who were setting up the paraglider while fighting a cold, cold wind.

Fifty-Eight

Tuesday, 0915 Hours, 27 October 2009, Texas Hill Country

Sitting in the passenger seat of Stefan's Challenger, Lan thought about the sheriff's parting comment: *Thanks for your cooperation.*

"Cooperation, my ass," Lan said.

Stefan took his eye off the road and cocked an eyebrow.

"What? You think I do not curse. I live with Kannon, remember?"

Her stepson grinned.

They were on their way home from the Williamson County Sheriff's office in Georgetown, each wearing the same clothes as the day before—Belynda in her embroidered dress, Stefan in jeans and Wrangler shirt, and she in sweatpants and a bulky sweater.

"How are you feeling, Lan?" asked Belynda, whose slender frame was squeezed into the back seat.

"Humiliated and relieved, but I am tired, so tired. It was good to talk with Kannon, though." She twisted her body to look at Belynda. "How are you?"

Her friend pressed her hands against her stomach and mocked vomiting. Lan curled her lip in agreement.

"Derrick's kidnapping seems unreal," Lan said.

"It's hard to imagine what you're going through." Belynda patted her arm.

"Derrick, Kannon, and Đăng Đạo are experiencing much worse." Life without her new family would not be worth living. *I must remain positive. Kannon will succeed.*

Lan faced forward and returned her attention to Stefan. Jaw set firm, cheekbones sharp, one hand was draped over the steering wheel, the other cradled the standard-shift gear knob. Her stepson's mannerisms frighteningly mirrored her husband's. "Stefan Ballard, first son of Kannon Ballard, why was I released so abruptly?"

"Yes, Lawyer Stefan," Belynda said, "what legal magic did you use to sway Sergeant Creighton to release her?"

"I didn't do anything. Obviously, they were wrong to bring Lan in for questioning in the first place."

Belynda flicked Stefan on the ear.

"Ow!"

Lan gave him what Kannon called *The Look*.

"Okay. Sindy Zeller got you released."

"What?" Lan blushed at her startled response.

"Whose side is Zeller on?" Belynda asked.

"Ours, I think, maybe," Stefan said meekly. He adjusted the rearview mirror and tilted his head as if to check on Belynda's expression. "What matters is that it worked."

Lan shifted sideways in the passenger seat. "We are still in danger, I feel."

"Yeah. We're not out of the woods yet." Stefan cut his eyes back to the road.

"Elaborate," Belynda said.

"Streak told Kannon—"

"Streak?" Belynda interrupted.

"He is on the team," Lan said.

"Oh, my Lord!"

"There's a chance Border Slot might pay us another visit," Stefan said.

Lan flashed Belynda a knowing look.

"The CID is sending over a seasoned detective for added protection," Stefan added. "It'll be twenty-four-seven until this situation gets resolved."

"We must be ready," Lan said, touching her stepson's hand. The pressure to remain quiet about what she knew weighed her down, just as in Việt Nam when made aware of her pregnancy, and, not knowing whether she would ever see Kannon again, felt confined regarding her feelings. *And here I am again, wondering, worrying, but this is different. I do have support. Think about others.*

"Belynda, you have been through so much with us, but your life is at risk. You have classes to teach and a life to live. I cannot ask you to stay any longer."

"Are you kidding? I'm not leaving! I will be locked and loaded."

"I am grateful." She wondered if the Navajo had a phrase for steel will. That's how resolute her friend's expression appeared.

Stefan remained mute, but Lan felt his solidarity as well.

The click-clack of the turn signal blinker distracted her. Stefan slowed and turned off Highway 29 onto her driveway. And just as quickly conflicted emotions arose along the drive leading to a house absent her husband and son.

Inside . . .

"You two get some sleep," Stefan said after the women had finished showering and dressing.

A pouch of extra shells at his feet, he was holding Kannon's shotgun, a Browning over- and under-twelve gauge that he had removed from his dad's gun cabinet in the study. "I'll hold the fort until Detective Hamilton arrives."

* * *

Disoriented, Lan awoke to the sound of three men talking in the kitchen. Glancing at the clock, she saw that nearly two hours had passed since arriving home. Her time-frame reference was as messed up as if cobwebs were clogging her mind.

Groggy, she groped her way off her easy chair, belted the terrycloth robe, and started for the sofa, where Belynda had been sleeping and was now stirring. "I think the detective has arrived."

They headed for the kitchen. Sergeant Creighton was there with a man she did not recognize. He was holding a slim canvas briefcase. Stefan, wearing man-sweats and rubbing his eyes, was there too. All three were sitting at the table drinking coffee.

Creighton nodded his hello. "This is Detective Hamilton from our criminal investigation division. He'll be watching for intruders and monitoring the landline. Miss Lan, go ahead and cancel the rerouting of your landline to your cell. Any calls—"

"You're on our side now?" Belynda asked, with bitter sarcasm.

"Not going there again," Creighton said.

"Ladies?" Hamilton rose from the table and shook hands, "I'm here for twenty-four hours, then my replacement will handle the next twenty-four, and so on."

Lan's initial impression of the new arrival was positive. His deep tone radiated confidence. Standing about five feet ten with cropped, slicked-back hair, the new detective was clean-shaven with narrow cheekbones, a broad nose, and bushy eyebrows shading green eyes. Appearing fit and agile, he wore loose chinos and a purple Polo shirt.

"Normally, we'd have two men assigned," Creighton said, rising, "but we're short on manpower." Specifically, to Lan, a sardonic smile on his face, he added, "Of course, we don't really expect any calls, do we, except maybe from your husband."

"How could I know in advance!" Lan postured her unreadable face.

"Our belief is your husband is tackling the recovery of your son on his own," Hamilton said. "Is that true?"

Belynda slunk into the background and crossed her arms.

"He is," Stefan said.

Lan arched her eyebrows.

"They have to know," Stefan said, "since there's the possibility of reprisal here."

"He's right, Lan," Belynda said, dropping her arms at her side.

"Where is your husband, ma'am?" Creighton asked.

"I do not know," Lan said.

Creighton and Hamilton looked to Belynda, who shrugged, and Stefan, who said, "We really don't."

The deputies' expressions read of disbelief, but they seemed to accept the answer, at least for now.

Belynda fronted Hamilton. "Our understanding is that you are here to protect us."

"You are correct, Miss Belynda Blu," Hamilton said.

"I just wish your husband had put his faith in us," Creighton added.

"My husband has a history of handling things on his own," Lan said.

"So I've been told."

"Kannon was troubled because he and I did not feel you were taking us seriously. In hindsight, maybe we were all too quick to judge. But my husband is a warrior. So are those who are with him."

"Jesus," Creighton said. "All right. What's done is done.

We're on the same team now, here to help. Just understand we have lots of questions to clear up."

"Thank you." Lan let out a grateful sigh, inferring, though, the deputies were far from placated.

"Let's get moving." Stefan rolled up the sleeves of his sweatshirt. "Where do you want to set up?"

"Got a cordless phone for your landline?"

"Yes."

"Got a dining room table?" Hamilton asked.

"Adjacent to the den." Lan pointed it out.

"That'll work."

"Turn on your alarm after I leave," Creighton said, "and stay inside." To Hamilton, "This is real. Remain alert."

After Creighton left through the patio door, Lan armed the system on the back-door console.

They filed into the den, except for Belynda, who headed for the kitchen. Stefan and Lan sat on the sofa. Once the detective moved to the formal dining table and occupied himself with the cordless and setting up his equipment, Lan straightened her back and whispered to Stefan, "I am tempted to tell them more."

"I wish we knew what they knew," Stefan said, twisting, popping his back.

"I worry less about that now." Lan rose from the sofa and balled her fists. She felt like a Machiavellian puppeteer was pulling her strings.

She walked to the front window, spread the curtains, and looked out. The sky was overcast, blocking the sun, creating colder temperatures. Colder temperatures brought misery. With misery came depression.

Lan closed the curtains. She marched to her piano and pounded the keyboard, startling Stefan. Seeing his reaction, Lan realized keyboarding was not going to solve anything. She strode to the coffee table in the den and examined the turquoise-filled wooden dolls lying on the table. There was one unfilled depression on the baby. She wet her index finger, reached into the tiny leather bag, and removed a turquoise bit. After placing it in the hole just below the navel, she set the baby doll back on the table and knelt before it.

"Stefan, please get Belynda. I want to say a prayer."

When Stefan returned with Belynda from the kitchen, they knelt beside her. The three clasped hands and Lan began her trilogy.

"To Almighty God, all-knowing Buddha, and Navajo Faith Healer, I pray to you from the deepest of my heart that you protect Kannon and Đăng Đạo as they attempt to rescue my precious Derrick. Keep them alive and healthy. Even though my son is only six years old, give him the strength of the water buffalo, the wisdom of the ancients, the perseverance of, yes, the perseverance of his father's enemy—the Việt Cộng. God, speak to Derrick through your Holy Spirit. Buddha, teach my son the lessons of Nirvana. Faith Healer, let the turquoise stones placed in the curing dolls' holes heal all physical and emotional wounds to my son. Let Derrick feel the strength of my love, a mother's love that began in my womb, a love that grows stronger each day." And forgive me for the information I continue to withhold from the authorities.

Fifty-Nine

Tuesday, 1100 Hours, 27 October 2009, Border Slot Compound, Montana

A blast of cold wind curled over the edge of the cliff and whipped the lapels of Kannon's parka. He stepped away from the precipice and found shelter within a maze of granite boulders and upright stones that reminded him of Stonehenge, a reverent setting for untangling his thoughts. For him, wrestling with the weight of Derrick's kidnapping, the loss of his brother, and his wife's vulnerability was akin to being crushed by a steamroller.

Someone tugged on his shoulder.

"The sky is falling." Quán gestured upward.

Kannon frowned as he followed Quán back to the others. Snowflakes began plummeting like battalions of paratroopers. Đăng Đạo's glasses frosted over. So did Streak's. The brothers were shivering, their camouflaged parkas dusted with nickel-sized crystals. The temperature registered sub-freezing, and the blustery wind amplified the chill factor. On the plus side, the blizzard-like conditions should aid their concealment.

"Build a fire," Kim said.

"Unless you know how to build a smokeless one, we'll have to tough it out. Do some jumping jacks."

Kim rolled his eyes while Quán, cloaked in his bulky parka, proceeded to exercise. Kannon pictured a mid-sized sumo wrestler trying to flag down a taxi.

"Couldn't you have stolen some portable heat packs?" Kannon asked, trying to inject humor into their grim situation.

"My wilderness store did not stock them," Đăng Đạo said.

"I hope you are as unperturbed as you sound."

His nephew winked.

Wanting another look at the compound roughly half a mile below, Kannon walked to the edge of the cliff. He wiped the moisture off his binocular lenses and looked down. Mist still obscured the compound, fostering the impression of a dead zone. Pressing the binoculars hard against his eyes, Kannon wanted to *will* his son into view. What if the Border Slot group, with Derrick in tow, had abandoned stakes and moved to another location?

He lowered the binoculars and shielded his face from the wind. Streak and the brothers were still working with the paraglider, the wind playing havoc with their efforts.

Đăng Đạo approached him from behind.

"About last night," his nephew said, "I understand why you were *túc giận*."

"Yeah. I was angry. As I said, though, you were right."

"Ironic, you and I working together, just like you did with my dad." A look of admiration filled Đăng Đạo's face.

"Look in the mirror, and you'll see your father's face."

His nephew cracked a blue-lip smile. "Derrick is my cousin. His mother is my aunt. We will succeed."

Kannon cuffed him on the shoulder.

"I am glad Lan has been released," Đăng Đạo flicked at the falling snowflakes, "but you must not think about her now. You must remain sắc bén."

Kannon furrowed his brow.

"Sharp."

"Got it," Kannon said.

Uplifted by the brief conversation, Kannon lowered himself to the ground for a steadier view of Border Slot. The crypt-cold granite was like lying on a slab of ice. He brushed icicles off his mustache and raised the binoculars. Fortunately, the ice fog was lifting, affording a decent topside view. Both evergreens and leafless deciduous trees dominated the compound. Before launching a rescue attempt, he had to know whether Derrick was there.

Kannon stared beyond a thumb-shaped rib of granite. According to Streak's map, he was directly above the armory. Craning his neck, he could barely detect the chopper pad and the obstacle course. Kannon switched to wide angle and swept the rest of the compound. Three smoke plumes spiraled from chimneys. *Someone was home.* Then he noticed an outdoor grill, long and rectangular, with flaming red embers.

"Streak, what's the smoke coming off that grill tell you?"

Kannon asked.

"Crandle likes to celebrate a successful mission by holding a banquet."

"The frying of Kalispell," Kannon muttered.

A small, bundled-up figure emerged from the main cabin. Adrenaline pumped through Kannon's veins, but the energy burst quickly died. The person's footprints were too far apart to belong to Derrick. Male or female? he wondered.

"Take a look down there and see if you can tell who that is," Kannon said to Streak.

The defecting militia pilot walked over and took the binoculars. He dropped to one knee and held the powerful glasses to his eyes. "That's Anh."

Hearing the name gave Kannon some comfort. Ever since Streak had described the woman, Kannon pictured her as Derrick's guardian angel. He hoped this wasn't a pipe dream.

"This pisses me off!" Đăng Đạo said through clenched teeth. "It is wrong for the SOB to imprison this Vietnamese woman."

Kim nodded. "Very wrong. She should cook him on the grill."

Quán didn't say anything, which surprised Kannon. But he was grateful for Kim's and Đăng Đạo's perspective toward Anh.

There but for the grace of God, Lan—

"The bastards destroyed my cabin," Streak spat out.

"Hell, you weren't going back anyway." Kannon again brushed ice off his mustache.

"Point out their power supply," Quán said. Ice particles beaded along his scar.

Streak did, noting the generators and solar panels.

"And the fuel depot?" Kim rotated his hands in a cycling motion.

"The above-ground fuel tank and pump are near the chopper pad." Streak handed the glasses to Đăng Đạo.

"Ah, I see them," he said. "They're surrounded by a cyclone fence, with coiled barbed wire on top. Better than Quán's and Kim's father had," Đăng Đạo added.

Listening between the lines, Kannon figured the brothers' father must have been a VC. He remembered how Việt Cộng conscripts manned bicycles in enlarged underground tunnels to power their generators.

"Kim should blow the fuel tank," Quán said.

"Yeah." Streak used a stick to draw a diagram in the snow. "Solar panels, there," he pointed. "Maybe Kim could destroy those too."

"I'll add the idea to my contingency list," Kannon said. "But timing is a concern. I'm not sure we'll have enough of it to destroy the panels. Besides, there would be a power reserve, would there not? And they've got generators. Not sure we'd gain anything."

"What about Internet?" Kim blinked rapidly, eyes like twin cursors.

"No service," Streak said.

"What is antenna for?" Kim asked.

"The ham radio," Streak said. "Remember, Crandle has access off his bedroom."

"I wonder who comprises Crandle's worldwide circle of contacts," Đăng Đạo muttered.

Kannon shrugged.

"What puzzles me," Streak said, "is how Crandle plans to maintain the perks of his compound by destroying everything electronic."

Kannon thought a moment.

"Maybe he doesn't care. Perhaps he's preparing to live completely off the grid."

"I wonder if all his men share that view," Đăng Đạo said.

"Good question," Kannon said.

"Is the armory penetrable?" Đăng Đạo asked.

"It's sealed by a hinged steel door," Streak said, stuffing his hands in his pockets. "The doorframe is embedded in reinforced concrete, with steel rods extending from the frame into solid rock."

"Who has access?" Kim shouldered his brother as if wedging open a door.

"Only Crandle and Whitehead," Streak said. "Rumor has it that there's a large safe in there."

Kannon and Đăng Đạo exchanged glances.

"Maybe, Streak Man, Crandle's armory has a back door."

Kannon recalled their discussion during the flight about the possibility of tunnels. What if Crandle had mapped a way out using the network of mine shafts? And what if he took Derrick along with him? The thought was almost too much to bear.

Observe. Plan. Execute. Trash the negatives.

Kim, with binoculars strapped around his neck, crept to the edge of the precipice, and knelt. Quán moved behind his brother, also knelt, and grasped his brother's ankles. Kim unfurled like an inchworm and extended his body prone, flat as an ironing board, with only his thighs and lower legs maintaining contact with the granite-laden cliff.

Kannon figured they were deciding on the best way to approach the chopper pad. Much depended on the direction and strength of the air currents that would carry Kim on his flight. Kannon, who had piloted a paraglider a couple of times, couldn't imagine doing it in a snowfall, much less at night. Not wanting Kim to get blown off course if the wind velocity increased, Kannon might have to abort the paragliding phase.

Kim signaled he was finished, so Quán dragged him away from the edge. The brothers stood and stepped away from the abyss.

"There is enough clearance. I can hit the LZ." Kim emulated another imaginary flight.

Feeling buoyed by Kim's confidence, Kannon fended off second thoughts regarding the younger brother's ability to fulfill the flight mission. He thought about basketball players envisioning the ball swishing through the net before releasing the shot.

Execute the glide. Land undetected. Toss a white phosphorus grenade at the fuel tank. Then navigate to Anh's rear window.

"Đăng Đạo, remind me, what's the range of those PRC-148 radios?" Kannon asked.

"Three- to six-kilometers, sufficient to cover the distance between the ground and top of the cliff."

Depending on the weather and terrain obstacles, Kannon knew. He turned his attention to the gate and the chain-link fence below. If only Streak hadn't chunked his remote-control unit for the gate when defecting from Border Slot.

The electrified fence and gate were connected to an alarm,

344

Streak had said. The control unit was mounted inside the bunkhouse. Cutting through the fence meant severing the electrical current, which would activate alarms and forfeit the element of surprise. He wished for his own EMP weapon.

Using explosives would also announce their presence, of course, but the shock value might disrupt the militiamen's response. Which brought up a question he should have thought of before.

"Streak, do they have CCTV cameras?"

"Not that I'm aware of."

No known surveillance cameras. A plus for our side, he hoped.

Kannon returned to the cliff's edge for another scan. Despite the cold, he was perspiring. He raised the binoculars to his eyes and peered through them. A large, redheaded man filled the frame.

Crandle.

The visual gave life to the man, put a face on his target. Despite what Streak had told him, Kannon couldn't imagine what sort of guy he was, couldn't imagine living in that prick's world.

"You're lucky I don't have a fifty-caliber sniper rifle," Kannon muttered.

He resumed panning the area. Other militiamen loitered in the yard. One person stood at the grill, Anh, probably.

And there he was, a small figure wearing a camouflaged jacket, his child, Derrick. He was wearing the look of the lost. Something flitted into Kannon's scoped view.

What the hell?

Kannon adjusted the focus. A goddamn lasso was looped around Derrick's shoulders. As the rope grew taut, the bastard at the other end of the rope yanked his son to the ground.

Sixty

Later Tuesday morning, at 1100 hours, Crandle unlocked the door to his ham shack, sat in his swiveling wood chair, and turned on his transceiver. He rotated the tuning dial to the band containing emergency nets. After adjusting the beam antenna and settling on a frequency, he sat back and listened. Today's aircraft surveillance reports confirmed the chaos in Kalispell. From various ham radio reporters:

"Authorities have determined a freak dry lightning storm knocked out Kalispell's electrical grid."

"The National Guard is setting up checkpoints on all access roads."

"Refrigeration and water treatment facilities have been knocked out."

"Food and water are being trucked in."

"Electrical fires have broken out."

"Looters will be shot."

What got Crandle going were the uncensored comments and questions.

"There weren't any effing storms hitting Kalispell last night."

"It was al Qaeda. Dropped some kind of new-fangled bomb."

"This the beginning of Armageddon."

"Concerns about lack of ice & perishable food . . ."

"Some diesel-fueled engines operate."

"Place smells like shit."

"I've been telling you guys. Watch out for man-made lightning strikes."

"What the crap does that mean?"

"Lines of people are streaming to the airport looking for outbound flights. There aren't any."

"How do I get money out of my Kalispell bank?"

Crandle chuckled as the comments continued. Residents had broken into grocery stores, hardware stores, and service stations. Shattered glass everywhere. Random shootings had occurred. One guy even took a shotgun to his computer.

The EMP op had been executed as slick as dog shit, except Whitehead had shot a cop. That was okay. It needed to be done.

Garrett fell to his death due to a frayed lanyard. That was not okay. His loss hurt. He was a good man but should have tested the strength of the lanyard beforehand.

Enough of this crap. Crandle switched off his ham set and swiveled in his chair to stare at the picture of Patterson hanging on his wall. He thought about his son's death, the look of horror on his face, and that of Patu's. And Garrett . . . what had been the final look on his?

Damnit, Patu. If not for you, Garrett would be alive.
* * *

Crandle left his cabin amid a persistent snowfall. It was time for the debriefing. His men stood around a roaring fire, waiting for him to begin. Brick, the wonder dog, was asleep on a snow-covered redwood stool. Anh stoked the coals in the nearby grill while Patu puttered around her.

He stepped onto the podium and raised his left fist. "To electromagnetic weapons."

"Lightning in a jar," Whitehead said.

"Hooah!"

Praise the Lord and pass the ammunition.

"We've suffered a big loss, our first from the Border Slot Headquarters Group. Garrett was a good soldier, but we expect losses in combat. Bow your heads in silent prayer to Garrett and give thanks to God. White Might is Right."

Seconds later, Crandle broke the silence. "Time to get down to business. This is a somber occasion, so I'll make my comments brief. Team leaders—written reports due tomorrow morning. Include what went right and what needs improvement."

Grabbing a stack of thick envelopes, Crandle left the podium to walk among his men. Each packet contained the thirty thousand he'd promised to the ground assault teams. After handing them out to

347

Porter, Smitty, and Timmons, he said, "I've split Garrett's share by three. He'd want you to have it. You'll get a full share once you execute a successful mission."

"Good enough," Porter said. Smitty and Timmons smiled their approval.

"Whitehead and Badger. Up front. On the double." Crandle returned to the podium.

"Ten-shun." For this momentous moment, Crandle displayed two medals made from the vein of silver he and Whitehead had discovered in a mine tunnel. His design: A one-inch-diameter-sized silver disc mounted on a solid, triangular-shaped metal base coated in black enamel.

"Listen up," Crandle said to his unit. "For the first time in Border Slot's history, I'm awarding Silver Discs—For Courage and Sound Execution for Inflicting Damage on the Enemy."

"Hooah."

Crandle pinned the medals on Whitehead and Badger and exchanged salutes. Then he addressed the others. "This is the level of performance I expect."

"You'll get it, sir," one of his guys said.

"Hooah!" Crandle said. "Chow line at fourteen hundred hours. Dismissed."

Whitehead strode toward his cabin while the other militiamen headed for the barracks. Crandle picked up his lariat and walked toward the grill. *I'll be damned if that roasting moose meat doesn't smell good.*

"The meat will be ready in time, Commander."

Anh, despite the little peckerhead clinging to her, was on target.

"Let go of her leg, you little shit. She's got work to do."

Patu didn't move.

Crandle tossed the rope over Patu's chest and yanked him to the ground. As he started toward him for a swift kick in the butt, Anh jumped in front and took the blow. Backpedaling, she went down flat on her ass. Patu, wearing a heavy coat, struggled to get up but couldn't. Crandle laughed.

Anh rose and brushed herself off. *"Con lợn!"*

"What the fuck did you say?" Crandle shoved her back down.

"She called you a pig," Patu said, still lying where he'd fallen.

"You little turd." Crandle couldn't believe the boy had translated.

Anh rose again and helped the boy up, shielding him behind her.

"Listen, bitch. If not for your tight ass and your cooking, I'd throw you out." Crandle scrabbled around Anh and grabbed Patu again. He lifted him in the air. "You keep sassing me, boy, I'll strip you naked and cook you on that grill."

"Let me go."

He shook Patu. Then, holding him with one hand like a hot dog on a spit, Crandle approached the grill and held the kid over the intense heat. The boy yelled bloody murder, but Crandle didn't care. He lowered Patu further. His face reddened to the color of blood and his screaming continued.

Anh jumped on Crandle's back and pounded him with her fists. Hardly feeling it, he brushed her off with his other hand. Backing away from the grill, he lofted Patu ever higher, and roared, "You understand me now, boy?"

"Yes . . . sir!"

Crandle tossed him to the ground. "Thirty minutes," he said to Anh. "Have the table ready."

Fuming, Crandle approached the barracks. Just then, Porter emerged, holding a satphone to his ear. Brow furrowed, his militiaman wasn't saying anything, just listening. "Who the hell you talking to?"

"It's Johnson, from Whitefish. He just returned from his deployment—"

Crandle snatched the phone away. "Welcome back, Johnson." Though he was no longer under Border Slot's control, the loyalty factor filtered in. "What's going on?"

"You guys didn't have anything to do with what happened in Kalispell, did you?"

"No comment. Keep this short."

"I heard you were looking for Streak."

"Bet your ass."

"I saw his Jeep last night, rather, early this morning."

"You sure?"

"It was dark, hard to see. But its mirrors were missing. Side-mounted spare tire. It was Streak's. The thing is, he wasn't driving."

"Who was?"

"A short dude. He could barely see over the steering wheel."

"Doesn't sound like anyone I know or would recognize."

"I think he was Asian."

"Streak could've sold it," Crandle said, "to fund his getaway." Still, Johnson's comments struck a chord. "Thanks for the heads-up. Come see us."

Crandle handed the phone back to Porter, trotted to Whitehead's cabin, and told him about the call. "What do you think?"

"We'll crank up the fucking watch after the banquet."

Sixty-One

Seeing Crandle hold Derrick above the heated grill blew Kannon apart. It spawned a spasm of emotions, the strongest of which was a searing, raging hatred so vile his knees buckled.

Dehydrated, he gulped down half a canteen of water. Still, it took another fifteen minutes before he calmed down enough to become halfway rational. But amid his range of emotions was hope. His son was there, alive.

Đăng Đạo took him aside.

"Chanel your anger into positive energy, planning, and action," his nephew said. "Use it smartly to destroy the bastard."

"You're right, of course. Let's get after it."

Shaking off the negatives, his team concentrated on map study and simulated attacks on the compound, using rocks to represent its various structures. One way or another, this would soon be over.

"Okay, guys, let's huddle and run through this again."

Kannon spread out Đăng Đạo's topographical map on the hood of the Willys. The topo map provided more detail than Google printouts. The others gathered around, each man also holding a copy of Streak's sketch of the compound.

"I'm figuring on ten militiamen, maybe eleven, that we'll have to neutralize."

"You mean, kill," Đăng Đạo said.

Despite struggling to keep hate from corrupting his soul, Kannon no longer harbored any doubt. He realized his initial thinking had been naïve. Đăng Đạo was right. Considering Border Slot Militia's track record at revenge, he couldn't afford to let any of them live. This was war. "Yes. I mean, kill!"

"I think the majority of the guys will be in the bunkhouse," Streak said.

"Surely, they will post a guard or two at the front fence." Quán tapped the front gate on the map.

"I agree," Kannon said. "Again, here's the deal. Quán and I will pair up as Team A, Đăng Đạo and Streak as Team B. A will approach from the southwest, B from the southeast." Đăng Đạo was a leader, Streak a follower. Pairing this way seemed the most effective way to utilize his assets.

I just hope my nephew and Streak will maintain their tenuous peace.

Kannon penciled in military symbols for the squads' positions on Streak's hand-drawn map. After making a few more notes, he continued, "Kim will paraglide from the cliff at zero two hundred hours. He'll radio Teams A and B once he's touched down at the chopper pad. Kim, repeat what we talked about earlier."

"I have one minute to target fuel tank area after landing. Toss white phosphorus grenade. Blow up objective."

"It's essential you radio us just before throwing the grenade. Simultaneously, our two-man teams will take out any gate guards. Then we'll use the plastic explosives to breach the gate and chain-link fence. Understood?"

Everyone nodded.

"Next step?" Kannon wanted to ensure there were no misunderstandings.

"Work my way back through woods to Crandle's cabin." The paragliding pilot-to-be mimicked stealthy footsteps.

"Không!" Đăng Đạo shouted.

"He's talking about the minefields," Streak said. "You'll need to stay on the trail."

"Got it. Got it. Got it."

"The militiamen will have rallied and most likely will be racing toward the fuel tank. Kim, you must avoid them."

"If necessary, hide in what's left of Streak's hut," Đăng Đạo said.

"All-in-all, you'll have about three-minutes to infiltrate Crandle's cabin from the time you hit the ground," Kannon added.

"A tight window," Quán said.

"Depending on weather and equipment . . . I think okay," Kim said.

"Go on," Đăng Đạo said to Kim.

"I go to Anh's window." Kim looked at his brother. "'Tight window.' Quán make pun."

Đăng Đạo mocked smacked him.

"Try not to alarm her," Kim continued. "Explain purpose . . . if she not in room, I smash window and enter. Look for Anh and child. Radio what I find."

Kannon shook the topo map to rid it of accumulated snow. He worried about the time it would take to traverse the twenty yards from the tree line to the fence—three times—once to place the C-4, the second, to take cover, and the third, to sprint through the breached openings and cover the fifty yards from the fence line to Crandle's cabin. There had to be a better way.

"I forgot to mention they've got a German Shepherd. Answers to Brick," Streak said.

Kannon glared at Streak, irritated that he hadn't mentioned this before. Still, he should've thought to ask. A guard dog or two seemed probable in a situation like this. "Only one?"

"Yep. Brick usually stays with his handler in the bunkhouse but occasionally roams the grounds at night. He's well trained," Streak added.

"Vicious?" Kim asked through clenched teeth.

"Can be. But Brick knows me."

"Yeah, well, he doesn't know us," Quán said.

"What worries me is what else you might have forgotten," Đăng Đạo said, frowning.

Streak crossed his arms and scowled.

Kannon cast a look of disapproval at both men. "If the dog interferes, shoot it."

No one objected.

"Another thought," Streak said. "These boys can put away the beer. If they're full, drunk, and happy, then they might be slower to react to alarms and explosives."

"Wishful thinking," Kannon shot back. "Normally, I'd agree with you. The timing of the militia's celebration couldn't happen more fortuitously, but, as we discussed, they're likely expecting a rescue attempt."

"I agree," Đăng Đạo said. "Two to one this self-anointed commander will limit his militiamen's drinking to one or two beers. Presume the men of Border Slot to be one hundred percent prepared."

Kannon thought about this as he rolled up the terrain map. "If these militiamen are a little tanked up, they might be more reckless and aggressive, harder to take down."

No one said anything. Streak and Đăng Đạo exchanged glances, then brushed snow off their glasses.

Finally, Quán broke the silence. "If Kim does get Anh and the boy out of the cabin, we must be careful not to place them in a crossfire."

"Absolutely," though easier said than done. The use of the word *boy* reminded Kannon of the need to objectify his son and remain detached in order to succeed. "Quán and I will take the lead."

"Streak Man and I bring up the rear," Đăng Đạo said, squatting.

"Crandle's mine," Kannon said.

"Understood," his nephew said.

"Okay. Now to Plan B. Let's review what'll we do if Derrick is *not* in Crandle's cabin, or if Kim is unable to make the jump." Kannon realized how much of this mission depended on Kim's success. If he didn't hear from Kim by 0210, they'd have to attack, regardless. "Pick it up—"

"I will jump," Kim said indignantly.

"Okay. Pick it up after Kim blows the fuel tank and we breach the perimeter."

"If the boy is not in the room, leave cabin same way I went in. Join with Đăng Đạo and Streak Man outside," Kim said.

"What about Anh?" Quán asked.

"Adapt on the fly," Kannon said. "If she's in her room, bring her out."

"After that . . ." Đăng Đạo shot a measured look at Kannon.

"The surviving militiamen will consolidate," Kannon said, pacing. "We'll likely find ourselves in the middle of a hellish firefight. Team B, augmented by Kim, will set an ambush for any of Crandle's men returning from the fuel tank, and keep a watch on Whitehead's cabin. Quán and I will storm the main cabin, then the bunkhouse."

"Afterward, if any of us are still alive," Kannon started to say.

"And, of course, find Derrick," Đăng Đạo said, rising from his squatting position.

"Roger." Kannon ended the prep by identifying the rendezvous area for escape and evasion. If all went well, there would be six adults, one child.

"Then I'll fly us out," Streak said.

"Anything else?" Kannon searched their frost-laden faces. All were somber.

"Kim, it's getting colder. You got everything you need up here?" Quán asked.

The ranting snowfall continued, not quite a whiteout, but close.

"Got radio. The sleeping bag for warmth. And I've got enough food and water." Kim didn't pantomime this time.

"Before the rest of us head down the mountain, I want another looksee," Kannon said.

Even though the plan seemed reasonably sound, he dreaded the possibility of missing something. He remembered another line from Sun Tzu. ". . . one who knows the enemy and knows himself will not be endangered in a hundred engagements."

Did he know either one well enough?

Sixty-Two

Tuesday, 1430 Hours, 27 October 2009, Texas Hill Country

Propping the shotgun against the closed bathroom door, Stefan took a quick but much-needed shower. After toweling off, he put on jeans and a Henley long-sleeve T-shirt. Feeling refreshed, he returned to the den, lugging the weapon and extra shells with him.

Lan had slipped into a traditional áo dài, white silk pants and a short black tunic, slit at the sides, while Belynda had changed into khaki shorts and a tie-dyed T-shirt. The women were sitting together on the sofa, holding hands. He marveled at the depth of Lan's and Belynda's quick-bonded friendship.

With those images in mind, Stefan leaned against the mantle, closed his eyes, and summoned a verse from Lan's prayer, her version of the Trinity. *I pray to you from the deepest of my heart that you protect Kannon and Đăng Đạo as they attempt to rescue . . . Derrick.*

Let it be, he thought.

In these last few days, he had spent more time with Lan than on any other occasion during her residence in the U. S. He didn't understand his stepmom but grasped that she and his dad loved each other, which made him care for her more. Loving Derrick was a no-brainer. He would do anything for him, which underscored his disappointment at being left off the rescue team.

Wish I was up there with you, Dad. But if anything happens here, I'll be ready.

Stefan wondered what Detective Hamilton thought about all this—a Vietnamese, a Navajo, and a Caucasian huddling around antique, wooden dolls. The detective had cast curious looks their way but hadn't commented.

Stefan approached him. "Anything going on?"

Hamilton shook his head. "Have a seat."

Grabbing a straight-backed chair, he flipped it around and straddled it, joining the detective at the dining table. "I know these things usually don't end well."

"Keep the faith," Hamilton said, though he was a bit slow to respond. "That was some prayer from Miss Lan."

"I've never met any women like those two."

Hamilton smiled. "Belynda Blu? She your lady?"

Stefan rested his forehead on top of the chair back. Between girlfriends, he wouldn't mind connecting with Belynda, even though she was a few years older, but now was not the time. He looked up and shook his head. "We've just met."

"I'm good at sensing things," the detective said. "Once things settle," Hamilton paused, "about your dad. Is it true what I've heard?"

"You mean about what happened in Việt Nam years ago?"

"Yeah."

"It's true. Until six years ago, I probably wouldn't have cared what happened to him. But after learning all the reasons for his awful behavior, primarily drinking, I've forgiven him."

"Understandable. I lost an uncle to PTSD. Suicide!"

"I'm sorry."

"Me too. Back to business. For what it's worth, at the theater where you saw the Pigeonaire's Magika, the Artist Palace has added closed-circuit video monitoring."

"Good." Stefan thought about his Uncle Roger's death and Derrick's kidnapping. "I don't know if you're aware of everything that happened there, but I got a sinking feeling—premonition, or whatever—when one of the doves crash dived into a ceiling fan."

What could I have done differently to prevent the horror?

"I know what you're thinking. And no, you couldn't have done anything to prevent it."

"I appreciate that."

"Okay," the detective said. "I want to take a looksee and get more familiar with the premises before it gets too dark. Can you shut off the alarm?"

"Will do."

While the detective was outside, another verse from Lan's prayer trickled into Stefan's consciousness: "*Let the turquoise stones placed in the curing dolls' holes heal all . . . wounds.*"

He remembered examining the curing dolls the day before and hadn't noticed any unfilled holes. Had Belynda notched another, symbolic of Derrick, for Lan's comfort? If so, was this tempting fate?

Sixty-Three

Tuesday Noon, 27 October 2009, Border Slot Compound

Standing over the five-foot-long barbeque grill, Anh tended the burning hickory. She had timely fired the wood and maintained the coals at the proper temperature for roasting moose. The meat would be ready on time.

She imagined roasting Commander Crandle. What would his meat smell like? Not sweet and tender like barbequed moose meat, but tough and rotten.

Anh brushed a wisp of hair away from her forehead. She liked her hair. At times, when she looked into the mirror and smiled, she thought she might even be pretty. Would she ever have a husband? Could she bear children? Or had Commander Crandle ruined her?

While in the Thai refugee camp, she had overheard a woman talking about dying from a broken heart. Was this happening to her— dying from a broken heart? Tears filled her eyes. She was a human being, with feelings, and knew she was not supposed to live this way.

Anh was not even sure how old she was. She thought perhaps, around forty. When old enough to understand, she had been told by an uncle about the Việt Nam War. But no one could explain the disappearance of her parents. To survive, she and her sister took to the streets, until a kind family smuggled them out of the country on a sea vessel. But they had run out of fuel, run out of drinking water, and drifted.

Then the Thai pirates boarded and violated the adult women. Anh could never remove the stink of that horrible, dirty attack. The pirates killed the Vietnamese men and tossed them into the sea. She and her sister were separated when the pirates scuttled their boat. Anh and two grown women found a floating piece of the bow and clung to it until drifting onto the shore. Her sister was not among them. How do you wash away the pain?

For the millionth time, Anh entertained the prayer about escaping this hell on earth. But where would she go? And how would she get there?

So, the sickening reality of her current fate homed in again. Even the Thai refugee camp was better than this. Each time Commander Crandle ravaged her body, Anh prayed he would have a heart attack. Every day he made her shave her legs, even her pubic area.

It hurt the most when he entered her the other way. At least she did not have to sleep beside him. When Commander Crandle was done, he wanted her gone.

Anh remembered a war tale from Sài Gòn. As a street child, she had overheard a story about women placing razor blades in their vaginas to wound American GIs. Anh did not know if that was true or not but thought she might like to try it on Crandle if only she could figure out how. Then she could set that part of the Commander on the grill.

Hearing the rustling of tree branches, Ann looked to the sky. Low clouds, dark like her hair, flew fast with the wind as if portending another, far worse storm. It made her nose tingle.

Derrick, wearing crisp camouflage fatigues and black combat boots, came outside and joined her. Beneath an OD baseball cap, his head was shaved, and his face was red from when Crandle held him over the grill.

Anh had plastered his cheek with salve.

"Little One. It is too cold for you to be outside without your coat on. Go back and get it."

"Yes, Miss Anh."

She watched him trundle off, then checked the coals and decided they were ready. She placed slabs of meat on the grill. Here was a piece of Commander Crandle's thigh, a breast for those who liked white meat, an arm, a leg. What should she do with his brain?

Sixty-Four

Kannon mouthed a silent prayer as the four team members vacated the clifftop and piled into the Jeep. Streak started the Willys and they drove off. The road meandered and wound up and down like an abandoned roller coaster. Scrub chokecherry flattened under the wheels and thin aspen branches yielded to the Jeep's front end. The damp smell from saturated humus flooded the area, despite being covered by snow. After crossing a rickety wooden trestle bridge, they weaved their way down the leaf-covered forest road that T-boned at an expansive stand of spruce.

Kannon sat glued to his GPS screen. Daylight, if you could call it that, was waning. Storm clouds hastened the oncoming darkness.

Quán reached forward from the backseat and tapped Streak on the shoulder. "There is the junkyard."

Streak stomped on the brake pedal, and the Willys skidded to a stop on the dirt and gravel road. The fenced-in enclosure, roughly the size of a tennis court, was topped off with coiled barbed wire. It appeared unoccupied.

The four of them jumped out. Kannon walked around to the back of the Jeep and retrieved a pair of bolt cutters.

"Hope there are no dogs inside," his nephew said, squatting on his haunches at the edge of the fence.

"Or any other vehicles passing by," Kannon added.

Streak returned to the Jeep and repositioned it to shield their break-in from any roadside view.

Kannon knelt and snipped an opening for Đăng Đạo and Quán to wiggle through. Five minutes later, each returned, holding a full-length exhaust pipe to be used as a canister for making improvised explosives.

"Hit the dirt!" Streak hollered.

All of 'em did. A logging truck blaring its horn roared past, leaving in its wake the ugly clang of metal on metal.

"Shit! I left the driver's door open."

Fortunately, the body and engine compartment weren't

damaged.

They resumed work. As the Vietnamese duo slid the exhaust pipes through the hole in the fence, Kannon made a cursory inspection. Most of them had rotted through and were useless. The stainless-steel pipes, though, were in better condition. Several short sections seemed serviceable.

"We can use these," he said.

Thirty minutes later, the team had cut four twelve-inch-long cylinders, packed the four tubes with explosives, and crimped the jagged lips to seal one end. They pinched the open end of each Bangalore, leaving enough room to insert blasting caps into the pliable C-4 before connecting timed fuses and igniters. When finished, they stashed the improvised weapons inside the Willys.

Streak sat in the driver's seat, rubbing his chin. "Think I've come up with a better way to breach the compound."

"What's that?" Kannon asked.

"Tape these Bangalore torpedoes to the front bumper of this baby. Smash the gate."

"I like it," Đăng Đạo said.

"You don't mind?" Kannon asked.

"Hell, there's not much left of the Willys anyway."

"How do we escape?" Quán asked.

"I'll fly us out on the helicopter." Streak started the Jeep.

If the chopper was out of commission for some reason, they could commandeer one of Border Slot's vehicles. Choose the most opportune field-expedient available.

"Time to move to our final staging area," Kannon said.

* * *

By the time they reached a sheltered clearing south of the compound—one that Streak had selected in advance—it was 2200 hours, four hours before their targeted strike time. Streak nudged the Willys against the needled branches of a spruce tree and killed the engine. They remained inside the Jeep and discussed final preparations. All of them rubbed their gloved hands for warmth. The missing door didn't help.

For the time being, they'd leave the Bangalore torpedoes and the detonation mechanisms in the Jeep, counting on the tall trees to

361

serve like gigantic sentinels while they plowed a trail through the forest to the assault line.

"About Kim," Quán said, "before we move out."

During their last radio contact, Kim had reported the award ceremony had ended shortly after they departed the clifftop. Kannon had been able to hold his gut in check and not ask about Derrick.

They hadn't heard from Kim since.

Kannon checked the frequency on his PRC-148 field radio. After adjusting the squelch, he exited the Willys and extended the radio's antenna.

"Yaak Three. Come in."

No response.

"I told him to keep the radio nearby. That's two attempts in the last hour." Kannon worried Border Slot might intercept if he kept transmitting.

"Kim may be meditating," Đăng Đạo said.

"Or freezing to death," Quán shot back.

"Maybe he's not receiving the transmission." Streak cupped his hands and blew into them.

Kannon regretted leaving Kim up there so early, alone. His bowels tightened. What the hell had he been thinking, planning to go forward with the rescue operation in this lousy weather?

Then his radio squawked.

"Yaak One. Yaak Three. Over." It was Kim.

"This is Yaak One. What's your status? Over."

"Yaak Three. It looks like the militia is posting . . ." The transmission faded.

Damnit!

Kim's voice sounded weak, slurred like a drunk's, or a person suffering from hypothermia. Or maybe it was just interference from the shit-ass weather. Kim was his eyes and ears up there. What had he been going to report?

Border Slot's perimeter was armed with 60-caliber machine guns. Reinforcements had arrived. Unable to paraglide after all.

Kannon was tempted to drive back to the plateau and check on him.

Quán, teeth chattering, said, "He's too cold to talk."

362

"Should we abort?" Streak asked.

"He's got a down sleeping bag, food, and water," Kannon said as he got back in the Jeep.

"Not good enough. We must get my brother."

Đăng Đạo arched his eyebrows. "Kim knew the danger involved. You did too, Quán."

Quán's eyes narrowed. "He is my brother."

"I understand, Quán."

Kannon almost added, "I know what it's like to lose a brother." Fortunately, he didn't. The words would have been counterproductive, escalating the rising tension within the team. Still, rescuing his son came first for him, if not for them.

"What do you think?" Kannon asked Đăng Đạo.

His nephew's lips grew taut. His jawbones looked like chiseled rock. Đăng Đạo turned to Quán, "Pussy."

"I am no pussy," Quán said, glaring at Đăng Đạo.

"Then stop acting like one," Đăng Đạo said. "We are all concerned about Kim."

"We're in this together," Kannon added.

"Okay. But after the mission, I deal with you, Mister Kannon."

"Is that a threat?"

Quán glowered.

All I need is more dissension.

Kannon nodded to Đăng Đạo.

"Let's you and I have a quick discussion outside the Jeep."

Kannon got out of the Jeep again. Đăng Đạo followed. They whispered.

"It's more than just his brother, right?"

Đăng Đạo looked him in the eye. "Yes."

"Fill me in."

His nephew removed his iced-over glasses, wiped the crud from his eyes, then replaced the specs and said, "Quán feels responsible for Kim, yes. But the real problem is his jealousy."

"Of what?"

His nephew held up his palms.

"You."

"Me? Of my leadership?"

"I overheard him saying something to Kim about your being married to a Vietnamese."

"As in, he doesn't approve?"

"Right."

"Think I should talk to him?"

"This is not a good time."

"You're right," Kannon said with a sigh. The pressure was eating at all of them. Interracial marriage *was* a delicate subject, not one to broach here. But, could he count on Quán? Should he realign the teams? After reflecting on the *keep your friends close and your enemies closer* mantra, he left things as they were.

Sixty-Five

"You guys ready to blaze a trail?" Kannon asked.

Somber nods.

"Let's set our watches." *One mile between his team and the Border Slot compound. One mile between him and the bastards who held his son.*

Three and a half hours remained before 0200.

Timepieces in sync, the team kitted up. They belted radios and navigation devices, pocketed the three types of grenades, then slipped Pulsar Edge night-vision goggles over their eyes. Each man holstered a semiautomatic pistol. Each man slung his rifle over his shoulder. Each man carried a two-quart collapsible canteen.

Streak snagged some MREs and protein bars they had stashed away for an emergency.

"Shooting gloves." Đăng Đạo handed each man a pair.

When it's go time.

As a final step, Kannon wedged his Sig P238 inside his right boot.

"Let's go."

Roiling clouds blocked the moon. Snowflakes snaked through the trees, blotting Kannon's greenish field of vision with miniature space balls. Pine trees exuded a Christmas-like smell, an aroma inconsistent with his objective.

Knowing the terrain, Streak led, followed by Đăng Đạo and Quán. Kannon logged the rear. The topography ranged from mild depressions and rises to sharp inclines as the team moved deeper into the dense forest.

Silence was impossible because the snow-covered ground hid fallen limbs and twigs. They couldn't avoid stepping on them. In addition, footwork was slippery.

Due to the change in plans on how to deploy the Bangalores, at least they didn't have to transport four twelve-inch long explosive-packed tubes through treacherous terrain. Still, Kannon labored as he slushed through the snow. He worried that by the time he reached the open space fronting the compound, he'd be too wiped out to mount a successful attack.

Kannon considered his team's motivations. His was a no-brainer. Streak's was conscience-driven guilt. Đăng Đạo's, passion and loyalty. The two volunteers—or were they draftees—was it the combat high, money, what?

Distracted by his wondering, Kannon skated on a patch of ice. Trying to regain balance, he tripped over an exposed root and plunged headlong into a snowdrift.

Streak and Đăng Đạo helped him up.

Kannon caught his breath, dusted the snow off his weapons and body. "Thanks."

"We're fifty yards from the gate," Streak said, reading his GPS.

"Let's stop here and rest," Kannon said. They had hiked nine-tenths of a mile.

"Are you all right?" Streak asked, his voice staccato, like it had acquired static.

"Will be. Rip open those MREs. We need fuel."

They huddled in the middle of a fir- and spruce-rimmed clearing as if in a makeshift corral. The temperature had long ago dropped below freezing. Everyone wore moisture-resistant, layered clothing, and all of them should've built up body heat by now due to their exertion. However, all of them were exhausted.

For fear of being detected, they couldn't risk a wood fire down here either. Even if no one noticed the flames, the smell of smoke might be detected. Its odor traveled fast and far. Relying on an old Army trick, Kannon lit a chunk of C-4 for hand- and food-warming purposes. The heat was minimal but warm enough to restore feeling to hands gone numb when constructing the Bangalores.

For food prep, not so much. The spaghetti and beef stew iced over as soon as they were removed from the heat source. They munched on crackers and peanut butter instead. Better than nothing.

It was now 0045.

"Hydrate," Kannon said.

Everyone did, except Quán, who remained sullen.

Kannon hoped the agitated brother wasn't planning to eliminate him with extreme prejudice. He shifted his gaze to Streak, whose body shook like it had last night when the Border Slot chopper flew over.

"You just cold, Streak, or nervous?"

"Both."

"Eat a protein bar, Streak Man," Đăng Đạo directed. "And hydrate your body more. You too, Quán."

"I'm going to recon," Kannon said. "You guys stay here and try to warm up.

Except for the goggles and two semiautomatic pistols, Kannon left the rest of his gear with the team. He moved forward at a crouch. As he got closer to the compound, the forest thinned out, so Kannon dropped to his knees. Once he reached the edge of the tree line, he went prone. His heartbeat palpitated against the snow-covered granite like a clapper inside a bell.

On knees and elbows, he ratcheted forward in hopes of getting a better looksee. No shining floodlights. Strange, he thought. He flipped his night-vision device into place and panned the compound. Snow and ice clung to the chain-link fence, making it difficult to see through.

Nothing moved. The compound was quiet, seemingly deserted. Of course, it wasn't. Rolling to his side, Kannon stared up at the cliff edge, trying to discern anything definitive, hoping to see Kim ready to take flight. It was useless. The distance was too great, too damn blurry.

Kannon removed the goggles and rested his head on his arm. Three days had passed since Derrick was taken. It seemed like a year.

His gut told him cold-hearted sociopaths occupied the compound. His gut told him Crandle expected a rescue attempt. And somewhere inside that Border Slot den of evil, his son lay frightened, probably injured, if not worse.

The wind escalated and the volume of snowfall increased—both a plus and a minus. Kannon replaced the NVD over his eyes.

Shortly, one sentry approached the gate from Kannon's right, then reversed his direction. There was no sign of . . . no, wait. Another militiaman patrolled from the left. So, there were two sentries, one on each side of the gate. He watched their protocol for several minutes. Their timing was irregular. That meant blowing up the fuel tank, killing the sentries, and simultaneously crashing the Bangalore torpedo-laden Jeep into the gate became more problematic.

Kannon rehearsed the initial assault. Team A: He'd drive the Jeep, Quán, take out the sentry on the left flank. Team B: Đăng Đạo and Streak shoot the sentry on the right flank. Storm the compound. Hook up with Kim. And Derrick. And Anh. No problem, right?

Before returning to the staging area, Kannon panned the compound again. The area behind the fence line looked like a cresting ocean wave. Just as he scooted back, the sentries stopped and turned their attention toward the compound's interior. A third man approached the guards.

Big. Tall. Crandle!

Kannon considered drawing his Sig .40-caliber. No, not at night. Not at twenty-five yards with no laser sight. He couldn't chance a miss. Even if he could take out Crandle, it wouldn't guarantee the safety of his son.

As if sensing his presence, the three militiamen turned and faced in Kannon's direction. He pressed his forehead against the cold granite rock. Had he been seen? Still lying prone, he inched backward until finding concealment in a thicket of spruce and pine. They must not have detected him, or they would have reacted.

Kannon breathed relief into his lungs. He started to rise yet sensed a presence. A dark shadow loomed, blotched the snow on his right. Then the hands . . . one clamped over his mouth, the other clinched Kannon's shoulder.

Sixty-Six

"She . . . it's me."

Kannon's heart beat like a bass drum. He craned his neck and saw Streak kneeling beside him.

"Christ! You scared the crap out of me. Get down!" Kannon said in a harsh whisper.

"Sorry."

"What the hell are you doing here?"

"Quán said he was going to a different location and try to reach Kim on the radio. Didn't return."

Kannon swore. His skin prickled as if stabbed by porcupine quills. Quán's absence would screw up their rescue attempt. "Let's get back to Đăng Đạo. Stay low."

Boiling clouds sealed off any moonlight. The wind kicked up wild and fierce, blowing from north to south, driving the snow horizontally. Kannon shielded his face. He waited until Streak vacated the area, then, placing his forearms, chest, and thighs flat to the ground, slid back.

Once he and Streak reached the safety of the trees, "What happened?" Kannon asked.

"I don't know. Đăng Đạo went after Quán."

"And?"

"Lost his trail."

"Not good."

"You think Đăng Đạo was mad before, you oughta see him now."

Kannon shook his head. The situation just kept getting worse. "Is Đăng Đạo back at the staging area?"

"Yeah."

With the wind howling, Kannon made no effort to mask the racket he made during the return. Đăng Đạo was on the radio, probably trying to contact Kim or Quán. His nephew lowered the PRC-148. His eyes were like fire on ice. "Nothing like this has ever happened before."

"Maybe Quán got disoriented," Streak said.

369

"No way, Streak Man." Đăng Đạo clipped the radio to his belt. "He is too good to get lost."

"He could've gotten hurt. Or maybe his radio doesn't work," Streak said with concern.

Standing at the edge of the open area, Đăng Đạo glowered.

"He could've been captured," Kannon said, stomping his feet in the snow. "But it won't do any good to speculate."

"What do we do?" Streak asked.

"Continue without him, damnit! Are you in or not?"

"In," Streak said.

"Đăng Đạo?"

"Dumb question," he said, "but we can probably kiss Kim's flight goodbye."

"Yeah. No way could he paraglide in this weather." Kannon considered their timeline. "What if we went after Kim? Streak, could we get back up there in your Willys?"

"No guarantees," he said. "The bottom layer of snow would be iced by now. It's a steep ascent. And no tire chains."

Kannon sighed. "We can't afford to get stuck."

"Quán might still return," Đăng Đạo said.

"True." *At least his nephew wasn't giving up on him.*

"All right," Kannon said after taking a deep breath. He noticed Đăng Đạo scanning the woods. Despite Quán's not-so-veiled threat, Kannon would've never predicted the guy would bolt.

Đăng Đạo executed a one-eighty and faced Kannon and Streak. Red-faced from the cold and maybe anger, he asked, "What did you see on your recon?"

"There are two sentries. They maintain an irregular pattern. Crandle came out to check on them. I'm confident they're expecting *someone*," Kannon said, wiping his nose.

"Muddies the water for our attack," Streak said.

"Looks like we're a three-man assault team," Kannon said, frustrated because his plans kept changing before any shots were fired.

Đăng Đạo, his teeth clenched, nodded.

* * *

Crandle left Whitehead's cabin and entered his own.

370

Johnson's sighting of Streak's Willys in Whitefish stoked his adrenaline.

He changed into woolen trousers and a pair of insulated, waterproof boots. After donning three layers of upper body shirts, he grabbed a parka and put it on. He extended the length of his pistol belt to fit over the parka and snapped it in place. Finally, he rammed a Colt .45 into his holster.

Leaving his bedroom, he passed through the den, where dying embers glowed in the fireplace. Crandle entered the kitchen and grabbed a handful of chocolate chip cookies. After stuffing them down, he drank a glass of milk.

He put extra cookies in his jacket pocket for his men out front. Then he started toward the front door, stopped, and turned toward Anh's room. She was sound asleep, as was Patu. Despite Whitehead's good intention, the boy had proved to be nothing but a liability. Crandle harbored mixed feelings. Should he dispose of the boy or keep him? Dumping him would be easy. Changing the boy's mindset over time presented more of a challenge. He liked challenges. Besides, the name Patu had a nice ring to it.

We'll see how the next few hours play out.

He thought about Garrett. Deep down, Crandle knew it had been his piloting errors that caused the militiaman to fall from the chopper, that and a frayed lanyard. Which made him even madder. Streak wouldn't have mishandled the controls, and Garrett would be alive.

Crandle checked his watch. It was too early to hear from Bull, who should reach Ballard's place by midmorning. It may be a non-issue. Due to the sequence of events, Crandle's intuition said something was up.

He went back outside. The wind hadn't let up. It was almost blizzard conditions, and the storm showed no sign of lifting.

Motherfuck, it's cold.

He walked toward the bunkhouse and entered. One of his militiamen had better be on watch. Inside, it sounded like a damn snoring competition. It also smelled like a shithouse. *Must be a farting competition too.* A faint neon glow appeared from the back of the room. Hatfield sat by the radio and the monitors, looking bored.

"Who's on the fence line?" Crandle asked.

"Porter and Badger. They're in a bad frame of mind, sir."

"Gonna check on 'em."

Crandle cuffed Hatfield on the shoulder. "Stay alert!"

Crandle left the bunkhouse and marched straight to the gate. Damn snowfall was so thick he couldn't see shit. It wasn't until he reached the gate that he bumped into Porter and Badger, who were huddling for warmth.

"Commander. Surprised to see you outside."

"Cold enough for you?" Crandle asked.

"Freezing my ass off," Porter said.

"Colder than a witch's tit," Badger added.

Crandle reached into his pocket. "Have a cookie."

"Thanks."

The militiamen devoured the treat.

"Expecting trouble, sir?" Porter asked.

"Good chance."

"I don't think anyone in their right mind would be out on a night like this." Badger followed up his cookie with a drink from his canteen.

"Normally, I wouldn't either. We've kidnapped a boy. His father's a soldier, or was. If I were him, I'd choose a night like this," Crandle said, staring at the tree line. "Loan me your goggles."

Crandle trekked along the fence, studying the green-hued tree line. He saw movement. Could be an animal, a wolf maybe.

Or a crawling human.

Sixty-Seven

Wednesday, 0120 C Time, 28 October 2009, Texas Hill Country

The last few hours had passed slowly. Stefan didn't know what was worse, the confining boredom, or the tension from waiting for something to happen. They had snacked and chatted, nothing substantive.

The patio door opened. Detective Hamilton returned from another walk-around. "Nothing out of the ordinary," he said.

"That's a good thing," Stefan said, hastily putting away the burner phone. Every time Hamilton went out, Stefan checked it for messages from Kannon.

"It's time for post-midnight coffee," Belynda said. "Detective, you want a cup?"

"Sure."

Belynda headed for the kitchen. Stefan followed, the self-defense weapon at his side. He tapped her on the shoulder. "Something's bothering me."

"What?"

"I'd examined the three curing dolls earlier, you know, before Lan filled the last hole in the baby one. I don't remember seeing any unfilled nicks."

Her eyes flashing, Belynda gave him a closed-lip smile. "What of it?"

Stefan flinched. "Just saying, if you did *add a hole*, would that change the psyche of its intended purpose? You know, to bring Derrick safely home."

"Has your withholding information from the detectives altered the sequence of events, you know, to bring Kannon and Derrick safely home?"

Jeez! Stefan didn't know how to answer. All he could say was, "Touché."

"What matters is that Lan believes in its power."

"Like a placebo."

"Exactly."

JACK LYNDON THOMAS

Belynda flipped her ponytail from side to side, her brown eyes glistening. She's cool, he thought. Not only was she attractive, she was also tough, feisty, and smart.

"Sit," she said. "Keep me company while I refresh this brew."

He obliged. Belynda set a coffee cup in front of him before taking the others theirs. Once she returned, she filled her cup and took the chair at a right angle to his.

"Lan is an extraordinary woman," Belynda said after taking a sip of her black coffee.

"Just seen glimpses in the six years I've known her. But I'm getting a better idea. And Derrick—"

"He's a jewel," Belynda added.

"I love my little brother." Stefan paused. "What do you think of my dad?"

"Except for what I saw at the magic show," Belynda said, smiling, "I don't know your father. Part of me wants to scalp him for getting you all into this mess."

"Actually, I understand that."

Belynda patted his arm. "Tell me . . . how are you doing?"

"I feel as if I'm inside a whirring blender."

"Your body language shows it."

"You're not worried?"

"Of course."

"You hide it well."

"I have faith."

"So do I." His tone was harsher than intended.

Belynda arched her eyebrows. "No need to get defensive."

Stefan tipped the chair back, then set it down. Perspiration beaded through his sweatshirt. He massaged his temples. "It's just that . . ."

"What's bothering you?" Belynda said, drumming her fingers on the table. "You can tell me."

Stefan's mouth twitched. Tears clouded his eyes. "I . . . I should've done more at the magic show."

"Oh, my God. You feel guilty?"

"Yes."

Belynda scooted forward in her chair such that their knees

374

touched. She grasped his chin and turned his face directly to hers. "Listen to me. You did what your dad told you to do. Helped get the sliding walls open."

"If I'd have stayed with you and Lan, Derrick wouldn't have been taken."

"You don't know that. You might've been shot, too." She paused. "Look. I've worked with Navajo combat vets from Desert Storm. One of the most common feelings is guilt. You followed orders and did what you could."

"Detective Hamilton said something similar."

"How much reassurance do you need?"

"Are you speaking as a friend or as a counselor?"

"Friend. As a counselor, I'd give you a harder time. Don't beat yourself up."

"Yeah, but—"

"You're not that powerful, Stefan. Get over yourself."

"Who are you to tell me!" he started to say. Then he remembered the number of times his birth mom had storied him about the apple falling close to the tree, as well as what Lan had said recently about him being like his father.

"Jeez! I really am like my dad."

"Awareness! You're making progress," Belynda said with a tight smile. "I'm going to check on Lan."

"Okay."

After she left the kitchen, Stefan rose and entered the den, carrying the shotgun and the pouch of extra shells. His stepmom and Belynda were sitting beside each other on the sofa, engaged in quiet conversation. He walked past Hamilton in the dining area. The detective was sitting with his elbows on the table, head resting on his hands, looking bored.

"I hope you won't need that," the detective said, draining his coffee cup.

Stefan presented the shotgun at port arms and frowned. "Me too."

"If someone uninvited shows up, I'll take care of it."

Stefan padded to the front picture window and, like his stepmom had done, peeled back the curtains and gazed into the darkness. It was hard to see any distinctive shapes beyond the throw of the floodlights. Feeling tired and useless, he shook his head and closed the curtains.

Wearing the same blue jeans and Henley shirt, Stefan took a seat in an armchair. He breached the shotgun and checked the load, removing the two shells and then reinserting them. Put the weapon on safe.

He was good at shooting skeet, but how would he react if attacked? Could he pull the trigger? Or would he freeze?

Soon, his eyes grew heavy. Closing them for just a moment, he thought about Belynda's words.

Get over yourself.

Sixty-Eight

Wednesday, 0130 M Time, 28 October 2009, Final Preparation-Border Slot

Backtracking over the faint impressions left from their earlier trek, Kannon led Đăng Đạo and Streak back to the Willys. The air, thick with ice crystals, smelled heavy, like tundra, and hindered breathing. His feet and hands were numb. If the chill spread to his chest, he'd be in trouble. To make it worse, his bowels were crying for relief. The last thing he wanted was to have to crap in this weather.

Finally, they reached the vintage Willys, which was coated in an ivory blanket, including the exposed driver's seat. Đăng Đạo and Streak set down their gear. Kannon propped his AK against the crook of a tree and looked for signs of Quán. There were none.

"Hand me your knife," he said to Streak. Taking the knife, Kannon bent over and probed the depth of the snow.

"What are you doing?" Streak asked.

"Following up on your previous comment about ice forming underneath the snow. It hasn't."

"What's your revised plan?" Đăng Đạo asked.

"You two will have to take out the sentries. I'll drive the Willys to the gate . . . and bail."

"Give yourself enough time," Streak said.

"Good thing the door is missing. I saw a movie once where this guy snagged his cuff on the door handle," Đăng Đạo said. "He went off the cliff with the car."

Đăng Đạo's humor was as black as his. Kannon removed his gloves and ran his hands over the ice-blanketed windshield.

"Streak, lower the windshield. Đăng Đạo and I will bundle the Bangalore torpedoes."

"Underway." Streak grabbed a toolkit from beneath the front seat and set to work.

Kannon could no longer deny the urge to take a shit.

"Back in a moment, guys." He double-timed into a copse of fir trees and dropped *trou,* barely in time. It was the first time he'd

377

ever wiped his ass with snow. His damn balls seemed frozen.

He returned to the Jeep. While Streak worked on the windshield, a gloveless Đăng Đạo was configuring two sets of Bangalores from the original four. Kannon removed his gloves, saying, "We'll need two detonation devices."

"Right," his nephew said, wiggling his fingers to keep them nimble. "Duct tape or bungee cords?"

"Bungee cords. The cold reduces duct tape's tackiness." Tape might also reduce the explosive impact, Kannon reasoned.

After arranging the four torpedo tubes into two sets, they wrapped each set in three strands of bungee cord. Then they crimped the blasting caps into the timed fuses and connected them to the fuse igniters. Đăng Đạo hefted the assembled explosives and set them on the front bumper. Kannon secured the Bangalores to the Jeep.

"My fingers feel like sticks of ice," Đăng Đạo said.

"Mine too." Kannon inserted the ignition string—blasting caps, igniters, and timed fuses set for one minute—into the C-4. He tossed a roll of tape onto the driver's seat, intending to stabilize the steering wheel with it before he bailed.

"Here is a branch to wedge between the accelerator and steering column," Đăng Đạo said.

Kannon tossed it onto the passenger seat, then hopped up and down, trying to warm up.

"I'm done," Streak said. "Looks like you guys are too."

Stepping away from the partially stripped-down Willys, Kannon eyeballed Streak. The skilled chopper pilot wasn't shaking anymore, which was good, because once this was over, and weather permitting, Streak was to fly them out of Border Slot.

Kannon raised the PRC-148. He was about to speak into the mouthpiece when a bulky figure emerged from beneath a pine bough.

"Hey, hey." Quán lowered his head.

Christ. He's acting as if nothing has happened. But when Kim's brother got close, Kannon saw differently. His eyes were puffy. Frozen tears streaked Quán's face like glazed rivulets.

Đăng Đạo spat. "You are a deserter."

Quán shook his head. "I have returned."

"You have dishonored Kannon's team," Đăng Đạo said.

"No, I—"

Đăng Đạo kicked Quán in the balls.

"Jesus." Streak backed away, stared at the sky.

Kim's brother doubled over but didn't fall. Quán gasped for air, sounding like wind howling through a turbine. He struggled to raise his head. "I . . . I was meditating."

Quán withered under Đăng Đạo's glare.

Kannon swore.

"We don't have time for this." His team was on the verge of breaking up. "I don't care where he's been. We've got to roll."

"He is unworthy," Đăng Đạo said, his eyes still fixed on Quán.

An owl hooted, an ill omen in Vietnamese lore.

"Let me run the vehicle," Quán said, still gasping.

"Do it," Kannon said, thinking this would be the right way for Kim's brother to regain face. "After Quán delivers the Jeep bomb, he bails, joins me. We head straight for Crandle's cabin."

"Works for me," Streak said.

"All right." Đăng Đạo shrugged. "It is your call."

"What about Kim?" Quán said, his breathing quick. "I could not contact him."

"At this point, we can't count on him." Kannon filled his lungs with air, then released it. "It's almost time to move out. Streak, you and Đăng Đạo establish position twenty yards east from where you scared the crap out of me. Get in place five minutes before kickoff."

"Got it," Streak said.

"Let's warm our hands before moving out." Kannon lit another chunk of C-4. Everyone exposed their hands to the tiny blaze.

In its specious warmth, Kannon saw himself with his alluring, lavender-scented wife and their son Derrick, all sitting in front of the fireplace. Their connection, their right to live as an unburdened family, seemed the truest path under the laws of order in the world. Yet, from his Việt Nam experience, he had learned that government-sanctioned killing did little to alleviate his ensuing guilt and sorrow.

And this time, it was him doing the sanctioning. If successful, Kannon knew he would suffer. Lesson learned from Việt Nam!

They donned their shooting gloves.

379

Sixty-Nine

After alerting Porter and Badger to what he saw, Crandle trotted back to Whitehead's cabin, his lungs sucking for air. It was 0115.

Not bothering to knock, he barged in. "We've got company."

Having slept in battledress, Whitehead gathered himself, smiled, grabbed his AK and sidearm. They headed to the bunkhouse.

"Get your asses out of the rack," Crandle hollered. "Fucking jackals in the lions' den."

"Huh?"

"What the fuck!"

"Whazup?"

"Whitehead, rub snow on these bastards. Get 'em moving."

His number two snatched a spittoon and ran outside. Seconds later, Whitehead returned with the container stuffed with snow. Crandle took the spittoon from him, held it aloft, and threatened to sling the contents at his men.

"We're up! We're up, for god's sake," one of his guys said.

Now, all his militiamen stood before him.

"Whoever's out there, I want 'em alive," Crandle said.

"Sir. What if we have no choice but to kill?" Hatfield asked.

"You have a choice." Crandle again raked a finger across his throat.

* * *

"Yaak Two. This is Yaak One. Commo check. Over." *Come on*! Đăng Đạo and Streak should be in position by now. Kannon's heart pounded loud and fast, like an angry drumbeat.

"Yaak One. Yaak Two. In position. Ready to commence," Đăng Đạo said.

Good. At least something was going right. Five minutes . . .

Kannon walked to the Jeep. Quán sat poised behind the steering wheel, one trembling ungloved hand fingering the ignition key, the other on the choke.

The icy wind escalated. Snowfall thickened.

Two minutes . . . enough time for key elements of Kannon's

life to accelerate through his mind. Much of it was ugly. He'd left too much wreckage in his wake. He thought about Crandle's launchers, the death discs Streak had mentioned. What would it feel like to be sliced to pieces—his blood spilled all over the frozen ground? If he died, would he reach heaven? Would he have an infinite vision of past events? Future events? Watch Lan and Derrick in their everyday life for all their lives? Their aching? His aching?

His radio crackled.

"Yaak One. Yaak Three. Over."

Kim! Kannon wanted to know what the hell had been going on but now was not the time.

"It would be suicidal to lift off," Kim said.

Kannon peered through his Pulsar Edge goggles but couldn't see a damn thing.

"Yaak Three. Yaak One. Understood. Hunker down. Will extract you later. Over."

"Yaak One. Yaak Two. Advise situation. Over."

"Bird unable to fly," Kannon radioed to Đăng Đạo and Streak. "Rest of mission intact. Continue as planned."

Kannon signed off and clipped the PRC-148 to his belt.

Quán stared straight ahead and said nothing as Kannon informed him about his brother. This surprised him. He thought he would be relieved, at least show some emotion. His behavior wasn't insolent. If anything, Quán exuded unreasonable calm and determination. Or was it resignation?

"Remember," Kannon said, "after you start the Jeep, I'll activate the igniters and set the fuses for one minute, which gives you about fifteen seconds to bail and run before this baby strikes the gate."

Quán gave a slight nod and then said, "Boom!"

* * *

Crandle worried. With Bull in Texas, Garrett dead, Porter and Badger manning the front fence, and Hatfield on radio watch in the bunkhouse, that left five militiamen, excluding Whitehead, who he wanted beside him to thwart any rescue attempt. Was that enough?

What if Ballard had joined forces with the Feds? What if Streak was leading them here? Maybe the rescue team included a mortar squad, or stinger missiles, or tanks, or even a drone. He was

381

sorry now he had sent his newbie to Texas, but it was too late to bring in reinforcements.

Naw! Come on! Don't be an idiot. I would've heard tanks. A drone couldn't fly in this weather. My men are ready. And I hold the trump card, Patu.

Seventy

Conditions worsened as the wind escalated and racked the branches overhead, dumping clumps of snow on Kannon's head. Wind-driven sleet blitzed his face as if shot from a Howitzer.

Despite the arctic-like cold, Kannon unzipped the cumbersome parka and checked his weaponry—the grenades clanking against each other in the outer coat pockets. The .40-caliber Sig was strapped to his waist, a round chambered, safety engaged. Kneeling to one knee, he removed the 9mm semiautomatic rig wedged inside his boot. He massaged his ankle, press-checked the pistol, re-holstered it, and then rewrapped the rig tighter around his ankle. After slinging an AK47 over his shoulder, he strapped on his night goggles, which he could flip into place when needed.

At 0155 hours, Kannon approached the driver's side of the Jeep for a final word with Quán, whose profile was exposed due to the discarded door. The near-paralyzing wind howled, chafing the man's cheeks. Absent the lowered windshield, Quán's face was being pelted by sleet, yet his expression remained impenetrable. His knuckles were white from the cold. *Or were they white from gripping the steering wheel too tight?*

"Đăng Đạo and Streak are in position," Kannon said. "Got the duct tape and wedging stick?"

Quán nodded. His iced-over facial scar twitched as if charged by an electric current. "Any further word from Kim?"

"No, sorry to say."

"Well, there's no way Kim will jump unless the weather breaks. You and Đăng Đạo look after him."

"Will do." A strange comment, Kannon thought. He needed Quán to concentrate. "Look, I know you're worried about your brother. It's not too late to switch out with me. Are you sure you want to drive?"

"Yes. But I have one more question."

"I'm listening."

"How do you treat your wife?"

Kannon arched his eyebrows, unprepared for the question. It

wasn't a total surprise considering what Đăng Đạo had passed on regarding Quán's comments about his marriage to Lan. Regardless, Kannon realized he was being tested and answered truthfully. "I'm still learning to treat her with love and respect."

With that, Quán proffered a half smile, then pulled the choke and turned the ignition key. The Willys rattled to life. Kannon hustled to the front of the Jeep, took a fuse igniter in each hand, pulled the two cords, then stepped away. The Bangalores were set.

"You've got one minute. Hit it," Kannon said.

Quán shifted into first gear and released the clutch. The blacked-out Jeep crawled forward, leaving a trail of retching exhaust and dirty snow, the engine sound masked by a near gale-force wind.

Worried that Đăng Đạo and Streak might not be able to see the vehicle, Kannon activated his radio. "Yaak Two. Yaak One. Package released for delivery. Over."

"Roger that," Streak radioed back.

Kannon repositioned his night goggles for protection against the driving sleet, but the lenses kept frosting over, so he flipped them up. Using his hand for a shield, he looked up at the edge of the cliff, hoping for a break in the wintry storm—no such luck.

He followed Quán.

Trailing ten yards behind the Willys, Kannon scanned the fence line for signs of the sentries but didn't notice them. Had they vacated their posts? Or, had they taken up concealed positions? The vacuum didn't feel right. Absent any visuals of the guards meant the teams couldn't kill the sentries outright, which exposed the mission to more risk.

The Jeep reached the clearing. Its boundary was twenty yards from the Border Slot gate. Poor visibility made it seem farther away. This was where Quán was to strap the steering wheel in place with duct tape, wedge the stick between the steering wheel and accelerator, then reset the Willys in motion—and jump.

Kannon's heart rate amped up. He detected a crouched figure moving west along the edge of the parking area. Was it a man or the dog Streak had mentioned?

A militiaman! Shit! Quán was a sitting duck.

Kannon rushed forward.

"Quán! Get out of the damn Jeep!"

Instead, Quán gunned it, and the Willys lurched forward.

Muzzle flashes erupted from Border Slot's left and right flanks, piercing the darkness. Đăng Đạo and Streak returned fire. Due to the raging wind, the automatic weapons could barely be heard, like heat lightning without thunder.

Kannon spun toward the Jeep. It was only five yards from the gate and moving fast. Where was Quán? He should have jumped free by now and been sprinting toward Kannon. Wasn't happening.

Tufts of snow-laden earth kicked up at Kannon's feet. Weird, Kannon thought.

Shit! I'm being shot at.

He unslung his AK and dove to the ground as muzzle flashes erupted from the roughed-out parking area. Rounds peppered the ground around him.

But the shooter changed targets. Kannon shuddered at the pinging sound of rounds striking metal. The shooter had zeroed in on the Willys.

Still lying prone, Kannon returned fire, using bursts of three as taught by the Army years ago. The shooter adjusted his firing from the Jeep to Kannon. Lead whistled overhead and thudded into the trees behind him. Kannon fired another burst. This time his AK silenced the militiaman. *Did I hit the bastard, or is he lying low?*

A furious firefight continued between Team B and the militiamen posted in front of Whitehead's cabin thirty-five yards distant. Attuned to the sounds now, Kannon heard the sharp retorts of the militiamen's rifles. They sounded like stick-beats on a hollow log.

One-minute fuses. How much time has passed?

Kannon returned his attention to the Willys and the Bangalores. The Bangalores should have exploded by now. Were they duds? Had he wired them wrong? With the timing screwed up, Kannon worried the shooters at the front fence would be reinforced. He hoped he, Đăng Đạo, and Streak had enough ammo.

The Jeep finally struck the gate. Kannon hoped to see Quán racing for cover. Still wasn't happening. He shouted again! "Are you hit?"

No response.

"Damnit."

Rounds continued to ping into the Jeep's body. Frantic, Kannon rose to a crouch and raced forward to find Quán. Rifle shots struck near his feet from both directions, ricocheting off rocks, kicking up clumps of snow. More muzzle flashes erupted from the compound. But no pinging. The shooter must've finally zeroed in on Quán instead of the Jeep's front or rear. Bullets couldn't ping off a passenger door that wasn't there.

The torpedoes, the gate, the Willys, exploded. The blast rocked Kannon backward, knocking him flat on his ass. Bits of metal whistled past like shrapnel from an artillery shell. Hot shards rained around him, on him, in him. Singed clothes. Singed flesh. Flashes of explosive light seared his ears and scorched his eyes. The smell of gunpowder and the stench of burning fuel stung his nostrils. Until he could no longer feel, see, or smell.

* * *

Crandle, still at the bunkhouse, and alarmed by the firing volume, tried reaching both Porter and Badger on the radio. Neither man responded. "Wolfhound, you and Smitty hightail it to the front fence. McAfee, you and Timmons get your asses over to the chopper pad!"

"Yes, sir," came the reply in unison.

"Nolan, take up a position in front of my cabin, which is where I'll be."

The militiaman nodded.

"Whitehead. Do your thing. Check all positions. Remember, I want 'em alive."

"A tough order, sir."

Crandle hightailed it back to his cabin. He needed to take a dump. Just as he sat on the commode, an explosion ripped at the front of the compound.

* * *

Anh jolted awake.

Gunshots!

"Oh, my God. We are being attacked. Derrick, come here!" Anh refused to call him Patu. A given name was sacred. She honored that whenever Crandle was not near.

Out of the darkness, the boy came to her. Her mind raced back to the stories she had heard in the Thai refugee camp about the American war in Việt Nam. Her people shot. Her people blown to pieces. Her people burned alive by napalm. Her people decimated by both sides.

"Daddy K is here," Derrick said.

Could this be true?

Jumping from her bed, Anh reached for the light switch and turned it on. She grabbed a set of man-clothes and donned them, then pulled on a pair of boots. Derrick was sitting on the floor beside her bed, dressed, his back against the wall. His little arms cradled his knees, which were drawn up to his chest. His jaw fixed, the boy stared not at her, not at anything, but through time and space. Anh understood this look. It was the look of knowing.

"Daddy K is here," he repeated.

Could she trust his knowing? She knelt beside him. "Little one. I cannot know if your father is here. Your vision is not available to me."

Derrick turned to her. His breath smelled like apricots. He rested his head on her thigh. Anh leaned forward and slipped one arm under his tender legs and her other arm around his waist. She lifted him. "We must hide," she said. Like a snow rabbit burrowing into a hole, Derrick nestled against her breasts.

An explosion shook the cabin. "Come. We must hide."

"Are we going to die, Miss Anh?"

An unfamiliar feeling swept over her. *Is this what a mother feels—an all-powerful love and concern over a child?*

Although Commander Crandle had forbidden entry into the room that contained his ham radio, one night he got careless when thinking she had fallen asleep in his bed, which rarely happened. She observed his hiding place for the key to his study. Several times since, she had tried making calls like she had overheard him doing that night, but her efforts never worked.

One night, when Crandle was on maneuvers, she was sitting at the desk and accidently knocked the key to the floor. On hands and knees in her scramble to find it, she discovered the wall switch under the desk. Curious, she flipped the switch and heard the click that led her to the secret door underneath the tacked carpet. The iron-wrung steps led down into a deep, dark pit. Remembering stories about booby-trapped tunnels in her country, though, Anh was afraid to enter.

Now, she would overcome her fear and imagine the tunnel as a safe place. Anh opened her bedroom door. The horrible battle noises sounded louder, closer. Taking Derrick by the hand, she paraded to Crandle's bedroom and entered. Just as she was reaching for the key to the ham shack, Derrick's mouth and eyes opened in horror. He pointed at the bathroom door. As Anh followed his outstretched arm, the hairs on her neck became like arrows that pricked her body.

The bathroom door opened.

"What the hell do you think you're doing?"

"Protecting this boy."

Crandle slapped her harder than ever. She fell to the floor, blood forming in her mouth, streaming between her lips. He swung at the boy, but Derrick ducked. Anh watched as Crandle snatched the key to the study. Next, he grabbed her by the ankles, dragged her into the hallway, and threw Derrick on top of her.

Crandle locked his bedroom door and left.

Seventy-One

Kannon opened his eyes. What the hell had happened? He was lying face down on snow and mud, his mind a jumble of cobwebs, his head aching as if he'd been TKO'd in a boxing match.

Turning over, he blinked. Blinked again. His vision was fuzzy, like peering through an out-of-focus lens. An unwavering, piercing siren sounded in his ears.

He lolled his head from side to side. Despite the snow, heat from an unknown source warmed Kannon's face. He raised his head and stared straight ahead. A splash of light as bright as a solar flare blinded his corneas. Only then did he realize his NVD was in place. He shucked the goggles, then reached for a clump of snow and scrubbed it against his forehead. Slowly his reality returned. Vision focused, as did his thinking.

I was flattened by an explosion. There was a firefight.

Telling flames engulfed the Jeep. Scorched tires emitted noxious black fumes. The stench of burning flesh was nauseous.

As a frigid gust dispersed the smoke, Kannon sank into horror and disbelief. The cab resembled a blackened skeleton. Pieces from Streak's Willys lay strewn over the snow like smoldering chunks of charcoal. And Quán? Quán wasn't whole anymore.

More of Kannon's soul emptied. What would he tell Kim, if there still was a Kim? Having lost his brother Roger three days ago, Kannon understood.

I can't focus on that now.

He looked to his right. An AK lay a few feet away. His AK. He crawled toward his weapon as two vague shapes raced toward him. Just as he gripped the rifle, the two men reached him. Đăng Đạo and Streak. Thank God. They grabbed him by the shoulders and dragged him back to the woods.

"How long was I out?"

"Seconds," Đăng Đạo said.

Kannon rose to one knee, realized the firing had stopped. "What about the sentries?"

"We got 'em," Streak said.

"Good work, but it won't be quiet for long. We've got to move." Kannon stood erect. "Any word from Kim?"

Đăng Đạo shook his head.

Kannon gritted his teeth.

He led Đăng Đạo and Streak forward across the snow. Frozen pellets stung his face like hordes of angry wasps. Kannon stumbled over a severed leg that could only have belonged to Quán.

They drew abreast of the destroyed Willys.

"Good Lord. Look there," Streak said.

Quán's upper remains occupied the driver's seat. His hands clung to the steering wheel in their death grip. Flickering firelight revealed the dead man's face, his eyes white globules fixed upon a never-ending road. The stench of seared flesh hung close, but the Bangalores had done their job. The gate was blown.

Kannon felt as if columns of ants were crawling underneath his bite-injured hand. He removed his gloves and rubbed the stricken area. Pulling his gloves back on, he said, "Onward!"

They double-timed through the breached gate. Team B broke right toward Whitehead's cabin. Kannon dropped to one knee.

Floodlights popped on and turned the night into shrouded daylight. Devil light. Automatic rifle fire chewed the earth in front of Đăng Đạo, who lunged behind a tree. Unable to see Streak, Kannon flung himself prone and released a burst from his AK, suppressing the militia's automatic rifle fire. Đăng Đạo leaped into the open and charged toward Whitehead's cabin. Streak materialized and fell in behind.

Again, incoming rounds from the thirty-five-yard gap between the two main cabins raked the ground. His nephew, barely visible, stumbled. *Christ! Not him too.* Kannon pulled hard on the AK's trigger, sprayed a stream of hellfire toward the distant muzzle flashes.

Militiamen responded with controlled three-round bursts. If nothing else, the bastards exercised discipline. Driving snow continued to mask visibility. Regardless, Kannon fired a reckless three of his own.

Rounds pinged overhead. Still maintaining focus to his left, he shouted over his right shoulder. "Đăng Đạo, are you hit?"

Ice-cold laughter sprang from deep within the compound. God all mighty, he had led his guys into a death trap. Kannon rolled to his side. Like a ghost, Đăng Đạo rose and zigzagged toward Whitehead's cabin. His nephew threw a frag grenade. Streak followed suit, then both disappeared, either into the cabin or to the right side of it. Another explosion rocked that area. Gunshots followed. Then an agonizing scream.

Jesus! Sounds like Streak.

Bullets continued raking Kannon's position. He flipped to his stomach, splayed one leg out for a better firing position, but snapped it back after a bullet creased his boot heel.

Then the firing stopped. What was going on? He pulled out his radio.

"Đăng Đạo? Streak! Answer for God's sake," Kannon hollered, dispensing with protocol.

No response . . . except for the roaring gale-force wind. Kannon hesitated. Should he check on his guys or continue as planned?

He rose to a crouch and pushed across the snow-covered, uneven terrain toward Crandle's cabin. Quickening his pace, Kannon stood and high-stepped forward, gulping down breaths of cold, mountain air. As he swatted away a chest-high branch, his left foot with the shattered boot heel struck a splayed root and he went sprawling.

Kannon sat up. Shook his head. Brushed snow from his eyes.

To his front . . . Kim, in battledress, wearing a safety helmet, stood in the middle of the path ahead, cradling Derrick, who mouthed soundless words.

Daddy K . . .

Seventy-Two

And then there was nothing. Disoriented, Kannon looked front and rear. There was no Kim. There was no son. All had been his imagination.

His chest heaving, Kannon collected himself and probed into nearby clumps of snow for his AK. He located the weapon, shook the rifle free of debris, and scrambled to his feet.

"Shit." The Border Slot Militia could've planted a damn garden from the time of Quán's death to now. Where was Crandle? Where was Derrick?

His radio crackled. Kannon lifted it to his ear.

"Yaak One, Yaak Two, Over."

Đăng Đạo.

Kannon squeezed the push-to-talk switch.

"Yaak Two, Yaak One. Thank God you're alive. Where are you?"

"Whitehead's cabin is empty," Đăng Đạo said.

"I heard a scream."

"Streak took a round—"

"What? Streak took a . . ."

Radio contact cut out. Had Streak been killed?

Automatic weapons fire resumed. It peppered the trees, ripped the ground near where he stood. Kannon again flung himself flat.

Shielding his eyes, he tried to bore through the shrouded floodlights. Two silhouetted, formless masses approached. Took shape. There, strutting down the middle of the path, illuminated in his satanic world, came the man called Crandle. His red hair appeared aflame. His head sat upon a neck that might've been cut from a telephone pole. The man's chin looked like a battered anvil, grayish cheekbones like chipped granite. His lips were locked in an undying snarl. Molten lava could flow from Crandle's eyes. Two militiamen, smoke pouring from the muzzles of their automatic rifles, walked beside him. Crandle held a squirming Derrick in one arm. His other hand gripped a pistol, its barrel jammed against the boy's head.

Kannon rose slowly. A bullet grazed his scalp. It happened so

392

fast he didn't see Crandle's trigger finger move. Staggering, still cradling his AK, Kannon fell to his knees. Sticky blood streamed down his forehead.

"Daddy K!"

Kannon looked up to see his son's outstretched arms. Tears flooded the boy's face. "You motherfucker! Let Derrick go."

"You mean Patu?" Crandle roared. "He's our boy now."

"Like hell he is!" Kannon's guts roiled as if a cherry bomb had exploded inside his stomach.

"Drop your popgun." Crandle sneered. "Else I open up a large hole in Patu's head."

With two weapons aimed at Kannon's midsection, what action could he take? At best, he could fire a burst of AK rounds from his hip, but the result might be disastrous. The bullets could stray, hit Derrick. And there was no way he could drop the rifle and draw the .40-caliber without getting drilled.

Kannon dropped his AK.

Do they want me dead or alive? Alive! Else they would've already shot me. That gives me an advantage. Time to work my way out of this mess. So . . . stall.

"Obviously, you want me alive."

Crandle nodded. The other militiaman remained mute.

"Why?"

"To watch you die on the disc range," Crandle said.

"There's nothing to gain—"

"You've messed with Border Slot."

Đăng Đạo and Streak, where are you?

At this point, all Kannon could do was try to negotiate.

"All I want is my son. You want money? I'll pay. We both walk away from this. Never meet again."

Crandle paused, seemingly thinking it over. He nudged one of his sidekicks with his foot. "Nolan, get with Whitehead. Find out if Porter and Badger are okay."

"You're lucky the Commander wants you alive," Nolan said as he walked past Kannon.

How is that lucky?

Crandle waited until Nolan rambled off. To Kannon, "How

much?"

"One million dollars."

"You can do that?" Crandle said through compressed his lips.

"Yeah, I can do that."

The remaining sidekick smirked.

An additional militiaman materialized from the harsh, illuminated darkness. The newcomer, about six feet tall, with wavy brown hair, handlebar mustache, high cheekbones, and a bulge in his cheek, matched Streak's description of Whitehead. Behind him were three more men, one of them, Nolan. They were hard-looking men, strong as if cast in bronze.

"Porter and Badger are dead," Whitehead said.

Kannon shuddered. Confirmation of their deaths would make things worse. Crandle's face turned redder than his hair. He held Derrick upside down by his legs. Screaming in anger and frustration, his son twisted wildly, trying to get loose. Helpless, Kannon stood confronted by six militiamen.

"Give me Patu," said a soft voice.

Crandle turned.

Kannon hadn't noticed the smallish woman approach. Speaking with a Vietnamese accent, she must be Anh.

Crandle tossed Derrick to the turf.

"Take him and get your ass back inside," Crandle said

Anh picked him up and slogged toward the main cabin.

"Where the hell have you guys been?" Crandle yelled.

"Ease up, Commander." Whitehead fixated on Kannon. "Wolfhound and Smitty were flattened by the explosion at the gate."

Too bad it didn't kill them.

"Porter and Badger are dead?"

"Afraid so, Commander."

"Motherfucker!" Crandle turned to Kannon. "You killed two of my best men. And one of them was Brick's handler. His dog's not gonna like that."

As if on cue, the dog approached. It sat on his rear haunches, growling in hate as if it knew Kannon's team was responsible for killing his keeper. As if that wasn't enough, two more militiamen emerged from the direction of the chopper pad.

"McAfee and Timmons, meet Kannon Ballard," Crandle said. "Everything okay at the pad?"

"Yep," said one.

"No problem," said the other.

Crandle nodded toward Whitehead. "Search Ballard."

The militiaman patted Kannon down, relieving him of the grenades, pistol belt, night goggles, and of course, the Sig .40-caliber.

Exclude the boot. Exclude the boot.

"He's clean."

Kannon breathed a sigh of relief.

"Not so high and mighty now, are ya, *war hero*," Crandle said, pocketing his handgun.

No, Kannon didn't feel high and mighty, and definitely not a war hero, more like a fool.

The eight militiamen tightened the circle, eyes glaring. Crandle compressed his lips, stepped forward, grabbed Kannon by the lapels and jerked him forward. On instinct, Kannon turned to his left just as a sharp blade slashed his left side.

"Agh!" The cut seared as if he'd been gouged by a streak of lightning. Kannon reached for the wound, but a militiaman grabbed his wrists and cuffed his hands behind him, cinching the ties tight.

Crandle drew his pistol, cocked his arm, and pistol-whipped Kannon on the right temple. Collapsed to the ground, close to blacking out, Kannon heard Crandle say, "Meddling bastard. I could've used you in the militia, but now your blood's gonna splash all over my training range. And Patu is gonna watch."

Seventy-Three

Wednesday, 0315 C Time, 28 October 2009, Texas Hill Country

Bull stashed the Dodge Ram camper alongside a dry creek bed that ran beneath a bridge located two miles from Ballard's property. The furious pace that had brought him here—thirty hours driving straight from Border Slot—wore him out.

However, the twenty-five grand he'd earned for surviving the killing range and the additional fifteen thou he'd get for completing this mission was more dough than he'd ever made in a year. He patted his pocket to ensure the five-grand advance was still there. He liked that. It comforted him. It energized him.

Bull geared up. He dressed in black fatigues and combat boots, then smeared charcoal grit over his face and donned a black baseball cap. He placed his Armasight N-15s, a pair of Minolta binoculars, plus water, crackers, and a pull-tab tin of tuna inside a backpack. After setting his satphone on vibrate, he clipped it onto his belt, then rolled up his shirt sleeves.

He unzipped his canvas rifle case, removed his gleaming AK47, and slung it over his shoulder. Bull tucked a Colt .45 semiautomatic into his back waistband, placed flex-cuffs in his right front pocket, and holstered his Sling-Hawk at his left side.

Kneeling, he opened the camper door and squeezed through the opening. Satisfied the vehicle was hidden, he edged into the woods. The night was mild under a sparsely clouded sky and a half-full waning moon. A light wind rustled the leaves.

He crossed the highway and worked his way through the vegetation and trees covering the rolling terrain. Ten minutes later, he stood on a knoll overlooking Kannon Ballard's house. The rise offered a different vantage from the one used days earlier with Whitehead. It was time to earn his stripes.

His satphone vibrated. Turning his back to Ballard's house, he answered in a whisper.

"Bull, here."

"Crandle."

"Yes, Commander?"

"We've got Ballard. I think Streak's nearby."

What about my fifteen grand?

"Sir, I've got some things to talk—"

"Not now!"

"Well . . . what do I need to do to satisfy the mission?"

"Destroy the house and anyone in it. Document your kills. Then get the hell out."

"Yes, sir."

Bull was upset. To learn Kannon Ballard already had been captured and that Streak might've been too pissed him off. Did that mean the promised fifteen thousand dollars was off the table?

He'd also wanted to ask about the EMP attack, wanted to talk about the unnecessary beating Whitehead had dished out. It was the first fight he'd ever lost. Only it wasn't much of a fight. He'd been sucker punched. His jaw still ached. He'd like to use his Sling-Hawk and plant a spinning disc in the middle of Whitehead's ugly face.

So far, he'd been loyal. Hadn't revealed to anyone he was OT's brother. Or that OT had helped him develop the Sling-Hawk. It was from him Bull learned that the killing discs were outsourced from a Canadian firm.

Sure, he had endured all this militia crap, knowing he might have to face the discs if he didn't graduate after initial training. He took the risk because it was more important that he measure up to OT. And now, the promised payoff from Crandle was uncertain. What should he do? What would OT do?

OT wouldn't quit.

At least Crandle hadn't rescinded the kill order. The Commander wanted evidence of the kills. Okay, he'd give him proof. *Pictures? How about body parts! White Might is Right! Hooah!*

The thoughts mollified his crappy mood.

Atop the knoll, silence reigned. Outside floodlights rimmed the rafters, negating any need for the Armasight goggles. Shaded light from inside poured through two windows.

He put the binoculars to his eyes. A Volkswagen beetle sat in the drive next to the garage door, and a polished Dodge Challenger convertible was parked in front.

Neither had been there on his earlier recon. Had the vehicles been in the garage then? Or, maybe guests were inside the house now. It didn't matter. Bull screwed a silencer onto the barrel of his AK, chambered a round, and took aim.

Seventy-Four

Wednesday, 0220 Hours M Time, 28 October 2009, Border Slot Compound

The winter storm had abated. Tree limbs were motionless, the air fresh, the compound quiet—a tranquil setting that begged to be painted. Yet, Kannon's situation was far from peaceful. Dazed, shivering, and surrounded by the eight militiamen, he lay on his back where he'd fallen. A bullet-grazed scalp, throbbing skull, and punctured side—nothing he couldn't survive. His breathing, though labored, seemed unobstructed, so, no pierced lung. Small blessings.

McAfee approached. He stooped, ripped open Kannon's jacket where the blade had penetrated, then roughly bandaged the gash. Yeah, they wanted him alive all right, only to be sliced to death by razor-edged discs. The worst part, though, was Crandle's threat of having Derrick witness his father's slaughter. It was too frighteningly real to dismiss. The potential impact on his son was unfathomable.

"How many of you are there?" Crandle asked.

Kannon didn't respond.

"How many?"

"My thinking's fuzzy. Can't remember."

"Answer my fucking question. Else I'll waterboard you."

"Okay," Kannon gasped. "Give me a moment."

Despite his numbed hands cuffed behind his back, Kannon rolled over and struggled to gain a kneeling position. "Agh!" The sharp pain from the knife wound bit hard.

The damn dog leaped and clamped its jaws on Kannon's ankle. It was a control technique, not a bite. The dog was probably as disciplined as the militiamen. "Keep that stupid mutt away from me."

"You're lucky we don't turn Brick loose," Whitehead said, grabbing the dog's collar and restraining him.

Again, how is that lucky?

"Blood's seeping through your *medic's* pitiful bandaging. You want me to bleed to death?"

"The bandage is good enough for what's in store for you,"

399

McAfee said.

Crandle kicked Kannon on *that* side. "Answer the question."

"Oh, God!" Kannon collapsed. Bile rose in his throat. He couldn't contain it and vomited. Brick licked it up.

"Hooah!"

Kannon regained a kneeling position, then shakily rose to a stance. In doing so, he noticed another figure lying supine, hands and feet bound by a rope. He appeared unconscious, not dead, because the man's chest heaved.

Đăng Đạo!

"My partner," Kannon nodded toward Đăng Đạo. "There's no one else."

"Bullshit!" Whitehead smirked and shook his head. "You obviously had a driver."

"He's dead. Scattered in pieces."

Đăng Đạo opened one eye. Winked at Kannon. Hell, in this fix, he'd be better off never regaining consciousness. Yet, what if his wink meant—

"Was Streak the driver?" Crandle asked.

Whitehead shook his head. "I searched through the blast area. It was Streak's Jeep, all right, but I don't think it was him, or what was left of him. The body parts looked more gook than white. Streak's a traitor. But I don't think he's changed into a slant-eye."

Crandle laughed, a dark, deep, menacing laugh. He pulled a cigar from inside his parka, clipped and lit it. He studied Kannon, drew close, and blew smoke in his face. "You and two slant eyes, just three of you infiltrating our compound? Don't think so."

"Đăng Đạo's the only person who agreed to help rescue my son. He's the boy's first cousin. The other guy—"

"Such a perverted family!" Crandle said, poking Kannon in the side. "There's no way you could've found your way here without Streak. Where is he?"

"I don't know."

Crandle placed his thumbs on Kannon's temples and squeezed like a mechanical vice.

"I'll ask one more time."

"Don't know," Kannon gasped.

"McAfee, bring the board. Let's give our boy a bucket of water and some towels."

"My pleasure, Commander."

"I think you'll remember soon enough." Crandle arched his eyebrows and gazed at his men.

How the hell am I going to get out of this!

What would be worse—suffocating or being sliced to death? But he wouldn't give up, not with Derrick's life at stake. His only hope was to find some way to gain access to the Sig 9mm wedged inside his boot.

McAfee returned with the board, bucket, and towels.

"Place the fucker on his back," Crandle commanded.

One militiaman kneed him from behind. Another pushed, and Kannon went flying backward. Before he could protest, four militiamen pinned his limbs.

"Strap him to this nice slab of redwood," Crandle said.

They did and then raised the aft end so that his feet were higher than his head. He was helpless and scared—really scared.

"Last chance," Crandle said.

"I don't know where he is. He contacted me after you bastards took Derrick. Streak told me about Border Slot, your ridiculous agenda, the EMP weapons—"

"He told you about those?"

"Yeah."

"Who'd you tell?"

"No one!"

"Hand me the fucking bucket and towels," Crandle said, kneeling beside Kannon's face. "I'll suffocate you if you don't talk."

"I've told you all I know." Kannon took in a deep breath.

McAfee punched him in the stomach and forced him to exhale. Kannon lost control of his bladder.

Crandle slapped two ragged towels over his nose and mouth. Then came the water, lots of it. Kannon inhaled, sucking the saturated towels tighter against his face. Water, not air, flowed into his nose and mouth, into his lungs. He struggled against his bonds but couldn't move. He tried to exhale, which was futile. Panic! Nausea! Crandle poured more water onto the towels. Kannon's brain began dissolving in blackness.

The towels were removed.

"Where's Streak?"

Kannon tried to speak but coughed up water instead. Gasping . . . gasping . . . gasping. "I don't—" He threw up.

Crandle slapped the towels on him again. More water. Blurred vision. It seemed as if his eyes were rolling into the back of his head. His mind swirled in dizziness. More nausea.

I'm drowning.

"You're overdoing it, Crandle," one of the militiamen said. "He's asphyxiating."

Militiamen flipped him upright, tilted the board against a tree. Kannon wheezed . . . and wheezed, vomited again.

"Where's Streak?"

"I paid him . . . to disappear . . . get the hell out of my life."

"He may be telling the truth."

It was the same voice, one of authority. Whitehead's?

"Asking one more time . . . who did you tell about this?" Crandle waved the wet towel in Kannon's face. "I'll do this again. And you will talk."

How long had the waterboarding gone on? It seemed like forever.

I can't take another round.

"Lower the board."

Once more, Crandle slapped the towel across Kannon's mouth and nose. He tilted the bucket and slowly poured more water onto the towel.

Kannon sucked in what he could. His muscles spasmed in protest. His lungs were bursting, his synapses screamed for relief. Militiamen's faces swirled like waterspouts, and it felt like his brain mass had turned into a sponge. He opened his mouth to speak but then, nothing but darkness.

Seventy-Five

Murmurs worked their way into Kannon's consciousness. The swirling faces in his vision finally stilled. The voices grew sharper. His ragged breathing steadied. It seemed to Kannon as if everyone was exhausted—the post-torture lull.

"Last fucking time. Who'd you tell about this?"

It was Crandle. Of course, it was Crandle. Even in his blackout, he saw the *Commander*. Was there a shred of humanity left in him?

"Look," Kannon said in a croaky voice, "I understand you lost a son and a wife, Crandle. I'm sorry that happened, but there's nothing I can do about it. Life's hard. At times, it sucks. But Derrick is as precious to my wife and me as your son was to you. Yeah, *Commander*, he's got a mother and father who love him, and you have nothing to gain by keeping us here."

Whitehead shook his head, almost as if warning Kannon not to go there.

"Shut the fuck up!" Crandle puffed on his cigar, then flicked ashes on Kannon. "Listen up, faggot. Fathering that half-breed, you're as bad as the niggers, Jews, slope heads, spics, ragheads, and all the other impure cocksuckers."

I'm kidding myself. How do you reach a man who has no conscience? There are no bargaining chips.

"I asked you a question," Crandle said, poking at Kannon's insured side with a rifle.

"The . . . the . . . Feds."

"I told you, Whitehead!"

"He's bluffing. Like I said, Commander, guys like him don't contact the Feds. Ballard's a lone wolf. Operates alone. And Streak's in the wind."

"Shoulda put Streak on the training range in the beginning," Timmons said. "Would've ensured his loyalty."

"I know that! Don't want to hear anything else about it." Crandle scowled at Timmons. "As for Ballard and his gook, I'm gonna enjoy watching them die."

"What's next, Commander?" Whitehead asked.

"Ready the training field. I'm going to send out a ham radio alert to all contacts to be on the lookout for Streak."

"Why in the hell do you want my son?"

"Young and trainable, just like white kids who got captured by Indians. He'll survive the beatings, the hostile wilderness, or die. Right, Whitehead?"

Whitehead didn't respond.

"I've already gone through that thought process, Crandle. My son's tough. He'll survive."

"Doesn't matter. You're never going to hold the kid again." Crandle kept twisting the virtual knife.

"Don't forget about Bull," Nolan said. "Wonder what he's doing to Ballard's woman about now."

"What?"

Crandle grabbed Kannon's lapels and jerked him to his feet. "Think about that—Patu watching you get ripped apart while Bull's coming into every hole of your slant-eyed bitch."

Blood rushed to Kannon's head, propelling him into dizziness. Crandle's taunting was working. The thought of Lan being raped sickened him further. Even a deputy sheriff and an armed Stefan might not prevent it.

"You're all sociopaths."

Crandle snuffed out the cigar on Kannon's nose. "You shouldn't have screwed with Border Slot."

Seventy-Six

Wednesday, 0320 Hours C Time, 28 October 2009, Texas Hill Country

Bull lined up the crosshairs of his mounted Leopold MK4 scope. Applying light trigger pressure, he took one breath, let it out, then another, and released half. He squeezed the trigger on his muffled assault rifle. The first floodlight shattered, then another and another and another. After taking out the smaller porch light, he set the rifle down and grabbed his NVD.

Facing the front of the house from his position on the knoll, he scanned left to right, paying attention to the metallic-silver Dodge Challenger parked in front. Who does it belong to? he wondered.

Peering through the NVD's ghostly green display, Bull tracked the curved driveway to the attached garage situated on the left side of the house, where the Volkswagen bug sat parked for the night. He scanned past the garage side door and settled on the front alcove.

Come on, Bitch. I wanna see your panty-clad ass again.

Instead, someone else emerged—a man. One Bull didn't recognize. Squinting, the stranger stared toward the rise. He must've heard the impact of the shots.

Can't see me, you stupid ass. What's that on your hip? A fucking pistol. Gotta be a cop.

Bull's pulse quickened as though his veins had been injected with adrenaline. Confident of being unseen, Bull eased forward, right hand on his pistol butt, left one on his Sling-Hawk.

The cop shrugged, then turned and patrolled away from the garage along the house front before disappearing around back. Bull moved to the alcove and waited.

A couple of minutes later, the cop completed his round, paused, and headed toward the knoll. Bull pulled the Sling-Hawk from its sheath. "Hey, asshole," he said, keeping his voice low.

The cop stopped, drew his weapon, and turned toward the alcove. "Show yourself. Hands above your head."

"Fuck you!" Bull cocked his arm and thrust it forward,

releasing the disc at head level. The cop never saw it coming. The disc flew through the darkness and embedded in his forehead. He flopped to the ground.

The man's eyes and lips were locked open. Blood trickled from his fatal head wound. Bull rifled the man's pockets and lifted his wallet. Flipping it open, he found a badge and photo ID and pocketed them. He reached for the disc stuck in the cop's forehead and wiggled it back and forth to pry it loose.

"You won't need this anymore," Bull muttered. He wielded the disc to cut off one ear and smiled—proof for Crandle of kill number one. As a final measure, he slit the cop's throat and snapped a photo with a pocket-sized point and shoot.

Gathering the rest of his gear from the knoll, he carried it to the Challenger and placed the pack against the driver's door. He wouldn't lose this vehicle like he had Streak's motorcycle.

Bull moved to the garage. He leaned his rifle and pack against a crape myrtle tree, which bookended the bordering flower bed. Since he didn't have to worry about Streak or Ballard, he could take his time with the woman. He got a hard-on thinking about it. Tie her up, come on her face, then in her pussy.

Another thought struck. Hell! Take her to Border Slot. Crandle had a woman. Why shouldn't he? Then a chill crept along Bull's arms. What if someone besides the cop heard the bulbs shatter, or bullets strike the rafters, or wonder why the cop was gone so long? He or she might've already called for help. The sheriff could be on the way.

No way could he afford to repeat what happened the first time. Bull wanted to prove to Crandle he was as good or better than his brother, OT.

He bit a fingernail, cocked an ear for sirens. Nothing.

Fuck this. I barely heard the glass breaking. No one's coming. Get it done.

Bull examined the VW. It was locked. Looking through the driver's window, he noticed two glasses sitting in placeholders.

What's a good way to scare the hell out of anyone inside? A big Molotov Cocktail.

Using the butt of his .45-caliber pistol, he broke the passenger side window—no alarm sounded—then took the glasses and examined them. They were composed of hard plastic. Even better, each held twenty-four ounces. He set them beside his pack by the crape myrtle.

A thin garden hose lay coiled against the far side of the garage. Bull sliced off four, inch-long pieces, and wedged them between the facing and the garage door to keep it from opening. Next, he cut a five-foot-long section from the hose and stuffed it through the gas cap filler. Before siphoning gas, he slipped the manual shift into neutral and muscled the car into the front alcove, not an easy chore with a locked steering wheel.

He retrieved the glasses, returned to the VW, and sucked on the open end of the hose to start the flow. It tasted, well, like gasoline. He coughed up globs of phlegm and wondered: If by holding a flame in front of his mouth and exhaling, could he become a dragon?

After filling the glasses, Bull doused the garage side door with gasoline, flicked his lighter, and set it aflame. Needing to work fast to cover all the external windows, he ran to each one, doused its wooden sill with fuel, and ignited it.

Bull returned to the VW, removed his fatigue shirt, and hacked off the sleeves. He tied the fragments together and saturated the cloth with gasoline. He plunged the braided sleeve as far down the VW's fuel canal as possible, lit the fuse, then hauled ass to the back door.

Ten paces outside the door, he assumed an offensive tackle's crouch. And waited. Nothing happened. *Shit!* His legs were cramping. He stood. Maybe the fuse had gone out. He trotted back toward his big Molotov cocktail, when . . .

BOOM!

The explosion knocked him to the ground. His ears rang from the deafening sound. Shaking his head, he rolled over and got up, raced around back. Roaring, he charged toward the framed-glass patio door.

Seventy-Seven

Wednesday, 0700 Hours M Time, 28 October 2009, Border Slot Compound

Kannon opened his eyes. Early morning sun rays struck his retinas like multiple bursts from a camera flash. His mind instructed him to blink and rub his eyes. He blinked with some success, but couldn't move because he was tied to a tree trunk with his hands cuffed behind him.

Pinned to a nearby tree, his nephew was in the same fix.

"Đăng Đạo." Kannon raised his voice. "Đăng Đạo!"

No response.

Is he dead?

Fighting off a sickening dread, Kannon fixed his eyes upon the open, snow-covered field to his front. To his right, snowcapped trees dotted the terrain, punctuated by the chopper pad and the remains of Streak's hut. Beyond those lay the undamaged fuel tank, obstacle course, and Lord knew what else.

The compound loomed to his left.

Slowly, the rest of his senses returned. Voices. Metal on metal—the sound of hammering. The smell of his body odor and dried blood stung his nostrils. His nose was raw, and his head throbbed as if blunt nails had been pounded into his skull. His right ankle hurt because of the Sig Sauer in his boot. The knife wound bit sharp, destined for infection if not treated. Hell, at this stage, he wouldn't live long enough for his side wound to become infected.

Kannon retched—again, the dry heaves. And he couldn't stop shivering. Icicles hung from his mustache.

Kannon returned his focus to the killing field. Militiamen moved in military precision, muttering like men in a barracks preparing for inspection. They were unrolling steel mesh screens and erecting support columns to set up field boundaries to contain the killing discs. As Streak had described, the field was about the size of a basketball court.

Other men were positioning five disc-launching machines

behind a three-foot-high berm fronting the killing field. The throwing arms of the disc launchers just cleared the berm. The only advantage Kannon saw was that the angle of fire might be limited to three feet high and above.

He turned to his nephew.

"Đăng Đạo! Talk to me."

"K . . . Ka . . . Kannon?" His nephew's word dribbled from his mouth. So did blood.

"Thank God you're alive. How badly are you hurt?"

"Do not . . . know. I . . . I am freezing."

He saw the pain in Đăng Đạo's eyes. It sickened Kannon to think of him being slaughtered on the killing field. Worse, forsaking Derrick to the whims of these bastards was more than he could bear.

And Lan? Was Bull raping her?

Stefan's and Belynda's presence provided some comfort, but they too would be in the line of fire. He hoped and prayed that the onsite detective could protect all three of them. Bull was only one man but, according to Streak, an extremely violent, dangerous one.

Kannon looked again at his nephew, whose disheveled long hair and sunken cheeks made him look like a discarded corpse.

"Đăng Đạo, I screwed up. Big time. I'm sorry."

"Not your fault. I volunteered."

That doesn't make me feel better.

Kannon shifted his gaze east toward the helicopter pad. On it sat the Jolly Green Giant that Streak had piloted before defecting. Kannon visualized that a special ops squad led by Sindy Zeller would stream from the chopper and perfect their rescue.

Fat chance.

"Do you know what happened to Streak?" Kannon asked.

"Last I saw . . . beneath Whitehead's bunk."

What? That doesn't compute. "Say again."

"Streak got hit as we approached Whitehead's cabin. I thought," Đăng Đạo had a coughing spasm, "I thought it was just a surface wound. But once inside the cabin, he collapsed. I could not bring him to consciousness. The cabin was empty, so I slid him under the bunk."

"So, we don't know if he's dead or alive."

409

"Right."

Or if he'd been found. "How'd you get captured?"

Đăng Đạo shook his head, slowly. "I was reaching for my PPK when Whitehead took me from behind, halfway between his cabin and Crandle's. My bad."

"Shit happens." Kannon's hope was evaporating like the morning fog. "I offered Crandle a million dollars."

"I overheard, but how is he going to get it if you are dead?"

"His sadism overrides any monetary concerns."

Kannon closed his eyes, seeking control. Feeling the sun warm his face, he recalled the signature message from Viktor Frankl's *Man's Search for Meaning*. It was about Jews who maintained dignity while standing in line to be gassed or incinerated during World War II.

Dignity. He could muster that. Kannon flexed to try and loosen the ropes that tightly bound him against the tree. He straightened up best he could. Held his chin high. "We're going to get out—"

A gong sounded, reverberating off the cliff wall.

I don't want to die on a sunny day.

* * *

Crandle strapped his pistol belt around his starched fatigue shirt. A knife hilt extended above its sheath. Two grenades hung from his pistol belt. He holstered his ceremonial, pearl-handled .45, the one reserved for special operations. After slipping on an ear-muffed woolen hat, a shooting glove on his right hand and insulated mitten on his left, he was ready.

"Commander."

"Yeah, Whitehead, be right out."

Crandle opened his bedroom door and entered the den where his second-in-command waited.

"Looking sharp, Commander."

"Bet your ass I do."

"The men are setting up the field," Whitehead said.

"No sign of Streak?"

"Nothing. If he was out there, Brick would've found him."

"Join the men," Crandle said. "I'll be out in a minute. And

Whitehead!"

"Yes, Commander?"

"Once this is over, organize a patrol and find Streak."

Once Whitehead left, Crandle walked toward Anh's bedroom door. He flung it open. Standing, she wore only her bathrobe. She also wore a purple bruise and a split lip. The boy wasn't dressed.

"You ever try to enter my study again, I'll flay you."

"Flay me. It cannot get any worse than this."

"You probably don't even know what that means. I'll skin you alive."

Ann visibly shuddered. That pleased him.

"Get Patu dressed in his camos. And get that sour look off your face."

She didn't.

"I should have stayed in the refugee camp."

"Yeah. You didn't even have a roof over your head. I've given you food and shelter. Made you my woman—"

"I am not your woman."

"Yes, you are, and you'll do what I want. That's the way it is here."

"If not for that dear boy," she came close and spoke to his ear, "I would kill myself."

"If you meant that, you would've done it long ago. Admit it. You like what I've given you . . . good sex."

"Rape is not sex."

"Anh . . ." He turned and touched her shoulder. She brushed him off.

"Bitch." Crandle slapped her cheek. It turned crimson. "That's the thanks I get."

"If you took the worst parts of all the bad men in the world and combined them, that person would not be as evil as you."

"You'll make up for it tonight," he said, thinking of hot, angry sex.

The boy cowered in the corner.

"Stop bawling, Patu. Today's a big day. You'll get to watch people die."

"I hate you," Patu said.

"You'll learn about survival."

"Daddy K is better than you."

"Your *Daddy K* is soon gonna be dead—"

"No!" Patu rushed him, his pathetic arms flailing, his fists hammering at Crandle's thighs. Crandle laughed and tossed him aside. "You little shit! I do like your spirit, kid." To Anh, "Get cracking."

* * *

All Kannon and Đăng Đạo could do was squirm and watch the construction of the death field, which lay beyond the chopper pad and Streak's destroyed quarters. Past that lay a berm.

Whitehead sauntered over. "You two fuckers piss me off. It's a pain in the ass to set up this field."

"Take it down," Kannon said.

Đăng Đạo let out a guttural chuckle.

"Funny," Whitehead said.

"If you have courage, white man full of hate, you will turn us loose. WE FIGHT! MAN-TO-MAN." Đăng Đạo's inflection sizzled with vitriol.

"Nice try, *Gook*. It wouldn't be much of a fight." Then to Kannon, "You might as well have brought a nigger."

Even though Whitehead's prejudice disturbed him, the guy's tone lacked malice. He didn't seem evil. Crandle reeked of it. Not this guy.

Whitehead's face was chiseled but not harsh. His almond-shaped eyes showed a life-light. Sure, the hair was a bit unwieldy, but the mustache was trimmed, and yeah, a chaw was in his mouth, but he wore starched fatigues, the pants bloused into Jump Boots. What if Kannon revealed Đăng Đạo's tangled story or even his own! Would Whitehead care?

Jump Boots.

Paratroopers wore jump boots, the kind with the thick double seam that set apart the toe, the part you spit-polished. Kannon remembered now that Streak had mentioned this.

"You were in the military," Kannon said.

Whitehead gave him a measured look. "What of it?"

"Wondering about your experiences, that's all. How you

412

wound up here?"

"You washed out of Special Forces," Đăng Đạo said.

Shit! Kannon wished his nephew hadn't said that. The last thing he wanted was to antagonize the militia further.

"Shut up, motherfucker. Another word from you and I'll cut out your tongue." Whitehead turned back to Kannon. "Keep him quiet. Or I'll skin him alive."

"What is the difference?" Đăng Đạo asked.

Whitehead pulled a knife from his sheath. He fronted Đăng Đạo and slugged him in the stomach, reached in and grabbed the tongue.

"Wait!" Kannon said. "His father was my interpreter in Việt Nam. That's how I met my wife. For God's sake, man, I served my country. Just like you. It's where I learned people are people."

For an instant, a look of shame swept over Whitehead's face. "It doesn't matter anymore. It's too late."

"No, it's not. SF training is tough as hell. It must've meant a lot to you," Kannon said.

The militiaman swallowed hard. Did a lump form in Whitehead's throat? Maybe there was a chance—

"Whitehead! Get your ass over here." It was Crandle.

"Duty calls." Whitehead let go of Đăng Đạo's tongue and turned to go.

Kannon hollered after him.

"Why?"

"It's my job," Whitehead said over his shoulder.

"You are wasting your breath talking to him," Đăng Đạo said.

Kannon sighed. "Yeah, I guess so."

He lifted his gaze and looked skyward. The dramatic weather change amazed him. If only the weather had been like this last night instead of near-blizzard conditions. The attack as planned might've worked. And Kim would've been able to make a successful jump.

Maybe he had tried and been blown miles off course. Or driven by the wind into the cliff face and died. If alive, where was he?

Holding his skyward gaze, Kannon saw a large-winged bird take flight. *I'll be damned.*

Seventy-Eight

Wednesday, 0330 Hours C Time, 28 October 2009, Texas Hill Country

Stefan marveled at the Christmas bulbs burning bright, the joy spread by each color. Then his dad walked into the den.

One by one, the Christmas bulbs burst. Stefan wanted an explanation, but none came. Instead, his father said: "Get to bed!" Returning to his room, Stefan climbed into bed, grabbed his baseball glove and buried his face in the pillow, crying. Why are you being mean, Dad? I didn't break the Christmas bulbs.

An empty feeling worked into his stomach. He wanted his dad to comfort him. Needed his mother's soothing words. Neither happened.

He got up and went outside, seeking solace in nature. A jackrabbit bounded along a red-brick road before turning off into the woods. Stefan chased it. When he got close, the rabbit stopped and turned and said, "Your family needs you."

Stefan returned to the house and found his mom and dad sitting in the den. A fire was burning. Music was playing. The stimulating aroma of wood smoke filled the room.

The music reached a peak. The fireplace became a campfire. The den became a tent standing among tall pine and aspen. Burbling rapids sang from behind the tent. A mountain slope fronted them. And then the slope moved, swirled, and coned into a volcano. Erupted. Molten lava . . .

Stefan woke up coughing. The armchair upon which he'd straddled and fallen asleep tipped over backward. Eyes centered on the ceiling, he noticed a thin layer of fog gathering. Fog? Inside? Carrying the acrid smell of burning wood? No, it was smoke! From where? What in hell was happening?

The fire alarm was sounding.

"Lan! Belynda! Detective Hamilton!"

"On the den floor. By the sofa." It was Lan's high-pitched voice.

Stefan scrambled to his feet and ran to the wall switch by the front entrance. Only there was no door, just a jagged opening where it once had been. Lan's VW bug was in flames. The VW didn't get there by itself. That was the crescendo he'd awakened to in his nightmare.

Chunks of the ceiling begin collapsing. Embers dropped like fiery rain. Stefan dove to the floor, only to see the foyer fill with a mass of fire and billowing smoke. No way could they get out that way.

"It's the militia! We're under assault," Stefan yelled, stumbling toward the den in a crouch. Glass popped. Window frames burned as if entrances to hell. "Have you seen Hamilton?"

"No!" Belynda cried out.

Flames licked at the living room walls. Visibility was limited, the odor nauseating. Stefan again dropped to the floor and crawled toward the women.

The patio door shattered. More windows imploded, and shards flew like salvos of darts.

Lyn and Belynda screamed, only to be throttled by the gathering bank of poisonous smoke as fire sucked oxygen from the room.

Stefan paused and yelled, "Hamilton! Where are you?"

No answer. Stefan tried again. "Can you hear me?" Thinking he heard a clattering in the kitchen, he ran in to check. It was vacant.

The garage! They could get out through the garage.

"Crawl toward the kitchen," Stefan hollered.

Inside the garage, he ran to the control panel. Pushed the open switch. The motor whirred and strained, but the overhead door remained shut. He tried again—same result. Stefan raced to the manual override lever, yanked the chain, and then scuttled to the handle at the bottom of the door. With all his strength, he tugged at the handle but to no avail.

Engulfed by the smoke pouring in, Stefan scrambled back to the kitchen. He dropped to all fours and reentered the den.

"Lan! Head for the patio." He needed to get the women out, then find the detective.

"I cannot see the way," Lan shouted.

"Help us!" Belynda's voice reeked of panic.

Stefan crawled toward their screams. "Ow!" Glass fragments pricked his unprotected hands as he moved forward, leaving droplets of blood pooling on the floor.

Shouts from a male voice he didn't recognize reached his ears. Quickening his pace, Stefan bumped into Lan's rear. He grabbed her and spun her around. "This way!"

Both women trailed Stefan as he led them in the right direction. *Damnit!* He remembered the loaded shotgun and the extra shells he'd set beside the chair where he'd fallen asleep. He worried about the rounds cooking off. Worse, what if he needed the weapon once they escaped the fire, which was closing in like a scalding vise.

"Keep going!" he told them.

Stefan scampered back to the chair. He grabbed the shotgun by the barrel but immediately let go. *Mother* . . . It was sizzling hot. Ignoring the burn, he seized the wooden stock and stuffed the pouch of extra shells into his pocket, surprised the rounds hadn't already cooked off. He started toward the patio door in a low crouch. He stopped, his mind snagging on something else he wanted to retrieve.

Locating the items he was looking for, he wedged them inside his shirt and rushed for the patio. His foot caught on the leg of an overturned table, and he stumbled onto his hands and knees, dropping the shotgun. He skittered over the floor like a spider trying to find it.

Lan screamed again, then Belynda.

* * *

Bull halted his charge toward the glassed patio door. The fire was spreading much faster than he'd anticipated. He feared becoming engulfed by the flames if he smashed through the door. *Damn! How am I gonna get that bitch?*

The glass door exploded inward. Instinctively, he hit the ground. He lay there a moment, deciding what to do.

The explosion allowed him a partial view of the interior. Shadowy figures thrashed inside the smoke-filled room, trying to find their way out. He couldn't tell how many people were in there but heard a female voice, and maybe a male's too. He'd already taken out one detective. Was another one inside?

He thought about the fire alarm and how much time he had before the fire department, and maybe more cops arrived. Then two figures materialized out of the smoke. Damn! Two broads. Just as quickly, they disappeared. Had he seen what he thought he'd seen?

Bull entered the inferno.

* * *

The draft created by the smashed patio door fueled the fire but was clearing the den of smoke. Stefan saw the shotgun lying near the kitchen door. Just as he started for it, he saw feet, large feet, and looked up. A looming hulk stood silhouetted just inside the patio entryway. Stefan stood and looked into the eyes of the broadest barrel-chested man he had ever seen. He must have been what triggered the women's screams.

"I am the BULL!" The man spoke in a husky, baritone voice. "Who the fuck are you?"

Stefan didn't answer. He assessed.

Bull had one huge arm clamped around Lan's head. Her eyes bulged. Belynda lay on her stomach, pinned by the man's foot planted in the middle of her back. She flailed her arms like an overturned turtle but couldn't get free.

Stefan slowly switched his focus to what the man held in his other hand—a large semiautomatic pistol. He backpedaled and desperately sought the fallen shotgun.

"Stand as you are! Hands high," Bull said.

Reluctantly, Stefan complied. The shotgun lay perhaps three feet away, out of Bull's line of sight. "What the hell do you want?"

Bull smiled an ugly grin. "These two whores." The man removed his foot from Belynda's back, nudged her to roll over. "Get up."

"Go to hell," Belynda said, rising.

Bull backhanded Belynda, and she crumpled back to the floor. Lan tried to break free but remained pinned to Bull's side.

"Belynda, I am so sorry for getting you into this," Lan cried.

"We'll get out of it." Belynda wiped the blood from her lips.

"Shut up, Whore."

"In case you haven't noticed, the house is on fire," Stefan yelled. "We're all going to burn if we don't get the hell out of here." He moved forward but froze when Bull cocked the hammer.

"Who owns that Challenger out there?"

"I do," Stefan said.

"Give me the keys."

Stefan calculated his options. He was taller than Bull, but not as broad, and probably not as strong. But he could punch and dance, the boxing skills he'd learned by taking out his anger after his birth mom threw out Kannon's drunken ass those many years ago.

"They're in my pocket."

"Get 'um."

Stefan reached into his pocket, slipped his index finger through the keyring, and withdrew the set of keys. He dangled them in from of Bull.

"Toss them at my feet."

Instead, Stefan flung the key chain toward the now-burning kitchen door, near the shotgun. A bullet whizzed past his ear.

"Murderous bastard," Belynda said.

Bull kicked her.

Stepping forward, Bull placed the big, squared-off muzzle of the semiautomatic against Stefan's forehead. "Get the keys, pussy."

Stefan's knees shook. "There's another way to settle this."

"There is no other way," Bull said, his eyes twitching in recognition. "Hey. I recognize you. From the magic show. You were with Ballard."

"Yeah. And you were the one who shot and killed my uncle."

"You're next, asshole, unless you get those damn keys."

Flickering flames reflected off Bull's wide, dark eyes. Stefan was staring at one of Satan's disciples. "Go ahead. Shoot. Then you get the damn keys."

Bull shot him in the thigh.

"Damn!" Stefan collapsed to the floor. "Ah, Jesus!" Blood flowed from the wound and saturated his jeans.

"Stef—" Bull mashed Lan's face tighter against his side. Her mouth was nothing but a slit. Belynda groggily attempted to rise.

Stefan's vision blurred. Grew darker.

Concentrate. I can't pass out, or we'll all die.

Bull threw Lan aside and knelt in front of him, grabbing his chin in a vice. "Get the keys!"

"You shot me in the leg, asshole."

"Get the keys." Bull jammed the muzzle against Stefan's forehead. The hammer was back, his finger on the trigger.

"All right. Don't shoot."

"Move it."

Stefan turned onto his uninjured side and started to sidestroke toward the kitchen. Flames spurted all around him. The hot floor singed his already burnt hand. Out of the corner of his eye, he saw Bull holding both women in headlocks, stumbling toward the exit to escape the fire. This was his chance.

Blocking the stabbing pain, Stefan rolled to his stomach and continued scooting toward the shotgun. His lungs labored. His shattered thigh felt as if the bullet had erupted inside.

It's taking forever to crawl one foot. Keep on keeping on. If Dad can do it, so can I.

The fire lapped closer. Stefan couldn't see Bull or the women any longer, but from their screams knew they were in the backyard.

"My stepson will burn to death," Lan screamed.

"Let him burn."

Stefan grasped the shotgun. After ensuring the safety was off, he wrapped his fingers around the trigger housing, then latched on to the keys. As he turned back to his good side to slide them into his pocket, he stuck his hand into a pocketful of blood. He looked down. His pants leg was saturated.

His head was swimming. He had to staunch the bleeding. *God, please don't let the blood flow stem from my femoral artery.*

Stefan ran his hands around his thigh. No exit hole in the back of his jeans. Which meant the bullet had lodged inside his leg. Which dictated where to place the tourniquet.

He removed his belt from his jeans. It was thick-leathered and wide. Hard to secure around his leg. But the belt was long, with a western-style buckle. He wrapped it twice around his thigh, above the wound, and winced as he pulled it tight. He was able to plug the belt post into one of the holes. The pressure numbed his agony only slightly.

The wound still bled. Stefan withdrew a bloody pocketknife from his front pocket and a handkerchief from his back pocket. He cut off a strip and used it to plug the wound. He draped the remaining sleeve around the entry wound and tied it to secure the plug.

All the while screams from outside continued. Time was short. Stefan placed his left hand on the forestock, his right on the stock. Keeping his good knee to the floor, he used the shotgun to paddle his way forward, dragging his bad leg behind him.

He gagged from the sickening odor from his singed hair. His scalp got so hot he was afraid it might combust. The heat was nearly unbearable. He kept on. Nearing the exit to the patio, Stefan saw that Lan and Belynda, both naked, had their backs to him.

Bull, standing opposite the women, held them at gunpoint. He stepped forward and forced plastic flex-cuffs into Belynda's hand, then stepped back. His eyes darted from high to low, from Belynda's breasts to Lan's crotch.

"I'm not gonna tell you again, Bitch. Cuff that there slanty-eye's hands and feet. I'm saving her for last."

"Go fuck yourself," Belynda shot back.

Bull fired a round at her feet. The bullet ricocheted off the concrete floor and whistled above Stefan's head. Apparently, the militiaman had decided to forego the Challenger, and *him*—possibly figuring Stefan had burned to death—just to rape the women.

Bull approached Belynda again, grabbed her elbow, but hesitated.

Stefan cocked an ear. *Sirens!*

"You whores are coming with me."

I can't let that happen. Using the shotgun as a crutch—not a good idea in the best of circumstances—Stefan rose and hobbled forward.

"Hey, Motherfucker, I've got the car keys. Let the women go."

Bull snapped his attention toward Stefan. It didn't seem to register to the big man that Stefan held a shotgun . . . until it did. Glowering at him with coal-black eyes, Bull laughed the crazy man's laugh. He drew his handgun and leveled it at Stefan.

Stefan tossed the keys in the air, hoping to distract Bull. Lan and Belynda hit the ground and rolled away.

Dropping to his knee, Stefan steadied the shotgun and fired, blasting twelve-gauge lead *shot* from the top barrel. The projectiles tore into Bull's gut and knocked him against a tree trunk.

As if in disbelief, Bull gaped at his exposed intestines, his lips quivering. Blood gurgled from his throat down his chest. Bloodied hundred dollar bills full of holes lay strewn around him.

Bull slumped to a sitting position like a once-cocky felon found guilty. Stefan rose and limped forward.

"How does someone become a man like you?" he demanded.

"God and country . . ." Bull's head lolled side to side.

"God and country, my ass. You're done. Any last words?"

"Tell . . . Crandle and OT I'm . . . I'm sorry."

"For?"

"Not . . . not killing you bastards."

"That's it, then?" Stefan asked.

"Oh, God, I didn't want it to end like this." Bull was sweating profusely. Color drained from his face. "Please, I'm hurtin' bad. Don't let me suffer no more . . ." Bull moaned in an emotion-choked voice.

Stefan pulled the trigger. This time the muzzle flash flared from the shotgun's under barrel. More lead *shot* riddled Bull's chest. Shocked at what he'd done, Stefan gawked at the body. An undercurrent of shame swept over him.

Belynda came to his side. She took the shotgun from him and offered her shoulder for him to lean on. "You had to do it."

Lan, too, approached. "You saved our lives. Your father will be proud."

Stefan managed a grim smile. He was embarrassed by their nakedness but comforted by the warmth of their words and presence. He tried to imagine how scared and vulnerable Lan and Belynda must be feeling. And he wanted to . . . "Oh, God." The pain arced from synapse to synapse from his leg, up his spine, and to his brain.

Lan and Belynda led him further away from the fire and laid him on the ground. They elevated his wounded leg on a patio stool, his pants leg plastered to his skin by sticky blood. Lan tended to his wound while Belynda went to search for a water hose.

"I believe the bullet missed the femoral artery," Lan said, "and help is on the way." She cupped his cheeks with her hands, and said, "I am going to make you a Purple Heart and a Silver Star."

Seventy-Nine

Wednesday, 0730 Hours M Time, 28 October 2009, Border Slot Compound

A flicker of hope ignited in Kannon as he watched Kim soar off the cliff edge into a clear, blue sky. Seconds later, a lump formed in his throat as Kim, like a fledgling falcon kicked from its nest, struggled to maintain control.

Thermals caused by rising warm air mixing with thinner cold air above were wreaking havoc with Kim's flight. Had any of the militiamen noticed? With their attention focused on the killing field, it appeared not. Any minute, though, the Border Slot militia would complete their setup, then march him and Đăng Đạo to the killing field.

Kannon silently urged Kim on as he tacked between port and starboard, trying to stabilize the paraglider.

"Đăng Đạo," Kannon whispered. "Look up."

His nephew raised his head. "We are not done."

"We're not."

"Kim better have his damn weapon." Đăng Đạo's voice sounded as if his vocal cords were lined with sandpaper.

"I'm sure he does. I'm just worried he might slam into the cliff face."

"Still got the nine mil?"

"Inside the boot." Even if he could access the weapon, seven rounds wouldn't offer much fire support.

Kannon noticed Kim bank away from the cliff toward the eastern tree line. He steadied his rig and gathered speed, racing through the air. If Kim landed undetected within the trees, it would take him several minutes to trudge across the snow-covered ground and reach the compound. His effort, though admirable, might come too late and only provide another victim for Crandle's vicious game.

"They are coming for us," Đăng Đạo said.

Reality . . . we are outmanned and outgunned. This is it. Quán has been blown to bits. My brother Roger is dead. Derrick, if he survives, will become a victim of Stockholm Syndrome. The rest of us will die, and Lan will join the ranks of broken-hearted widows.

The militiamen marched in formation, rifles at right-shoulder arms, Whitehead counting cadence in a quiet, solemn tone. A German Shepherd accompanied them.

Whitehead halted his men. "Brick, sit." The dog sat on its haunches.

"It's time," Whitehead said.

Heaven is for good people. Am I good enough to get in? Well, maybe God will be in a good mood today.

The militiamen broke ranks and surrounded Kannon and his nephew. Two men loosened the ropes binding them to the trees. Whitehead formed a double column, three men on either side, and positioned Kannon and Đăng Đạo in the middle.

"Forward, march."

Feeling stiff and sore, Kannon could barely move, but his hands were free. As he flexed them, he and his nephew exchanged a glance.

"You don't have to do this," Kannon said to Whitehead.

"Shut up, motherfucker. No talking in formation. Another word and I'll tape your fucking mouth shut."

Kannon turned abruptly and caught Whitehead's eye. As before, malice wasn't reflected in his face, but then the militiaman averted his eyes. Whitehead's tone, the expression on his face, puzzled Kannon. He wondered again if a militant could feel shame? If so, no one showed the guts to change the direction of the pending execution.

The formation trooped forward, boots on the crusty ground the only sound. Kannon worked his limbs as best he could, wishing the march would last forever.

Five modified skeet throwers were lined up and ready to go. Each projectile arm contained a six-inch, razor-sharp glass disc, with additional discs stacked in autoloaders.

"We are about to be sliced apart," Đăng Đạo said.

Crandle strode from the compound area, wearing unrecognizable medals on a field jacket—*must've designed them himself.* The *Commander* surveyed the field and then addressed his

423

men. "Well done."

Kannon thought again about appealing to the *Commander's* good side. Hell! There was no good side. Baiting him hadn't worked. Maybe it was time to accept his fate.

"Have your fun with me, Crandle. Just let Đăng Đạo return my son to his mother."

Crandle smirked and stepped aside. There to the rear stood Derrick, outfitted in camouflage fatigues for God's sake.

"Daddy K!"

"Only a coward could do what you've doing to my son."

"I'm teaching Patu to obey."

"Don't put him through this," Kannon said in a cry of anguish.

"Ah, but he will watch, every bloody second while you bleed out. I've lost three men because of you, including one who died because of this little shit. Never have I wanted to watch a man die more."

Eighty

Agony ripped Kannon's soul. Blinding pain pulsated inside his head. Rage boiled away any tears he might shed.

Đăng Đạo, a glazed look on his face, stood beside him as they waited to be escorted onto the killing field. Nearby, Derrick was crying uncontrollably, his tears staining the camouflage fatigues Crandle made him wear.

"Don't force my son to watch this!"

"Ah, but I am." Crandle was sitting on a makeshift bench beneath a canvas awning, puffing on a cigar.

"You're one sick devil."

"To the contrary, God and I are one," Crandle said. To Whitehead, "Give these two a practice round."

"The velocity's set at one-hundred-forty feet per second," Whitehead said to Kannon and Đăng Đạo.

"That's ninety-five miles an hour," Crandle added.

Whitehead pointed at one militiaman, who broke from formation and kneeled behind the control console. The remaining five militiamen stood at port arms behind Kannon and Đăng Đạo.

In unison, five glass discs sliced through the crisp air.

Christ!

"Trời ơi," Đăng Đạo said, his mouth agape.

Kannon faced him. He needed to steady his nephew. "Think of it like dodging a hard tennis serve. You stand a better chance because you're younger."

A sardonic smile crossed Đăng Đạo's face. "We dodge the discs . . . then what?"

Then what indeed?

"I am proud to know you, Kannon Ballard," Đăng Đạo said.

"I'm honored to have known your father . . . and now you."

Kannon's limbs were tight. Every movement hurt. Even if in his best condition, Kannon couldn't access his handgun quickly enough before being riddled with bullets.

"Have fun, boys." Crandle's guttural laugh was sadistic, derisive, condescending, and arrogant.

"May you fall into a den of pit vipers," Đăng Đạo said, his glare capable of smelting iron.

"No matter what happens, Crandle, you're finished," Kannon added.

"Listen up, assholes." Crandle stood and picked up a coiled lariat, looped it around Kannon's neck, and jerked him forward. "I'm taking the world back to where it belongs. No one's stopping me."

"Why do you not just shoot us, Neanderthal man?" Đăng Đạo spat at Crandle's feet.

"It's not as much fun, Gook."

"I've got an implanted tracking device. The Feds have your coordinates." Kannon realized his tone lacked conviction.

Crandle's eyes widened for a moment. "Then where are they? You're fucking bluffing."

"You'll see."

"Bleed well, my friends." Crandle lifted the coiled lariat from around Kannon's neck.

Whitehead nodded toward the field. The militiamen broke formation. Two trotted forward. The guy at the controller maintained his post while the other three trained their rifles at Kannon and Đăng Đạo.

"Derrick," Kannon said, his voice choking, "always remember your mother and I love you."

"Daddy K, I want you safe. I want Mama Lan. I want to go home." Derrick, his little body trembling, puffed out his cheeks and made his trying-not-to-cry face.

The two militiamen, with Brick alongside, grabbed Kannon and Đăng Đạo by the elbows and shoved them onto the field. His nephew shook off the grip, held his head high, and marched forward. Out of the corner of his eye, Kannon saw Anh approach Derrick from the direction of Crandle's cabin and pick up the boy.

As a diversion . . . Kannon pretended to stumble, tried to reach his handgun, but was jerked upright.

"The boy is not watching this," Kannon heard Anh say.

Crandle turned. "Put Patu down and get your ass back to the cabin."

"Go to hell."

"McAfee, get behind the bitch. Make her and the boy watch."

"Yes, sir!" McAfee double-timed and moved in behind the two. He grabbed each by the hair and yanked downward, wrenching their faces up toward the killing field.

"Close your eyes, son!" Kannon understood those might be the last words he ever spoke to Derrick.

"Get those guys in position," Crandle said to the two militiamen escorting Kannon and Đăng Đạo.

They led them to the center of the field, about fifty feet from the launchers, and trotted off toward the berm. Steel mesh screens formed the eastern, southern, and northern boundaries. The one possible exit led through the row of machines, a futile effort because a fusillade would cut them down.

He and his nephew edged to the rear while the two escorts returned to the throwing platform, joining their mates.

"Stay balanced on the balls of your feet," Kannon said.

Holding their rifles at port arms, three militiamen positioned themselves behind the five launchers. A fourth, his eyes glued on Crandle, sat at the controller, the guard dog at his side. Whitehead, his jaw bulging with a chew, stood beside Crandle, who was blowing smoke rings. He raised his arm, then lowered it.

The catapults released their projectiles. Killing spinners shot toward them. Like bailing away from a high inside fastball as he had advised Đăng Đạo to do, Kannon hop-skipped sideways. His nephew mirrored the move in the opposite direction.

Kannon barely had time to catch his breath before a second round launched. He flung himself to the frozen ground and slid beneath a disc that whistled above his flattened body like an artillery shell. It shattered against the backstop.

"Đăng Đạo, are you—"

"I am okay," Đăng Đạo said.

Bullets peppered the ground.

"Stand up, you fucking cowards," Crandle shouted.

"Screw you!" Kannon hollered back.

"Can Crandle adjust those damn things?" Đăng Đạo asked.

"Move the skeet throwers to the top of the berm and adjust the trajectory," Crandle commanded.

"There's your answer," Kannon said.

Once the militiamen executed Crandle's command, the controller adjusted the pitch angle of the throwing arms. The next salvo of discs sailed forth, but the trajectory was low and to their left. The discs skipped off the surface and ricocheted into the steel mesh screen.

Crandle hollered at the controller.

The time was now. The lull would be brief.

"Roll in front of me and get up slowly," Kannon said.

Đăng Đạo pretended to stumble. Kannon reached inside his boot, grabbed the weapon, and then rose in sync behind his nephew, the palm-sized pistol cupped in his hand. He engaged the slide to chamber a round and moved away from Đăng Đạo.

Crandle signaled as soon as the controller confirmed adjustment made. The next round of killer discs shot toward them. Kannon dodged on instinct, but a disc nipped his thigh. Still, he edged forward, past the centerline.

Another round launched. Đăng Đạo wailed but didn't fall.

Fearing he was still too far away for accuracy, Kannon moved to within twenty feet of the berm as a disc cut into the ice beside his leg with the damaged boot heel.

Militiamen exchanged glances as if inferring he was crazy.

Kannon halted and brought the Sig P238 to eye level. He snapped off a shot at the controller.

"Wolfhound's down," a militiaman hollered.

"Who fired that round?" Crandle yelled.

"Ballard!"

Brick broke loose and charged. Kannon felled him with another shot. Five rounds left. He glanced behind him and saw that Đăng Đạo had fallen. Damn! How badly was he hurt?

"How'd Ballard get a goddamn weapon?" Crandle sounded stunned.

"Must've come out his ass."

"Gun 'em down. Whitehead—"

An explosion rocked the bottom of the cliff.

"The armory," Crandle exclaimed. "We're under attack! McAfee, get your ass over there."

428

The armory is less than a hundred yards away.

Automatic weapons fire erupted from the front edge of the killing field at the base of the cliff. Kannon went prone. Two more of Crandle's men dropped, blood spurting from one guy's gut, the other collapsing from a black hole drilled into his forehead.

Who was shooting? It had to be Streak or Kim. They must've hooked up and executed a two-prong assault. With McAfee headed toward the armory, that left four militiamen present, including the two leaders.

Friendly fire continued from Kannon's right, pinning down Crandle and the others.

Kannon crawled toward his fallen nephew. He heard Crandle holler, "Maintain discipline, damnit! Return fire." His voice seethed with frustration.

Rounds sizzled over Kannon's head. Another explosion came from the direction of the armory. Militiamen ceased firing for a moment, then resumed. Keeping their heads down, Crandle's men propped their weapons on top of the berm and fired wildly. The rounds splayed everywhere, kicking up snow and pinging against the steel mesh.

Wild but dangerous.

"Smitty! Timmons! See what's happening with McAfee," Crandle yelled. "We'll take care of these bastards. Whitehead! Get it done!"

Smitty and Timmons sped off, their boots tossing clumps of snow in their wake. Kannon wished his man shooting at the edge of the killing field could cut them down, but the berm shielded them.

Now, only Crandle and Whitehead remained as immediate threats.

Kannon continued low crawling and reached Đăng Đạo, who lay in a shallow depression. He noticed a crude tourniquet wrapped around his nephew's forearm. "You hurt bad?"

"It is all right. I will not bleed to death." He stared at Kannon. "Your thigh—"

"Just a scratch."

Staccato bursts from AKs sounded like hail storming a tin roof. As Kannon helped Đăng Đạo secure his tourniquet, rounds

429

zipped overhead and passed through the steel mesh or bore into the frozen turf.

"Oh, no. Look!" Đăng Đạo grabbed Kannon's arm.

Derrick had broken loose and was running toward the field, exposed, with Anh clumping through the ice and snow trying to corral him.

Kannon rose. "Derrick. Go back! Go back!"

His son kept running.

"Hold your fire! Hold your fire!" Kannon yelled. "My son's in the open."

The supporting firing ceased. Anh snagged Derrick and shoved him to the ground.

"Cover me," Kannon heard Crandle say.

The *Commander* rose to a crouch and charged toward Derrick and Anh. Whitehead, too, rose. Retreating, he kept his back to Crandle's while firing his automatic rifle at Kannon. The rounds sailed high.

"It's now or never," Kannon said to his nephew. He, too, went into a crouch and scrambled to cover the roughly twenty yards to the berm.

"Crandle!" Kannon hollered.

The lead militiaman stopped and turned aside. Whitehead tripped over him, spraying a burst of bullets into the sky. Kannon raised his weapon. Crandle reached for his holstered pistol, but the snapped strap securing the sidearm hindered his draw.

Kannon squeezed the Sig's trigger just as the *Commander* grabbed Whitehead off the ground and jerked him into place as a human shield. The round slammed into Whitehead's chest. Eyes wide, mouth open, he slumped to the ground.

His nerves a bundle of adrenaline, Kannon cast darted looks for Derrick and Anh. No luck. They had vanished. At least they were out of the line of fire. But where had they gone?

Eighty-One

Pursue Crandle? Chase after Derrick?

Kannon was torn. Instinct told him to find his son, but he wouldn't leave Đăng Đạo exposed.

"Behind you," Đăng Đạo shouted.

Kannon whirled. The hairs on the back of his neck spiked. One of Crandle's men who had been ordered to the armory charged toward him. Kannon raised his Sig, but the slide was locked open. He had spent his one magazine.

Now on his feet, Đăng Đạo was rushing forward but didn't possess a weapon. The militiaman, who Kannon figured must be Smitty, switched his gaze from Kannon to his nephew as if unsure which one to shoot first.

Out of the corner of his eye, Kannon saw Kim emerge from the path between the cliff wall and northwestern edge of the killing field, carrying his AK47 at port arms. He couldn't shoot because Kannon stood in his direct line of fire.

Smitty aimed at Kannon.

"Hey, hey!" Kim shouted, distracting Smitty.

The militiaman turned and fired a burst at Kim.

"Trời ơi! I've been hit."

Damnit!

Smitty turned away from Kim and Đăng Đạo, shifting his attention back to Kannon. The militiaman pulled the trigger, but the AK didn't fire. He released the magazine and reached into a pouch to grab another. Kannon did the only thing he could. He charged Smitty, who dropped the rifle and withdrew a long knife.

"You're going to die," Smitty hissed. He brandished the knife and lunged.

Squaring his shoulders, Kannon parried the blow with his left arm and raked his Sig across the militiaman's face. For all the effect it had, he might as well have kissed him on the cheek. Smitty thrust again. Kannon warded it off.

Despite his wounded forearm, Đăng Đạo charged in, feinting left, right, stooping, rising, snapping kicks, using finger jabs like flint-

431

tipped spears. Smitty was small, but quick and wiry, avoiding contact. His eyes were lit up like a wolf's, counting on a kill. He thrust his knife again, first at Đăng Đạo, then at Kannon.

Gasping, on rubbery legs, Kannon could barely catch his breath. His balance was affected by the shattered boot heel, and his adrenaline was fading.

"Get Whitehead's weapon," Đăng Đạo said. "I will take care of this poor excuse for a man."

Kannon hesitated.

"Go," his nephew said again.

His nephew's command finally registered. Additional militiamen might return.

Kannon backpedaled and picked up Whitehead's AK. He darted glances between the cabins and the cliff, then spun toward the chopper pad. Seeing no threat, Kannon rotated back to fixate on his nephew's battle.

Đăng Đạo, too, appeared to be running out of steam. Kannon steadied the rifle, but the combatants' gyrations prevented a clear shot. His nephew dropped to one knee, his head bowed. Smitty seized the opportunity. He cocked his elbow and swung down at Đăng Đạo's neck. Kannon fingered the trigger just as his nephew grabbed Smitty's outstretched arm, snap-kicked him in the stomach, and flipped him over his shoulder. The militiaman went down hard, conscious, but with the breath knocked out of him. Đăng Đạo leaped on Smitty, grabbed the knife, and plunged it deep into the militiaman's chest.

Kannon removed his finger from the trigger and set the AK down. There was no need to shoot. Panting, he leaned over and rested his hands on his knees. A moment later, he looked to Đăng Đạo and said, "Quite a feint you pulled there."

"I am a ninja."

"Christ! Your arm is soaked in blood. You need a medic."

"I will seek aid later. First, I must see about Kim."

"Right," Kannon said.

He surveyed the compound, the dense forest, and considered the condition of his two team members, who were in no condition to help. It was his to do alone. "I'm going after Derrick."

"Wait!" Đăng Đạo grabbed Kannon's arm. "Your thinking is

muddy. The *Commander* most likely has your son now. He wants you to pursue."

"No choice. I've got to save Derrick."

"Getting ambushed will not do it," Đăng Đạo said. "Crandle is out there . . . with lots of bullets."

Bile clogged Kannon's throat. He'd been so close, ten yards away from Derrick. But his nephew was right. *Restraint!* Cold, fatigue, and mental fog had clouded his clarity.

"Thanks for holding me back," Kannon said, *as well as for your toughness.*

Đăng Đạo relaxed his grip. "Drink some water. Calm down."

"Okay."

As his nephew turned to check on the fallen Kim, Kannon found a full canteen left by one of the men. He unscrewed the top and drank heavily, then, rehydrated, capped the canteen.

Kannon pivoted in time to see Kim limping forward, an arm draped around Đăng Đạo's shoulder. The two collapsed on the ground once they reached him, Kim offering nothing but a grimace. Despite the sun, a shiny layer of ice glazed Kim's cap and jacket. How long had he been sitting in the cold?

"How bad?" Kannon asked.

"He has a leg wound," Đăng Đạo said. "I will take care of it."

"Great job, Kim. You saved our asses." Kannon ached for him because soon he would learn his brother Quán had been killed.

As Đăng Đạo reached for the canteen, Kannon glanced toward Crandle's cabin. "The explosion at the armory, did you—"

Kim shook his head and pointed in that direction. "Streak Man set a time-delay fuse with C-4 . . . Boom!"

Kannon spun to his left. Two men, hands clasped behind uncovered heads, trudged on wobbly legs in their direction, Streak behind them, an AK supported by a sling over one shoulder. A duffle bag dangled from the other.

"Streak Man!" Đăng Đạo said, raising his eyebrows.

"Damn, it's good to see you." Kannon never thought he'd say that. "I was afraid—"

"That I'd run! No chance."

Kim and Streak fist bumped.

"This one's McAfee. He's Timmons." Streak pointed from one to the other. "Hit the prone position, arms and legs spread."

Streak's earlier descriptions of McAfee and Timmons were spot on. McAfee's leathery appearance fit the environment. He was a couple of inches taller than Đăng Đạo and probably just as wiry. Timmons, by contrast, equaled Kannon's height, had smooth, pale skin, and piercing eyes. As Streak said, Timmons was built like a college tight end. Both wore fatigues and Nazi-style buzz cuts.

"How did you get control of them?" Kannon asked.

"You heard the second explosion, right?"

Kannon nodded.

"Got in behind them. Lobbed a flash-bang grenade."

"Good work." Kannon clapped Streak on the shoulder. "Based upon what Đăng Đạo told me, I figured you were out of commission."

"I was only out a few minutes. I didn't know where the hell I was at first. When my mind cleared, I crawled from underneath the bed and left the cabin. I saw you and Đăng Đạo were laid out and knew we were in trouble. But I had my radio and was able to contact Kim."

"Again, well done." Then Kannon brought Streak up to date.

"So, only Crandle remains unaccounted for," Streak said, setting the duffle bag down.

"Secure the prisoners," Kannon said. "I'm going to check on Whitehead."

"He took the bullet meant for Crandle," Đăng Đạo said.

"Not surprised," Streak said, rummaging in the duffle.

Swallowing hard, Kannon left the group and approached the fallen Whitehead. Raspy breath escaped from the wounded man's mouth. His eyes glazed over, and blood oozed from his stomach wound. Despite all that had happened, Kannon's humanity kicked in.

"You're dying," Kannon said. If he were Catholic, he'd make the sign of the Cross. "Clean it up while you can."

Whitehead's lips trembled. He looked up at Kannon. "I'm . . . I'm sorry about your son."

"Crandle . . . where would he go?"

"Tunnel . . ." Whitehead mumbled. "Tell the commander . . . to go to hell." Whitehead gasped his last.

Eighty-Two

Wednesday, 0640 C Time, 28 October 2009, Texas Hill Country

Tears rolled down Lan's cheeks as she watched firefighters search through the rubble. Clad in protective equipment, they had extinguished the blaze, but the structure of her home was a smoldering shell.

She had been clinging to her new life as she once had clung to her first family and home in Việt Nam. That was long ago, and all were gone. Would she once more lose everything?

"We'll salvage what we can, ma'am, during our investigation," one of the firefighters had said.

Investigation. What needed to be investigated? It was obvious her Volkswagen bug was the cause of the explosion. That and the gasoline-doused windows set aflame by the militiaman, as another firefighter had told her.

Bull! The chill from the rape attempt washed over Lan like a tsunami. His militant savagery did not surprise her. She had seen it all before. It was just that she did not expect to find this kind of violence in America. One war was one too many. No one was safe anymore.

Seeking solace, Lan gazed at Belynda, who was standing alongside Stefan's gurney near one of the ambulances. An EMT stood over him, dressing his wound, while another held a syringe.

Belynda strode over in an awkward gait. Both she and her friend were wrapped in blankets an EMT had provided to cover their nakedness. Both had burn marks on their skin from the violent way Bull had torn off their clothes, which were too ragged to wear.

"The EMT said Stefan was lucky. The bullet missed the major artery," Belynda said.

"Thank God!"

"He has something to show you."

"All right."

"How're you holding up?" Belynda asked.

"I have lost my home, perhaps my husband, my son, my nephew. Derrick's toys and games—the models he had *helped* build

435

with his father—my husband's memorabilia. My mementos . . . I feel so empty . . . violated."

Frustrated at not being allowed inside the cordoned-off area, Lan paused, turned, and looked back at her burned-out home. Her treasured piano was nothing but ashes, fused keys, and a jumble of wires.

One investigator was snapping photographs, while others sifted ashes and probed the remains with various tools. She understood they were following protocol, that it was too dangerous to enter, but she wanted to search for undamaged items, three in particular.

"I know you're down, but it could've been worse. You're alive. We're alive. We could've been raped, but we weren't."

Lan snapped too. She loosened her grip on the wraparound blanket, leaned toward Belynda, and kissed her on the cheek. And then behind a tearful smile, "You are right. It could have been much worse. I am sorry for being selfish. If not for you and Stefan—"

"And Kannon. Has your husband ever not come through?"

"I have faith in him," Lan said, her chin quivering.

"So do I. Look, you'll get past all this."

"You are a jewel," Lan said, brightening. "I wonder what Stefan has to show."

Her stepson sat up once they reached him.

"Idiot," Lan heard Belynda mumble. "Stay down."

"You are badly hurt," Lan said. "Do as she says."

"The morphine is kicking in," Stefan said with a lisp. His eyes were glazed over, his face the color of paste.

"Your contorted expression says otherwise," Belynda said.

"Wait." Stefan reached underneath the sheet covering the lower part of his torso as if to grab something. He withdrew his hands and opened his palms.

"The curing dolls!" Lan clasped them. "Oh, my God. Thank you. Thank you."

Belynda cupped his neck and smiled. "Head down, Mister."

"In a moment. Lan, here's the burner phone I've been using. I think it's safe for you to call Kannon now."

Lan compressed her lips. Tears welled up in her eyes. Then

she gave him the *look* again . . . "For keeping the phone from me."

Sergeant Creighton approached.

"Stefan's a hero," Belynda said.

"If not for him, we might all be dead," Lan added.

"Got it," Creighton said. "I can't comment on much right now, but these militiamen are vicious bastards. Slaughtered Hamilton. Set your house on fire. Attempted to kill your stepson, rape you two." He stirred the ground with his foot, then gazed at Lan. "I'm glad your stepson killed the son of a bitch . . . off the record."

Off the record.

"Wherever your husband is, whatever he's doing, I hope he gets your son back."

"Thank you." Lan smiled as she fingered the curing dolls. "Deputy Creighton?"

"Yes?"

"I am sorry you lost Detective Hamilton."

Creighton nodded. "Yeah, he was a good man." He pulled a notepad from his pocket and flipped it open, jotted down a note, mumbling something about Sindy Zeller and that it was a messy business all around.

"Come on," Creighton said. "I'll have a deputy take possession of your stepson's car. You two get in the ambulance. Take care."

Belynda whispered to Lan, "I think he just apologized."

* * *

Inside the ambulance . . .

"How come there's no exit wound?" Stefan asked. "The man used a .45."

"Probably a dumdum bullet," the EMT said. "I'm a former combat medic. Whoever applied the tourniquet did the right thing."

Stefan grunted.

"You've had quite an ordeal. It's going take a while to patch you up, though."

"It's been a nightmare." And it wasn't over.

I've never killed a man. A justifiable kill by reason of self-defense? Will a grand jury agree? Is this what Dad has gone through? Is that what I'm going to go through?

Eighty-Three

Wednesday, 0825 Hours M Time, 28 October 2009, Border Slot Compound

After taking a final look at Whitehead's body, Kannon returned to his team, which was hunkered down behind the opposite side of the berm. Streak, the only uninjured member of his squad, tended to Đăng Đạo's and Kim's wounds.

Kannon moved behind the two prisoners, who were sitting cross-legged, their hands tied behind them. He tugged on their wrist-binding plastic flex-cuffs to be sure they were secure. Satisfied, he retrieved a fallen militiaman's rifle and gripped it so hard his knuckles turned white.

"I was this close to Crandle and let him get away."

"You did not let him escape." Đăng Đạo gave him a reproving look. "He had the upper hand."

"Yeah. But he sacrificed Whitehead. Imagine what he might do to Derrick."

"I know you are frustrated, but we will get him back." A pause . . . "You were an infantry officer. Act like one. Do not go off half-cocked."

Touché!

"As Đăng Đạo said, Crandle probably has Derrick." Streak finished bandaging Kim's wound. Kim rose and tested his injured leg. "Otherwise, Anh would've brought him to us."

"If she was able," Kannon said. "Maybe he took her too."

"Wish we knew," Streak said.

"Get anything out of Whitehead?" Đăng Đạo asked.

"Crandle has a tunnel. That's all I got out of him."

"A tunnel?" Streak arched his eyebrows. "Hmm . . . there was a sealed interior door at the far end of the armory. I didn't think about it at the time."

"Could be a link," Kannon said, knowing Streak had never been inside the armory before. He adjusted Đăng Đạo's tourniquet. "If you guys need a medevac, Streak can fly you out of here now."

"I'm good," Kim said.

"Me too," Đăng Đạo chipped in.

Thank God. I need these men.

"About the tunnel," Kannon said, "has Crandle ever mentioned an escape route?"

"Maybe those two know." Streak jerked his thumb toward the prisoners.

Kannon knelt in front of McAfee and Timmons. "Where's Crandle?"

"Ask Whitehead," McAfee said.

Timmons snickered.

"Might improve their memory if I cut off a finger or two," Kim said, brandishing a knife.

"Don't touch me, you fuckin' gook."

Kim raked the blade across Timmons' skull. It left a nice red crease.

"You're dead, you slant-eyed fucker," Timmons said.

"Shoulda never let gooks in the country," McAfee added.

Đăng Đạo kicked McAfee in the chest and knocked him on his back.

"You don't know who you're dealing with," Timmons said.

"You don't either," Kannon countered.

"We don't know where the fuck the Commander is," McAfee said in a muffled voice.

"We will get nothing from them," Đăng Đạo said.

"Next stop is Crandle's cabin," Kannon said, rising. "No telling what we'll find in there." He looked at Streak. "What's in the duffle?"

"Colt .45s, ammo, tear gas canisters, smoke and concussion grenades, frags, night goggles." Streak reached inside the duffle and pulled out two gleaming .45s equipped with laser sights. He handed one to Đăng Đạo, who stuck it in his waistband, and offered the other to Kannon.

"Wait one."

Before taking the pistol, Kannon ripped away McAfee's pistol belt and buckled it around his waist. Then he took the .45, jacked a round into the chamber, placed the pistol on safe, and holstered the weapon. Streak handed each of them extra clips.

"Other than the interior door, you notice anything else in the armory?" Kannon asked.

"Sizable bombs. A large safe."

"More EMP weapons, more money, I imagine." Đăng Đạo said. He tested his arm injury by tossing a knife between McAfee's legs.

"About the prisoners?" Streak asked.

Kannon cast a disparaging look.

"Ought to let the bastards freeze to death, but yeah, bring 'em."

"Fuck you," Timmons said.

"I'm tired of hearing this crap. Gag 'em." Kannon grabbed the duffle.

Streak dipped into each man's rear pocket and fished out a bandanna. "Uniform of the day." He stuffed the kerchiefs in their mouths and secured them with duct tape. Then he grabbed hold of Timmons and pulled him upright.

Kannon yanked McAfee to his feet. The movement amplified the throbbing in his pistol-whipped, bullet-grazed skull and the sharp ache from the wound in his side.

His satphone buzzed. It was from Stefan's burner. "I need to take this."

Đăng Đạo and Streak stood guard.

"You okay?" Kannon asked.

"Yes."

"Lan?" That was a hesitant yes. Why hadn't Stefan called? he wondered. "Something's wrong. I hear it in your voice."

"What about . . . what about our boy?"

"We're closing in, Lan. I don't have time to talk."

"All, all . . . right." A pause. "But—"

"But what?"

"The Militia launched at an attack. A man called Bull is dead. Stefan saved us."

Lan's tone and hesitation suggested she had more to say.

"Stefan was hurt, wasn't he!"

"Yes."

"How bad?"

"He suffered a leg wound. The medics have taken him to the hospital. Belynda is with him. He is you, Kannon. He will be all right."

No time to think about that now.

"I need a bargaining chip. Call me back and leave a message about the militia's failure and Bull's death. Gotta go."

Empowered by the news, Kannon motioned the team forward. His legs regained stability as he hustled across the frozen ground. At the fork in the trail where one prong led to the armory and the other to Crandle's cabin, Kannon paused to visualize the compound's layout as depicted in Streak's drawing. Once satisfied, he moved on.

Kannon halted at the front door. If there was an element of surprise left, Crandle held it.

"What if the cabin's been booby-trapped?"

"I do not think Crandle has had time to set booby-traps," Đăng Đạo said.

"I agree," Streak added.

Kannon stared at them both. "You're probably right." He shoved McAfee and Timmons aside, unslung his rifle, and fired a burst. The lock shattered, and he kicked the door open.

"After you," he told the two militiamen.

Neither man budged.

Streak kicked McAfee's ass and sent him sprawling past the doorway. Kannon muscled Timmons inside. A hail of bullets didn't come.

A quick search cleared the den. Above the fireplace hung the words, *Posse Comitatus.* A framed photograph of a smiling young boy hung underneath their mantra.

"Crandle's son," Streak said.

"What a waste," Kannon said, shaking his head. He leaned his rifle against the wall and drew the .45. "Đăng Đạo, come with me. Streak, you and Kim stay put and guard these guys."

Kannon led the way along the short hallway to Anh's room. He opened the door and entered.

The hair on the back of Kannon's neck stood on end.

"Oh, my God," Đăng Đạo said.

Eighty-Four

The Vietnamese woman lay on the bed, either unconscious or dead. Purple bruises and ugly lacerations masked her face. Her body was crumpled, one leg bent at an awkward angle. Kannon rushed forward, placed his index finger on her neck, and felt for a pulse. There was one, steady and rhythmic. Anh moaned, moved her head. Her eyelids fluttered.

"She's alive. Stay with her, Đăng Đạo."

Dropping to the floor, Kannon searched underneath Anh's bed, his chest as tight as a wound spring. No Derrick. Rising, he walked to the closet and pulled the door open, hoping to find his son alive, even if cowering in a corner. No Derrick, just a few clothes hanging from a rod.

He approached the bathroom as if an IED might blow once he entered. Slowly, he pushed the door open. He ran his hands over the door jamb and along the threshold. No wires. Inside, a shower curtain shielded the tub. Did his son lie behind it? Cut up? Drowned? Kannon tore the curtain aside, expecting the worst. The tub was vacant. He didn't know whether to feel relieved or more anxious.

He grabbed a washcloth, wet it, and brought it to Đăng Đạo. "Derrick's not here."

His nephew compressed his lips as if in understanding, then took the cloth and gently wiped Anh's face. "*Hãy tỉnh dậy, người phụ nữ ngọt ngào và tốt.*" (Please wake up, sweet and good woman.)

"*Tôi ở trên trời?*" (Am I in heaven?)

"*Bạn đang còn sống và an toàn,*" Đăng Đạo said, smiling. (You are alive and safe.)

"She thought she had died," his nephew told Kannon.

The pair continued speaking in Vietnamese until Kannon's sense of urgency nearly leaped out his throat. *Translate! Translate!*

Finally, his nephew raised his head. "Crandle has your son. She thinks he took him to this tunnel complex Whitehead mentioned. Anh also revealed the location of the key to Crandle's ham shack."

"Good."

Anh spoke again. Đăng Đạo listened. "She says inside the

study, in the open space beneath the desktop, there is a remote-control switch on the baseboard. Flip the switch. A trap door, hidden by a rug, opens. A ladder leads down. Anh says she has never been below but thinks there may be another exit."

Kannon stroked his chin, recalling Streak's comment about the inside door within the armory. "Ask her whether she has any idea where the exit might be."

Đăng Đạo did. He turned and shook his head.

"Hell, there could be innumerable doors leading to mineshafts, and who knows where else," Kannon said.

Anh pulled Đăng Đạo close. He listened and nodded, then motioned for Kannon to grab a pad and pencil off Anh's night table. His nephew wrote something down and handed it over.

"It is a code, but she is unsure what it is for," Đăng Đạo said.

"Or a combination." Kannon put it in his shirt pocket. "Bring McAfee and Timmons in here," he shouted to Streak and Kim.

Streak arrived with Kannon's AK and the two prisoners. Kim trailed behind. He didn't look good.

Kannon herded McAfee and Timmons to a corner. Both militiamen wore looks of steel. Regardless, he needed one of them to accompany him into the tunnel. He glared at McAfee. "You owe me for the torture you gleefully participated in. You're coming along." Besides, McAfee was shorter. Kannon could see over his shoulder.

The militiaman's face turned red and his pupils dilated. Kannon took him aside and tightened the gag, then stole another look at Kim, who was favoring his leg wound. "Are you all right?"

Kim nodded, but the look on his face expressed what hadn't been verbalized. *Where is my brother Quán?* Kannon thought about Roger, but now was not the time to mourn.

"Kim, are you good to guard this piece of shit?" Kannon forced Timmons into a kneeling position facing the wall.

"I am, sir."

"If he moves, shoot him."

Timmons turned his head.

"No shoot. Castrate," Kim said, brandishing a knife.

Timmons' glower said, *Screw you.*

Kannon addressed his other two men. "Streak, cover the

chopper pad. Đăng Đạo, you're with me."

"On it," Streak said, hustling from the room.

Kannon turned to the duffle bag. Rifling through it, he retrieved two smoke grenades and clipped them to his pistol belt. Any other types of grenades could seriously injure or kill Derrick. A pair of night vision goggles, Armasight N-15s, caught his eye. After selecting a couple more magazines and a small flashlight, he slid the bag toward his nephew.

Đăng Đạo plucked out another N-15 unit. "I am taking the duffle along. It has other stuff we might need."

"Like C-4?"

Đăng Đạo nodded.

Kannon shoved McAfee ahead.

"To Crandle's bedroom."

Đăng Đạo trailed behind. At Crandle's bedroom door, Kannon reached around McAfee, flung open the door, and pushed him inside.

"Clear the room," Kannon said to Đăng Đạo.

Kannon stared at McAfee, who averted his eyes. Even though the militiaman was gagged and his hands were tied behind his back, Kannon remained guarded. He stepped away and took notice of Crandle's wall-mounted memorabilia: yellowed pictures of white-hooded clansmen, Samurai swords, a Nazi flag, and what appeared to be family photos.

"All clear," Đăng Đạo said. "But the key to the ham shack is gone."

"Which means he's either in the study or gone down below."

At the door to the ham shack, Kannon noticed only a standard dead-bolt lock secured it. As he'd done at the front door to Crandle's cabin, Kannon unleashed a burst from the AK47, which shattered the wooden door frame around the lock. There was little need for stealth now.

He nudged McAfee forward. "Into the ham shack." Once inside, "In the corner, on your knees, face against the wall."

The ham shack was small, orderly, and vacant, which Kannon expected. A sophisticated-looking ham radio set occupied the desk. The trap door was uncovered. And there was a sizable wall safe.

"You think the code Anh gave us is the combination to this

safe?" Đăng Đạo asked.

"Maybe." Kannon removed the slip of paper from his pocket and handed it to his nephew. "Check it out. Be careful. Could be wired."

"Right!" His nephew examined the safe closely, eyeballed it, then ran his fingers over the seams. "Clear."

The safe had a standard dial. The slip of paper contained four two-digit numbers.

"Try the standard turns, four left, three right, two left, one right," Kannon said.

As Đăng Đạo worked at the wall safe, Kannon pulled out the desk chair and knelt. There, just above the baseboard, was the release. He flicked it. A latch clicked. Kannon shuffled from underneath the desk and stood. The trap door had popped open.

His nephew uttered an exclamation.

"What is it?" Kannon asked.

"Money. Lots of it."

"Bag it."

Kannon rifled the desk drawers, wondering whether Crandle might have a laptop stashed away, even though Streak had said there were no computers.

"I'll be dammed. He does have a laptop."

"Wonder what's on it?" Đăng Đạo swept the remaining contents of the safe into the duffle.

"No time to examine it now. We've already spent too much time here." Kannon placed the laptop into the duffle, then shuffled to the trapdoor. He raised it and peered into an abyss, then glanced at his nephew.

"I'm going down. Watch McAfee."

"You should not go alone." Đăng Đạo hiked up his shoulders.

"You're wounded. No idea what I'll find down there. Besides, I have insurance." Kannon nodded at McAfee.

"You need an insurance rider. I am going with you."

Kannon appreciated his nephew's attitude and couldn't help smiling.

"Okay."

"Crandle sacrificed Whitehead," Đăng Đạo said, grabbing

McAfee's arm. "He will do the same to you."

McAfee's eyes opened wider.

"I'm removing your gag," Kannon said. "If you're smart, you'll reveal something useful."

"Good idea," Đăng Đạo said.

The militiaman coughed up phlegm and spit.

"Where do you think the tunnel leads?" Kannon asked.

"Guess, asshole."

"You should reconsider. We told you how Whitehead died."

"That's bullshit, man. Didn't see it. Don't believe it. He wouldn't betray any of us, much less Whitehead."

"Yeah? How come your eyes locked wide open at the news? It's all about Crandle. He's abandoned the ship. Deep down, you know that's true."

"Yeah, I thought about it but discarded the idea. I've seen how Crandle treated Whitehead. He wouldn't sacrifice him."

"Keep on believing that," Kannon said.

"You're fucked, Ballard. Kid's already dead. Give it up."

The comment jolted Kannon. It clouded his hope about Crandle leaving Derrick behind in his effort to escape. At this point, all he wanted was his son.

McAfee adopted a bemused expression as he gazed into the opening. "Crandle! The assholes are entering—"

Đăng Đạo snapped a side kick into McAfee's gut. He folded like a collapsed accordion.

Accepting he wasn't going to get anything out of him, Kannon replaced the gag. "Your *Commander's* not going to help," he said.

Kannon shined his flash down the iron-railed ladder, only to see the beam disappear in the darkness below.

Eighty-Five

Was the tunnel booby-trapped? Was Crandle lying in ambush? The questions flowed like hot lava through Kannon's consciousness. "After you," he said to McAfee. "Good luck climbing down with your hands tied behind your back."

The gag muffled McAfee's protest.

"Move it, or I'll throw your ass down there."

With his back to the ladder, the militiaman stepped on the first rung, then the second, catching one heel on each rung, then leaning against the ladder to steady himself before taking the next step. Not an easy task.

McAfee slipped, sounded a muffled curse, but regained his balance. Next rung down, McAfee lost his footing and fell to the floor. Another muffled curse . . .

Tough shit!

"Hope he landed on his head," Đăng Đạo said.

Kannon slung his AK over his shoulder and again checked the load on his .45. His nephew did the same before picking up the duffle bag . . . and winced.

"Your arm's bothering you. Let me check things out first," Kannon said.

He began his descent but hesitated at the fifth rung. A faint glow appeared along the corridor, stretching into the darkness. A series of dome lights illuminated the tunnel, reminding him of subway station lighting, though much more subdued. Motion detectors, powered by generators or solar panels, must have activated the lights.

Kannon switched off the flashlight and let his eyes acclimate to the new environment before continuing. Ten rungs later, thirteen in all, he reached the floor.

McAfee sprang to his feet and rushed him as quick and graceful as a head-butting ram. Kannon sidestepped and used the militiaman's momentum to slam his head into the ladder. The resulting clang echoed along the tunnel as McAfee landed flat on his ass.

"Kannon, are you all right?" Đăng Đạo asked.

447

"Yeah." He drew his .45. "Get up, McAfee! You really don't want to live, do you!"

Đăng Đạo clambered down, lugging the duffle bag.

"At least there is no ambush or booby trap . . . yet," his nephew said.

"Let's hope," Kannon said.

The immediate interior was roughly the size of a large walk-in closet, with room enough to stand. The passageway was from six- to eight-feet wide. The air was fresh, not rancid as Kannon expected. Fresh air meant vents and circulation. Construction was impressive. Rough-hewn timber jacketed the walls and ceiling. The floor, absent mining cart tracks, was laid in concrete. Stout eight-by-eight tar-treated wooden columns discouraged cave-ins.

The tunnel darkened. Its overhead lights dimmed as if someone had rotated a dimmer switch. *Unnerving.* Kannon positioned the Armasight goggles over his eyes to accent the dim lighting. Đăng Đạo followed suit.

"If Crandle has video, we're screwed," Kannon said. He motioned for Đăng Đạo to stay put while he walked along the corridor to search for surveillance devices. Not seeing any after twenty yards, he abandoned the effort and returned to his partner.

"Let's go, McAfee. Double time!" Kannon said.

"Fuck you," came McAfee's muffled comment through his gag.

It was all Kannon could do to keep from pulling the trigger. He prodded McAfee forward, a reluctant point man in a mini-pincher movement. The militiaman stumbled, then eased into a trot. Kannon followed, his gait in this double-time shuffle hampered by his shattered boot heel and nicked leg from the disc on the killing range. Still, he settled into rhythmic breathing as they hustled forward. McAfee appeared like a bobbling specter through the bluish-green light filtering through the NVD.

Đăng Đạo, trailing behind, spoke up. "We have covered nearly sixty yards."

"Sounds about right. But it's hard to tell. This tunnel curves like a backcountry highway with tight curves."

"Probably following the ore veins," Đăng Đạo said. "I bet

Crandle has constructed a reinforced underground bunker complex, complete with amenities."

"You mean like Hitler?"

"Yes," Đăng Đạo said.

"If so, I imagine it's well fortified. Derrick could be hidden anywhere."

"We will find him."

We will. Alive or dead? If the latter, he couldn't comprehend how hard it would be to tell Lan.

Their tête-à-tête echoed along the tunnel, as did their footfalls. They covered another fifty, seventy-five yards.

Cooler air greeted them.

Night goggles afforded a limited peripheral view, about forty degrees. And it was out of that narrow, right-side periphery Kannon saw a child-sized lump nested against a supporting timber. His heart rate quickened. His legs turned leaden as he drew abreast.

"Stop, McAfee!" Kannon dug his fingernails into his palms as Đăng Đạo edged him aside. His nephew set the duffle down and knelt beside the find. He examined it. "Nothing but a bundled tarp."

Kannon relaxed his fists.

McAfee attempted a muffled laugh, then mumbled something like, "Too bad it wasn't your kid."

Đăng Đạo punched the militiaman in the right kidney. "Your parents must be proud."

"Take off these cuffs, cocksucker," came McAfee's mouth-full-of-marbles response.

"Knock it off," Kannon said. "For the record, Đăng Đạo would turn you into a pretzel."

The militiaman didn't respond.

The tunnel straightened, then sloped upward. *Damn! How long's this thing?* Twenty yards further, the tunnel forked.

"Check out the left fork," Kannon said. He handed his flash to Đăng Đạo.

Two minutes passed. It seemed like an eternity. His nephew returned, shaking his head. "It is a dead end. Granite."

Strange, Kannon thought. "Nothing? No concealed entrances? No mineshafts?"

449

"None that I noticed, although it is possible."

Kannon held up a finger. "Wait one. I hear a whirring sound."

"I hear it too," Đăng Đạo said, "from the right fork."

"Let's go." Kannon prodded McAfee forward.

The hum increased. Must be a generator. The tunnel terminated at a massive door, which was secured by a ten-digit keypad lock. McAfee faced Kannon, his eyes a demonic green, his gag probably concealing a smile.

Kannon threw the militiaman to the concrete floor.

"Anh's code," Đăng Đạo said, handing the paper over. "Could it work here?"

"I doubt it but will give it a try." Kannon entered the eight numbers in the sequence used to open the safe door, hoping for a miracle Crandle might've gotten lazy here. No luck. He reversed the sequence. No luck. "Must take a different code altogether."

"Damn!" Đăng Đạo said.

"We'll have to blow it."

"I wonder if this is the back door to the armory or if it leads to somewhere else," Đăng Đạo said.

"Christ! What if this is the armory door and Crandle has already gone through it . . . with Derrick? They could be racing toward the chopper pad now."

Damnit! Be ready, Streak.

Đăng Đạo dug out the C-4 from the duffle.

"You want to move McAfee?"

Kannon thought a moment. "I'd rather him blown up, but yeah."

"Roger that." Đăng Đạo retrieved another set of flex-cuffs from the duffle and secured McAfee's ankles, cinching them tight. They dragged him back, then returned to the door.

Kannon prepped the explosive, careful to slice off just enough from the malleable white brick to blow the door and not eviscerate themselves in the process. After plugging in a nonelectric blasting cap and detonation cord, he set the fuse and activated the fuse igniter.

"Fire-in-the-hole," Kannon said. They shuffled past McAfee, whose smoked eyes spoke hatred.

Five, Four, Three, Two, One, Zero . . . KABLAM!

450

Eighty-Six

Palms over his ears, Kannon waited until the sounds from the explosion ratcheting along the tunnel walls in a cacophony of distorted echoes tailed off.

An alarm blared. Lights flashed.

Once the clamor subsided, he and Đăng Đạo approached McAfee, who appeared dazed.

"Stay with him," Kannon said as he advanced.

Reaching the door, he found it clinging to its hinges and standing slightly ajar. Kannon lowered his profile and widened the door opening. The blended scent of plastic explosives and detritus filled the area. Floating debris settled like silt from a stirred-up river bottom, but an expected hail of gunfire didn't come. Why? Did the explosion incapacitate Crandle? Or was he just waiting? Or was he even there?

The air cleared. The interior wasn't an armory but a bunker.

A five-foot-high standalone barrier obstructed Kannon's view of the interior. It was a natural formation instead of a constructed one. The Positive: It shielded him from a direct line of fire. The Negative: The barrier extended from its center by several feet in both directions yet left about five yards of exposure at each end, which would funnel intruders into killing zones.

Regardless, he was tempted to enter the bunker on his own. *Stay disciplined.* Crandle could be barricaded behind the barrier, just waiting for Kannon to do something stupid. Scooting back, he stood alongside Đăng Đạo and described what he'd observed. Once done, he heard a scuffling. It was McAfee, rolling onto his back.

"Cut his ankle ties and get him on his feet," Kannon said.

Đăng Đạo did so.

Kannon circled behind McAfee, grabbed his hair, and jerked his head up. He noticed a Christian fish tattoo on the back of his neck, tainted by a blood-red X over it. An appropriate symbol for him, Kannon thought. He tightened the gag and ensured the bond securing McAfee's hands was firm. Gripping the militiaman's belt at the waist, Kannon pushed him ahead.

"Once you're inside," he whispered to McAfee, "you'll find out where Crandle's loyalty lies." To Đăng Đạo, "If Crandle opens up, go low and roll to the right side of the barrier."

"Got it."

Keeping one hand on McAfee's belt and the other flat against his back, Kannon shuffled the still-dazed militiaman in front of the blown door. McAfee grunted and struggled as Kannon shoved him through the opening. Multicolored strobes fired from within the bunker, lighting up the interior like a revolving sphere in a 1980s disco hall. Feeling discombobulated from the piercing lights, Kannon shucked his goggles.

A volley of shots rang out, seemingly from an elevated position. Blood squirted from McAfee's chest as if pumped from a fountain with multiple spigots. The militiaman collapsed into a heap.

Seizing advantage from the distraction, Kannon dove over McAfee and rolled left behind the barrier. Đăng Đạo, hugging the duffel, mirrored Kannon's move and rolled right.

"Crandle, you shot McAfee," Kannon yelled, hoping to rattle the *Commander*.

The laser art show ended, and a bank of ceiling-mounted floodlights flicked on, fully illuminating the granite cavern.

"What the hell!"

"Confirming McAfee's death," Đăng Đạo whispered.

Taking advantage of the lull, Kannon craned his neck to get a better look at the interior. The bunker was the size of a country barn. Opposite the rock barrier stood a twelve-foot-high loft, which extended the length of the shelter. The ends of at least nine three-tiered rows of shelving faced him.

Various propane-fed appliances, fuel drums, filing cabinets, office equipment, and bedroom furniture occupied the bottom floor. Canned goods and flour sacks were neatly stacked on shelving.

"You're next, Ballard."

Crandle didn't sound rattled.

"Crandle's firing from the loft," Kannon mouthed to Đăng Đạo. "Can you get a bead on him?"

"Not without announcing my presence."

That's right. Crandle might not be aware of Đăng Đạo.

452

Regardless, we are pinned.

"Daddy K."

"Derrick!" The name reverberated. Kannon's heartbeat ramped to fully automatic.

"Shut up, you little fucker."

"Ow!"

"Damnit, Crandle. Let him go."

Five rounds cracked beside Kannon's position, none on Đăng Đạo's side. Another volley . . . the bullets pinged and ricocheted as if launched from inside a massive pinball machine.

The firing came from Kannon's right. The bastard was concealed, but where? And Derrick must be close by Crandle.

Shit. What's the best thing to do? Bold, be bold.

"We have to gain the advantage," Kannon mouthed.

"Be careful. He is just trying to draw you out."

"I know. Got a smoke grenade in that bag?"

"Roger that," Đăng Đạo said.

"If I toss smoke, can you use the cover to get beneath the loft?"

"Can do."

"I'll take out the bank of lights," Kannon added.

Đăng Đạo handed Kannon the *smoke screen in a canister*. He pulled the pin and let it fly. It bounded, rolled, and popped. A surreal-looking cloud of purple smoke mingled with beams of light, turning blackish in the odd lighting. Kannon rose above the barrier, aimed his .45, and emptied a magazine at the shrouded floodlights, which disintegrated.

"Damnit!" Crandle hollered.

Kannon ducked behind the rock wall as another volley of shots raked the granite behind him. Crandle wasn't done. Dim auxiliary lighting kicked in.

Kannon low crawled to his left.

I'm getting too old for this shit.

Yet, adrenaline fueled him. Chest and hips down, he kept his right shoulder against the rounded granite barrier and scraped his way alongside. There had to be an efficient exhaust system because the purple smoke dissipated rapidly.

Kannon peered around his end of the wall to try and spot Đăng

Đạo. Muzzle flashes and the tat-tat-tat-tat from Crandle's automatic weapon exploded from the loft, sparking off the concrete to Kannon's left front. Another volley rang out. Then another. The blasts and echoes were deafening. His ears rang in a continuous high-pitched chord.

Did Đăng Đạo make it across? Had Crandle seen him?

Another hail of bullets strafed the cavern wall to his rear. Crandle sprayed more rounds above the barrier. They ricocheted off the opposing wall, whistling overhead as had the discs on the killing field. Kannon covered his face and ears as more bullets slammed into the granite, gouging out pieces of rock and metal that stung his body like hot shrapnel. He didn't dare return fire for fear of hitting Derrick, who he assumed was somewhere on the loft.

I'll be riddled by ricochets if I stay here.

Kannon slipped into a sitting position, his back against the barrier, his feet extended. A red dot struck his damaged boot. But Crandle didn't fire as Kannon pulled his knees to his chest. Strange, he thought. Maybe the red dot hadn't come from Crandle.

The metallic clatter of a discarded magazine hit the floor. It would only take seconds for Crandle to reload. Kannon took advantage and looked straight across the bunker. A shadowy figure stood at the bottom rung and pointed up. It was Đăng Đạo, using his infrared sight to let Kannon know he'd reached the objective. His nephew began inching his way up the circular rock steps carved into the mountain's interior.

Hearing the click of a magazine rammed into its well, Kannon pulled back just as another volley peppered the area.

Time to play poker.

"Crandle!" Kannon shouted. "You're alone. All your men are dead." *Except for Timmons.* "Give it up."

"You're the one up shit creek. You've already lost the rest of your family."

"You don't know, do you?"

"Know what?"

"Bull failed."

"You're bluffing again." A somber tone belied Crandle's words.

"Really. Listen to this." Kannon pulled out his satphone and replayed the message from Lan, knowing that hearing his mother's voice would either comfort Derrick or further stress him. "All okay. Got that?"

"You damn bastard. You had to meddle, didn't you! Don't you think the world's overpopulated with scum! Government interference, rules and restrictions—"

"Anarchy," Kannon said. "You're preaching to the wrong choir."

"Screw you," Crandle said, still concealed.

Did Bull's failure have an impact? Kannon wondered. One way to find out. "Crandle! All I want is my son. Remember my offer of a million dollars?"

"I remember." The reply came in a harsh, guttural tone. "Patu is worth much more. Make it ten mil, and I might listen. In cash."

"Yeah, like I've got that in my pocket. One million is all I can get."

No response.

Kannon tried again. "We'll go outside, you, me, and Derrick. Give me the account info. I'll use my satphone to set up the wire. I'm sure your EMP attack neutralized the Kalispell banks. No doubt you have Canadian or offshore accounts."

"One mil, huh?"

"Yeah. And you'll release my son!"

"Other conditions will have to be met."

Is it possible to feel elation, fear, and hatred at the same time?

"What other conditions?"

The purple smoke had dissipated. Đăng Đạo had reached the loft floor and crouched behind shelving, which contained numerous bomb-shaped devices. Nearby was a hydraulic winch used to raise and lower them. According to Streak, more powerful EMP weaponry was stored in the armory.

"One. You will disarm. Two. You will be my prisoner until the wire transfer transaction is complete."

"What's the third condition?"

"Streak."

Of course.

"And any other surviving members of your team, especially that little Vietnamese fucker."

"They're all dead," Kannon lied. "Shot by your men."

"I'll need to see the bodies."

Yeah, right! Earlier, Kannon might've been willing to exchange a life for a life. If not for Streak, he wouldn't be in this mess. Roger would be alive, and Derrick would never have been taken. Quán would be able to walk beside his brother. But Streak was now an ally, and Kannon wouldn't have gotten this far without his turnaround.

Besides, Crandle wasn't stupid.

But I would be to trust him.

The *Commander* wanted to drain Kannon of *all* before killing him and everybody else. *Shit! A hundred million wouldn't be enough to satisfy this psycho's lust for power.*

Eighty-Seven

"You're holding the wild card," Kannon said to Crandle. *And maybe four kings to my four jacks. Đăng Đạo must be my ace in the hole.* "Why should I trust you, especially on the prisoner thing? I've experienced your training range. Can't say I care to repeat it."

"A masterful escape. I applaud you. Such a waste of intellect and talent. It's not too late to cross over."

"After seeing the number you did on Anh, no thank you."

"All right then. Let's settle."

"Okay. Deal! One million dollars. Streak for Derrick," Kannon said. "As for being held prisoner—"

"This bunker will be your cell. Lots of amenities."

"I want Derrick with me."

"Not until we consummate the wire transfer. And Streak is in my hands!"

Asshole.

"I'm coming out," Crandle said, "with the barrel of my pistol pressed against Patu's temple."

The *Commander* stepped into view. Clutching Derrick in his left arm, he clamped his meaty left hand over Derrick's mouth. With his right, Crandle thumbed back the hammer on his weapon.

"Show yourself, Ballard."

Holding his .45 downward at arm's length, Kannon emerged. He was relieved to see Đăng Đạo poised on the last step that led the loft.

Derrick squirmed and tried to wrest free. Crandle tapped the boy on the head with his pistol.

"Be still, Derrick. You're going to be all right," Kannon said in a calm voice.

"Remove the magazine. Eject the round in the chamber. Lay your weapon on the floor." Crandle flashed a sickening, sadistic smile. "You've got no choice."

Kannon stared at Crandle's hand. His finger rested on the trigger. In his peripheral vision, he saw Đăng Đạo had a clear line of sight to Crandle. Knowing a shot to Crandle's brain could inadvertently make the *Commander's* trigger finger flinch, Kannon trusted his nephew not to shoot.

Stooping, Kannon pressed the pistol's release button. The magazine clattered to the floor. He racked the slide and ejected the chambered round, then laid his .45 beside the mag.

Kannon's nerve endings prickled. The stab wound in his side throbbed. Someone was pounding on a bass drum inside his head. Time was running out, and Kannon did not want to lose the advantage of Đăng Đạo's unannounced presence.

I need to distract Crandle. But how?

His old bite wound itched. Instinctively, he stroked it.

Cắn. (Bite.)

"Lead me to Streak," Crandle said, keeping the muzzle of his weapon planted against Derrick's temple.

Kannon exhaled and rose from his stooped position. He rubbed his right hand again. *Bite! Bite! How do I get this across to my son?*

"I need to hear in my son's own words he's okay."

Crandle shrugged. He removed his hand from Derrick's mouth and repositioned it over his chin.

His son's blistered cheek was coated with a potion. Probably Anh's doing. Thank God for her.

"Talk to me," Kannon said.

"I'm okay, Daddy K," Derrick said in a frightened, unsteady tone.

Crandle alternated glances between Derrick and Kannon. His free hand was still clamped around his son's chin, while his index finger lay loosely on Derrick's lower lip.

"Derrick, are you hungry?"

His son looked puzzled.

Kannon raised his left hand and rubbed the scar. "Remember?"

"What the fuck are you doing?" Crandle hollered.

Kannon tapped his hand again. *"Cắn!"*

His son's eyes opened wide as saucers.

"Enough of this shit," Crandle said.

"Cắn! Cắn!"

Acknowledgment registered in his son's eyes. Derrick opened his mouth wide and bit Crandle's finger as would a hedgehog chomp on a snake. The *Commander* dropped Derrick, who tumbled to the loft floor.

"You little fuck—"

Đăng Đạo let out a whoop like a Native American and leaped forward like the ninja he was. He lifted his right leg and executed a snap kick to Crandle's upper back, which sent him sprawling. The Commander fell from the loft.

Eighty-Eight

Crandle's tumble from the loft seemed to take place in slow motion. He landed on a horizontally placed fifty-gallon drum and barrel-rolled onto the granite floor.

Kannon's eyes sought Derrick, who remained on the loft with Đăng Đạo. Fortunately, his son rose to his feet, appearing unharmed.

"Watch out!" Đăng Đạo shouted.

Crandle came up firing his semiautomatic. A bullet grazed Kannon's left shoulder, the same one that had taken a round years earlier. Shaking it off, he leaped for his weapon lying nearby. He grabbed the .45, rammed the magazine into the well, and jacked a round into the chamber. Đăng Đạo got off a couple of shots, but by then Crandle had fled down a hallway.

"He is probably heading for the armory," Đăng Đạo said.

"And then the chopper," Kannon shouted over his shoulder. His voice sounded as if he were yelling into a barrel.

"Roger!" Đăng Đạo said. "Get Crandle. I will take care of Derrick."

Kannon cast another glance at the two of them, then took off. *Hope to God Streak's where he's supposed to be.*

The hallway curved and proved to be short, culminating in a door like the one he'd breached earlier, only this one was open. Kannon found himself standing square in the middle of the damaged armory. In addition to the clusters of firearms and bombs Streak had mentioned, it contained a safe. But no Crandle. No surprise.

Stumbling over rubble from the explosion Streak had created, Kannon darted from the armory and barreled straight ahead. There was Crandle, running toward the chopper pad, parallel to the compound and the militia-constructed killing field.

Aching all over, his lungs burning, Kannon struggled to maintain pace but was losing ground.

Damnit! Keep going.

Clumps of snow shot into the air near the *Commander's* feet. Crandle hit the ground. Streak must have spit out a couple of rounds from a silenced rifle. Crandle rolled and returned fire, silencing

Streak, then leaped up and shifted away from the line of fire into the woods. Had Streak been hit? Was Crandle circling back to the compound area?

There are probably more weapons stashed inside the bunkhouse and the cabins. Come on lungs, don't fail me now.

He worried about Kim, who might be caught unaware if Crandle returned to his cabin. Kannon wished they had their radios.

Drawing in as much cold, thin air as he could handle, Kannon high-stepped on his toes through the snow, holding the .45 in his right hand. Crandle stopped, turned, knelt, and popped off three rounds.

Merely feet apart, Kannon lunged to the cold, hard ground, firing three rounds of his own. One of them struck Crandle's left leg, another, his chest. Blood sprayed from the wounds and stained the snow.

Crandle placed his left hand over his chest wound. Slowly, his right hand shaking, the *Commander* hefted the weapon and pointed the muzzle at Kannon.

Kannon rose to one knee and fired once, striking Crandle's gun hand. The weapon went flying.

"Fuckin' bastard."

"It's over, Crandle," Kannon said, limping forward.

As Crandle inhaled and exhaled, air hissed from his lungs. Blood bubbled from the hole in his chest.

"You've got a sucking chest wound. You're dying."

Crandle shot the finger.

Streak approached, his arms hanging loosely at his sides, probably from exhaustion. "I understand you wanted to see me again, you sick motherfucker."

Crandle's face contorted into a devil mask, inflamed, teeth bared, eyes bloodshot. He tried to rise, but Kannon planted a foot on his shoulder.

"Streak . . ." The word dribbled out like spittle.

"I'm done with your bullshit, Crandle."

"Tra . . . tra . . . tor."

Streak curled his lip, turned, and walked away.

Kannon tilted his head at the *Commander*. "Whitehead left you a message, too."

Crandle mustered enough energy to raise an eyebrow.

"He said, 'Go to hell.'"

Crandle slumped.

"Hey!" Đăng Đạo yelled.

Kannon looked up. His nephew was carrying the duffle bag. More importantly, he held Derrick's hand as they approached. The need to embrace his son washed through Kannon like a flash flood.

Just as Kannon turned . . . Pop! Pop! Pop!

"What the—" Out of the corner of his eye Kannon saw Đăng Đạo hit the ground. Streak, too, went prone as bullets tore into the snow-covered turf.

"Daddy K." Derrick broke free and ran toward Kannon.

"Who in the hell is shooting?" Streak hollered, plunging face first into the snow.

"Daddy K—"

Pop! Pop! Pop!

"Derrick's been hit!" Waves of horror flooded Kannon. His son flopped to the ground and remained motionless. A crimson streak creased the snow. Kannon rose, hop-skipped to Derrick, and covered him like a blanket. "Cover us!"

Streak and Đăng Đạo sprayed the area between the bunkhouse and Whitehead's cabin.

Kannon whipped out a bandana and applied pressure to the side of Derrick's head. "Border Slot has a long reach," he heard Crandle say.

More bullets peppered the ground. Kannon dug in, shielding Derrick.

Streak emptied a full magazine. Đăng Đạo tossed a frag grenade, and the incoming firing ceased. But for how long?

Đăng Đạo crawled over. "How bad is it?"

"I don't know. Derrick's unconscious."

"No!"

Kannon had never heard his nephew use a panicked tone, or was that his own voice? "We've got to get the hell out of here." He turned to Streak. "Ready the chopper!"

Streak rose and fired another stream of bullets as he backpedaled toward the path leading to the chopper pad. Again, there was no return fire. Maybe the shooter had been hit or had withdrawn.

"Đăng Đạo. Get Anh and Kim. Watch out for Timmons." Kannon wondered whether Timmons had overpowered the wounded Kim and gotten loose or if an unknown militiaman was doing the firing.

His nephew dropped the duffle and sprinted for Crandle's cabin. Streak picked up the discarded bag and headed toward the chopper.

Kannon gathered Derrick in his arms and followed Streak. The blades were rotating by the time Kannon reached the Jolly Green Giant. Streak assisted him in boarding.

"It's SOP to have a first aid kit and a case of bottled water inside the bird," Streak said.

Kannon found the first aid kit and inspected its contents. There was military-grade gauze but no hand wipes. He located the water, yanked off the plastic wrap, and opened a bottle. He poured the water onto his hands and scrubbed off the grime best he could. After grabbing a roll of gauze, he unrolled several inches and wrapped them around his hand. He repeated the process for another and then saturated the first strip with fresh water.

Kannon removed the bloodied bandana from Derrick's head. "Thank God the blood's not gushing."

He dabbed at the wound with the wetted gauze, but Derrick's hair was so damn thick he couldn't determine how deep the bullet had penetrated. God, please don't let there be brain matter. Using the other gauze strip, Kannon applied light pressure to the wound. His son's breathing and heartbeat were irregular, and his lips and eyes were closed.

Not now. Not after all this.

Holding Derrick, Kannon rose to his knees and stared out the chopper's windshield. "Come on, Đăng Đạo. Where the hell are you?"

"Hang on," Streak said. "He'll get here."

Two minutes later, Đăng Đạo trudged through the snow toward them. Kim was draped over his shoulders in a fireman's carry. Anh stumbled alongside.

The blades kicked up swirls of snow. The chopper groaned

463

and rattled as Streak ratcheted up the rpm. It was cold inside the cabin. Kannon pinned Derrick against his chest.

Đăng Đạo finally reached the cabin door. With one hand, Kannon helped his nephew place Kim onto the floor of the cargo hold. Anh tried to clamber aboard but was weak and fell to her knees. Đăng Đạo picked her up and muscled her inside the helicopter. He hopped aboard and positioned Anh beside Kim, making her as comfortable as possible.

Throttle open, Streak pulled on the collective. The helicopter rose. Once it cleared the trees, he pushed forward on the cyclic. The nose dipped, and their bird picked up speed.

Trembling, still cradling Derrick, Kannon leaned forward to close the side cabin door. He looked down and saw who appeared to be Timmons dragging Crandle toward the main cabin. Kannon drew his pistol and fired. By now, evergreen tree cover obscured his targets.

A burst of automatic fire raked the bottom of the fuselage.

Kannon reached into the duffle, which Streak had tossed into the back. He grabbed a frag grenade, pulled the pin, and dropped the grenade from the chopper. "Go!"

Eighty-Nine

Cradling Derrick in his lap, Kannon, along with Đăng Đạo and Streak, donned headsets, yet no one spoke. Two lives were on the line.

The chopper's pace heightened Kannon's dreaded sense of flying through a molasses-laden atmosphere, similar to what he'd felt when flying from Albuquerque to Montana.

He looked down at his son. Derrick's head wound had clotted, for which Kannon was grateful. He pressed his ear to his son's chest, praying for a stable heartbeat and steady breathing. Still stoked on adrenaline, Kannon found it hard to detect strong life signs. The rattling inside the cabin didn't help.

More alert now, Anh sat up, reached out, and clasped Derrick's hand. Leaning close to Derrick, she whispered in his ear. Kannon couldn't hear what Anh said, but he understood from the glow on her cheeks the words she spoke were soothing.

Derrick didn't respond, or did he? Did his lips just twitch? A flicker of a smile?

Pulling back, Anh dug into her pants pocket, withdrew a compact, and opened it. She dipped her index finger into a gooey substance and then gently applied the lotion onto Derrick's burned cheek. She didn't touch his head wound. Anh would make a great Godmother, Kannon thought, if his son survived.

If . . . God, he's innocent, precious, the best part of us. Derrick must not die.

* * *

"Passing over Kalispell," Streak said through the intercom.

They had been airborne over an hour. Streak had been able to contact the Glacier airport and was told that due to rioting and looting, Kalispell's Regional Medical Center's ER was swamped—from the destabilizing effects of the EMP attack. They were rerouted to Providence St. Patrick Hospital, a Level II Trauma Center located in Missoula.

Frustrated, impatient, Kannon stared out the window. It was hard to believe Crandle's EMP attack had occurred roughly thirty-six hours ago. Pockets of life glimmered in Kalispell now—various lights clusters illuminated parts of the city. Generator fueled, he imagined. The National Guard, the Feds, and who knew what other agencies were down there.

He cast a glance at Đăng Đạo, who wore a sallow expression, his eyes red-rimmed. Kannon understood his nephew was worried about Kim, who was in bad shape. His face had been battered into pulp. Timmons, somehow, must've gotten free and overpowered him, also aggravating the leg wound he had received in the firefight. Would Kim follow his brother Quán, who had died to protect Kannon's son?

They flew on. An hour later, the chopper hovered above the impromptu landing pad at Providence St. Patrick Hospital. The hospital's standard chopper pad was too small for them to land. Consequently, a section of the parking lot had been cordoned off, delineated by strobe lights.

Streak set the Jolly Green Giant down amid its self-generated dust storm. The whump-whump-whump of the rotating blades diminished as the chopper throttled down. EMT personnel poured from the emergency room wheeling gurneys. Techs loaded Derrick, Anh, and Kim onto mobile stretchers and wheeled them toward the ER.

"Jesus Christ," Streak said, ashen faced. "You're not going to believe who's here."

Kannon followed Streak's outstretched arm and saw a tall, thin woman dressed in civilian clothes. Her hair was cropped short. Her right hand rested on her hip, the hem of her jacket pulled back, exposing a gleaming service weapon.

"Let me guess. Sindy Zeller."

"Affirmative."

She approached, nodding first to Streak, then addressed Kannon.

"Do what you need to do for your son and the others," Zeller said to Kannon. "Take Đăng Đạo with you. Streak, you're with me. I want to know everything."

Streak arched his eyebrows.

"Do it," Kannon said, wondering how she knew all their names.

"Roger." Streak stuffed his hands in his pockets.

Even with the head bump suffered in the plane crash, and the grazing bullet or ricochet he'd taken during the assault, Streak appeared relatively unscathed.

Kannon, with Đăng Đạo in tow—he lugged the duffle—trotted after the gurneys. They reached the ER, its medicinal smell tainted by whiffs of wounded flesh and body odor.

"Sir, you can't come in here," a beefy orderly said to Kannon.

"He's my son."

The orderly took a spread-legged stance and folded his arms.

"Let the triage physicians do their work," Đăng Đạo said, pulling Kannon aside.

Kannon looked past the orderly at Derrick, so small and helpless among strangers. But these strangers could do what Kannon could not. As tension and frustration robbed his strength, he almost cratered.

A different orderly led them to a treatment room staffed with nurses. There they sat while being attended to.

A bespectacled clipboard-carrying doctor, with narrow-rimmed specs centered low on his nose, entered. Kannon explained the nature of everyone's wounds and what caused them.

"Bullet wounds, knife wounds, bludgeoning, rape . . . am I missing anything?" the doctor asked, peering above his specs.

"About covers it," Đăng Đạo said.

The doc looked skeptical.

"Christ! You guys must've come from a war zone."

"Pretty much," Kannon said.

The doctor shook his head and hustled out.

A nurse treated Kannon for the knife wound, then spread salve on his nose where Crandle had stubbed out the cigar. His bullet-grazed scalp required cleansing, no stitches. Another nurse examined the knot on his head and assessed his condition under the hospital's concussion protocol. He passed. All the while, Kannon worried about the procedures Derrick was enduring.

In the opposite cubicle, curtains open, Đăng Đạo frowned as a syringe-wielding nurse approached. "I do not need a painkiller."

The nurse shrugged. She cleaned his arm injury, washed it with antiseptic, and then stitched him up.

"Doesn't that hurt?" Kannon asked.

"Yes." Đăng Đạo looked at Kannon with a solemn expression. "When are you going to call Lan?"

"Once I have a more definitive diagnosis of Derrick's condition."

"Understood," Đăng Đạo said. He handed the duffle bag to Kannon. "Some stuff in here could come in handy," his nephew added.

Kannon nodded.

* * *

Two hours later, a man who appeared to be the lead trauma doctor entered the ER waiting room. Kannon rose, as did Đăng Đạo. Kannon's legs were wobbly, his nerves frazzled.

"Update," the doctor said, looking squarely at Kannon. "Your son has regained consciousness. The bullet didn't enter the skull, but he has a concussion. I don't believe there will be any permanent damage. We need to keep him in ICU a while longer."

Kannon's eyes moistened. "Is he talking? Can I see him?"

"Not yet."

"And the others?" Đăng Đạo asked.

"The woman was severely dehydrated and suffering from multiple blows to her head and body, but she's going to be okay."

"Thank goodness," Đăng Đạo said.

The doctor stiffened. A palpable tension filled the room.

"I'm sorry," the doctor said. "Your Vietnamese friend didn't make it. We gave him several transfusions—"

Đăng Đạo broke into tears.

"I'm sorry, man." Kannon put his arm around his nephew. "He and his brother were good men."

His nephew nodded.

"Both men sacrificed themselves to save my son. It wouldn't have happened without them."

"I know," Đăng Đạo said. "They were soldiers through and through." He paused to wipe away his tears. "Despite the trouble with Quán, he respected you. So did Kim. You earned it in the Sangre de Cristo Mountains."

"Thank you for that," Kannon said, choking up.

* * *

At five a.m. Kannon was standing alongside Derrick's hospital bed in a private room when Đăng Đạo returned from running errands, which included procuring a cellphone. His nephew handed it over. Kannon chose not to ask how he'd gotten it.

A nurse brought in a serving tray containing a plate of cut fruits and vegetables, the right post-concussion food for Derrick. He had mumbled only a few unintelligible words before drifting off in a doctor-approved sleep, which Kannon hoped was a peaceful one. The nurse nudged his boy awake. His lips parted into a sweet smile, his eyes dull but showing life.

"Daddy K!"

Kannon couldn't fathom how a woman felt after giving birth, but for him, the welling up inside must be as close as a man could get. "How are you feeling, son?"

"My head hurts . . ." he spied the fruit and vegetable tray and frowned. "I want pizza and a milkshake."

Kannon didn't know whether to laugh or cry. He leaned over and placed his cheek next to Derrick's. The soft warmth of his son's skin brought tears to his eyes. "We're going to get you well first. Pizza and milkshakes come later."

"Daddy K?"

"Yes, son?"

"Who is this man?"

"Đăng Đạo, your first cousin. He helped rescue you."

"The one in the underground bunker who kicked the bastard Crandle in the butt?"

Kannon chuckled. He wouldn't chide his six-year-old for cussing.

"Roger that," Đăng Đạo said, tenderly reaching for Derrick's hand.

Derrick began picking over the fruit and vegetable combo. "What happened to the Anh lady?" he asked.

"She's here in the hospital too, recovering," Kannon said.

"Anh will be fine," Đăng Đạo added.

"I want her to come home with us," Derrick said, his eyes both questioning and imploring.

Kannon and Đăng Đạo exchanged surprised looks.

"We'll see. I'll need to clear it with your mom first."

"I want to talk to Mama Lan."

"You've quite a story to tell but let me talk to her first." Kannon stepped into the hallway and placed the call. An exhausted-sounding voice answered.

"I've got him. He's okay," Kannon said, choosing not to reveal details.

Lan sobbed.

"Let me talk to him."

"In a moment. The nurse is checking his vitals." Kannon sensed Lan was holding something back.

"Are you and Đăng Đạo okay?" she asked through her tears.

"Yes."

"I am thankful." Lan paused. "I miss and love you . . . but I have bad news."

It was like her voice dropped into a well. "What?" Kannon almost dropped the phone. Đăng Đạo overheard his exclamation and joined him. Both put an ear to the phone. "Stephan is in the hospital with a serious bullet wound in his leg. Recovery will take time. Belynda and I are unharmed." Kannon doubted her last comment was one hundred percent accurate. "Stefan was heroic. Belynda is with him at the hospital. She will let me know when he's able to talk."

"Good lord."

"There is more."

Christ! Both sons at risk. What else could've happened?

"Our home burned to the ground."

Kannon listened as the sordid tale unfolded—the attempted rapes, the burning house, a detective murdered, and finally, more details about Bull's death.

"We lost everything," Lan added.

Đăng Đạo clutched Kannon's arm.

"All three of you were heroic, Aunt Lan."

"We're a family, but we have lots of healing to do," Kannon said, knowing he couldn't quantify the depth of their trauma. "The main thing is, everyone's safe," he started to say, but refrained, because, considering their losses, it might be inappropriate.

Instead, "Know what will make you feel better?"

"What?"

He and Đăng Đạo reentered Derrick's room. After Kannon handed him the phone, a banana-sized smile spread across his son's face. A few minutes later, the nurse indicated for Kannon to end the call, saying, "He needs to rest."

Kannon ended the call after reassuring Lan that Derrick, who was still undergoing treatment, would be fine.

I'll weather the full disclosure storm later.

Derrick fell back asleep with a smile on his face. Đăng Đạo left to forage for food. Kannon called Lan again. "There's this woman, Anh, I need to tell you about . . ."

His nephew returned with two vending machine sandwiches. Kannon met him with a tight smile. "Lan's all for it. Go see if Anh is willing to come with us to the Texas Hill Country."

Đăng Đạo smiled, the widest one Kannon had seen. His nephew left and returned a few minutes later with a thumbs-up.

"On a sobering note, we need to make funeral arrangements for Kim and Quán," Kannon said, though only body fragments remained of the latter at the militia compound.

"I know."

"Did they have a religion?" Kannon asked.

Đăng Đạo arched his eyebrows. "Cao-Đài."

Ah, the unique blend of Buddhism, Confucianism, Taoism, and Catholicism—an attempt to bring harmony.

"Tell you what," Kannon said. "How about we bring Kim's body to my property? We'll hold services and bury him there."

"And pray for Quán's soul," Đăng Đạo said.

"And pray for Quán's soul," Kannon repeated. He wished there had been time to collect Quán's remains in a body bag.

"I like it," Đăng Đạo said.

Wondering if Karen would ever forgive him, Kannon also pledged to hold a proxy service for his brother Roger.

* * *

"Does Streak know about the money we found in the safe?" Đăng Đạo asked with a quizzical look in his eye.

"Nope."

471

"That is your call."

"Roger that," Kannon said, choosing to leave Streak out of the loop for now. "Speaking of Streak, I wonder what's going on between him and Zeller."

As if on cue, Zeller appeared with Streak at Derrick's door.

"I'm glad your son's prognosis is favorable," Zeller said to Kannon. "Since he's asleep . . . nurse, stay with him while I talk with these men."

Kannon, Đăng Đạo, and Streak followed her down the hallway to a conference room. Zeller shut the door behind them and remained standing as the three men sat down. "My people have almost reached the compound. Streak has given his version of events. I want to hear yours."

Planting his palms on his knees, Kannon locked eyes with Zeller, the CIA operative who had seeded this nightmare by seducing Streak to locate Border Slot. The two-faced bitch who'd threatened Lan's immigration status, yet later got her released from the Williamson County Sheriff's Department.

Still, Kannon wondered if he was in trouble. He gazed at Streak. At least he wasn't in handcuffs, and all three were being questioned together, not individually. So maybe they weren't going to be spirited away to the nearest Federal *depository*.

"I'm waiting," Zeller said.

Here we go, Kannon thought. Except for their breaking into Crandle's wall safe and the uncounted cash in the duffle, he revealed everything, pausing on occasion to remember specific details while also allowing Đăng Đạo to interject. Even Streak chipped in. After revealing Crandle's ham radio set, Kannon concluded his tale.

"Streak told me about the large safe and the EMP weapons stored in the armory," Zeller said. "What's in Crandle's underground bunker?"

"More weapons," Kannon said. "It's also well-stocked with survival goods."

"We did not have much time to explore," Đăng Đạo added.

"I understand," Zeller said. "What about Crandle and his team?"

"Crandle, at a minimum, is incapacitated. But Timmons could

472

be alive. If so, no telling where he is."

"Or whether more of his guys appeared on the scene," Streak said.

"I get that." Zeller leaned against the wall and crossed her feet. "What about info on Border Slot graduates deployed outside the compound?"

"Other than what evidence might be in Crandle's office, nothing," Kannon said.

"The computer," Đăng Đạo said, pulling it out of the bag.

"Oh, hell. I almost forgot." Kannon took it from his nephew and handed it to Zeller. "We didn't even open it. No time. It's probably encrypted—"

"Jesus," Zeller said. "This could be a fucking gold mine."

"No argument there," Kannon said.

Zeller, in rapid-fire, punched her cell's keypad, presumably passing along the information to the field.

"What's happening in Kalispell?" Đăng Đạo asked.

"It'll take months to restore order from the EMP attack and bring the city's infrastructure up to snuff." Zeller pushed away from the wall she was leaning against and straightened. "Okay, that's all for now."

"Wait," Kannon said. "I've got a couple more questions for you."

"Shoot."

"Why the cloak and dagger? How come you didn't—"

"I lost a brother to Crandle's militia but didn't have enough evidence to present a case to my higher-ups."

Kannon eyeballed Zeller. "There needs to be an international link, right? For the CIA to become involved?"

"Correct."

Kannon suspected the CIA's boundaries for investigations might be a tad porous. He stared at her a moment, before reining in a sudden burst of animosity. "What pisses me off is your threatening my wife."

"I wasn't sure who was who or what part you played. And it wasn't a threat, just pressure." Zeller compressed her lips and stared down both Kannon and Streak. "If you two had come clean sooner, lives could've been saved."

Streak rolled his eyes.

"And prevent the EMP attack on Kalispell," Kannon said, reasoning from her implicating tone.

"Terrorism is terrorism," Zeller said.

No shit!

She tapped Kannon's arm.

"You guys inflicted lots of damage. Maybe they are done."

Her tender touch surprised Kannon.

"At least set back," Streak added.

"What else is in that duffle bag," Zeller asked.

"Anh's modest belongings," Đăng Đạo said, clutching it to his chest.

"Mind if I look?"

"I'd rather you—"

Zeller's phone pinged. She brought it to her ear. Stood. Listened. Bristled. Her expression turned knifelike as she pocketed the phone, then removed a folded piece of paper from another pocket and laid it flat. It was a copy of Streak's map. She planted her index finger in the middle of it. "There's nothing there but ruins."

Đăng Đạo and Streak exchanged alarmed glances.

"Jesus!" Kannon said.

"The buildings have been incinerated. The entrances to the mine tunnels have been blown up and sealed. There's no access to Crandle's tunnel fortress—no safes, no records, no EMP weapons. Nothing but smoldering embers and granite dust."

"Timmons must have rounded up some *friends*," Đăng Đạo said.

"C-4 and incendiary grenades," Kannon said.

"That's what it sounds like." Zeller grimaced.

"I wonder if they salvaged and moved the weaponry," Đăng Đạo said.

"This isn't over. They're still out there." Kannon balled his fists. "Hell, that mountain complex must be riddled with tunnels and mineshafts. You can bet your ass Border Slot's caches are accessible through additional gateways."

"Our official investigation's only just begun," Zeller added.

There was a collective sigh.

"Quid pro quo," Zeller said, frowning.

Kannon furrowed his brow. "About?"

"Based upon the latest input, and, since we're kinda letting you guys off the hook here, I expect you'll be responsive should the need arise for your services in the future."

"Regarding Border Slot, you mean? I presume you'll keep us posted."

An inscrutable expression crossed Zeller's face.

"If I consider there's a remaining threat to any of you or to your families, yes."

"Good Lord," Streak said.

Đăng Đạo smiled thinly.

"Understood," Kannon said through compressed lips, wondering what was on that damn computer.

"I'm off to Border Slot," Zeller said and walked away.

* * *

As Kannon returned to Derrick's bedside, he acknowledged some of his actions had teetered at the law's edge, if not occurring outside of it. So be it!

He needed, however, to make right innocent peoples' damages—compensate Tucker for crashing his plane, find the owner in remote Montana and replace his horse, and restore whole the wilderness store owner for Đăng Đạo's *borrowed* equipment.

Anh's release from captivity was a bonus. Stefan had performed courageously. Considering his severe wounds, though, along with aftershocks from the trauma suffered by all parties, recovery would take time.

Derrick's rescue was a success but at cost. There were losses Kannon couldn't replace: the brothers Kim and Quán, and his brother Roger, whose untimely death triggered enduring anguish for those closest to him.

As for the Border Slot Militia? It or something like it would resurface. Life is messy.

Truck on!

475

JACK LYNDON THOMAS

Author's Statement

The Second Amendment to the Constitution, passed in 1791, provided U.S. citizens the right to bear arms. When considering storylines, I got interested in the concept of the *Posse Comitatus* (power to the county), which came into being by a narrowly passed Act by the Forty-Fifth Congress in 1878. Its essence: Preclude armed forces of the federal government from being used for police actions. Law enforcement belonged under the purview of states and counties.

This Act, like any other, can be manipulated and taken out of context to *support* the ulterior motives of the perpetrator.

* * *

Research for the novel *Border Slot* involved devouring *The Terrorist Next Door* by Daniel Levitas. Published in 2002 by Thomas Dunne Books, the nonfiction work is both informative and frightening. One of the principal characters in Levitas' book is William Potter Gale, who had fifty percent Jewish blood and was an army lieutenant colonel [forcibly retired for medical reasons]. Gale was a principal proponent of white supremacy. Additionally, I became interested in the potential fallout to the U.S. should electromagnetic pulse (EMP) weapons be deployed against the electronic infrastructure of this country. It is a scary idea.

Except for Gale, who is merely used as a reference, all characters are fictitious. Technical information on EMP weaponry, helicopters, first aid, the construction of Bangalore Torpedoes, and other weapons was gleaned from the Internet and various publications. Errors in interpretation or misstatements are mine.

I have taken literary license with geographical locations and place names for this novel. The idea for the killing range came from a nightmare in which I was on the receiving end of the razor-sharp discs. Google Translate provided translations of the Vietnamese language.

www.ingramcontent.com/pod-product-compliance
Lightning Source LLC
Chambersburg PA
CBHW051507250626
47156CB00001B/3